Bread and Butter

Bread and Butter

A NOVEL

Michelle Wildgen

DOUBLEDAY

NEW YORK LONDON TORONTO

SYDNEY AUCKLAND

All rights reserved. Published in the United States by Doubleday, a division of Random House LLC, New York, and in Canada by Random House of Canada Limited, Toronto, Penguin Random House Companies.

www.doubleday.com

DOUBLEDAY and the portrayal of an anchor with a dolphin are registered trademarks of Random House LLC.

Jacket design by Emily Mahon
Jacket photographs by Andrew Purcell
Food styling by Carrie Purcell

LIBRARY OF CONGRESS CATALOGING-IN-PUBLICATION DATA
Wildgen, Michelle.
Bread and Butter : a novel / Michelle Wildgen. — First Edition.
pages cm
1. Brothers—Fiction. 2. Restaurateurs—Fiction. 3. Competition (Psychology)—Fiction. 4. Domestic fiction. gsafd I. Title.
PS3623.I542B73 2013
813'.6—dc23
2013005474

ISBN 978-0-385-53743-8

MANUFACTURED IN THE UNITED STATES OF AMERICA

1 3 5 7 9 10 8 6 4 2

First Edition

For Holly

After a good dinner one can forgive anybody,

even one's own relations.

—OSCAR WILDE

Bread and Butter

Every few months, in the grips of their parents' civic and vicarious ethnic pride, Leo, Britt, and Harry went on a forced excursion to the last Italian market in town. Most people in Linden would make a day of it and drive ninety minutes east into Philadelphia, to hit 9th Street or Reading Terminal, but Leo's parents were diehards. As long as Moretti's was open, they would insist it was the best.

Inside a butcher's case, denuded rabbits curled pink and trusting in white bins, while the sheep's heads appeared chagrined and surprised by the depth of their eyeballs, the narrow clamp of their own teeth. The display of calves' brains and kidneys, livers and tripe, repulsed Britt, struck Leo as regrettable but unavoidable, and entranced Harry, who was six. He stood with his hands on the glass, chewed-looking mittens dangling from his sleeves.

Britt and Leo, who were twelve and thirteen, were supposed to be watching their brother but were primarily lurking several feet away near the bulk section, peering over patrons' shoulders at the hooves and teeth.

Their father appeared beside them, holding a pink slice of prosciutto, which he did not offer. These Saturdays sometimes left their parents flushed and high-spirited in a slightly confrontational way.

"We're not even Italian," Britt pointed out.

"Since when are you purists?" their father asked. "Would you be happier if we were in a haggis store?"

"I was happy playing basketball," Leo said wanly. But the store was an invigorating riot of noise and meaty fragrance, and he found it difficult not to join in the hollering and sampling as his parents did with such mortifying enthusiasm.

"It smells like death in here," Britt said. "Death and spices."

"That's fennel seed," their father said.

Eventually their parents completed their tasting and shopping and returned, each holding a large brown paper bag.

"Where's Harry?" their mother asked. She craned her neck, peering through the crowd. Her red hair was coming out of its ponytail. "Boys? Where'd Harry go?"

"He was here," said Britt, and he and his brother both looked down to where Harry had been. The last they had seen of him, Harry was storming off into the sea of bodies, miffed that Leo and Britt refused to emote over the case of organ meat. They had not followed.

"Well, *look*," their father said. Their parents began working their way through the crowd.

The street was gray and quiet, cars rumbling past Leo on the pitted asphalt. What a terrible place for Harry to be wandering around, his vividness like a target. Why did their parents bring them here? Leo jogged up the block and around the corner, fruitlessly, before returning to the store, where he stood in the mass of people, sweating, his heart pounding, realizing that he had ruined his family.

And then the crowd shifted and Leo glimpsed them all: a cluster of ginger-colored heads back by the meat counter, his father's darker head in its Eagles cap. Harry was holding something wrapped in white paper. His parents' faces were a volatile blend of anger and relief.

As they left the store Leo glanced at Britt, who rolled his eyes in a way that conveyed complicity and gladness, the latter something Britt was clearly embarrassed to feel.

Harry refused to hold either parent's hand and was clutching his white package. Leo took in the oblivious bounce of Harry's shoulders, the round curve of his cheek, and the cowlick on one side of his forehead. He probably hadn't even gotten scolded. Leo took one lengthy stride, long enough to catch the heel of Harry's shoe, a punk-ass little gesture that almost made him feel better.

"Thanks for scaring everybody," Britt said.

"I was talking to the meat guy," Harry said. "He has all the good stuff."

"It's a lamb's tongue, by the way," Britt said to Leo, nodding at the white package. "He got a lamb's tongue."

"To eat?" Leo said to his parents. "You bought him a lamb's tongue?"

Their mother set her bag down on the sidewalk, pulled a stocking cap out of her pocket, and tugged it down over Harry's head. Then she straightened up and said, "*We* didn't buy it for him." Her eyelids lowered just slightly, slyly, because Harry hated to be laughed at, and she added, "He used his allowance."

Part I

LEO HAD IMAGINED A CAVERNOUS SPACE filled with sunlight and flaking pillars, but as he explored his brother's future restaurant, he feared he had overestimated Harry's ambition.

Britt trailed behind them as Leo followed Harry into the long, narrow room. Harry's shaggy red hair and his blue-and-green shirt were the only spots of color in the dusky room as he gestured, all lanky arms and skinny wrists, toward where he planned to put the bar, the tables, and the server station. Harry's forearms and wrists bore short faded purplish scars from hot pans and oven edges and errant knife blades, just like the arms on the cooks in Leo's restaurant.

Leo glanced behind him; Britt was not paying attention but was swiping at the screen of his phone and swearing under his breath about the linen service. Periodically Britt swatted his blazer, making Leo realize that he too was smeared with pale washes of dust at his knee, elbow, and shoulder, but he merely whacked perfunctorily at his clothes. This was why Britt ran the dining room while Leo ran the back of the house. Britt could sense a flaw from yards away— a spotty wineglass or a tablecloth scattered with pollen dropped from a centerpiece—and correct it almost without realizing he'd done so.

"What's the name?" Leo asked. His restaurant was called Winesap, the name a nod to the apple variety that grew in their parents' backyard.

"71 King. Same as the address," Harry said. He pointed up at fat ducts grown minty with age. "That's copper piping. And I think this wall is, like, three feet thick." He demonstrated the wall's soundness with a flick of his hand against the brick, a gesture that looked as if it hurt. But Harry shook it off and looked back over his shoulder. "You don't like the name?"

Leo chewed the inside of his lip. "It doesn't *say* a lot," he said gently. "It might be hard for people to picture what they'll get here just from the name."

"I guess it doesn't really fit," Harry admitted, looking thoughtful. "Although what does Winesap convey, exactly?"

"Well, for a while, not much," Leo admitted. "Heirloom apple varieties didn't evoke much in an old mill town. But now that we have more Philadelphia transplants I think it says farmers' markets and rarity and quality."

"Plus it's just a great word," said Britt. "Maybe it lets people forget for a second that they even got priced out of the suburbs."

"And anyway, now it evokes you, right? See, that's the thing," Harry said. "I'm hoping that soon this address *will* say something, something totally different from what it does now. I'm trying to get ahead of the curve. Or to set the curve. Call it what you will." He looked behind Leo. "Britt. 71 King. What's it say to you?"

Britt looked up from his phone. Whereas Harry's long, lean face was softened by his red beard and Leo bore a coarser nose and darker, down-turned eyes, Britt's face was elegant and spare, high-cheekboned and fine-lipped. "I picture a pit bull," he said apologetically. "Like a fighting dog named King."

Leo winced. Now that Britt had said it, he couldn't picture anything else.

Harry sighed.

"Listen," said Britt, "you haven't made any huge announcements, you haven't paid for any signs. You can still think about it."

"Okay," Harry said, but he'd lost a little of his spring as he continued the tour.

It was September now, and Harry had been back in Pennsylvania since April. He'd allowed only bits and pieces about his nascent restaurant to emerge during the basketball games the three played a couple of times a month, until the build-out began and Harry was too busy to play. He'd been secretive and cheerful on these Sunday mornings in the park, reluctant to lay bare the details until the whole thing came together. Leo had the feeling that Harry both hoped to surprise them and somewhat dreaded the opinions of two brothers who'd already logged ten years—more in Leo's case—in the restaurant business. Harry was still quite new to it.

Leo had worked hard not to pry. He understood how fragile these early ideas could feel, how easily you could get off track if you got input too soon. Instead he had contented himself with coaxing along his own creakily returning jump shot. Britt, who in their teens had painstakingly honed a swooping outside shot until it seemed effortless, tended to lope easily around the court, more concerned with form than points, while Harry had never lost the wiry zeal that could have carried him into an athletic scholarship instead of an academic one. Neither of his brothers would ever admit this. What they said aloud was that Harry could have gone as far as second string on an emerging semipro team in Iceland.

Now they finally got to see the restaurant space and to see Harry, who'd been out of communication for several weeks. To Leo, the entire space seemed more like a hallway than a dining room, and the farther into the building they went, the darker and more forbidding it became. The ceiling seemed to descend as they walked. The west wall was brick, the east wall flaking plaster, and the wall facing the street was three-quarters glass. At the back of the rectangular space was a thick steel door painted a military green.

"That was carpeted," Harry said, glancing down at the floor.

"That's maple," said Britt. "Refinish it."

Harry looked to Leo, who shrugged. "It's probably maple," he said.

Britt said, "What was this space before, anyway? A bar? Apartments? If you found carpet in here, you've got to assume that food and crumbs were ground into it for a while before you tore it out. Could mean mice."

Leo watched Harry gaze doubtfully at the floor for as long as he could stand it, then clapped Harry on the back. "I'll give you the number of the exterminator we use, Hare," he heard himself say heartily. "This is an easy decision, trust me." Around his youngest brother he became bluff and jocular, issuing definitive statements he only occasionally believed in. Somehow he never affected the same persona with Britt; they were too close in age, had grown up playing on too many of the same baseball teams and going to the same parties.

Harry nodded. "You may be right." It was clear he was deciding which way to go—to allocate money to a potentially mythical rodent problem, to laugh it off, or to argue. He settled for shaking his head, and then took a sip from Britt's coffee, which had been left on top of a stepladder, and considered the mouthful. Then he said, "See, this is why I need partners, Leo. You guys know all this stuff already."

"And I'll tell you for free," Leo said, deliberately keeping his tone light, "you don't need me."

"When this place gets huge, you're going to wish you were in on it," Harry said, almost matching the playful tone. "Besides, how's it going to look if I open a restaurant without you? People will think we're feuding. They'll think you have no faith in me."

"I do have faith in you," Leo said. "You just jumped in really fast. You've set yourself a real climb." This was as far as Leo would go in expressing his fears. Leo himself had worked for years in the restaurant business before he'd finally gathered financing and opened his own place. He hadn't put together a few years in the food industry in between graduate degrees and other endeavors and then decided to start a business.

"I think it seems faster than it is," Harry said, unperturbed. "Besides, an industry needs new blood. Britt didn't have any experience when he started working with you."

"I had spite," said Britt. "That'll carry you further than you'd think. I got to quit a job I hated *and* I was upset with Frances for walking out on Leo."

Leo was circling the room, only half listening to his brothers. The conversation made him realize how long it had been since Harry had come home.

Their parents still lived in the house where all three had grown up, a three-bedroom white Colonial with red trim perched on a sloping hillside. His father used the steep side yard as a terraced garden, green beans, tomatoes, squash, carrots, onions, and herbs all fenced in with grapevines. At the top of the yard were the two eponymous apple trees. The neighborhood was a tightly packed grid of older houses kept in careful though elderly repair, beginning to age out and turn over once again, and there would come a day when the next wave would mean renovation instead of mere upkeep. But for now their father patrolled his yard and garden and made wine in his basement. Their mother hauled out a giant wooden jack-o'-lantern sign in the fall and red and green Christmas lights in December.

They'd been older parents for their generation. Their father had retired years earlier from engineering and their mother from being the principal of a local junior high school, but well into their seventies they remained bustling and flustered, talking at one another about different topics at once and lamenting their lack of free time. The house alone seemed to require all their attention. Every time Leo spoke to his father, he was on his way to the hardware store for some minuscule item: a hinge, a flange, a yard of weather stripping.

Leo and Britt were eleven months apart, a lingering intimation of their parents' sexuality that never ceased to cause both men some embarrassment, and perhaps because of the closeness in age their parents were forever conflating their two older sons, forgetting that Britt had not put in years of restaurant work in high school and college, thinking that Leo was alert to sales on good suits. Only Harry, six years younger than Britt and seven younger than Leo, seemed entirely distinct to them. They kept careful track of his many endeavors, enumerating his degrees, years later still talking about the goat he had served them when he was working on a farm in upstate New York. ("Gin!" their father would exclaim. "He added gin to give it a piney flavor. Who thinks of such a thing?")

Leo noted how the sun poured into the restaurant space behind Britt and pooled on the brick before them. Britt's closely clipped reddish blond hair was alight with it; the lines around his eyes had taken on a powdery fineness. The room was tight, but the space was not *all* wrong. Harry would be able to fit three rows of tables if he turned them diagonally to allow servers to swivel through. There was little room for a bar, much less the great zinc *J* that was currently propped up against the east wall awaiting its moment, and what Leo assumed would be the kitchen, back behind that mossy-looking door, was too cramped for more than two cooks or three at the very most, who would be elbow to elbow, knife handles knocking over each other's prep dishes. Yet the dining room was not appalling. The length offset the width—you had the feeling of journeying deep into the old building toward a cache of '66 Bordeaux and a scattering of dusty jewels—and the wood floors would look good refinished. There would be patched corners and spaces between some of the floorboards—try getting crumbs out of *there*—but it would feel welcomingly worn and intimate. This place would be more casual and rough-edged than Winesap, but Leo felt that for Harry, this made sense.

Of the three, Harry was the tallest and the truest redhead, a throwback to the great-grandmother who'd spent years lecturing all three on the meanings of the family tartan. To this day none of the brothers wore plaid. Leo favored pinstripes so faint as to be theoretical, Britt preferred some mix of charcoal or beige set off by blocks of saturated gray-greens or citrus, and Harry bought vintage cotton button-downs for ten bucks a handful, the sort that were printed with typewriters, horses, or paisley. All the brothers had gone to college, but only Harry had collected, as if by accident, several more college degrees than most people required. Leo was equally chagrined by and proud of his little brother's roving and uncontainable intelligence. Harry had strong opinions on pierogi and loved to read terrible popular novels about werewolves or hit men for the pleasure of analyzing their mass appeal, right down to the verb choice. Harry wanted to revitalize Linden—which had long ago lost its steel and textile mills and never quite replaced them—not through its citizens' altruism but through their appetites.

At the moment, however, Harry was exclaiming over Britt's diner coffee, trying to get him to inhale the staleness. Leo believed that Britt drank shitty coffee for the irony of it—that he liked to be the guy in a cashmere sweater with a blue-and-white Greek-patterned coffee cup from the dingy corner pastry stand. Once a week, on Tuesdays, he also bought a square of baklava made by the wife of the Ethiopian guy who sold the coffee, and left the pastry in its butter-spotted white paper package on Leo's desk.

"The river's what, two blocks from here?" Leo called over the sound of his brothers' voices. Harry joined him at the window, peering out at the Irish bar across the street and the corner store—bodega, really—down the block. A few blocks away the river ran south, and just north of them was city hall, the DMV, the restored old mansion of some robber baron where the mayor now lived, and beyond that a mix of abandoned houses, chain-link fences, and bars with plywood on the windows.

The compact city of Linden perched on a tributary of the

Schuylkill, the town shaped in an arc of gentrified neighborhoods and new construction fanning outward from the struggling downtown where Harry had rented his space. Several blocks from 71 King Street, the rest of Linden was becoming aggressively charming. All those city transplants hadn't left Philadelphia so they could be pioneers in some crumbling town center but for velvety green lawns and newly built mock Tudors. Harry's neighborhood was forever expected to gentrify; during the time it had been poised for renewal a slew of businesses had sprouted and wilted. On some blocks, Leo could believe in the hope for a moment, but then he'd take a left turn and discover the prehistoric limbs of the industrial equipment still blocking the riverfront, or the lines of tired civil servants and spiritually battered auto owners smoking cigarettes at the DMV. Harry wanted to charge eight bucks for spiced almonds and quince paste.

"Yeah," Harry said. "There's talk of a new development on this block, new business to use the waterfront."

"Mixed-use condo and commercial, right?" said Britt. Harry nodded. "It always is," Britt continued. "I just hope it's not just another mall."

"Say they put in a Target," Harry argued. "Ugly, sure, but people would come." But his cheer had lessened once again.

"Come on," Leo said softly. "It's getting late." He went back to Harry and patted him on the shoulder, momentarily surprised at the hard planes beneath his palm. As a boy Harry had been so round and freckled, until he stretched out at thirteen. Leo still found it startling sometimes. "Britt's tired," he said. He looked over his shoulder. Britt was leaning against the window, plucking the cuffs of his shirt so they showed beneath his jacket. "Long hours."

Harry walked away from the window and knelt beside the zinc bar top. "I know," he said, tipping a bottle of polish onto a rag. "I know the hours will be long."

Behind them, Britt slurped his coffee pointedly. "You want

me to find out the distributor for these coffee beans?" Britt asked. "Since you like it so much. I can even write up some tasting notes for the menu. 'Boxy, with top notes of resin and defeat.'"

Harry rubbed creamy greenish polish on the metal and didn't look up.

"Come spring this stuff will make your name," Britt went on. "'Bursting with the freshness of the Linden waterfront. A lingering finish of stevedore.'"

Leo stepped to the side so he could see Harry's profile. Harry was still covering the grimy zinc surface with polish, but Leo saw the smile at the corner of his mouth.

"An intriguing balance of sparkling acidity and robust municipal corruption," Harry said, and Britt laughed. He crouched next to Harry, picked up an extra rag, and rubbed at the cloudy polish, opening a circlet of blurry light on the metal, glowing somewhere between silver and pewter. All three of them gazed at the circle, the shiniest spot in the whole place.

"It'll fly," Britt said.

"Even if it doesn't," said Leo, "it won't be the end of everything." Both brothers turned to stare at him. "Well, what business did you think this was? A lot of great places fail. Don't think I'm all smug—a lot of successful places go downhill and fail later too."

"I'm kind of regretting asking you guys over here," said Harry.

"It's just risky," Leo said. "You weren't living here when we were first getting Winesap off the ground."

"Come on. You're doing great."

"Now we are. It takes a while. You don't know how scary it is. I'm worried we made it sound easier than it was."

For years Leo had admired his brother's basic optimism and the sheer energy with which he plunged into any new endeavor. Maybe Harry's forays into graduate school fellowships and overseas trips and a stint in a salmon cannery had been just as treacherous as this but too foreign for Leo to have realized it. But now Harry was plunging into Leo's own business, the demands and financial cruelties of which would daunt even a veteran if he ever stopped to think about it. Maybe he should have been urging caution all along. He feared that the restaurant business, which outsiders adored and thought would be so relaxing and congenial until they waded in and found it was all oil spatter and mayhem, might spell the destruction of Harry's many, if poorly applied, gifts. For once, Harry might have come upon a task where sheer energy and will might not be enough.

Harry leaned back on his heels and looked up at Leo. "I do know," he said.

"Okay," said Leo. "Hey, who'd you get for investors, anyway?"

"Mostly the landlord. He gets to have a long-term tenant for once, he hopes, and he can swan in anytime he likes." He paused. "Then a small business loan. Mom and Dad chipped in a little too."

Britt's head jerked back in surprise. Leo's eyebrows darted up as he said, "You took Mom and Dad's money? They're retired. It's enough you're staying with them."

"They offered. Insisted, even. I didn't clean out their savings. It was very modest. And you know I'm paying them rent, right? More than what they wanted me to pay, if you must know. I didn't just show up and ask Mom to do my laundry." He delivered the last part with equal measures of defensiveness and amusement, and was rewarded with a collective snort at the idea of their mother doing laundry for any of them. There'd been an individual laundry policy in place since Leo was still standing on a chair to reach the washing machine.

"But, man, Harry," said Britt, "we never asked them to invest in Winesap."

"I know," Harry said. "They didn't pay for any schooling for me, though. I did it all with scholarships and work-study. I think they felt it was unequal."

"Oh," said Leo. Britt, who'd also long forgotten about the

expenses of his education, looked sheepish. For Winesap, Leo and Britt had cobbled together their own small business and personal loans along with money from a few wealthy investors who liked the tax break and the special treatment. No one in his right mind bet on a nonfranchised restaurant to be a moneymaking investment, but now and again people got lucky.

There was a silence until Britt said, "Tell him where you got the bar top, Harry."

"Craigslist, for a hundred bucks," Harry said, his voice lightening. "Some lady in Pottstown's grandfather died and this was in his attic, can you believe it? I'm going to have people cooking behind it, since the space isn't big enough just to use it as a straight-up bar."

Leo shrugged, more to himself than to anyone else. It was not a bad solution. He didn't love to watch cooks at work when he went out, but other people were into these things. He gazed at the round of light on the metal, which was widening as Harry polished.

"It's amazing," Leo said.

BRITT HADN'T COME TO THIS NEIGHBORHOOD in years, and as he drove away from Harry's restaurant space, with Leo brooding in the passenger seat, he remembered why. This section of town had always had a certain amount of . . . call it grit, he decided, but when they were kids, even teenagers, it had felt more gruff and working-class. No frills, but not dangerous. Now the bars he drove past looked not like shot-and-a-beer joints where you might go after a shift but crooked and grimy, with more than one window boarded up, the kinds of places frequented by the real alcoholics, the ones who'd made a profession of it.

"Did you try to talk him into another location?" Britt asked. He glanced toward Leo, who was peering out his window with a frown.

"He'd already signed the lease," Leo said. "I didn't realize the landlord was the main investor. I told him he could break it. I told him he *should* break it."

"How'd that go over?"

"About like you'd expect."

Britt nodded. Harry had waited until he was deep into this venture before bringing it to them. He suspected that Harry didn't really want their input at all.

He hummed under his breath as they entered the greener, cleaner part of town on the way to their restaurant. The sugar maples were turning crimson and golden. Leo was quiet as they neared the gray stone façade of Winesap and pulled around the back. He seemed to become focused and inward as they began each day at the restaurant, so interior that when summoned, he often looked at Britt for a split second before he took in who was speaking to him and why.

Britt looked forward to each day's fresh scan of the dining room, the bar, and the maître d' station, the straightening of its crooked tables, polishing of its liquor bottles, and dispatching of its droopy flowers. He liked a space in which flaws could be whisked away, order and grace visibly restored. He liked walls the color of some creature's muted underside or the soft inner petal of a plant, slippery leather banquettes and a silky curl of gravlax served on a slick white plate. Britt knew that some people found the repetitiveness of the restaurant business rather crushing, but to him it was rhythmic and satisfying. Somehow Leo must have known he would find it so.

The first time the *Daily Journal* had covered Winesap's opening, many years earlier, the photo that accompanied the article had showed Britt in a sand-colored linen suit and a tangerine tie, looming before the bar seeming taller and more handsome than he was in real life, a mirthful, conspiratorial expression on his face. Leo was in the photo too, hunched and rumpled on a barstool, with his dark auburn hair showing too much scalp.

The article was respectfully interested, the *Journal* unwilling to tip its hand before the dining critic (who was also the arts editor) had a chance to eat there. She'd attempted a bit of a disguise, but Britt had recognized her in spite of the hair stuffed beneath a hat and what appeared to be extra sweaters to add bulk.

This was the sort of thing you ended up obsessing over: not only the critic in halfhearted costume in your dining room, but the fact that critics sometimes relied on such dowdy disguises. Britt didn't believe in relegating poorly dressed people to the back tables, but there was no denying that people walked into a new restaurant and judged their company as they considered whether to join it. A dress code had seemed too off-putting for a new place back when Winesap opened, so they'd just had to concentrate on outfitting the staff and space as stylishly and simply as they could, so that anyone who showed up in running shoes or a T-shirt would be sufficiently aware of the contrast to step it up if they returned.

He had considered not telling Leo that the critic was there. He'd considered not even telling the kitchen or the server or the backwaiters, as an experiment. It shouldn't matter who this woman was; there should be no higher standard reserved for VIPs, but of course there was. It gave customers something to aspire to: the martini materializing as soon as they were settled, the reserving of one last lamb loin for a late reservation known to be partial. Guests who dined out only now and again might not even realize such a possibility existed, but those in the industry and its frequent visitors would have felt slighted by having the same experience others had every day, one in which they were forced to verbalize every wish and then received no more than what they'd asked for.

In the end Britt had entered the kitchen and told the executive chef about the critic. Kenneth was expediting rather than cooking that night and smelled perceptibly of gin even back then. Britt still marveled that Leo had been right about Kenneth—he'd hired him saying that they might get a few years out of him before Kenneth imploded somehow, but that those impeccable years might be enough. How did Leo know these things when he spent his time squirreled away in the upstairs office like a dotty aunt? But there was nothing to be done about it right then: the critic was in the house; Kenneth seemed sober and brisk and so maybe he only reeked of the booze from the night before; and the servers, summoned, had stood before Britt in a dark-clad phalanx in the kitchen, hands clasped behind their backs. Once admonished to be unobtrusively perfect, the servers melted back out into the dining room, where they gave no sign they knew who had just asked for the rillettes au lapin and homard à la vanille. (They had flirted with French menus at first, a wish of Leo's that Britt had indulged for a few months before it became too ridiculous and dated to continue. Say what you would about Leo, he was gracious when he'd been wrong.)

And so the article heralding their opening appeared, and the review a few weeks later was so good it drew not only local papers but even a mention in the *Inquirer*'s "Neighbors" section. Britt found it hard to believe they'd managed such attention, but Leo had shrugged. "This city is just starting to climb out from a sinkhole," he said. "They want to be able to cover an economic recovery. Do you see anyone else insane enough to open a restaurant in Linden?"

Britt had swayed for a moment—somehow he had not realized how big a risk Leo had so easily talked him into. Britt had replaced Leo's ex-wife, Frances, who was supposed to be in charge of the front of the house but had left Leo and the business before the opening, and at the time Britt had found this reassuring: surely Leo would not risk the livelihoods of *two* family members. He'd assumed that Leo had some knowledge he did not, some secret that assured him the restaurant would be a success despite the city's teetering municipal services and seedy downtown, but now he realized Leo had been banking on the fact that they were going to be pioneers. Perhaps Linden could join other outlying cities in being revitalized even after steel and textiles were gone. It had the advantage of distinct neighborhoods that still bore a faint ethnic imprint. It had a waterfront with some commercial potential, and it had a nearby college that helped bring in a few more adventurous eaters and support the local farmers' markets. For years anyone who wanted to eat a good meal had gone into Philadelphia while Linden concentrated on eggplant parm, diners, and grungy but tasty Asian or Mexican food. Now, spurred by Winesap's success, a few local restaurants were venturing further afield, with seasonal cuisine or menus showing cross-pollination of various countries.

But it was always precarious. Linden wasn't close enough or rich enough to be one of the posh suburbs, and businesses like Winesap would either grow fat on the gold rush or be forced to eat one another during the pitiless winter. This rather stately place was balanced on the head of a pin—that was why the *Inquirer* thought it worth a mention.

For the first two years they were alone in the endeavor. The local diners kept slinging eggs and soggy toast; the local taco joints kept delivering grease-soaked paper bags. And meanwhile Winesap operated out of a converted old stone house on the edge of Linden, where, not coincidentally, the city's most upscale neighborhood clung to the adjacent town like a barnacle, still shamefaced about its Linden mailing address.

They were carefully positioned between blowout expensive and pleasantly upscale. To some extent, Winesap had to replace that sense of occasion people got by driving into Philadelphia, and so certain requirements were nonnegotiable. In choosing the location, Leo had ensured that no strip malls were nearby, for example. Even expensive places near Linden often operated out of strip malls. The concession horrified Leo, who communicated this horror to Britt until Britt accepted it as his own. Because it *was* awful, walking into a mall and dropping two hundred dollars on lamb shank and Barolo in the shadow of a Radio Shack.

Slowly, other places began to open. Britt began to receive press requests for quotes not as the ingénue but as the elder. For it was Britt they called: Leo had taken one look at the photo that accompanied their first write-up, Britt looking so elegant and confident while Leo huddled homuncularly to one side, and entrusted Britt with the press. Britt did his best to live up to the task with the same alacrity with which he had shouldered so many demanding yet rewarding endeavors: high-strung girls who dabbled in modeling and French, a degree from Penn, a weathered barn door that turned out to be dark golden cherry and that he made into a grand dining table. He liked to talk, he liked making his seamless way through a crowd of people, he liked to know what was happening, and he'd found that reporters were always willing to dole out bits of city info in exchange for his take on, say, a revered pizza place opening a branch in Linden. Britt's take was often actually Leo's take first, but Britt generally agreed. Of the pizza place, Leo had said, "They don't need real estate, they don't need ambience. Serious pizza goes anywhere—it's currency." And he was right. In any city of mildly Italian extraction, a truly fine pizza transcended every class stratum. Italians could be counted on to influence everyone that way. Leo loved Italians. It crushed him not to be one.

When the restaurant was about three years old, Leo had told Kenneth to start making his own pasta, and two weeks later Britt entered the kitchen to find two women, one ancient and one about forty, set up near the walk-in, chatting in Italian and rolling satiny yellow sheets to be cut into tagliatelle. At first Britt thought Leo had imported them from Sicily like a case of plum tomatoes, but it turned out they spoke English and were Kenneth's landladies. Britt phoned a reporter he'd been talking to now and again and off-handedly mentioned the growing trend of Linden discovering its own pockets of culinary talent for economic gain, embodied in the heartwarming story of the Torsini family, and then everyone knew

Winesap served a glorious dish of tagliatelle as well as a perfectly crusted sea bream. Weeknight sales rose accordingly.

He was made for it, just as Leo was made for the position of watcher and string-puller. If the arrangement bruised Leo's ego, he never said so. And Britt believed that occupying the less heralded role would never bother Leo. This was one of Leo's greatest strengths: he knew himself.

WHEN BRITT AND LEO ENTERED the kitchen door, evening service was gearing up to a bad start. In the dining room, servers swabbed grimly at the crumbs left on the floor from staff dinner while Alan, the bartender, observed them and polished a snifter. He stood very straight, motionless but for a slow, murderous circling of his thumb.

Watching him, Britt shuddered. "What the hell is wrong with these people?"

"They keep sleeping together," Leo said. "Annette never trades shifts with anyone and now she can't find people to cover her vacation. And Alan's pissed that Helene never pushes people toward the bar to eat. He wants the tips."

Britt rubbed the bridge of his nose. "Have you been holding roundtables with the front-of-the-house staff about their romantic lives?"

Leo said, "My office window is right above the dining room. You think I don't open that up?"

In the kitchen the cooks were frantic and silent, the Hobart mixer batting at a vat of butter in one corner, while across from it a stainless steel prep table held two hotel pans of putty-colored cow's tongues, steam swirling off them as they cooled.

"Where's Thea?" Leo asked the room at large. Manny, his dishwasher, jerked his head toward the walk-in. Inside the fridge he found Thea with one clog braced on a sealed bucket of chicken stock, counting sardines. Leo closed the door behind him.

Thea glanced up at him and then returned to marking her checklist. The sardines were layered in a flat pan of ice, crescents of blood threading from their gills. "Hector quit," she said.

"Shit. Really?"

"Really. We have to keep a dessert chef more than six months sometime."

"We have," Leo said. "We will again."

"He got bored silly doing warm chocolate cake." Thea flipped a sheet of paper over in her binder and began noting the dates, written on masking tape, that marked every item in the walk-in and freezers.

"There's room to maneuver," Leo said, slightly stung. "Every workable idea Hector had, we served. He just gave us a lot of stuff we couldn't use. The place is what it is. We couldn't serve tobacco as a garnish, no matter how avant-garde he felt that week." None of it made him feel any better. He'd known he'd never keep Hector forever, that Hector would go to New York, Philadelphia, or Chicago, but he'd tried. He gave bonuses. He was judicious in his criticism.

"He's not big on workable," said Thea. Hector would spend a week perfecting a sesame grapefruit mousse that Britt had described as the union of grainy and puckering, but then ditch the mousse and debut a flawless napoleon of crackling pastry layered with coconut and kaffir lime custard. He'd sprinkled it with a vivid emerald powder that sent Leo's mouth alight when he tasted it, a fragrant tartness that intensified the creamy custard and the buttered shards of crust. It turned out to be sugared lime leaf powder. No one knew how he'd made it. Leo had tried at home, just to see, and turned out a murky, unchewable paste. They'd all learned to wait out dishes like the sesame grapefruit mousse, the servers exchanging glances at each tasting but tactfully silent, because the two weren't unrelated. Thea had pointed out that Hector seemed to need to work a bad dish with his hands while he worked his way through a stunning dish in his head.

"Oh well, I guess. That's how it goes." It was a blow. Hector had begun knocking away the restaurant's reputation for classic but staid desserts, but no one kept the best talent forever. You found the next guy. Leo was already thinking about pouring a cup of coffee and getting upstairs, forgetting about Hector's departure in a mountain of invoices. "Where'd he go, anyway?"

Thea shrugged. "He said he was going to take a vacation and travel for a couple months." She hefted the pan of iced sardines and bumped open the walk-in door with her hip.

The door closed behind her, but Leo stayed in the walk-in. He poked idly at a plastic bag of demi-glace, gleaming mahogany cylinders like a row of sliced horn. Thea liked to add a calf's foot for texture. Maybe next time he came in Thea would be handing in her notice too. Leo would have to promise her a mountain of calves' feet.

No. Thea was happy here. She had a three-year-old daughter and an ex-husband; she'd be loath to mess with a well-established routine—a routine Leo was as much a part of as, say, the ex-husband, if you really thought about it. Britt handled the front of the house and channeled Leo's directives to the kitchen staff, but it was Leo who had noticed Thea as a quiet, focused prep cook slowly emerging each day from behind a mound of carrots, celery, and shallots, which she turned into great bowls of perfect dice.

Back then, Kenneth was still executive chef. He'd made the restaurant's reputation, but the drinking problem had curdled his brash personality into an abusive one, and it was Thea, by then the sous chef, who'd slowly taken on responsibility, developing the nightly specials and training new staff, whom Kenneth either threatened or ignored. Leo had been upstairs all day and night, or out front watching the service, and for months he hadn't seen that Kenneth was deteriorating. When he finally did realize whose dishes he'd been praising and whose guidance had been steering the back of the house, he'd called Thea up to the office, expecting protectiveness of her boss or total self-effacement, in service to a kitchen's military protocol. Neither appeared: Thea had run the place because she hated disarray and she hated failure, but she had also seen a chance and taken it, and she expected recognition. And Leo gave her what she'd earned. He still did.

Harry might have youth and energy and possibly vision—it was too soon to tell; Britt could charm journalists and angry patrons; but did either of them have any idea how to wrangle the kitchen that kept them all employed? Because the most dedicated, talented, and downright martial kitchen staff were still crazy. They were inked with full-sleeve tattoos and they picked fights about offal; they wore scuffed leather jackets and smelled of smoke and whiskey; they spent their meager salaries on top-shelf brown liquor and execrable fast food; and they placed bizarre wholesale orders for items like duck tongue, Jew's mallow, persimmons, and blood clams, which they paid for in crumpled bills and then took home to create menus for the decadent, spiteful, all-staff dinner parties they would then dissect throughout service for the rest of the week. Even stern, responsible Thea had joined in, sensing a threat to her authority after a particularly successful paella party hosted by a previously unknown prep cook named Jaime. She'd packed off her kid to her parents' house and set about breaking down an entire pig into a twenty-four-hour feast of barbecue and charcuterie that had left the whole kitchen staff awed and overstuffed, with a respectful chartreuse tinge lingering in the whites of their eyes.

Britt might get to be the face of the restaurant, but Leo knew that he, Leo, was the brains. Now Leo paused, just out of the way of the swinging kitchen door, to look over the staff: Thea moving into place at the pass to expedite, a towel tucked into her belt and one tight curl of dark brown hair disappearing into her collar; Manny humming to himself while he raised and lowered the door to the dishwasher as decisively as if it were a guillotine; Dennis slicing the tongue into circles with that gelatinous starburst in their centers, horrid but also rather beautiful; Suzanne at the fish station tasting a spoonful of fish stock; and at the meat station the sous chef Leo had found in a pasta place up in Bingham, where the cavatelli was gluey but the lamb shank had silenced him for a whole minute: Jason, an automaton, a pale bearded carnivore with a preternatural sense for meat temps.

The call-and-response of the first orders had begun; he listened to Thea firing one tongue, two ceviche, one venison, one escolar, one gnocchi, all day. He liked to stay for a few minutes during service—later he would return for more coffee and would stand silently near the espresso machine, observing—because when Leo was up in his office he would hear muted servers' chatter but not this, not the rhythm of the kitchen as orders shuttled through it, the steaming roar of the dishwasher and the click of metal hotel pans on stainless steel counters and the constant verbal assertion and confirmation between the expediter and line cooks, like an animal talking to itself.

CHAPTER 2

L EO SPENT THE BETTER PART OF that autumn preoccu-
pied with the belief that somewhere near Linden lurked an
unknown pastry prodigy just waiting to be discovered. Britt, meanwhile, devoted himself to concealing his fixation on one of Winesap's new regulars.

She had appeared at the end of the summer, a few days before
their first visit to Harry's restaurant space. She arrived wearing a
charcoal sleeveless dress that could have been dull except that it was
fitted so snugly, with tall heels and dangling, faintly Egyptian gold
earrings. When she turned, the skirt flared and Britt saw a flash of
a lime silk lining. At first he assumed she was a visitor from New
York or Philadelphia, but bigger-city dwellers tended to radiate
an air of parental delight at having uncovered a decent place. She
might look like a transplant from some larger, chicer city, but she
behaved like a local.

The woman handed a credit card to Alan and snapped her purse
shut with a brisk click, shaking back a heavy, shining length of
maple-colored hair. Alan looked dazed. He had assumed the slightly
openmouthed smile of a Labrador retriever, and Britt stepped forward to save him.

"My father," she said, when she saw Britt approach. "It's his
birthday, but he'll still try to pay."

"Not mine," said Britt. He raised an eyebrow at Alan, who murmured, "Table eight," and Britt gestured for her to precede him to

her table. As they walked, he added, "My father would drop a few hints about college tuition and order a dozen extra oysters."

They paused at her table and Britt pulled out a chair for her. He was about to introduce himself when she said, "Ah, there they are," and he turned to see a couple who were an older version of her enter the restaurant, followed by a man his own age. Maybe a brother but more likely a husband. And yet not much of one that he could see: the man was shorter than this woman, who stood eye to eye with Britt (hers were a tawny brown), and he was balding. Disappointed, Britt returned to Alan and told him to send out glasses of champagne.

It was a Friday evening, and Britt was lurking about, observing Alan's first solo night running the dining room. They had struck a bargain after several shifts of Alan's carefully reasoned arguments for a trial as maître d'. Britt assumed that Alan was only campaigning out of spite for Helene, the maître d' who never let people eat at the bar, but Helene was going on vacation and needed someone to replace her, and Alan, who was ABD in philosophy, made a first-rate argument. But now Britt was having doubts. Alan was relaxed and genuine as a bartender, but as a maître d' the weight of responsibility seemed to get to him, and he took on a peculiar pan-European accent and kept clasping his hands before him like an undertaker. Britt was petrified that he might bow.

She returned the next week, occupying a table of five with two couples, and then a few days later with three heavy-shouldered young men of a sort of collegiate-warehouse hybrid. Then Britt didn't see her until the end of September, when she was there with a blond, reedy man in his forties, and a week after that with a group of women who appeared to be very much like her: midthirties, chic, with smooth hair and notable eyewear. Britt greeted her the same way each time, warm but professional, never quite willing to turn her over to Alan or Helene but too baffled by her companions to try any further innovation. The two couples had seemed ner-

vous and sweet-tempered, all ordering chicken. They had brought
a large box with them, which sat tucked beneath the table until
dessert, when they'd opened it and pulled out prettily wrapped
jars of jam, handing each to this woman for her examination. The
young men, who gave the impression of wearing baseball caps but
who in fact were suitably dressed, had listened to her speak with
rapt attention, pausing only for the burliest one to order an obscure
bottle of gruner veltliner to accompany the mushroom flan. And
the blond man, who looked familiar to Britt though he could not
quite place him, had ordered cheese as an appetizer and foie gras
terrine as a main course and spent the dinner dabbing at his eyes
with a transparent ivory handkerchief—too distraught and bilious
to seduce anyone, Britt decided. When she turned up with the
group of women, Britt circumnavigated Alan and bounded forward, delighted to see her in a recognizable configuration. They
ordered champagne as an aperitif, slurped at the heads of shrimp,
and leaned back languidly in their chairs, flashing the scarlet soles
of their expensive shoes. They seemed to have more and whiter
teeth than the rest of the diners. Entranced and perhaps faintly
threatened, Alan had sent out an extra amuse-bouche without even
asking Britt first.

What did this woman do? Was she a therapist, an etiquette
coach? She did not dominate the conversation at any of her dinners, but she was nevertheless clearly central in some way to all—
her companions oriented their bodies in her direction subtly but
unmistakably. Watching each set of shoulders angled toward her,
Britt was not sure it was even conscious. She ordered last and differently from the rest of the table but always shared tastes of her
rabbit ragù with pappardelle, her saddle of lamb with potatoes dau-
phinoise. With the two couples she seemed solicitous and gentle,
almost maternal, and she let the weeping man talk at her for an
hour, nodding calmly, but then just before the chocolate truffle she
reached over and tapped his knuckle. Whatever she said made the

man rear back and drop his handkerchief. A passing server swooped in, folded it, and placed it at the edge of the table. Britt made a note to compliment her on the grace and subtlety of the move; the man seemed unaware that he had dropped it, and therefore that anyone had noticed whatever little shock had caused it. The woman just signaled for the bill.

Britt made a point of being accessible each time she departed so they could discuss the finer points of whatever she had chosen that evening. He made casual circuits of the room, noting the details of her frame with what even he could tell was a strange and orthopedic kind of attention: the diagonal sweep of her jaw, the length of her fingers, the smooth cup-and-ball of her bare, gleaming shoulder.

At the time, Britt was distracted and defensive thanks to a dying relationship, and the appearances of this woman were a respite not only from that but from arguments with Leo over finding a new pastry chef and from unreliable suppliers and the kitchen's latest turf war with the servers.

She was also a useful barometer for Alan's progress as a maître d', a position he had continued to occupy a few nights a week after Helene returned from vacation. Alan was slowly abandoning his Continental undertaker mode and honing his instincts for how and when to woo a guest with small displays of welcome, which had to be dispensed judiciously or else the guest would expect some free thing every time.

By this time Britt had learned her name, and so despite his general distraction he brightened when, just after Halloween, he saw her on the reservations sheet, slated for a window table overlooking the half-leaved trees and the darkening gray sky. He had noted a *BC* next to her name, which was Camille.

BC no longer stood for an actual blue index card but for a file on the computer system of frequent guests and their habits. A note on the servers' ticket would alert them to check it before approaching the table, so they would know who hated salmon, who was allergic to gluten, who adored soft-shell crab, and who liked to linger over coffee. It was a habit Leo had picked up years ago, at a place where he had worked in college. There the staff had kept a small recipe-card box at the bar, containing alphabetically arranged blue index cards with additional notes jotted on, crossed out, and amended. The cards bore family names and configurations, the dead and the divorced neatly crossed out, new names in fresh ink to one side. They knew who married, separated, and gave birth. They knew birthdays and anniversaries and wonky food issues like an aversion to onions but a love of chiles, a rotating circuit of odd diets, favorite cheeses, and beliefs about meat temperature. However wise a business move the files were, scrutiny of them revealed lives in a way that was also oddly moving, and sometimes—perhaps—unflattering.

The staff was continually admonished to keep the cards' language simple and neutral. No jokes, no giving in to moments of rage. Nevertheless, unable to resist, several servers had amused themselves by writing cards for one another: *Often leaves table to weep in lavatory*, read Alan's file, *likes server to offer brave smiles upon return*. The file for a longtime server named David was nearly a novel, from *Likely to arrive with chorizo in pockets; do not be persuaded to cook it for him* to *Frequently unmanned by hiccups*. No one had made a card for Leo, who was just distant and intimidating enough that the servers weren't sure how he'd take it. Britt would have told them to write one for him—Leo would love it—but the cards were not the kind of thing one could direct. Every now and again Britt read through them, hoping to see one for Leo appear. Britt's blue card file read simply, *Mouth breather.*

When they first set up the filing system, Britt had had the idea to try to configure it so that descriptions could be sent to a portion of the servers' tickets but would not print out with the final bill.

The idea was to eliminate a step, precisely the sort of efficiency that kept a restaurant lean and quick. And it might have worked quite nicely except for a glitch that left the notes on the bill, forcing Britt to be summoned by a woman with silver hair in a brutal little knot at the back of her head, who opened her billfold and read aloud, "'Likes to talk, but not to server.'" He'd had to buy her table an additional round of cognac to smooth it over, and afterward Britt and Leo had accepted the need for a less efficient filing system and an additional procedure even on the busiest nights—whatever it took to safeguard their guests from knowledge of themselves.

The blue card for Camille was no help at all. Britt stood at the maître d' podium, watching Helene rearrange flowers and the servers nudge place settings into alignment, and opened her file. *Often dines with business (?) colleagues*, it noted. *Omnivore*. And that was it. The servers she'd dealt with were as baffled by this woman as Britt was.

Britt stepped away from the podium, shutting down the blue card, as Helene returned. "How many covers tonight?" he asked, solely to redirect his own attention. He knew how many.

"One twenty-nine," Helene said. "Good night." She paused to look around the room—at the bar, Alan was holding a jar of cocktail onions to the light—and then gave a satisfied nod. Helene was as small and neatly turned out as a carved figurine, with a short, chic flutter of dark hair and a superhuman tolerance for high heels. She had returned from two weeks in France with a smattering of sun-induced freckles across her nose and a cool polish on her tableside manner.

"Who did the blocking?" Britt asked. The computer program handled the basics for booking reservations, but he insisted that a live brain reexamine the books each evening as well.

"Alan," Helene said, "and he did a nice job too, I have to say." Both of them glanced discreetly over at the bar. Alan had pointedly set out two place settings at one end and was now refusing any acknowledgment of Britt and Helene. "I think he got some of his friends to book the bar," she added.

Britt nodded but said nothing. Overall he preferred to leave territorial spats to the participants. Like Leo, he felt it was undignified and unnecessary for the owners to get involved. "What's the deal with Camille Lewis?" he asked. "Her blue card is no help, but she's been coming in a ton."

Helene eyed the reservation list. Camille was on it with a two-top for eight thirty. "I have no idea," she said. "I'm trying to get a handle on her myself. She's very easygoing, I can tell you that."

Britt nodded, a bit embarrassed to have asked. He shouldn't be, he knew—it was his business to ask about guests who had all but declared themselves regulars—but he feared some new interest showed in his expression. Helene was eyeing him, alert as a rabbit, her dangling earrings vibrating with attention.

"I'm going upstairs to chat with Leo," he said, and, ever discreet, she simply nodded.

Upstairs was where they kept a small library of cookbooks and culinary guides, two rooms filled with dry goods, and climate-controlled wine storage. In the dressing room the later shift of servers and backwaiters had arrived. David was standing in a white undershirt and unbuttoned black pants, ironing his shirt for service while around him several servers twisted their hair into knots or looped ties around their necks. They saluted Britt as he passed.

Leo was in their office, which perched over the front dining room. Two desks faced each other, one Britt's, one Leo's. Leo was concentrating on the computer screen. "What's up?" he said without turning.

"Just checking in," Britt said.

Leo glanced up and considered Britt for several seconds. "Helene may be too chic," he said.

"Chic is good."

"Chic is good, intimidating not. People go to bigger cities for that."

"I'll ask her to warm it up a notch," Britt said, and Leo nodded, satisfied.

"You want to grab dessert tonight?" he asked. "I've been checking out this kid at Hot Springs. She's a little up-and-down, but she might have something."

"Sure," said Britt. "Just let me stick around till the eight-thirty turn."

"Invite her if you want," said Leo.

"Who?" Britt said stupidly.

"This Camille person you keep hovering over. You'd better change things up. At some point she's going to tip you for something and then you're fucked."

"You're right," Britt said. "I can't quite figure out who she is."

"That's what dinner's for," said Leo. Britt nodded and stood there, waiting to see if Leo had divined anything else up here in his aerie, but Leo flipped over an invoice with a decisive thwack, said, "They're nuts if they think we'll pay four hundred a case for that Oregon plonk," and ignored him until Britt headed back downstairs.

WHEN CAMILLE APPEARED A COUPLE OF hours later, the night was in full swing. The bar was three deep and Alan was neglecting his patrons in order to mix an elaborate nineteenth-century cocktail under the direction of a guest who was obviously making it up as he went along. The newest backwaiter was zooming around with a generally hunted aspect, and Helene was striding between the tables, pouring water, whisking away soiled napkins and crumbed plates, and calming people by virtue of her faint scent of laundered linen and her very presence. Britt delivered a cognac and glanced up to see Camille through the scrum near the door: a swirl of brown hair, the white flash of an incisor. He made his way back to the maître d' station, where Camille, color in her cheeks from the chill outside, was shrugging off her coat. He was looking forward to seeing what peculiar assortment she had collected this evening and—galvanized by Leo's prediction—whether it would be easy to extricate her from them for dessert, for champagne, for some late-night wandering.

She waved, and Britt smiled and extended a hand as he neared, because the opened hand could do anything, really—it could become a kiss on the cheek, it could be a simple clasping of her hand, but either way it was a clear invitation and yet a thoroughly appropriate welcome, an approach he had perfected long ago. And so it was all the more disconcerting when she did in fact lean into him for the briefest and silkiest of cheek brushes, and even more so when this motion revealed behind her Britt's brother Harry.

Britt nodded at Harry, who could be counted on to understand a delayed greeting when a woman was there, and returned his attention to Camille. "It's been too long," he said.

"I know," she said. "I tried out that Italian place on Sommers, which I probably shouldn't tell you."

"Not at all," said Britt. "How was it?"

"Prefab." Camille glanced behind her.

"This is my younger brother, Harry," Britt said, and Harry and Camille both laughed.

"I know," she said. "We're having dinner."

"Oh," Britt said. "Well. I didn't know you knew each other."

Britt was rather warm inside his suit now. Was this development helpful or not? Out of his work boots and paint-splattered jeans, Harry was looking altogether presentable. He had trimmed his beard, appeared to have gotten a haircut, and had finally found a decent suit long enough in the limbs.

As the three of them made their way to a table by the front window, Britt heard his own voice saying various things, but he had no idea what any of them were. He seemed to be recommending the pasta. When Harry and Camille were seated, Britt stood for a moment gazing down at them in the avuncular way in which he often regarded Harry, which was, catastrophically, now directed at Camille as well. Then he told them to enjoy and departed for the kitchen to inform Thea that his brother was in the house.

Thea was expediting, standing with her feet planted well apart, hands braced on the stainless steel counter before her, observing the line cooks at work. She wore houndstooth pants, a white chef's jacket that tied like a robe instead of being buttoned or double-breasted, and the surgeon's cap she preferred to the house baseball cap with the restaurant's logo on it. She believed the surgeon's caps were more effective, and they did somehow contain the untamable headdress of dark brown curls that was the bane of her existence. People touched her hair compulsively, unable to believe the spirals weren't formed of metal filings or some resinous material; when they reached up for her hair, Thea would go as still as a cat and endure it. She was sturdy and long-limbed, broad-shouldered and slim-hipped as a swimmer.

On the line she radiated a steely calm that had taken some time for the kitchen to adjust to after Kenneth. At first many cooks had been unaware that they were being chastised for an uneven sear or an insufficiency of acidity. They thought she was commiserating. Where was the name-calling, the hoarse roar, the flash of the spatula Kenneth had wielded, ridiculously yet effectively, like a chef's knife? Yet this misapprehension worked in her favor: the understanding of their failures surfaced later, over cigarettes and bourbon at Mack's, the shithole bar around the corner, where around one a.m. a cook would often go quiet and stare at his knees in humiliated comprehension. When they returned the next day they found Thea already in the kitchen beside a vat of some vegetable awaiting their attention, a reminder that in the end they were there to peel, mince, blend, or sear, to be yeomen and craftsmen, whatever she asked them to be, and slowly they settled in and reoriented themselves to the kitchen as the seat of a controlled burn instead of a constant apocalypse. Britt had taken tremendous pleasure that first month after Kenneth's ouster, watching Thea bring the kitchen staff in line one by one, like a game of psychological Whack-A-Mole. She had done it without raising her voice or losing composure; she had done it all by subtext.

Britt also found her rigid and distant—he was always thrown off by an uncharmed woman—but he trusted her with everything, and in a way he felt the two of them had the same job. Britt might be part owner, but to some extent he and Thea both executed Leo's vision, internalized his tastes and hatreds and sensitivities, and smoothed their respective staffs into the same mold.

He was just about to let her know which table Harry and Camille were at when Thea looked beyond him and smiled. Britt turned, expecting to see Leo, but instead found it was Harry, strolling right through the kitchen doors to shake Thea's hand and kiss her high on the cheekbone.

Harry clapped him on the shoulder. "Am I in the way if I say hello?" he asked. "Leo said it was okay."

"Not at all," Britt said. "It's good to have you back here again."

Harry was nodding, taking in the kitchen. He raised a hand in the direction of Suzanne and Jason. "Nice to see you guys," he said.

"You too," they said in unison. Britt frowned, wondering where they'd met.

"I'm dying to get my hands on that lamb," Harry told Britt. "And the foie. I don't think I'm going to be able to get away with serving that anytime soon. You guys can do those really high-end things over here. Maybe if I keep it casual it'll hide the learning curve."

"I'm not even all that big a fan of foie gras," Britt said. "I feel like we kind of have to serve it. You'll get more flexibility."

Britt had always thought of Harry as the freest one of all three, unhindered by the same nervousness or expectations their parents had had for Britt and Leo. And so Harry had been gone for a decade, his extensive education punctuated by stints at the Alaskan salmon cannery, an organic farm, a high-end food store, and finally a restaurant on a tourist island. Meanwhile Britt had toiled in a PR firm and Leo had worked his way through restaurant after restaurant. Harry returned for Leo's wedding and for a commiserating lost weekend when Leo divorced. Over the years photos had arrived: Harry looking like a serial killer in bloody coveralls at the cannery, or on a boat before a glacial backdrop, his hands thrust beneath the flared scarlet gills of a great silver salmon. He clustered with a group of rumpled scholars before a grand stone library in Ann Arbor or stood, hands on hips, in a field where two spotted goats nosed at his denimed knees, his red hair lifted by the breeze. He was no sap, though; those goats had been braised with juniper berries and thyme not long afterward.

Britt had realized guiltily that he'd ceased paying close attention to these missives, nor had he kept up with answering them. By the time he replied that the farm sounded great, Harry was eating raw salmon straight out of the Alaskan waters, then had landed a research grant for his dissertation. All that resourcefulness made Britt feel old and staid.

But then again, Harry had never appeared to have a long-term plan, either, and Britt was discomfited by the suspicion that Harry's path to opening his restaurant was just a little too random. Britt didn't believe in randomness; he did not believe in serendipity. He felt a dark turn of uneasiness every time he really thought about Harry hoping to save the waterfront and awaken the city's palate all at once. Britt was afraid Harry had gotten the impression that there was some single obscure trick to opening a restaurant, as there was to unhinging a mussel. It wasn't like making a few great meals or decorating one pleasant room. Leo had drilled that into Britt before they'd opened Winesap, because back then Britt had been more of a newbie than Harry was now. But Britt had approached it with lists and spreadsheets and research, because although he found it important to appear effortless in all things, few things truly were.

Maybe Harry had a pile of spreadsheets and research at home that Britt didn't know about. He was a scholar, after all.

Out in the dining room Britt could see the vivid blur of Camille's dress. "So how do you know Camille?" he asked.

Harry smiled mysteriously. "Oh, you might call it a professional relationship through one of my investors," he said. To Thea he added, "She's a knockout."

Thea nodded. "I know," she said, "I saw her résumé." Harry and Britt looked at her in confusion, but Thea only shook her head, disappointed in them both. Jason handed her a plate of rabbit ragù, and she inspected it before finishing it with a fresh grating of Parmigiano-Reggiano. She snapped a damp towel from her belt and wiped a smear of sauce off the plate, marked the dish on the ticket, and reached for a fish plate from Suzanne. Most of the time she was quiet, but now and again she noted a plating that displeased her, a mirepoix on the verge of being unrefined. Thea was not charmed by rusticity or idiosyncrasy.

"I was going to take her out for sushi," Harry was saying. "I wanted to introduce her to this place I just found with the most incredible toro. Did you know most toro is *days* old, *and* it's thawed? It'd shock you, man, it really would. Anyway, I think my guy has a line on some black-market toro or something—you should see his little unmarked restaurant door. This tuna is like heroin. It's like *sea* heroin. I think she'd love it. But I haven't been here in so long, I couldn't go somewhere else first."

"It's been a while," Britt agreed. "Since Kenneth? No, that can't be right." But he was distracted, thinking that Harry knew the secrets of Camille's desires and tastes, while Britt, after months of observation, was still grasping sadly at details. Britt glanced down at the line, where a halibut and a venison had joined the rabbit ragù and been wiped clean by Thea, finished with a drizzle of olive oil, and capped with a metal dish cover. The backwaiter had left a scattering of breadcrumbs near the cutting board, and Britt brushed them into an empty basket and stashed it beneath the counter. He turned back to Harry just as Alan came bustling into the kitchen to retrieve his dinners.

"Completely purposeful," Alan was saying. "Finally she seats the bar, knowing perfectly well I'd get slammed. Where's the brittle?" Thea silently handed him a plate with a shard of salty pistachio brittle to accompany the venison. It had to be placed on the plate immediately before serving or else it softened up. Harry was eyeing the brittle closely as Alan remembered himself, said to Thea, "Thank you, chef," and dashed away.

"Salted brittle?" Harry asked thoughtfully.

Thea smiled. "It's actually pretty savory."

Harry crossed his arms and bent forward. "How do you do that? Brittle *is* sugar."

"I know!" Thea said. "It took forever to get the proportions right. Our pastry chef actually came up with it. Well. Former pastry chef. Anyway, it's not that there's no sugar, it's more that it's so caramelized that you perceive the salt and nuttiness and roastiness. But also there's the tiniest bit of dried currant. Tarts it up."

"You should try it," said Britt.

Harry said, "I'd love it. I don't know if Camille's a venison person."

"I think she's had the venison here before," Britt said.

Harry peered back into the dining room. "She's gorgeous, don't you think? I'm still looking for an in. Maybe tonight. Maybe some wine."

"You know what?" Britt said. "Let us take care of ordering tonight. Don't even bother looking at your menus."

"Really?" Harry said. "We'd love it. I mean, I want to try the venison—"

Britt interrupted him smoothly. "Not one look. Go relax, and we'll plan it all from here."

Harry's eyes darted between Thea and Britt, a tentative smile working at his mouth. "Okay, then," he said. "That's fantastic, you guys. Thanks." He gave Britt a winning smile, punched him on the arm, pointed a finger at Thea, and said, "You. Me. Brittle. Later," and then headed back out to the dining room. Britt watched him go, feeling guilty but also faintly relieved to have a little control again after the careening sensation he'd had when he'd seen Harry with Camille.

"What's he doing back in town?" Thea asked. She had returned to work now, firing the next round of dishes. She had always been fond of Harry, who joshed her and teased her in a way no one else was allowed to. Certainly no one at Winesap would dare to flirt with Thea. Britt suspected even her ex-husband had never enjoyed the privilege.

"He's been staying at our parents' house since April, while he gets settled," Britt said. Then he lifted one shoulder and admitted, "And he's opening a restaurant." Thea glanced sharply at him.

"You're kidding," she said.

"I am not."

Thea's face clouded, and Britt experienced a rare flash of genuine warmth for her. It *was* ridiculous, he was about to say, for his brother to assume that he could so easily step right into what Leo and Britt had built. Of course it was!

"Why wouldn't I have heard about this?" Thea said. "Are you guys in it with him?"

"Nope. We may have offered an idea or two, but that's it. We didn't want to mention it till it was clear he was really going to do it."

She shook her head. "Jason! Did you know about this?"

Jason handed her a plate. "Yes, chef."

"You did?" said Britt.

"Yeah," said Jason. "We heard over at Mack's. He came in to buy drinks and meet the locals."

"Tell them what they're calling it," said Suzanne. Jason shot her a look, but Suzanne had served up a plate of fish and turned back to the range, leaving Jason to his fate.

"Crab Apple," Jason admitted. He wiped a sheen of sweat from his ivory forehead, looking faintly ill, but Jason always looked faintly ill. "I heard the real name is 71 King."

"Goddammit," said Thea. "People are going to compare us, whether it makes any sense or not. I need to be aware of it. If my own sous chef hears something like this, I should know." She looked at Britt accusingly. "Now I have to hang out at that dive bar once a week or else I'll be out of the loop."

"I'm sorry," Britt said. "I should've told you." Britt thought of the front table, the window table, where he had installed Camille and Harry, where even now Camille would be working her way through a glass of champagne. The taut pull of her throat as she swallowed, her fingers curled around the stem. Professional acquaintance or not, Harry would be laying some groundwork, a glancing touch on the shoulder as he returned to the table, a disarming opinion of some recent movie.

"Oyster fritter," Britt said. Thea whipped out a pad and began to write. "Oyster fritter, then the foie gras terrine, then a little taste of the pork rillettes." Thea raised an eyebrow. "The sea bream with potato-truffle galette, the lamb, and a half course of the venison. And a half course of the rabbit ragù, before the bream. What's the soup situation?"

"Plenty of the bourride," said Thea.

"Well, then, a little bourride early on as well," said Britt. "Finish with the rib eye, and give them the works on dessert. I'll have Helene do the cheese."

Thea had finished writing—the meal order had gone on to a second page—and now she looked at him. "No halibut?"

Britt blanked. "What's the prep?"

"Clementine gremolata, saffron broth."

"Oh," he said, disappointed, "it's the light-bright." This was their term for the dishes that were high in acidity and low in cream; every night's menu had one, to appease the dieters and the faint of heart. "Nah. Make it a full order each of bourride and we'll take it from there."

He headed back out to the dining room, where the tenor had shifted slightly. It had taken him a full year, maybe even longer, to calm down during the madhouse period of a Saturday night and accept that it would always eventually smooth out into this: Britt thought of it as the acceptance phase. The pace was no less frantic, but the servers had settled into their groove and the backwaiters remembered how to think only three or four tasks ahead instead of trying to see their way through the whole evening. Alan was pouring out martinis in a perfect silver thread, with not so much as a pause between glasses, and Helene was removing the empty plates from the diners at the end of the bar. They would all keep going like this until a couple of hours from now, when the last turn would filter in and the room would suddenly be dotted with a few blessedly empty tables and the welcome sight of coffee cups and brandy snifters. The moment always arrived as an abrupt shift in perception, marked every night by the instant when Britt realized the music was now too loud. Inevitably, at the very same moment he would see Helene reaching inside the maître d' stand to lower the volume on the sound system.

THEA WATCHED JASON PLATE a venison rib chop, curious how long he would try to avoid looking at her. He finally looked at her as he handed over the plate. "I thought they told you, chef," Jason said. "Sorry." Thea waited. "Leo didn't say anything?"

Thea shook her head as she placed the ticket for Harry's table at one end of her board.

"Can I get a down-the-road?" Suzanne asked.

"Yup. Ordering one fritter, split," Thea replied. "Firing two amuse. That's all you."

"One fritter, split," Suzanne replied. "Firing two amuse."

Thea sighed. "You know how Leo is. If we hear anything from anyone, it'll be Britt. And it should've been them. I shouldn't give you guys a hard time. So I won't, but still—you hear anything further, you let me know."

"Of course," Suzanne said piously.

Thea decided she had taken it as far as she could. She was more concerned about Leo—either he didn't think she knew the local scene, minimal though it was, or else he didn't think she needed to know. He was hard to catch hold of these days, weaving his way through the restaurant silently and unexpectedly, ever-present but difficult to pin down. Often the cooks looked up to realize he'd been standing by the espresso machine for who knows how long, observing the movement of the kitchen with a look of calm, if unsmiling, contentment. Yet he rarely spoke at staff meal or offered more than polite greetings when she ran into him in the office. It was tough to believe that his brother was Harry, who seemed to like everyone and who over the years had stopped in to charm the staff whenever he was in town. Apparently he'd strolled into Mack's and started introducing himself and within a night or two had had cooks practically fighting to name the best staff in the local industry. Even Britt, whose charisma was so professional and yet so unconscious, gave only the impression of intimacy, the constant promise of it. But she could imagine Harry leaning back in his plastic chair, listening as intently as a therapist. Yet he too kept some silences. It seemed he hadn't said much about the kind of place he was opening. Maybe those three were related after all.

A new ticket spat out of the printer. "Ordering three venison, firing one bourride, split," Thea called. Jason nodded and repeated the venison portion of the order, pulling chops from the reach-in to let them come to temp. Only when Thea fired them would he begin to cook each dish.

"Sure you want to split these dishes?" Jason said. "I think Britt wants us to double 'em up."

Thea laughed. "We should send out an extra course too, come to think of it. Poor Harry. He's gonna end up sleeping here."

CHAPTER 3

Hot springs was the venture of a couple who had been around the restaurant scene near Linden for years. The Makaskis had started out in the late eighties with an Italian place that was not a chain but cooked like one, with pesto cream and skinless chicken breast and frozen ravioli. They'd hung a painting of a tiny, black-clad old woman over the bar and offered the impression that she was a maternal grandmother of either Barbara's or Donnie's—the story seemed to change, but Donnie Makaski liked to glance fondly up at the image when he passed. At the time, Leo was working for a seafood place in the same neighborhood, while Britt was still strategizing campaigns for outpatient aesthetic surgery clinics. They stopped in for a drink once and sipped flaccid Valpolicella while watching Donnie pour himself a half glass of wine and knock it back. On his way to the kitchen he'd looked up at the portrait's sweet, round-cheeked smile and touched the edge of the gilt frame as if it were the robe of a saint. Leo decided then and there that they had bought the picture at an estate sale or out of someone's garage; any genuine portrait of a Makaski ancestor would have included what Leo believed to be the Makaski familiars: Kalashnikovs, maybe, or a vampire bat.

Hot Springs had opened a year earlier, touting itself as Northern California fare, and Leo was as surprised as anyone to find himself there late on a Saturday night. But as the Makaskis had opened and sold places, they'd learned a few things. While the decor was rather bland, all ivories and slate accents, it did not resemble a hotel lobby or an Atlantic City reception for the pope, as their first few places had. The menu bore fewer overtly silly touches; the pesto cream was long gone, and the dishes looked reasonably edited: roasted figs and prosciutto, grilled sardines with capers. Though Leo was still fairly certain that the Sysco truck backed up behind Hot Springs in the dead of night to deliver everything from linens to chicken breasts the Makaskis swore were free-range or mesclun greens they advertised as local, the Makaskis had learned to hide such shortcuts. And now somehow they had obtained this new pastry chef who had earned them the best part of a recent review. In the wake of Hector's departure (Hector had recently sent a note from Guatemala, accompanied by a photo of him wielding a machete and a purple cacao bean the size of a football), Leo didn't think he had any right to snobbery. Besides, Leo used Sysco too, where it didn't matter. He was no purist.

He hoped that by showing up late on a Saturday, he'd miss Barbara and Donnie, who might already be in the back doing book work or even at home if things were going well enough. But when he and Britt walked in, Barbara was there at the host's podium, sweeping the dining room with a martial gaze, offering them a view of her Roman general's profile and her frozen magenta hair. She was taller than Britt and Leo both, with ropy limbs and muscular freckled hands with short unpolished nails and a single ring: an inky, pointed stone clawed in yellow gold. Tonight she wore a black wrap dress that exposed the planes of a chest that looked like hammered copper. She came out from behind the podium to press cheeks, clouding Leo with the dark fragrance of sawed wood and nightshade. Sometimes Barbara scared the shit out of him. She gazed at them searchingly. "How divine to see you both," she said. "Simply divine. How is everything at Winesap?"

"Fantastic," said Britt. "Throngs. I've had to add a velvet rope out front."

She laughed abruptly. Britt was very good with Barbara—he stayed with jokes and exaggeration, which meant Barbara spent all her energy trying to ferret out hidden meanings and secrets about their purveyors, their service, their vinaigrette. The Makaskis were known to quiz guests about their experiences at nearby restaurants, usually menacing them with a glass of grappa first. It would never occur to them simply to have dinner at Winesap.

"Divine," she said again. "Dinner tonight?" Already her hands were on their shoulders, steering them toward a table, but Leo gently wrenched himself toward the bar.

"Just a snack," he said. "How's everything going here? Donnie?"

She allowed them to choose seats at the bar, then said, "Donnie is astonishing. The man's instinct for business, for inspiring loyalty—you can't imagine. It's new to me every day, really." She shook her head, pondering Donnie. "He'll want to say hello, of course. He thinks—*we* think—so highly of you both."

"Love to," said Britt. Barbara bowed slightly, as if in the direction of a dueling partner, and departed.

Leo picked up his menu while Britt scanned the wine list. "She's probably dispatching the busboy to slash our tires," Leo said.

"She smells a rat," Britt murmured. "I'm still not wild about this. You never know when we might need that proverbial cup of sugar."

"We're just doing research," said Leo. "I want to know who's out there. Anyway, I don't seek them out. If someone comes to me, that's a different story."

Britt smiled. "And if the pastry chef just happens to hear you were in for dessert, maybe she'll come over to Winesap to say hello. Very nice. What do you want to try?"

Leo took a deep breath and examined the dessert menu for a few seconds, chewing the inside of his lip. "Let's try the chocolate quills, the roasted pear, the sour cherry cake, and the ice cream trio. You think she put up sour cherries? Dried them?"

"Maybe," said Britt, shrugging. They ordered desserts from the bartender, plus decaf for Leo and a port for Britt. They watched the bartender pouring cocktails for a few minutes. Leo caught a glimpse of Barbara gliding into the kitchen. Donnie would be out soon. They could have ordered something besides dessert if they had wanted to be a bit subtler about checking out the competition, but Leo figured there was no point in hiding it. He didn't need some poor sap thinking he was there to see what someone could do with rolls of prosciutto on an antipasto plate. The pastry chef might as well know why they were here. Britt was sipping his wine, gazing out over a still-full dining room.

"What'd you send out to Harry?" Leo asked.

"Oh, a bunch of stuff," Britt said, not looking at him. "Kind of a tasting menu."

"Lot of wine pairings too, it looked like," Leo added.

"I thought they'd like it. Camille never drinks much, though, have you noticed? Does she drink at all?"

"She sips," said Leo. "But I don't think it's her thing."

Britt nodded. "That's what I thought."

As he and Leo had prepared to leave the restaurant, they'd stopped by Harry's table, where Harry and Camille were midway through the marathon. Several wineglasses in varying states of fullness sat before each of them, and Harry was sniffing at a glass of red while Camille took a minuscule bite of cavatelli off the very tips of the tines of her fork. The two were talking quietly, unsmiling, as Britt approached, and when he and Leo stood next to the table, both Harry and Camille had started slightly, their gazes unfocused by wine and animal protein, before they recognized who had joined them. That was the error in strategy, of course: Camille was now just as woozily ensconced as Harry. There was no chance of inviting her out for anything, except perhaps sleep or insulin.

Now Britt rubbed his fingers on the edge of the bar top and glanced at them surreptitiously, hoping to detect dust or cleaner residue. There was none. "You gone over to Harry's new place lately?"

Leo shook his head. "Not since we saw it in September. It keeps getting away from me. And he didn't even mention it last weekend."

The three of them had met up for a game of basketball, at Harry's behest, early on Sunday morning before Harry returned to the restaurant space. He'd been on a roll on the court, weaving silkily around the other two and sinking layups. He didn't bring up the restaurant. When Britt asked after it, Harry had said, "Oh, it's fine. I just need a break from thinking about food and places people go to buy it." Then he sank a three-pointer and added, "Aha! Now that's the shot that's going to take me all the way to Reykjavik."

"I never saw him in this business," Britt mused now. "I figured he'd be a professor by now. He could've been, too, if he hadn't kept taking off to gut fish."

"You never saw yourself in it either," Leo said.

"I know. It's just that for someone who always liked to wander, he's tying himself down pretty tightly. Since when does he settle down?"

"And he always said he'd never come back. Though I guess he was a lot younger then."

Britt snorted. "In college, I never thought I would, either."

Leo looked away. He'd gone to college not far from Linden; both of his younger brothers had made a big deal of going to more demanding schools.

"It's not that his idea's bad," Britt was saying. "I don't know if it can work around here, or in that location, but small plates of something a little interesting—I can see it. I can see it somewhere. It's something new."

"New around here," Leo pointed out. "You go to a bigger city and trust me, none of this stuff is really new. Still, someone has to bring it here, I guess."

"He really wants to get a farmers' market going in Linden," Britt said.

"Well, who doesn't?" Leo cried. Britt looked taken aback, and Leo lowered his voice a notch. "How long have we been name-checking every remotely local producer on the menu? For years. I happen to find it kind of obnoxious, but it works, so I'll do it. I may not chase every trend that filters through, but sometimes I think Harry thinks we're serving veal Parmesan or sun-dried tomatoes or something." Leo sipped his coffee and sighed, disliking the sound of his own voice.

"The space has possibilities," Britt ventured after a brief silence. "And maybe this time the waterfront really will improve."

"You should tell him that. We should quit giving him a hard time. He'll carry a lot of debt for a while. It's not a casual thing. Plus, he admires you."

"He thinks I'm shallow," Britt said.

"Yes, but he also trusts your taste."

The bartender refilled his decaf and Leo nodded his thanks. The Makaskis didn't run a sloppy operation. The bar was whisked clean and the bartender wore a spotless white tuxedo shirt and bow tie—he looked like an elevator operator, but crisp and neat.

"Why did he and Shelley split up?" Britt said. "I thought they'd stay out there in Iowa or Michigan or wherever they were forever."

Leo shook his head. "I only know she quit that island thing they were doing and left Harry to clean it up."

"Ugh. I always thought he was just too smart for her. He was too nice to notice."

"I think she went off with a baker to open a pizza place in the Bay Area."

"That's even worse! He's opening a rebound restaurant."

"Oh, I don't think it's that simple," Leo said.

"Listen, she did him a favor, not marrying him. He'd never have divorced her and we'd still be dealing with her at Thanksgiving."

"Jesus. Those weird little tempeh pie appetizers."

They sipped their drinks, smiling. The truth was, they loved discussing Harry and felt a sort of backhanded pride in his eccentricities and the way he saw new projects where others saw only the same old systems.

For all Harry's intellectual flexibility, however, he could be unexpectedly fierce once he'd homed in on a goal. When he was about ten, in Little League, Harry had once forced a home run out of what should have been a triple, and he still sometimes displayed the same clenched jaw and narrowed eyes he'd had then, as he rounded third and hurled himself mercilessly and foolishly into the kid at home plate. They'd ended up with bloody faces and elbows, Harry with a swollen cheekbone and a finger's length of raw skin on the bridge of his nose. Leo had been seventeen, at the game with Britt on orders from their parents, and the two of them had exchanged a glance half of amusement, half of alarm, while next to them their parents had cried out over the dust and blood.

The only other woman in Harry's life who'd ever seemed serious had been the one before Shelley, a Ph.D. in history whom Harry had lived with in Ann Arbor. Catherine had been reedy and dark-haired, with large eyes in a foxy, elegant face, given to slim-cut pants and striking old jewelry and heathery tweed blazers. From behind she had looked like an English schoolboy in need of a haircut. Catherine was almost freakishly brilliant but too polite to flaunt it; they understood how meteoric her career track was only when Harry mentioned that she was deciding between jobs at Oxford and Harvard. It turned out she'd wanted to set up her new life alone, however (she chose Oxford), leaving Harry bereft, in possession of a collection of arcane books he no longer wanted to own and a cat soon revealed to have feline leukemia. Not long after the cat's demise Harry left Ann Arbor for the island. Leo and

Britt assumed that he was healing, that after Harry had enjoyed the company of someone as particular and graceful and intelligent as Catherine, he would be drawn to ever greater heights of romantic accomplishment. They had waited in pleasant anticipation of some divine creature, and instead they'd gotten Shelley, she of the goat's milk soaps and endless balls of smelly untreated wool, which she ferried about in badger-sized lumps; she of the joyless dietary theories and miasmic dinner table silence; she of the pallid limbs and midday naps and whispered arguments with Harry and hateful rye flour and maple puddings. The first time she set one before Britt, he'd looked as if she'd stabbed him through the back of his hand. When the rest of their family played a hand of poker, Shelley would meditate. When they divvied up the preparations for some elaborate holiday meal, Shelley inevitably expressed disappointment over the authenticity of the local ingredients or the source of a recipe. No one had ever seen her smile. Britt and Leo were too dismayed to discuss her even with each other until, several months earlier and right before Harry reappeared in Linden, she had finally, mercifully, removed herself, like a virus that dies off for no discernible reason.

"Can you imagine what that wedding would have been like?" Britt mused. "Instead of a toast, she would have made people stand up and confess how they've contributed to the patriarchy."

"I wish Frances had met her," Leo said. "She would have hated her." The joy of being able to discuss Shelley, unafraid of summoning her presence, never lessened.

Britt watched Leo for a beat. "How is Frances?" he asked. "You never talk about her."

"I don't?" said Leo. He thought Britt was being sarcastic—he felt as if he talked about Frances all the time—but Britt's face was open and sincere, his green eyes intent. Britt had heavy reddish gold eyebrows and deep-set eyes; they made his stare a little penetrating. "She's in Portland," Leo said. He shrugged. "They're having a baby."

Britt waited for more, but Leo only lifted his chin in the direction of Donnie and Barbara, bearing down on them with an array of dessert plates. Leo and Britt set down their drinks, picked up their forks, and braced themselves.

Leo's ex-wife, Frances, had been in the restaurant business too, training as a sales rep for a wine importer when Leo was managing a bistro. Leo and Frances rented a little house, painted the rooms, weeded the garden, and hosted Thanksgiving. Around Frances Leo had felt as close to relaxed as he ever did. She was small, round but compact, with curling dark hair and snappy black eyes, given to showing off her olive skin with white halter dresses and a Slinky's worth of wire-thin silver bracelets. But after five years, right about the time they were completing the build-out, Frances moved out. She said she'd come to hate the wine business and the restaurant business too, its booziness and brashness.

What seemed to clinch it was New Orleans. She and Leo had gone to a convention where the culinary community converged annually for a combination of professional development and Roman orgy. They drank Sazeracs with some new brand of absinthe, martinis showcasing new brands of gin and vodka. The drinks were usually embellished with weird striving garnishes like cantaloupe batons, which floated in the booze looking, fatally, like fingers. After several of these, Leo remembered seeing Frances gaze slowly around her for what felt like hours, from face to face to face, while people talked at her. He had been listening to her boss go around the room person by person and enumerate their professional failings. Frances had been nodding and nodding, fingering a pendant on her necklace and talking to a boy-wonder chef who'd released a cookbook that year and was now dumping the remains of abandoned cantaloupe drinks into his own glass. They'd gotten swept into a crew heading out for gumbo z'herbes and had crowded into a run-down old house turned restaurant with a bunch of strangers. After the bread pudding, the boy wonder had tried to kiss first Frances and then Leo. The next morning Leo had woken up with a vivid flash of memory, the boy wonder's scratchy chin against his, Frances laughing, and the smell of smoke in the air. The hangover had descended on them both like a fever, and when it had gone she'd been distant and morose.

Every year they all headed down there, closed their eyes, and splashed in, and Leo actually liked the annual madness. He liked the chance to behave like a frat boy when no one even noticed, and now that he and Frances were opening a restaurant and working a staggering number of hours, he'd enjoyed it all the more. The rest of the year he was measured and calm and drank wine paired with each course, and once a year he and Frances tore the lid off and then stuffed it back on. He liked the randomness of each year, the conviviality of Frances with a few cocktails in her, when she could and did talk to anyone. He liked the gumbo. He liked the fact that Frances was the one who'd shown him around the event, since she had been attending for her job a year or two before Leo went; he associated the place with Frances in her most Circean element, three days spent eyeing her through a constant, glowing buzz. But that year she'd said she hated the whole business, actually, that she wanted to go home at six o'clock like a normal grown-up, and that she was sick of discussing food as if it were art or a cure for AIDS. "But I don't do that," Leo had protested on the plane ride home. "Food's our craft, that's all. I just want to do it well." "But all those assholes, arguing about ramen broth," Frances had said. "We'll never get away from those people if we stay in it, you know. They'll break our spirits and we'll end up running an Olive Garden." "I think there's a third way," Leo had said mildly. He'd snapped open a magazine while Frances turned toward the window. Frankly, he was insulted. He didn't enjoy the rabid foodies any more than Frances did, but he recognized that they would provide a livelihood. Let people caress their slices of pork and argue about seasoning. What did he care? They could photograph their food all they wanted. Leo thought Frances—who'd spent a few years rolling wine around her tongue and gazing at the ceiling herself—was being snobbish and reactionary. Leo liked being out among people he knew; he liked to finish a shift and go out for late dinners of a few first courses and a free glass of grappa or a comped dessert. Frances just wanted to go home and wake up early to go for a run. She was a morning person. Sometimes Leo thought it all rested on that.

The rupture took on other forms, but within a year she'd gone back to school to be a teacher and moved out.

Now and again it hit Leo all at once, the fact that of the three of them, him and his brothers, not one was happily married or attached, and any lessons from their parents' long marriage must have passed them by. Leo feared that he and Britt were just getting too old now to reorder their lives for a woman, and he feared even more that Harry would follow their example.

THE DESSERTS WERE NOT BAD. Once the Makaskis disappeared, Leo and Britt looked hard at their plates and tried to be subtle about poking around in them. The ice cream trio arrived on a black plate scattered with fruit. A tuile, rolled at the edges like a potato chip, perched on top. The roasted pear was halved and opened, filled with something creamy; the sour cherry cake a little golden loaf in a pool of compote. The chocolate quills arrived tied up in a strip of orange peel and set in an upright bundle.

They started on the ice creams: cinnamon, crème fraîche, and Damson plum.

"Ever had Damson plum ice cream?"

"Nope. Nice color." The plum ice cream was vanilla marbled with a rich winey purple.

"By 'cinnamon,' do they mean cinnamon the spice?"

"As opposed to what?"

"The candy. Try it. Plus, it's pink."

"Oh."

"I would have plated this differently."

"Yeah. The plum is perfect, though. So's the crème fraîche."

The quills were filled with a boozy ganache. "Do we eat them with our hands?" Britt asked. Leo shrugged. They tried them both ways: Leo ate a quill as if it were a French fry, and Britt ate one with a fork. It shattered easily under the tines, and Britt found himself absorbed in trying to get every shard of chocolate. Leo's fingers were printed with chocolate after the first bite. "It tastes pretty good," he said. "A little uniform. But it's kind of impossible to actually eat."

At the other end of the bar, Barbara was in conversation with a server, her eyes trained on them. When Leo smiled at her, she inclined her head respectfully and turned away.

They set aside the quills and inspected the roasted pear, which was filled with mascarpone and scattered with pistachios. Leo considered. "The mascarpone's a good idea," he said. "It's not sweet. There's some cardamom in there too."

Britt nodded. The tuiles that accompanied the pear were caramelized and sparkling with coarse dark sugar. He took a bite of pear and mascarpone and a bite of tuile and chewed, still nodding. Leo took one more bite. "That's actually really good. I hate a mushy pear, but this is just right."

They moved on to the sour cherry cake, which was moist and fragrant with almond and some herbal note that quieted both of them. They sat, tasting and thinking, for several seconds, until Leo said, "Hyssop."

They finished all the cake, two of the ice creams, half the pear, and only a couple of the chocolate quills. Leo left a big tip and they waved to Donnie and Barbara, who were swooping down on another table with a great platter of prosciutto. Outside, Britt said, "Well?"

"I thought it was mostly pretty nice," Leo said. "Couple missteps." He shrugged. "I'll file it away for now. Where you headed? Are you still seeing the brunette? Maria?"

"Maren. Kind of. I was supposed to see her tonight but I rescheduled, and now I'm not really missing it. I think we're at that stage after three or four months where it feels a little depressing to state the obvious. Now it's just hanging over me. You headed home?" Leo still lived in the house he'd shared with Frances.

"Yeah, it's late." Leo glanced at his watch. "We've been gone two hours, which means Camille and Harry are probably about a third of the way through that banquet you inflicted on them. You should stop back and see if they're awake."

CHAPTER 4

S UNDAY MORNING, BRITT DRANK AN ESPRESSO at one end of his massive barn door table, then ran six miles. Then he did a quick scan through Craigslist to see what was being sold on the cheap.

He'd reached the point at which he could discern in seconds whether there was anything of worth. His eye skipped over curlicues and egg-and-dart detailing but might pause over painted wood. This was how he'd found out where to have peeling old radiators sandblasted and freshly painted to look like new. It was where he'd unearthed a massive Wolf range—he wasn't much of a cook, but it had been sold cheaply and he believed in the real estate value of a serious stove—as well as a Stickley chair and his beloved barn door. People had no idea what could be done on the cheap, and Britt prided himself on the fact that no one looking through his apartment or his restaurant would suspect he knew, either.

This was one of the vexations of the restaurant, and the reason Britt obsessed about his suits, treating each with as much care as if it were a royal corgi. He and Leo courted clientele who thought little of dropping hundreds of dollars on a meal, or who expensed ridiculous dinners for a gaggle of doctors in order to stuff them with steak and wine and give them free pens and logo pads. And Britt moved among them with a modicum of power, because he had the ability to make them seem more important and respected than they might actually be. But his income, though good, as was that of his busiest servers, was nowhere near that of his clients, and nowhere near what he took great care to project. The false parity was crucial, but it was a strain at times, and one felt by the entire staff. They were there, servers and cooks alike, because they knew what good wine was, what excellent food could be, and had sought out ways to obtain it despite the limits of time, education, and income. They were working at Winesap not only for tips and pay-checks and even career integrity, but to get wine, fish, cheese, or the occasional white truffle at cost, to be paid to taste the lobster prep, and to dine out under the restaurant's aegis and reap its benefits.

When any of their staff, be it backwaiter or prep cook, traveled or went to a big-name restaurant, Britt, Leo, or Thea would phone ahead and call in favors, owner to owner, chef to chef, to ensure that they were known as fellow industry people and treated accordingly: esoteric extra courses, obscure wines, and bits of culinary info to which the average diner, however wealthy, was not privy. "They're massaged and fed beer each day," confided a server at one astronomically priced place where Britt had eaten the previous year. She had placed the last plate of wagyu beef—scarlet meat threaded with ivory fat, ringed with a rich browned crust—before him and glanced around, lowering her voice. "But also, to ensure they aren't stressed by the slaughter, they're periodically thwapped with the flat of a sword. They get so used to it that when the time comes, they're totally unfazed. And the meat, of course, stays as ten-der as ... well, as this. Of course I can only say this to you—you'll appreciate it." It wasn't just about freebies, though that helped. This was the reward for working when everyone else was relaxing, for treating the petulant and ignorant with grace, for learning to give the appearance of toadying to the kind of ass who needed it while retaining one's self-respect through the occasional subtle retort.

There was nothing of note online today, and he didn't need much of anything. Restless, he went out to a coffee shop to read the paper and get a snack, but the place was full and the pastry was wrapped in plastic. As he left, on impulse he turned into the bakery down the street, bought six sfogliatelle, and drove to his parents' house.

When Britt arrived, he was relieved to see Harry's truck at the curb; for all Britt knew, Harry might be young and energetic enough to have muscled his way through that meal and spent the night with Camille anyway. But inside he found Harry at the stove, flipping pancakes. Their parents were standing in the kitchen in matching khaki pants and plaid vests, hands on hips, watching him work. For a moment after Britt walked in they seemed unable to disengage entirely, watching Harry peek at the crust on a golden cornmeal cake before being satisfied it could be turned. Their father observed until the pancake was safely flipped before he turned his attention to Britt.

"Ahh. A surprise!" He inhaled at the edges of the box. "I almost don't want to know."

"Sweetheart." His mother kissed Britt's cheek, smelling faintly of hand cream. Her hair had been the same ruffled auburn cap since they were children, though her cheeks were now downy and tender as overripe fruit. His father had taken his pocketknife from his khakis and was slicing through the red-and-white string that tied the bakery box.

"How was Hot Springs?" Harry asked.

"Good. Pretty good. A couple missteps, I guess, but some great spots too."

"Good to know," Harry said. "Leo leave his card on her windshield?"

"Of course not." Britt laughed, slightly offended.

"Doesn't mean she won't hear you were in and wander through Winesap some evening," Harry observed.

"True. Hector's off harvesting cacao, so we'd better find some-one."

"Oh, *Hector*," said their mother. "He did such intriguing things with fruit."

Harry slid the last of the pancakes onto a plate. He held up a plate in Britt's direction. "No, thanks," Britt said. "You go ahead."

Harry laughed. "I'm not eating. Are you kidding?"

Embarrassed, Britt picked up a corn cake and tore off a bite. Now that massive meal seemed so childish.

Their parents seated themselves at the table and busily spooned some sort of preserve onto their pancakes. The sfogliatelle were arranged prettily in a circle on a white plate. "It's very carby in here," Britt said. "I should have brought you lean protein. Some tofu." His mother waved this away, pouring coffee from a carafe into his father's cup and then her own.

"I'm going to see if anything's left in the trees," Harry said. "You coming?" Britt nodded, trying to come up with a reasonable excuse for the previous night's excess. Harry had barely met his eyes so far. Maybe he was angry, maybe he was still a bit hungover, maybe he was thinking ahead to a day at the restaurant.

Outside the back door, Britt picked up a flat cardboard box from a stack beneath the eaves and followed Harry up the hill to the apple trees. For a few minutes the two of them parted the remaining leaves of the trees, peering into the branches for fruit. It was early November now, and the trees were giving up their last meager harvest. Their mother would make apple butter and give it away for Christmas.

Harry circled a tree, reaching up occasionally. He had new glasses, Britt realized, tortoiseshell horn-rims that gave him a professorial air. He wore a red corduroy shirt and brown work boots. His face seemed older, the beard neatly trimmed beneath sharp cheekbones. What was he now, thirty-one? Thirty-two? Britt wondered how long Harry intended to stay with their parents—he couldn't be paying as much as if he'd had his own place—while the restaurant siphoned off as much cash as Harry could give it. These things had a way of becoming permanent if you weren't careful. If Leo hadn't dragged Britt out of the PR agency and into the restaurant, he might still be there.

Then again, their parents and Harry seemed to be enjoying each other, playing cards and puttering around the house, anticipating Harry's latest test of some new dish. Britt was even feeling slightly intrusive, which reminded him in a disquieting way of having had the same sensation in college. Then, his visits home had revealed that whereas in high school Britt and Leo had been furtive and absent, off sneaking weed and trying to recall where they'd hidden the condoms, Harry was a brash but winning teenager who was allowed to split a beer with his father, his curfew tacitly extended well beyond his brothers' old ones; a teenager who felt no need to lie about parties or to stay in the family room when a girl was over. Britt had been torn between envy—why not have Harry go through the same motions of rules and secrecy as his brothers had, just for form's sake?—and admiration for Harry's sheer finesse.

"*We* were never allowed to have girls in our rooms," Britt had once noted. He'd been visiting from Penn then, where he was a senior and free to take a girl to his apartment whenever he liked, yet for a moment he had felt that his little brother commanded more freedom in his parents' house than Britt enjoyed miles away from home. "They don't even have to keep the door open."

"Well, they never stay in there more than an hour or two," his mother had said, turning the page of her novel.

"Mom, how long do you think it takes?"

"Oh, Britt, don't be crude. You can't police people forever."

She'd bestowed on him an understanding smile, which had the effect of shifting Britt's halfhearted envy into regret. Harry wasn't getting the fun of being sixteen, he realized, of sneaking around, the exhilaration of slithering out a bedroom window and jogging down the block to where a car wouldn't wake his parents, the extra snap of the night air long after curfew. He decided to make up for it that weekend. He told their parents they were going to a movie and then took Harry out for a tour of accommodating dive bars, where Harry charmed the waitresses, bought a round of shots for a mangy crew of guys Britt would have crossed the street to avoid, and finally came in second in a pool tournament, winning a beer cozy and a free pitcher of Bud.

Feeling nostalgic, Britt took off his jacket and laid it carefully on the grass. "Hey," he said. "You're not so far from that dive bar I took you to once. The Tip-Top. You see if it still exists?"

For a second Harry looked confused, then his face cleared. "The *Tip*-Top," he said. "If it's not there anymore, then there's something just like it. I still have a soft spot for dive bars for some reason."

"You must, if you went to Mack's. Now that's a dump."

"Yeah, but it's like a Linden restaurant convention. Pretty handy for research. And they have an okay jukebox."

Britt climbed onto a stepladder his parents kept propped against a tree trunk during fruit season and reached further into the branches. These apples tended to be tart and hard, better for cooking than eating out of hand, but he sometimes tried a bite, just in case something had changed from year to year. He broke them off by the stems, then realized he'd left the box on the grass. He was about to climb down when Harry appeared below him, holding out the box, and took the apples from Britt's hand. "Hand 'em down," he said.

They worked that way for a few more minutes, Britt climbing a step and then another further into the tree, bracing one hand against the trunk while he reached. The remaining leaves gave way and drifted to the grass. The air smelled faintly of grill smoke from the neighbors', and the sun kept flashing golden through the branches, like a reflection off metal.

"So," Britt ventured. "You ever find your in?"

Harry glanced up. "What do you mean?"

"With Camille. How was dinner?"

"Oh, right. Yeah, dinner was great. Maybe I'm finally getting somewhere with her. I owe you."

"Great," Britt said, sounding toneless even to himself. The intensity of disappointment caught him off guard. Maybe that rugged, well-read cannery worker thing was Camille's style after all. Britt felt fussy and sheltered in comparison, a state of affairs so unexpected that he stopped, one arm midair, just identifying it. He was jealous of his kid brother. Jesus.

He redirected the subject, not wanting to hear any details about why Harry thought he'd gotten somewhere but still enjoying a little reminiscence. "Remember the O'Connor kids? We used to play kick the can with them," he said. "Terri O'Connor came into the restaurant a few weeks ago. She married a banker or something. She got all sleek. I didn't even recognize her."

"I think I got to play, like, one summer before everyone else got too old and quit," Harry said. "I remember Terri, though. 'Sleek' isn't the first thing that comes to mind."

Britt laughed. "Tell me about it." Terri O'Connor had had dark-lined brown eyes and uncontainable flesh, her hair thrillingly roughened with hairspray and cigarette smoke. Britt had made out with her once at a party when she was a senior and he a junior. She was surprisingly sweet to kiss, mentholated and tentative, her hands resting lightly on his back. It was a little disappointing, actually; for years he'd entertained fantasies about the carnal riot that must be Terri O'Connor. "She was nice. Two kids."

Harry nodded. "What'd she order?"

"Fish in saffron broth with the aioli on the side. Her husband was not impressed by the wine list." As Britt looked down at his brother, he saw Harry open his mouth as if to speak and then shrug. "What?" Britt said.

"What do you mean, what?"

"You looked like you wanted to say something."

Harry stepped back from the tree. "Come on down," he said. "We've got them all. Dad won't break his neck trying to pick them, at least."

Britt jumped down and brushed at his hands. "Hey," he said. "What?"

"It's just something I've been thinking about," Harry said. "Not the wine list—that's good."

"I know it's good," said Britt. "Terri's husband was the sort who thinks it's sophisticated to harp on rosé."

"You guys really did a serious meal for us last night," Harry said. "And I appreciate it. Helene wouldn't even charge me what she should have. Which you don't have to do."

"I know, you don't want to feel like you're using a coupon in front of Camille," Britt said.

"Camille wouldn't care—she'd be glad to see it," Harry said, mystifyingly. "It's just that I've been coming into Winesap for years, obviously, and I've always been proud as hell of it." He hesitated, and Britt realized that Harry might be angry at him for not being equally proud of Harry's ventures. Britt was so used to needling Harry that he forgot to do anything else, even when Harry really did impress him.

"I'm still proud of it," Harry went on, "but I just think there have been a lot of changes." He hesitated again and then lifted one hand as if to give up altogether and said, "I think you've lost focus, to be frank."

"You think what?" Just when Britt had been feeling so nostalgic and familial.

"I don't know if it would have seemed as clear if we hadn't eaten pretty much every dish on your menu. Well, that's not true. A look at the menu does kind of make it clear. But when you wade in like that, it becomes really evident that it just needs some *editing*. Like that toro dude—he doesn't make soba, you know? He doesn't do any pan-Asian crap, he doesn't even do pan-Japan. He learned how to source and cut sashimi and sushi and that's what he does. That's what you get, fucking perfect fish and rice. It's a little austere. But it feels all of a piece, it feels right for the place, you know."

Britt couldn't decide whether this was wisdom or effrontery. Harry had a way of ostensibly explaining his own learning process when in fact he was aiming to educate the listener. It was always a rather galling attitude for a younger brother, even when he was saying something genuinely insightful. And while Britt liked to think of himself as open to criticism, at the moment his indignation felt so piercing and vital that he went with that instead.

"I get it," he said. "You like the toro. But do you really think I don't know about *fish*? Have you even started talking to your purveyors yet? Do you even know who they are around here?"

Harry shook his head. "The toro's not my point. My point is that you walk into that place, or a pizza place, or whatever, and you know exactly where you are. There's a clarity of vision that you trust, because it's clear the chef has done the hard work, made the choices, and you can relax and you can get a little excited too, to see what they're going to show you. But I don't even know if you guys know. You do everything now. I mean, Jesus, the venison brittle is this kind of molecular gesture, I guess, and now you do your own pasta, and then you get kind of Alsatian on the foie gras, but then there was rösti with something else, and it's too much, Britt. That's what I'm trying to tell you. It's all over the place."

Britt picked up his jacket and shook out the grass from its sleeves. He shook his head. "Your restaurant isn't even open yet," he said. "Harry, you've done all this stuff over the years, you bounce from idea to idea, and you land on *my* idea and start correcting me about focus?"

"I know," Harry said. "I'm not really one to talk about laserlike focus, but I'd rather tell you than not. I think Leo is the one who's lost some focus. Leo's the one who created it in the first place. And

Leo's brilliant. But I don't want you to hear from a reviewer that your pistachio currant brittle doesn't work. Wouldn't you rather hear it from me?"

"You were psyched about the brittle!"

"I thought I would be. But it's a little off-putting, to be honest. It softens in a really gluey way. I get the idea, and the flavor was good, but texturally, it's a failure. Thea's usually on that kind of thing. I'm actually kind of surprised at her."

"Well, thanks, but you really might want to worry about your own reviews." Britt tried to sound unconcerned, but it came out catty instead. "Because that's the fun part. Soon you're going to experience the joy of working your tail off so every single person can nitpick your brittle."

Harry gave a bark of laughter. "Okay. Britt, where did I live for the last three years?"

Britt stopped brushing at his jacket sleeves. "You were in Michigan or something. Iowa."

"I was on an island in Lake Michigan," Harry said. "And what was I doing?"

"Come on."

"No, seriously, what was I doing?" Harry set down his box of apples and crossed his arms. For a moment Britt almost laughed at them, sparring beneath an apple tree. At times the food business wasn't exactly a roar of masculinity.

"You and Shelley were working at some restaurant," he said, more softly. He was feeling foolish. So Harry needed to take him down a peg—so what? He understood. It couldn't be easy to enter the fray when your brothers had already done it.

Harry smiled at him. "Shelley and I were managing a restaurant and cooking for it too. And it was fun because we did whatever we wanted. Amanda had us just branching out in any direction we wanted to try."

"I have no idea who Amanda is," Britt said.

"She was the owner and the chef," said Harry. "I sent you that article."

"Blond, flinty-looking, chef-on-the-cusp kind of thing?"

"Exactly. She had this concept for years, but she had a hard time getting funding till she got nominated for a James Beard. It was completely different from what you guys do, and yes, it turned out to be unsustainable over the long haul, but it was also like getting a Ph.D. in restaurants and food. We grew a lot of what we served. And forget all this fish distributor shit—I caught fish. Or I hired someone directly to catch it. If we wanted flour, we got a local guy to grow the wheat and then I bought myself a mill and ground it. Chefs from all over the place were trying to buy the stuff, except no one had time to hire another person to grind it. Shelley made her own butter, I made my own ricotta, and we figured out how to cure our own bacon. And it was really shitty bacon at first because I got the wrong breed of pig, and it turns out I have no aptitude for cheese-making. But I really wish you guys had seen it. If you'd come up then, you'd see why I'm doing this now."

"Well, you never told us *that*," Britt said uncertainly.

"I don't know, I thought I did. I could've sworn I e-mailed you guys about it, or at least I figured Mom and Dad would tell you. The point is, you think I have no idea what I'm doing, but I do. To some extent. And I'm telling you, every now and again you could listen to me."

"Okay," said Britt, holding up his palms.

"Not really," said Harry.

"No, really," said Britt. "I get it. I'm sorry."

"Thank you."

"Okay."

There was a long silence while they looked around the yard uncertainly, wondering what the next thing should be. Maybe a handshake. "I have to say, though," Britt began. Harry looked sharply at him, tilting his head, and Britt went on. "No, I really mean this. Harry, you don't have to make life so hard on yourself. You're not going to make it so difficult here too, are you? Let the world sell you flour. Pounding your tablecloths on a rock in the river isn't going to make it a better restaurant, you know? Get a linen service and call it a day."

Harry laughed and handed the half-full box of apples to Britt. "Now you tell me. No, listen, half the reason to come back here is that there's just more infrastructure. But when we were getting it right, we were making better food. It's a lot of Sysco around there, that far from the farms. And that island was struggling economically. Why not try to build more than just a restaurant? That was the idea, anyway."

"Okay," said Britt. "I get it." They began walking back to the house.

"I'll tell you what, though," said Harry. "We could bring a little of that here. Build up some relationships with the farmers."

Britt sighed. "We do a little of that," he said. "Thea's the one in charge of it."

"You guys helped start that here. You take a town like Linden that was in a downturn for so long. I always wondered why Mom and Dad stayed."

"Their parents were still around then. And Dad's attached to Linden. I think he still sees it the way it used to be."

"I suppose. And to be honest, now I feel attached to it in a weird way—you know, I even feel fond of the crappy sections. The Tip-Top! Now I have to go see if it's still there."

"Probably with all the same patrons," said Britt. "But listen, Harry, if what you were doing out there was such a great idea, why'd you stop?"

Harry held open the side door for him. "Amanda closed it down. It just didn't make enough money. And I think she just got so fucking tired. We all did. I loved it, but it was pretty lethal.

That's why I'm not doing the same thing here, not on that scale. I'll make it manageable—I'll make it fit the town. I know you guys are afraid I'm in over my head, but I have a good feeling. It's going to be great."

"We don't think that," Britt said, but it was for form's sake. "I didn't quite see your plan before," he admitted.

In the kitchen their parents were just finishing breakfast, and their father shooed them out of the kitchen when Britt tried to help with dishes. Harry disappeared into his room, and Britt watched his parents move about the kitchen, putting lids on jars and covering up the leftover corn cakes. He watched his father wrap half a slice of bacon in plastic and set it in the fridge. Harry took good care of them when he was here; there was no denying it. And so when he appeared again wearing a jacket and holding his keys, Britt said, "Let's go see how it looks," and followed his brother to the waterfront.

IN THE TWO MONTHS SINCE BRITT had seen it, Harry's restaurant had developed from an empty space with glimmers of possibility to a place that looked almost ready. The most amazing part was the ceiling: Harry had had it opened up, the beams exposed, raising the height of the room by three or four feet. It changed everything. Suddenly the room was airy and industrial, lively and unfussy. The tables were in; the long zinc bar was installed and ringed by stools with cracked saddle-colored leather seats. Behind the bar at one end was a beverage station and at the other, toward the back, were the grill, the oven, the salamander, and a fryer. The refinished floors glowed a warm honey. The east wall was freshly drywalled and painted the color of vellum. The wooden support beams were a rough chestnut color, sturdy and grand against the brick wall and the old leather seats, the gleaming curve of the bar and the tall windows and pale linen. A grandly proportioned mirror with an old gilt frame was propped against one wall. Harry gestured at it and said, "I still have to get that hung." He paused before it, cocking his head. "I wanted a darker frame, though. But it's really expensive. I could strip it, I guess."

Britt shook his head. "The frame is beautiful," he said. "It picks up the zinc. If you get too much dark rough wood in here, it's going to stop feeling modern and feel Hobbity."

He looked around, touching the tables, jostling the chairs to see how sturdy they were. He gazed up at the clear bells of glass in the pendant lamps. Harry watched him move around the space. After a minute he uncrossed his arms and looked around too, as if seeing it for the first time.

At a huge old hutch that Britt guessed would be a server station, he paused. "Why do you have a pancake griddle in your server station?"

"Oh," Harry said, embarrassed, "I grabbed it at Bed, Bath and Beyond to warm the coffee cups. It's nicer than pouring hot coffee into some cold porcelain cup. This is just a stopgap."

"And you can have the waiters grill cheese on it. Let's hear the menu," Britt said.

Harry got out his laptop and set it on the bar. "It's a work in progress," he said. "It has to be simple, just because of the space limitations, but I don't want it to be too simplified. On the island we did pretty stripped-bare stuff, you know—wood-fired-oven breads and pizzas, roast chicken. We kind of had to up there. I think I can do a little more here."

Britt was nodding, scanning the page Harry had opened for him. Pan-crisped socca with baccalà and arugula. Nduja toasts with sardine and blossomed caper. Lamb's neck with gremolata and artichoke. Korean glutinous rice stick with crisp pork, grilled scallion, and house-made chile sauce.

"You might want to pull back on some of the culinary terms," Britt mused. "Call it crispy chickpea pancake and whipped salt cod, you know? People zone out if they don't recognize enough words."

Harry looked at the page, nodding. "You're probably right. But I don't want to condescend to the people who'd know."

"In this town that's about a dozen people. Leave a few in there for interest, but if you don't think most people can pronounce it, reword. You should've seen us when we first started. Leo went hard-core Francophile. That first menu was all sauce bordelaise and entrecôte—no one knew what we were talking about, and the waitstaff kept mispronouncing it anyway. In a year, you get your clientele, you start calling it socca again."

Harry looked cheered by this. He had gone back around the bar, opened a toolbox, and taken out a level and a pencil.

"All small plates?" Britt asked.

Harry began marking the wall. "I think it has to be," he said over his shoulder. "For one thing, people spend more on a bunch of small plates than on one entrée. But also if you put entrées on, they make people feel cheap if they don't order that instead."

"Uh-huh." Britt returned to the menu. He kept getting stuck on the Korean rice stick. "Why just one Asian influence?"

"There'll be more," said Harry. "The rice stick doesn't even seem super-Asian when you eat it. I mean, yes, that gooey texture does, but I thought, why not use that starchy soft component like you'd use, say, polenta? Serve it with contrast and heat, but not actually Korean flavors."

"Grilled scallion and chile sauce seems pretty Asian," Britt noted. "It's just—it's a little pizza, pizza, ramen bowl, you know. Talk about being a bit all over the place." He glanced up, smiling, to be sure Harry didn't take offense.

Harry looked stricken. "Maybe you're right," he said. "No wonder I'm sensitive to it on someone else's menu. I'm doing the same thing."

"Well, it's here to be edited. Nothing's set in stone."

Harry nodded, looking relieved. "I really like that dish, though."

"Okay. How are you serving the duck and potatoes? Just like a little entrée?"

Harry set down his pencil and returned to the bar. "The duck is very cool," he said. "We confit the leg and serve that with roasted fig and butternut chips, whatever, that's a different prep. But the breast we sear off, right, and the potatoes we slice thick and roast with a little thyme. Crisp up the duck skin, let the fat render, and a minute or two before you take it off the flame to rest, you brush the meat side with some mustard thinned with a little olive oil. You let the breast rest on the potatoes, mustard side down, for maybe two minutes before serving. The juices mingle with the mustard and the thyme and the olive oil on the potatoes, and boom—dish has a sauce by the time you serve it. It's a self-saucing dish."

"Nice," said Britt.

"Nice? It's smart, that's what it is. Come on, say it, it's smart."

Britt laughed. "It *is*. Where'd you learn that, anyway? You go to culinary school when I wasn't looking?"

"I probably should have," Harry said with a grimace. "But I just picked it up over the years, on the island especially. People dropped like flies up there. I ended up learning everything, pretty much." He watched Britt for another beat, then took back the laptop, opened a file, and returned it to Britt. "Wine list."

Britt began to read, nodding. The list was focused and moderately priced: Arneis, Malbec, wines from Sicily instead of Tuscany, Austria instead of Bordeaux. He returned to the menu, picturing the meal he would choose from it. "You want a salad or some vegetable thing," he said. "Something crisp, something bitter."

"I know. I haven't quite decided yet."

"What about dessert?"

"Oh, I figured I'd just offer a nice rye flour and maple pudding and make it my signature."

"Funny."

"Ha. Okay, not really." Harry looked up toward the ceiling and closed his eyes. "What about pears and dulce de leche with salted almonds? Goat's-milk cheesecake with poached fruit—vanilla poached pears, or tart cherries, whatever, with the season. Corn ice cream with roast plums at the end of the summer. Something with basil ice cream, or basil cream, maybe. But it could all change."

"No chocolate?" Britt said, not looking up. "What, are you crazy?"

"Oh, there'll be chocolate. We've even been trying to work with fresh cacao liquor and butter and playing with that a little, but it's like a chemistry th—" Harry stopped abruptly.

For a moment Britt wondered why Harry seemed to have gotten so self-conscious. Britt was still concentrating on the wine pricing, which he found low, but he was also thinking how strange it was that this was the second time in recent days that he'd been thinking about cacao beans in desserts. Who else could possibly be working on cacao beans in a town of this size? Hot Springs, maybe? He was all set to say this—he had even looked up at Harry to ask him if he could recall who else could be working on such a thing— when he saw his brother's face. Harry's cheeks had gone red, the skin around his eyes a stark yellow-white. His lips were parted dryly as if to speak, but he was silent for another second before he swallowed and then added softly, "It's very tricky."

For some reason this dropped things into place. Britt set down the laptop and said, "I could've sworn I heard about somebody doing something with cacao beans. It's the same person, isn't it?"

"Listen," Harry said. "I didn't contact Hector. He e-mailed me."

Hearing this was the difference between suspecting the blow was coming and the sting of feeling it land. Britt actually winced. Why did Harry always find some way to make things harder on everyone? "Aww, Jesus. When?"

"After he quit. I didn't have anything to do with that. He just FedExed me some cacao beans and started e-mailing me all these ideas."

"Why not go to all your contacts from your old restaurant?" Britt said. "Was it so important to hire the one guy who just left our place?"

Harry was looking panicked. "I didn't think this would be such a huge deal," he said. "How many other good pastry chefs is a town like this going to have? I figured you guys would understand. Do you think Leo's really going to be that upset?"

Britt rubbed his eyes. "Beats me. It's never happened before. I just know you need to tell him."

"I know. Listen, why don't you guys come by next week and I'll try out some stuff on you? We can talk it through then."

"You want Leo to be your consultant at the same time you poach his pastry chef? Yeah, whatever, it isn't technically poaching, but he's still going to be pissed."

But Harry must have decided he'd apologized enough. He squared his shoulders and turned away to get two bottles of water from beneath the counter. He set one before Britt with a business-like thump that seemed to end the debate. "I think Leo can take it," Harry said. "You guys were just up at Hot Springs tempting fate with the Makaskis. Leo plucked that Jason dude right out of the Italian place—he knows perfectly well how this goes. I didn't take Hector—Hector got bored. He quit to travel and he heard through the grapevine about my place. That's it. Maybe if Leo hadn't made him do all those stupid chocolate cakes he'd still be there."

"Oh, everyone thinks they'll change the world with their chocolate bourbon soup or something, but I'm telling you, no one ever wants it. They say they want something interesting, but when it comes to chocolate, nobody does. Deep down all they want is cake or mousse or ice cream."

"Well, that's the place you guys have. You have a warm chocolate cake place. It's a better fit for Hector here and you know it. Maybe we *can* sell chocolate bourbon soup."

"Nobody can. It's disgusting."

Harry laughed, but quieted almost immediately. "You're right that I need to tell him. I know. I'll do it today, okay?"

Britt nodded thoughtfully. He was so used to being Leo's gatekeeper, to fending off ridiculous requests and useless purveyors and hack cooks and defending Leo's point of view as a matter of course, that it was surprisingly difficult to admit that Harry was right. Leo would have to understand.

Britt felt a pleasant jolt of energy being in here; it was the opposite of the soothing palette of Winesap's buff-colored walls and swooping white plates and shatterable stemware. Here one felt a little roughed up and alerted by the mix of stimuli, like a cat with its fur rubbed in one direction and then the other. The menu looked simpler than it was, he could tell already. Of the fifteen dishes, Britt saw only one or two he questioned, and even those he suspected would work better on the plate than on paper. Of course, Harry still had to execute it all.

He looked around the space again. "What's your POS system? Where are you putting the terminals?"

Harry leaned back against the counter, looking uncomfortable. "I was kind of thinking about trying to do it old school at first."

"You mean jotting down orders on pads? No. You can't do it."

"People do it all the time."

"Diners do it. Take-out joints do it. You have to be modern where it counts. Ask Leo sometime about what it used to be like keeping track of all your inventory and shit without an integrated system."

Harry shrugged. "I was just thinking about putting that money somewhere else."

"No." Britt felt this very urgently. "Just trust me."

Harry nodded. "That's what Camille said too. She used the phrase 'pound foolish.'"

For a moment Britt didn't even know whom he was talking about. "Harry, who the hell is Camille?" he said. "What's she *do*?"

"She's a consultant," Harry said. "I thought you knew that."

"A consultant? In restaurants? Or does she just have dinner with all her clients? And who the hell *are* her clients?" This was not at all reassuring. She might have been evaluating his restaurant for some future investor while he'd been doing the food equivalent of pinning down his little brother's arms and spitting on him.

"Food people. People who want to open restaurants or start food businesses. She consulted with Hot Springs when they revamped their menu, and she was the one who helped the All-Fresh stores create their specialty sections. She's not doing a lot of local stuff now, though. Too penny-ante."

Britt was recalling the odd assortment of people with whom Camille had dined that autumn: the group of young men, the couples. The young men, he guessed, might have been thinking about starting a craft brewery. The two couples must have been trying out a line of preserves, though at the time he'd thought maybe they'd brought them home from travel and were simply giving a gift. And then there was the blond man who'd looked so familiar.

"Is the owner of All-Fresh a blond guy who talks a lot?" Britt asked.

Harry laughed. "He's the son of the guy who started it. Camille would never say anything, but from what I hear, you practically have to tie him down to get him to make a decision."

That explained a lot. "What about you?" Britt said. "You're working with her?"

Harry looked embarrassed. "I can't afford her," he said. "But in exchange for dinner she said she'd do a little consulting for me."

"So you took her to Winesap," Britt said.

"That feast probably got me an extra hour or two at least.

Thanks. The mirror was her idea, by the way, and so were those leather-topped stools and opening up the ceiling."

"I thought you were seeing her," Britt admitted.

"Not yet," Harry said, and Britt felt his mood—so volatile since last night—settle lightly, like a robin landing on a branch.

"And you're cooking?" he said.

Harry rubbed a hand over his forehead, dislodging his glasses. "That's the plan for now," he said. "And of all the stuff I plan to do, that's the part I'm scared of. But I can't not do it. I don't trust anyone else, and I don't think I can pay them anyway. I cooked on the island. I can do it here."

"You need a good sous chef," Britt mused. "You've been interviewing, getting résumés?"

"Not yet."

"Well, get on it. If your opening is coming up soon, you'd better get your team together, get them cooking together. You can't chuck 'em in here on friends-and-family night and hand them some recipes. How many cooks—two, three?"

"Three, including me."

Britt looked over the menu once more and then got up and walked around the space. At the window he peered out toward the street. There was a liquor store, with a guy sitting on the steps out front. A bodega with a steady stream of people going in and coming out, holding two bananas, a large bottle of soda, or a box of cereal or cigarettes. He couldn't see the waterfront from here, but it was out there, with a couple of guys fishing from the pier, most likely. Maybe Leo was right and the location was tainted not only by past failures but by its sheer homeliness. Britt was worried that the area wasn't quite urban enough for the restaurant to feel like an exciting outlier—it might just feel downtrodden. He wished there were a boutique nearby, or one good bar in addition to the Irish pub. What had Camille told Harry about *that*?

Britt began to pace the dining room, moving the tables an inch away from the painted walls so they didn't scuff, looking up at the newly towering ceiling.

He was thinking about hours. Plenty of people opened a second restaurant when the first was going well. If he'd been asked yesterday, he'd have said Winesap was a well-oiled machine, but he was still stung by Harry's critique. He had the uncomfortable sensation of knowing some vulnerability of his older brother's that even Leo didn't know of yet, as if Leo were walking around with an unshaven spot on his jaw or a slip of soft flesh showing between an untucked shirt and his belt. Britt didn't know if he wanted to protect him or flee.

Winesap needed to be redecorated, he realized. He was feeling very annoyed with Leo all of a sudden. Their place was too muted; there was too much blue in its greens, too much fuss on its plates, shiny silver where it should be a cool tarnished pewter. He could picture the menu in his head, and even in his imagination it was too long, marked by too many random influences. Where was the elegant focus they'd started with? Now they had pasta, they had foie gras, they had the whole of Western Europe in there. Harry was right. Worse, they were older—Britt suddenly felt the restaurant's absence of youth and energy like a physical hunger. Winesap was a woman of a certain age wearing a statement bracelet and a statement ring and a careful painted coiffure, while this place—he couldn't remember the name, a bad sign—was some punky chick who had her Escoffier down cold, a rangy braless model with a silky tumble of untouched hair and a pair of scuffed-up boots.

Britt turned back to the bar, where Harry was marking off the wall with a pencil and humming under his breath. In this space, which he had all but conjured out of the air, he looked competent and comfortable, not like a student but like a professional. How amazing, that Harry's idea might turn out to be a good one—a *great* one—and Leo had almost persuaded Britt to miss out on it altogether.

Except that Britt had just gone along with his brother's opinion without even questioning it. Leo didn't have to say a word; he'd simply looked chagrined at the neighborhood, and Britt had accepted instantaneously that Harry was a goner.

"Listen," Britt said, almost as an experiment. "Would you consider changing the name?" If Harry refused to consider it, then maybe the two of them just wouldn't see eye to eye.

Harry didn't turn around. "I know, you guys hate the name. I've been thinking about some other ones since you got me picturing a pit bull."

Britt nodded, both pleased and discomfited. If he did agree to work with Harry, he was thinking, it would be a whole new job. He hadn't had a brand-new job in many years, and the truth was, he liked the pleasant, knowledgeable groove he'd worn for himself. That was why he was so rattled to find himself thinking this way.

"I don't *hate* it. But I'm glad you're open to ideas." Britt took a nervous breath, which he exhaled as a laugh. Maybe Harry wasn't even interested anymore. He had the distinct sensation of trying to date his brother. "If you still want a partner, I'm open to it, but I'd have to at least connect with the name."

Harry stopped moving, his hand still holding the pencil lead against the wall. Then he looked over his shoulder. "Don't start screwing with me," he said. "It's not funny."

"I'm not trying to be funny," said Britt. "Cook a meal if you really mean it. Let me see what you're doing."

"Of course I'll cook," Harry said. "You free tomorrow? Is Leo? I can get a lot done before then, even though obviously I'd have a different prep done when I have more time. I didn't think you guys would want to."

"Well, I don't know about Leo," Britt said. "I just meant me. If you want just me," he added. "You maybe wanted both."

"No no no no no," said Harry. "I misunderstood, that's all. Obviously I want you both. I want you too. All incestuous-sounding implications aside, I mean." But he looked away. He was getting very energetic about straightening up the bar top.

"Because I've been doing this for ten years now, you know," Britt was saying. "I know Leo's got, like, fifteen, but still."

Harry was shaking his head and wiping off the bar with great sweeps of his bar cloth. He began dealing out pieces of paper like playing cards, jotting down titles at the top as he spoke. "Here's what I'm gonna make," he said. "And listen, if you like it, maybe we do one big show for Leo, and maybe he likes it and maybe he doesn't. But we go from there. You did all that PR work, you know how to find a crowd. I was in academia—I just know how to talk things to death."

Britt laughed, slightly mollified, but he could hear the note of urgency in Harry's voice too. The overeagerness to collude, to diminish Harry's own experience—which, Britt was beginning to understand, had perhaps been formidable. Or at least Harry had made formidable use of his brief experience, which was more likely. For a moment Britt hesitated, thinking he had made a mistake in being even this enthusiastic. He looked around the space again, wondering suddenly if Harry needed a partner at all, or if his brother was so polite, or so desperate for capital and companionship, that he would accept even a redundant partner, even the partner he hadn't wanted terribly much in the first place.

CHAPTER 5

CAMILLE DIDN'T WANT TO MEET HARRY for a drink, which wasn't promising, but told him to come by her house, which was. He had been there for the first time the night before, to pick her up for dinner, but here he was, back again within twenty-four hours, almost as if it were familiar territory.

"I'm trying to get some work done," she said. She preceded him into her kitchen, her long chestnut ponytail flipped over one shoulder. The table was set with a number of open jam jars, spoons beside them, and a laptop and paper and pen. "You can help me taste."

"Well, I do owe you," he said, his voice coming out a little more enthusiastic than he'd meant it to. He was feeling slightly giddy.

"After last night?" she said. "Please. I haven't eaten all day."

Their introduction had been yet another gift from Amanda, who seemed to know someone useful in every city. So far Camille had walked him through the basics of protecting himself financially, forming an LLC, and writing up his agreements with the landlord and even his parents (who had gotten very crisp and professional when he presented them with the finalized papers, both of them setting down their coffee cups and whipping out reading glasses).

Harry had sometimes feared that Camille had helped him only out of pity or because of some debt she owed to Amanda, and that in fact she had some dreadful comprehension of his financial picture—his whole concept—that she was too tactful to tell him. But tonight he was feeling right with the world.

"That's what I wanted to tell you about," he said, but she was taking a handful of spoons from a drawer and handing them to him, telling him to try each jar.

"Do these taste Amish to you?" she said.

He took a bite of peach and ginger jam. It was tooth-achingly sweet, or maybe he too just couldn't eat yet. "I have no idea. The labels look Amish."

Camille was standing beside him, arms crossed, staring at the jars' ivory labels with their navy-blue script. Her feet were bare, her blue jeans aged as soft as suede, and she wore a long-sleeved T-shirt so tissue-thin that he could practically make out the ridges in the strap of her bra through the fabric. Sunday Camille was somehow more alluring to him than Saturday night Camille. Her daily self was so crisp and stylish that jeans and bare feet were more intimate than a low-cut dress.

"These are just prototypes. They're going for purity and home-made but not grannyish," she said. "I can't quite put my finger on how to help them capitalize on homespun without actually being dowdy."

"You could never be dowdy," he said.

She knocked her hip against his. "Not me, the jam."

"The jam either, then," Harry said, reaching for her hand. "Hey," he said. "I have some news. I think I have a partner after all."

She glanced down at his hand holding hers but didn't pull away. Instead she grinned at him. "No kidding. Who? When did this happen?"

"Today," he said. "I don't think I'd have gotten this far without your help."

"Of course you would have," she said. "All I did was go over a few things with you."

"Well, that was enough, I guess, because I'm cooking for him tomorrow and we'll see if he's in. I didn't think I cared anymore, but it turns out I'm pretty excited."

"You deserve it," Camille said, and she hugged him.

It was then that Harry did what every man does at some point in his life, which worked half the time and was a crashing failure the rest: he turned the hug into a kiss. He figured the odds were as close to being in his favor as they had ever been, and he was hoping that their friendly goodnight kiss after dinner the night before had been just for openers, that even if Britt seemed to have a thing for her, she might not have one for him. And for a second, a second in which the nape of her neck felt amazingly fragile and satiny beneath his palm and their mouths tasted of cooked sugar, he thought he had it. But then—there was no other way to describe it—the feel of her lips became thoughtful, as if he could feel her mind shifting in some other direction just by the change in pressure beneath his mouth.

He stepped back. Camille said nothing for a moment, then, "It's not quite right."

"No," he said, "I guess not." He was befuddled and slightly relieved, because she was correct, but there *had* been that glimmer. He wasn't sure where it had gone.

She took out a bottle of wine and poured a couple of glasses. She looked slightly embarrassed as she handed him one, seeming about to speak, but then she made a little face to suggest that she wasn't sure what to say and simply took a drink of her wine.

Harry understood that Camille was waiting to see if he was going to be hurt, if they could even stay friends. She was probably a veteran of ill-advised kisses and no longer wasted too much time trying to console their perpetrators. He decided the best course of action, one that would prevent them from drowning in awkwardness, was the simplest one.

"Listen," he said, "I still want to tell you about the restaurant.

Let's not let one kiss distract you from the fact that I've done something pretty impressive."

Camille laughed, her relief obvious enough to hurt Harry. "Oh yeah?" she said. "How so?" She moved aside the jam jars and gestured for him to sit down at the table with her. She concentrated a touch too much on placing the jars just so, and he knew he sounded a little too vehemently casual, but he felt okay. He felt like they'd tried and it was, maybe, no one's fault.

"I saw my brother again this morning, and he came over to see the space. He hasn't been there in weeks. And he was really impressed. I didn't think they'd ever come around."

"I knew they *should*," she said loyally. "Which one? Leo?"

"No, Britt," Harry said, and Camille blushed.

Harry was used to girlfriends having a certain level of interest in Britt. Catherine had loved him, perhaps a shade too much, and flirted with him by detailing the less seemly elements of British monarchical history. Shelley, on the other hand, bore an energetic antipathy spurred on by Britt's clothes, his well-clipped hair, and—Harry believed—his undisguised lack of interest in her. So was it really so surprising that the trip to Winesap would backfire in the end? He had intended it to be a grand seductive display, and instead the evening had felt more like being treated to dinner by his big brother.

Well, Harry wasn't going to let Britt sabotage the friendship too. He stayed at Camille's kitchen table and kept talking as if he hadn't perceived a thing, and she listened attentively. He was almost touched by their determination. They'd talk and drink and he would go home; they would barrel through this moment until they'd come as close to forgetting that kiss as they ever would.

LEO SAT AT THE BACK OF the dining room at Winesap, staring balefully at an individual chocolate cake in a pool of crème anglaise. It was the most boring dessert on the face of the earth, even though when it had debuted in the eighties it had felt like a revelation, all warm, sexy, oozing pools of chocolate. The trick was not simply to underbake a cake; the kitchen liked to place a truffle in the center that would melt during baking. But it had been years since the dessert was new, and whether restaurants called it mi-cuit or chocolate lava or whatever cute name they chose, it didn't change the fact that this little round cake now crushed Leo with a mighty ennui, nor that Winesap sold as many of them the kitchen could make.

"Is it even worth asking candidates to update this?" he said to Thea, who was sitting beside him with a pen behind each ear and a cup of coffee and a laptop before her. "I don't know if we'll even be allowed to tweak it, much less ditch it."

Thea unfolded her arms. "Can't hurt to try," she said. She opened several résumés and shifted the screen toward Leo. "I want to try these guys. If we don't feel it from this batch either, I have a few more backups in mind."

"How many backups can there be at this point?" Leo said. "I thought we'd seen every pastry chef in the state. How's Dennis been doing on it, anyway? Are you thinking about keeping him on?" Dennis had been filling in since Hector's departure, as had another prep cook hoping to be given more hours. Neither was really up to Hector's past dishes, and so during the search the dessert menu was less innovative than ever: the chocolate cake, tarte Tatin, even a few crisps and homemade ice creams.

"Leo, if we go ahead and put Dennis on it permanently, what was the point in giving ourselves time to do the search right? He's supposed to be a stopgap. Besides, he wants to move up to the line, not over to pastry."

"Good point. You line cooks are such snobs."

Thea shrugged. It was true; no line cook apologized for that.

"Well, listen, schedule the next round of meetings and I'll be there."

"Okay. Be hungry." Thea closed the laptop and stood up. She always seemed energized for her next task the moment she'd concluded the first, a trait Leo envied. Thea never seemed tired, bored, or beaten down by the weight of routine, afflictions that hit everyone else in the place sooner or later. Come to think of it, this reminded him a little of Harry, of Harry in high school darting from theater to basketball with equal intensity, or of the way he could often be found sitting on the couch, hunched alertly over a book and frowning at the pages. Britt liked to tease him for it, but really Britt was just as bad. He simply hid it behind insouciance and fine linen shirts.

Leo gazed up at Thea for a second, the blue pens on either side of her pale face, the green flare of her eyes. Leo was amazed they'd ever run Winesap without her—sometimes he even forgot where she'd come from, so ensconced was she here. But if Hector's departure had reminded him of anything, it was of how transient this business really was.

"Hey, how's your daughter?" he said. He felt the urge to convey to Thea her value, that she was more to the restaurant than just a sifter of résumés.

Thea turned back toward him, surprised. "My daughter?"

"Yeah. She'll start school this year?"

"Preschool," Thea said.

Leo nodded. He didn't know what else to ask. "Ex-husband good?"

Thea looked mystified but shrugged. "He's fine," she said. "He'll be done with his master's soon."

"Oh good." Embarrassed, Leo rose as well, picking up the cake plate and Thea's coffee cup. "Well, that's good. Just checking in."

"Okay." She frowned.

"All right." There was a pause, and then Helene appeared from the kitchen with an armful of flowers and both Thea and Leo seized on the chance to depart.

HARRY COULD REALLY COOK. Britt hadn't expected that, somehow. Harry's description of his work on the island had convinced him that Harry had learned to make bacon and bread and ricotta, but cooking on a line was a whole other ball game. Britt had thought perhaps his flirtation with this new place was like one with a gorgeous but unsuitable girl, just a moment's excitement, and the morning after he and Harry had talked about the menu and about Hector's defection, he'd left the new space trying to look forward to Winesap that night, its elegant systems and its balletic servers and Thea's stern profile overseeing the line.

He'd also surreptitiously searched through the reservations, looking for Camille's name. An embarrassing thing to do, admittedly, but he'd had an energized feeling of possibility that only intensified once he saw her name down for a three-top a couple of weeks out. Britt closed the file, humming to himself, and realized it was time to finish it with Maren completely. When he was younger he might have overlapped things a bit, but it just wasn't worth the hurt feelings and the deceptions. He didn't want to be hated by every good-looking woman in the region. He'd liked Maren, who sold software and had huge black eyes and slightly winged brows that always put Britt in mind of a hawk. She'd cooked for him quite a lot, but in a showy and exhausting way that made him wonder if she secretly disliked him, thought he disliked her, or harbored dreams of cooking at the restaurant. She had cut food into disks and squares and layered it precariously; she had sifted powdered sugar through stencils to make patterns on the plate; she had done things like garnish salmon with a single peeled and seeded grape. Just for a rest, he'd started offering to make pizza and scrambled eggs. These offers were not received well.

At least her approach was rare. Almost no one wanted to cook for you if you owned a restaurant; they thought you were judging them, and they apologized for serving baked macaroni and cheese or roast chicken, the very dishes everyone wanted.

After the dinner service at Winesap, he'd returned to Harry's restaurant space and found Harry already at work behind the zinc bar. A stack of papers sat beside a place setting, a notebook, a pen, a bottle of water, a goblet, and a wineglass. "Pour yourself a glass of that white," Harry said over his shoulder. "It's Sardinian."

Britt obeyed, removing his coat and pouring half a glass of a pale, grass-yellow wine that smelled faintly, not unpleasantly, of diesel and fresh greens. He let the wine swirl on his tongue for a moment, trying to free himself of the distracting remnants of Winesap, its scents of brown butter and wheaty, fragrant pasta, the seared steaks that had been ordered like mad that night, which always happened when the temperatures dropped. He flipped through the papers on the bar, realizing that they were diagrams of dishes, labeled in Harry's near-illegible hand. Harry had drawn the plates from a sort of side view rather than from above, with notes and exclamation points about temps and garnishes. Britt was admiring a particularly detailed rendering of a cauliflower floret when Harry set before him the same plate: a little mound of ivory cauliflower, its edges touched with brown, scattered with preserved Meyer lemon, wrinkled oil-cured black olives, and flat-leaf parsley. A drizzle of green oil ringed the plate. "Enjoy," Harry said, and then returned to his pans.

Britt ate slowly, first this dish, then a series of five more. He took notes, eyed the composition on the plate and compared it to the drawings. At first he offered commentary on the dishes, mentioning a pleasant balance of oil and acid, the ethereal crust on a goat cheese croquette over sharp grilled radicchio, the slight fibrousness of a cache of fried ginger batons. But Harry replied only briefly, not impolitely but clearly concentrating on his cooking, and so

Britt stopped bothering him and instead simply ate and watched his brother cook.

Somewhere along the way Harry had learned to move like a chef—or rather, he'd learned to cook, but he must always have had this grace, this economy of motion and lucidity of focus. You could learn all kinds of things—you could be a fine cook even if you were hulking in girth and jerky in your movements—but either you naturally moved the way Harry did or you would never learn to. That was it. Why had neither he nor Leo ever learned to cook, really learned to cook, professionally? Suddenly this failing seemed embarrassing to Britt, as if he and Leo had been merely posing as restaurant owners for years, pretending to know more than they did. He did not truly believe this—they had hired a real kitchen staff to do just that—but watching Harry, he now appreciated the brute self-sufficiency of being able to move easily from the front of the house to the back.

Harry produced the last dish with great fanfare. He drew something meaty and brown, dripping, from a braising pot and set it on a metal dish and slid it into the oven. Then he arranged some crisped root vegetables and broccoli rabe on a round white plate, placed the meat at the center, and scattered the whole thing with a blend of something golden and green and finely chopped. He placed this before Britt with the air of a cat delivering a freshly killed gopher.

It was clearly an animal part of some kind: the bones were there, interlocking like bracelet clasps through the center of the meat, and as Britt peered at the circumference of the item he saw an ivory cord running through them like a string through a necklace. "Is this a neck?" he asked, glancing at the dish plans.

Harry smiled proudly. "Lamb's neck, with Jerusalem artichokes, broccoli rabe, and gremolata," he said. "You're not going to wuss out on this, are you?"

"Don't be an idiot," Britt said. The meat shredded easily off the vertebrae. Just as he was taking a bite, Harry started and reached for a bottle of red and poured him a fresh glass.

"You have to have this with it," he said.

"Don't you want a little?" Britt asked, gesturing to his plate.

Harry shook his head. "I can't," he said. "I'm full all the time from tasting as I go."

Britt shrugged. He was chewing, thinking that the meat tasted delicious. The Jerusalem artichokes were rich and crisp, the broccoli rabe refreshingly sharp. It was a great dish, actually, but he was disappointed by the presentation of it. You saw this from cooks everywhere: they thought it gave them street cred to serve you a dish as a challenge. It tasted good, but people dined out for pleasure, for coddling, and they paid for the privilege, so why not give it to them?

He was full, beyond full, but he finished the lamb's neck anyway, leaving only a few Jerusalem artichoke rounds and the now scattered bones, looking like the remains in a prehistoric cave.

"Okay, then," said Harry. "So that's not the entire menu, obviously, but those are some of the dishes I think are central."

"The octopus was one of my favorites," Britt said, "except for the tough ginger, but that can be fixed. The goat cheese fritter's good but a little pedestrian. The cauliflower I love. The proportions are perfect. And the lamb's neck . . . I don't know. You can't get a nice shank in this zip code?"

Harry laughed. He poured his own glass of red wine and leaned back against the bar shelves. "I can get a shank," he said. "But no one's going to talk about a shank. They'll talk about a neck."

"And any press is good press," said Britt.

"I'm not quite that craven," Harry said. "But I'm not going to all this trouble to serve a nice burger. The goat cheese, I'll grant you, is kind of an easy mark. But you've also gotta give people something they haven't tasted, something they can't imagine and have to come in and try."

Britt shrugged. "True," he said. "But maybe this brings up a good point. What if you love a dish and I hate it?"

"*Do* you hate it?"

"No, it's really good. I just would skip the showing off and do a shank, that's all. What I'm asking is, what if we disagree? What do you picture, Harry? You picture me in the front, you in the back, and we leave each other's worlds alone? Or something more unified?"

Harry took a long drink of his wine, gazing out the front window at the dark street. Britt looked too, thinking that a big, stylish lighted sign was imperative.

Finally Harry said, "I'm not totally sure. I'd take your input. I won't guarantee I'll follow it. I guess I picture the same for you. Maybe I'd suggest something for the service you don't like, but maybe we agree not to dismiss it out of hand, even if we don't take orders from each other."

"It all sounds very civilized," Britt said. "I just don't know how it'll work."

"Why are we talking this way?" Harry cried abruptly. His wine sloshed as he set down his glass. "I just cooked you a meal, and you liked it, right? You like the space, you said so. Why'd we skip all the good stuff and go straight to planning for disaster?"

"It's a contingency," Britt said. "We plan for contingencies, not disasters. Get used to it, kid."

"Don't talk like James Cagney."

There was a very long silence. They watched each other across the bar.

Britt looked back down at the flared ivory bones on the plate before him. He gave in to the urge to pick one up and turn it over in his hands, to consider how the animal had been put together before Harry had so deftly taken it apart.

"Look," he said finally. "You want me in or not? Because I say if we want to do it, let's do it. If you want to, we can see if Leo wants to give it a try. Can you do this all again?"

Harry looked startled, as if Britt had broken some protocol. Then he said, "I'd better be able to do it again. Pretty soon I'll be doing this every night."

"True," Britt said. He got to his feet. "Well, we should hug or something, right?" They both laughed rather awkwardly, after which Harry walked all the way around the zinc bar to where Britt waited by his chair, realizing that he ought to have met Harry halfway. They reached somewhat confusedly in the same direction and then reoriented themselves, finally achieving a brisk, back-patting sort of embrace, talking over one another about nonsense as they did. Their voices echoed through the empty restaurant.

CHAPTER 6

HARRY HAD A PILE OF RÉSUMÉS, an obsession with his zinc bar, a kitchen filled with used restaurant equipment, and so many thousands in debt he couldn't bear to think about it. And now he had something else: he had a partner. Not the two he'd thought he would have—not yet—but still a partner.

Bringing his brother on board turned out to be a lot like winning over a skittish girl: only when he'd given up did Britt take him seriously. The night after Harry cooked for his brother, the two of them sat at Britt's kitchen table to decide on a restaurant name and prepare for their meeting with Leo. Harry was drinking seltzer by the quart. He hadn't eaten enough that day, and with each successive cup of coffee—he had had five—he got more jittery. He could not bear to eat after so much menu-testing; even his favorites were no longer appetizing. The lamb's neck was too rich and brutal, the octopus offered up a suspicious give between the teeth that made him uncertain whether it was tender or raw, and he kept encountering slippery pockets of fat in the duck. He'd been eating vegetables instead, and slice after slice of chickpea pancake, with its bland, soothing starch.

Sitting at Britt's table, gulping seltzer to settle his stomach, Harry listened to his own voice talking calmly about name ideas, uniforms, operating budgets, and division of labor, thinking that now that another person was actually listening to him, even the most quotidian details seemed too momentous to commit to.

Because of this sensation, he was drawing the naming process into a long, tedious affair. They'd sat down two hours earlier, with lists of names, themes, general ideas, and particular foods they liked, everything from geographical places to cuts of meat to words like "generosity," "variety," and "challenge." Nothing sounded right. Harry began to wonder how anyone named anything.

"How did you decide on Winesap, anyway?" he asked Britt.

Britt shrugged, looking at his laptop screen. "Leo already had it in mind," he said. "It was pretty much set."

"I wouldn't have thought Leo would be so sentimental," Harry mused.

"I know. Mostly I think he likes the PR—the tree in our yard, the apple butter. You know he wishes he could say Dad was from Calabria and cured prosciutto in the garage or something. Personally, I just think it's a good word."

"I loved climbing those trees. Mom used to make a pie when the first cold snap hit, don't you remember? That was how we knew it was really fall."

"She used those apples?"

"Of course. Here I thought I was the unsentimental one. Mom has one lone point of domestic pride, and Leo corrupts it for commercial reasons and you just don't care. Too bad we can't use it here."

"I care," Britt said absentmindedly. He picked up a cracker and broke it into little pieces.

"It's too staid for us anyway," Harry said. He stared up at the pendant light above the table. "Anything suggesting moms and home and pie is not it."

"Nope."

"It's supposed to sound more random, and more about traveling. More worldwide. Even if we do use heirloom this and artisanal that, I don't want to sound fussy about it."

"Traveler," Britt offered. "Wanderer."

"I dunno. I picture a hobo with a rag tied on a stick. Or a folk-singer getting beard hair in our food."

"Global. Globe. Globular. That doesn't even sound like a word, does it?"

"Too Shakespearean."

"How do you figure?"

"The Globe Theatre," Harry said.

Britt rolled his eyes. "Yeah, that'll be a common misconception."

"Too bad. I really thought you had it with 'globular.'"

A cracker crumb dinged Harry in the neck. "I was spitballing," Britt said with dignity.

"Drifter," Britt said.

"Murderer."

"Nomad."

Harry shrugged. "Middle Eastern food."

"Stray."

There was a silence. Harry said it, just to hear it, and typed it into his laptop in caps, to see how it looked. It looked good. "Is it too canine?" he asked.

"Maybe," Britt said. "But I think I like it anyway. I mean, it's not 'the stray dog,' it's simpler than that. It's kind of rough-and-tumble, though."

"I like that, given the location."

"Yeah, I actually meant that as kind of a good thing. Unless it also suggests fleas."

They added it to the short list, along with a few other words that instantly looked outdated. Harry kept staring at it, feeling as if the word were being carved indelibly into the screen. He tried out different fonts, closing one eye and then the other.

"We don't have to decide for sure right this second," Britt was saying. "But it'll be good to have a working name for interviews and whatnot." He glanced up at Harry, then focused on him piercingly. "You haven't told Leo about Hector yet, have you?"

Harry flushed. "Oh, right! Right. Not yet. I thought I could tell him in person."

"And then I have to tiptoe around it all week until you see him? This is exactly what I was afraid of, you making me your little secret-sharer. At least tell him before we all meet, okay?"

"I'll try." Harry truly meant this—it was just that he was so busy. It was hard to imagine popping into Winesap for this purpose.

"Harry."

"Okay, I promise. When are you telling him about you?"

"I guess this week. Or maybe when we meet. Whenever the moment's right, I guess." He kept tapping away at a spreadsheet, not looking up. Harry wasn't sure whether Britt was really unconcerned or just flawless at feigning it. As they wrapped things up an hour later, Britt appeared to be expansive and relaxed. "This is going to be good," he said to Harry. "You feel good?"

"I feel *great*," Harry said, too loudly. And sometimes he almost did.

LEO WENT TO HARRY'S PLACE the following Sunday afternoon, when Winesap was closed. This time Harry was going to cook his way through nearly the whole menu instead of a sampling, which hurt Britt's feelings just a bit.

He had never quite found the right moment to mention to Leo that he planned to be a partner to Harry. It seemed uncouth to discuss it at Winesap, and he'd had a vague idea that today would be a good day, but now that the three of them were here, Britt knew he ought to have spoken up sooner. As they shook out their napkins and poured water and wine, he found it hard to look at Leo. It would be better, he decided, to let Leo eat first and then tell him. Maybe he'd agree to be a partner and it would be one big fraternal celebration. But then Leo said, in response to a comment from Harry, "Stray, eh?" and Britt worried that the name sounded silly and a little mangy.

They watched Harry set out his mise en place. Harry's hair was held back in tufts by a folded bandanna and his brown T-shirt bore holes in the sleeves and a picture of a bowling ball on the chest, but his clean towels were folded neatly over the apron tied around his waist while he arranged squeeze bottles of mustard and vinaigrette and square metal bins of shallot and thyme, dishes of soft, slumping braised fig and thick chewy lardons. He laid out a garnet and white-fatted duck breast butchered as beautifully as a diagram.

Britt had learned enough over the years to know that a good prep was everything: a sloppy cook was a sloppy thinker; a jumbled workspace meant that the mind got stuck in the same disorder. Once again Harry cooked silently, gracefully, but with complete concentration. Britt shot a meaningful look in Leo's direction, but Leo gazed blandly back at him.

Harry served the first several dishes with only the briefest of descriptions, so that Britt found himself filling in what he perceived as the gaps. "This one actually makes me like cauliflower," he said at one point; later he offered an appreciation of the architecture of sardine skeletons. Harry had made a few little shifts in the plating and the proportions of some dishes, improving the entire experience in a way Britt found difficult to quantify. It all just felt sleeker and more finished, as in a real restaurant. If only Leo would talk more. Britt was so delighted as the meal continued that his conversation became less nervous and more simply excited.

But next to him, Leo ate quietly, offering little but nods and raised eyebrows. At the end of the tasting, Leo patted his mouth with a napkin and took his time folding it into a neat triangle before laying it back on the zinc bar. There was a lull until Leo said, "Coffee?" and Harry looked around a bit wildly, as if a coffee machine might have materialized without his knowing it. "Never mind," Leo said. "I'll be right back." He got up and headed off to the restroom, which Britt hoped was properly equipped.

Harry and Britt looked at each other, then Harry shrugged and began stacking dishes and pans. Britt looked toward the front of the building, where he now saw the dark silhouette of a man at the windows, hands cupped at his temples against the glass. The last rays of sun shone around him, glaring into the space, illuminating pinpoints through the man's rumpled coat and a hole in his hat. The deliciousness of the food didn't seem like enough right then; what guest would want to eat two inches away from a looming homeless guy, even one who mercifully shaded the chalky autumn sun? Then Leo returned and started talking almost before he sat down.

He didn't mince words: even though he thought the food was excellent, he still had his doubts.

Leo said, "It's a little overstated, maybe, and you're getting some chewiness in the meat. Plus your spices are on the raw side, and I think the portions are just *slightly* too big for the plates." He paused. Harry shot an appraising look in Britt's direction, and Britt could not help but feel abashed, as he suspected Harry meant him to. Why had none of these issues been obvious to Britt? Did he really know anything other than flatware and seating charts? He'd felt the same way back when he had first stepped in for the departed Frances and was just guessing at what he was supposed to do.

Leo went on. "But the thing is, it *is* fun. It's bold, it has range. Maybe too much range, but I'd eat almost all of it again, Harry. Maybe I can't be your partner, but I can definitely be your customer." Before Harry could bask in this slim praise, Leo moved on, gazing around the restaurant as he talked.

Now Leo aired his concerns about the space. It was beautiful, he noted, but it was hard to work in; the proximity of cocktails and line cooks struck him as dangerous. "And maybe I'm wrong," he was saying, "but there's something a little inelegant about divvying up your kitchen. Who gets stuck back there?"

"Desserts," said Britt, and as he spoke Harry looked up at him, his expression surprised and guilty, and Britt thought, *Oh no.* After Harry had agreed to tell Leo about hiring Hector, Britt had put the whole thing out of his mind. He'd been busy worrying about breaking his own news.

"Hey, Leo," Harry said. He coughed into his fist. "Something I keep forgetting to tell you." Leo cocked his head, looking from one brother to the other. "The dessert guy back there will be Hector, actually."

"You're not serious," Leo said.

Harry managed to turn a shrug and a nod into one motion. "Now you probably don't feel so bad about him being stuck back there."

"Is this how it's going to be," Leo said, "that I have to be afraid to have you in my place for fear you'll poach all my people?"

"I think that's a little rich," Harry said, "coming from someone who's done his share of poaching."

Leo said, "Not from my *brother*. And all I ever did was check out a place."

"Well," said Harry, "I didn't even do that. Dude tracks me down from Guatemala, obviously he was pretty interested in working with me, okay?"

Britt jumped in. As Harry got more combative, Britt got more nervous. Had Leo actually said no yet? Britt wasn't certain. He'd really only expressed doubts, and that wasn't the same thing. "I know Harry didn't seek him out," he said to Leo.

Leo rolled his eyes, no doubt thinking of Hector's vexing fickleness and the tensile beauty of his phyllo. "Fine, whatever, he left you no option. You'll find that Hector's not the most easygoing employee you ever hired."

"I know," said Harry. "I have no idea how long he'll last, but you have to realize that more familiar faces are going to apply here. It's not that big a city. I won't poach anyone right out of your kitchen, but if I can hire people who've worked for you, I probably will. I want them to have been trained well, and yours have."

"Thank you," Leo said, rather grandly.

Britt interrupted. "Can we get back to the restaurant itself? You're being kind of rough on the place. Nothing's perfect right from the get-go. Don't you remember our all-French menu? The tableside carving?"

Leo assumed a distant expression, as if trying to recall a busboy from many years ago.

"Those were things we could work through," he said. "We can't pick up this building and move it. I can't start neglecting Winesap for a place that might not even make rent."

Harry looked sick. He leaned back against the countertop with a thud.

"I did a little research," Britt said hastily. "There's a couple renovating that old theater down the block, did you know that? They're going to run independent movies. They got a license to serve wine and beer too."

Harry cheered up slightly, but Leo narrowed his eyes at Britt and said, "You've been helping, I gather. A lot."

"Well, yeah," Britt said. He decided just to lay it out there. "I changed my mind about this place. But I'm not leaving Winesap. I'm just buying in here."

"Really?" said Leo. Then he nodded for a very long time and cast a newly appraising look around the space before he settled on Harry.

"I still think it's going to sound weird if it's just the two of us," Harry said. "People will probably just assume you're part of it whether you actually are or not. Are you sure you don't want to give it a try?"

"Harry," Leo said gently, "it's not the kind of thing you just try out."

Britt had known all along that Leo wasn't likely to change his mind, but he felt the crumpling of hope nevertheless. He and Harry watched Leo gather his jacket.

"I guess you and I need to talk schedules," Leo said. He sounded very crisp and professional, so Britt simply nodded mutely. He'd expected to feel saddened by Leo's lack of vision, perhaps, or protective of Harry's feelings, but he felt abandoned instead. Leo had a way of making even this space, which Britt loved, feel a little dilapidated and ill-conceived.

"You'd better sweep," he told Harry when Leo was gone. "Or we'll get mice."

Harry looked at Britt bleakly. "You sweep."

CHAPTER 7

A FEW DAYS AFTER HIS MEETING with Britt and Leo, Harry invited Camille out to lunch. They met at a cheap noodle house where a dour Chinese man stood behind the counter, pummeling noodle dough and glaring at the customers. Camille ordered beef bone soup, and the name turned out not to be a euphemism. When the metal bowl was placed before her, she gazed into it at what appeared to be a cow knuckle and then reached into her purse, fished out a hair clip, and pulled her hair into a ponytail.

"You do find ways to challenge yourself," Harry said.

"I have to admit I thought there'd be more than bone," she said. "But I'm in it now." She sipped at the beef broth and considered it, her face showing such pleasure that Harry reached over and took a spoonful for himself. He had ordered noodles with pork and pickled mustard greens, and Camille took a chunk of pork from his bowl with her chopsticks. They ate quietly for a moment. Harry was tuned for any faint vibration of tension between them, just in case, but it was evident that now they were just pals as far as she was concerned, chomping at each other's noodle bowls.

"How's the new partnership going?"

"Okay," he said. "Leo passed. But Britt's still in."

"Does Leo care if you use their bookkeeper, their purveyors? Get a few economies of scale working in your favor?" She opened up a jar of chile sauce and spooned several dollops into her soup.

"I think he's fine with that," he said. "Britt brought up the same thing."

"Did he," she said. Camille stirred her noodles thoughtfully. The steam rising from the bowl had turned her cheekbones dewy, and her nose was faintly gleaming. "You know, I thought you'd have a hard time prying either of them loose. I mean, family or not, I didn't think you'd get Britt in with you unless he really believed in you. That's my impression, anyway." She gave a little shrug.

Something about the casual way she offered this opinion, with its suggestion that she was aware of Britt, that she had a sea of opinions and considerations of him that she kept private, wormed just under Harry's skin.

"I guess," he said. "It's actually thrown me a little. I'm used to doing it alone." He slurped a spoonful of spicy broth, thinking that putting it that way hadn't sounded so bad. More lone wolf than lonely idiot out of his depth.

"You're definitely going to have to find your way with that," she said. Harry glanced up, taken aback by the firmness in her voice. "Family's tough," she continued. "Have you guys ever worked together before?"

"No. Just him and Leo. We were too far apart in age for it to come up, I suppose."

"That's better. Clean slate. But you know—" She lifted the bone between her chopsticks and examined it, finally identifying an infinitesimal morsel of beef, which she nipped off with her front teeth. She made the maneuver look rather neat and elegant; even the angry noodle man looked mollified and hurled his ball of dough to the counter with a modicum of gentleness. "Don't fall into little-brother mode. You're never going to avoid it altogether, but it'll be tempting to take his opinions as gospel. And you're still the one who's really on the hook for this place, Harry. So remember that you have a point of view too."

"Of course," Harry said. "Have you seen some vein of weakness in me or something?"

"Not at all," she said. "I'm probably projecting my own family onto you."

Harry knew little about her family, though enough details—boarding school, a childhood horse—had emerged for him to perceive that she'd come from privilege. He knew that she too had two older siblings, a sister in Philadelphia and a brother in New York, and that her retired parents traveled extensively together, though they had lived apart since Camille was in high school. In a family of pianists, singers, and sculptors, Camille had preferred volleyball to pottery, math camp to theater camp, and she still found greater pleasure in a stack of orderly accounting books than in a painting. As a result she found it difficult to find a conversational topic with her family that lasted longer than fifteen minutes. She regarded families who worked together and were intertwined in one another's daily lives as exotic and perhaps a little frightening. For this reason she liked to hear about Britt and Leo's partnership and appeared to be continually intrigued that the Torsini women made pasta side by side each day and chatted all the while. Each time she saw Harry she expressed fresh surprise that renting a room in his parents' house was going just fine. Sometimes Harry found himself playing up his family's good side, as if no problems had ever occurred, just to enjoy her pleasure and disbelief. To hear him tell it, Britt and Leo had paid close attention to every one of Harry's travels and jobs instead of remaining consistently two endeavors behind; his mother had never once locked all three of them out of the house until they cleaned their crap from the yard or stopped annoying the life out of her, whichever came first; and his father had never been heard to utter Toyota-related statements like "The thing about the Japanese is that you just can't trust them."

"I'm sure my family is as nuts as yours," Harry said. "It's just that no one talks about anything long enough for it to show."

"Oh, you make it sound like you're all a bunch of silent farmers or something," she said. "You and Britt are both talkers! Leo, I can't tell."

"When you get Leo going, you can't shut him up," Harry admitted. "It's a question of finding the subject. For instance, he had plenty to say about my menu, which he agrees with you is too diverse."

"I said it was scattershot. Don't try to make me sound like a closet racist just because you don't want to edit yourself."

Harry laughed. After a moment he mused, "You know I said the same thing about *their* menu. I don't know. What do I know?"

"Just be pleased to have such an experienced partner." She waved a hand to dismiss the whole topic and took a long sip of her broth.

Harry returned to his soup, thinking that he had worked against his own interests once again: he'd snowed Camille into believing that his family was nothing but hugs and touch football games, and now he couldn't quite bring himself to explain why he had any doubts at all about this partnership. Any reservations he expressed about Britt would only look like he was trying to stem her interest in him, and any about Leo would look like sour grapes. So he said nothing, just chewed a slightly tough piece of barbecued pork and listened to the sounds of Camille sipping delicately at her broth, the clicking of plastic chopsticks on metal bowls all around them.

BY ELEVEN A.M. HARRY HAD WINNOWED down the line cook résumés to six, called to schedule interviews, and cleaned and polished the bar. Now and then he paused to test his kitchen equipment yet again. Harry's recurring fear was that on opening night the range would explode with bursts of gas, the oven would hover fitfully around room temperature, the dishwasher would stay cold and silent.

He sipped his coffee with a rueful smile. The new dishwasher was leased, at Britt's insistence. Harry hadn't known that no one ever bought a dishwasher; people leased them cheaply and bought the detergent through the same company. He had been all set to buy his own, used, off Craigslist from an out-of-business diner twenty minutes away, and when Britt found out he all but hurled himself at the phone to make Harry call it off. It was a relief to feel he'd avoided at least one mistake, but even more so to feel that one thing in this restaurant would be someone else's problem if it failed.

Not so with vendors, to whom Harry had to give a personal guarantee, an unsettling if unavoidable experience. People who dealt with restaurants didn't really give a shit about your LLC. They were so used to seeing places go belly-up that they went straight after the proprietor personally rather wasting any time on business niceties. Not that he intended to default on anyone. But he did keep picturing the burly, mustachioed vegetable guy, and the goateed fish purveyor, and the bearded meat guy—it was a facial-hair kind of business, apparently—lined up outside his parents' door.

Now he got up and circled the perimeter of the space, peering at corners and testing the shelves he'd hung in the server station and the prep areas. He was afraid to stack them with dishes. Britt would be interviewing waitstaff; people would be coming in. It had to be done. He got a couple of heavy sauté pans from the line and stacked them on the shelves above the server station. Then he grabbed a few more, plus a few notebooks and a box of napkins. The shelves held, but Harry felt only a slight relief. Still, the shelves were okay and the dishwasher company had twenty-four-hour repair. It was something.

The space was freezing; he had taken to wearing an extra layer until he worked up a good sweat. There was no way he was raising the thermostat just for scut work. He tried to start out with the most strenuous tasks and hoped that body heat would carry him through.

The restaurant space no longer looked like anything to him. It had looked like a horror movie when he had first leased it, then a construction site, and then—briefly and maybe delusionally—like a real restaurant. But months of nearly living in the space had taken away any objectivity he'd ever had, and he kept getting that sinking ache in the floor of his stomach, the one that said he'd lost his eye for all this long ago, that his carefully vetted fixtures and colors were as modern as polka dots and mint-green tea cozies. When Britt had walked around it looking pleased and surprised, even impressed, Harry had felt, for the first time in months, the lifting of abject terror. Britt was many things—egotistical and easily annoyed, judgmental of clothes and architecture, more limited in his palate than he would ever admit—but Harry knew no one with taste as flawless. Even as a teenager Britt had known to mess up his hair instead of feather it, to wear scuffed old work boots instead of Converse.

It was still difficult to believe he now had Britt as a resource. When Harry had first returned to Linden, he'd wanted to wait until he had a definite space to unveil to his brothers. When he finally had, he'd been surprised how hands-off they were. He'd thought they would be more help. If nothing else, he'd figured they'd have plenty of criticisms for him—and in truth they had, but few had felt like issues he could address. The first time he'd invited them over to see the raw space, he'd been expecting to hear about table configurations. Instead Leo had shrugged in the direction of the whole building, the whole block, the very river a quarter mile away. It was too painful for Harry—he hadn't spoken to them for weeks after that visit. He just got up each morning and drove to the restaurant space, stopped at the coffee cart and waved at the homeless guys, put his head down and worked. He knew it was childish and maybe disastrous to avoid hearing any more from his brothers, but he was this far into it; his deepest fear was that it was too late to back out and too late to make the most needed changes.

And yet after a while he'd called them up to play basketball anyway, deciding not to say a word about the restaurant. He knew they expected him to broach it again and had a feeling they dreaded it, so Harry had done his best to have a good game and just enjoy his brothers' company and the loose, easy feeling of a physical activity he excelled at, so different from the brute work of the restaurant build-out. Leo loosened up on the court, and Britt was surprisingly sanguine about losing a number of games. It had been a good morning, one that let Harry salve his hurt feelings over the restaurant.

Sometimes, when he hadn't seen them for a time, Harry's vision of his brothers grew warped. In his head, he might be so busy arguing some lost point from an old conversation, in this case about his restaurant, that he expected them to be cold and hostile when he finally saw them. But they never were; they were friendly, if not overtly affectionate, amused and amusing, apparently having forgotten whatever issue Harry was still perseverating about.

He often felt himself to be inside a little bubble of loneliness when he was around his brothers. At times Britt and Leo would turn toward him in unison, bemused and distant, an eyebrow quirked upward on each forehead. Those six and seven years hit in just the wrong place: closer in age and they might have felt more like friends, further and they might have felt more protective. Instead the three seemed to have grown up in two different households. His brothers' offhand conversation reminded him of just how intertwined their daily lives were, lives in which he had little place. It wasn't that he begrudged that intimacy but that he believed he had no claim to it, no more so than when they were in their late teens and he was ten. A part of Harry never stopped feeling like the little kid hopping around in the background, amazed when his brothers displayed any interest in him at all.

And sometimes their interest was worse than disinterest. These were the moments when Harry understood very clearly that he amused them. It had never occurred to him that all his work and travel over the years—the gathering, formless, but electric sensation he had had for so long that told him everything he did was connected and necessary, that he was amassing information, skills, viewpoints—to them looked like nothing, like fucking around.

Neither even asked why he'd come back, as if it were a given that one returned to one's hometown after years away. Harry had begun to wonder if his older brothers, whom he'd always viewed as more sophisticated and worldly than he was, were in fact as provincial as any other citizens of a medium-sized town that clung to its roots in failed industry and immigration with equal parts defiance and exasperation. Or perhaps Britt and Leo felt that they had already done what Harry was trying to do, that they had helped kick-start a bit of a revival in their hometown's fortunes and that anything Harry might add to it was just more of the same.

A lot of people never did leave Linden, or they left and returned, and for years he hadn't understood why anyone would come back. After Amanda's restaurant closed, however, he'd had to think about the next step, and Harry had experienced a longing for Linden for the first time, its gray downtown with its pockets of life centered around pubs, its cheap pizza places and taco joints. He got extremely nostalgic for Moretti's, which had closed years before. He craved pierogi, which he did not like. He stopped remembering some neighborhoods as blighted and saw them as picturesque.

If a place as isolated and territorial as a remote tourist island could try to revitalize itself, why not Linden? Linden was in a much more populated area, and instead of creating new infrastructure from the ground up, he could get what he needed from what was already there. His brothers had laid a lot of the groundwork with Winesap—groundwork Harry had never fully appreciated until then. That was the first glimmer he'd had, as he'd tried to figure out his post-Amanda life, that moving home need not be a failure but could be an opportunity.

Now, for some reason, he missed Shelley. Well, not so much Shelley herself. She had been melancholy and easily piqued and host to a frightening number of minor ailments and inner adversities to ubiquitous substances, but Shelley had known how to run a restaurant. She didn't want to know; she'd grown up in a restaurant family in St. Louis, and she hadn't intended to stay in the business, but Harry had begged. Amanda's restaurant had been too great an opportunity to pass up, and he'd felt he needed a companion in there with him. It was a chance to go from dilettante to pro, from occasional maker of ravioli to cook, and to do it all with a larger purpose. He hadn't been there just to serve some tourists a nice pâté. (Though he had done so, primarily out of defiance, after months of practice. When a table was being nitpicky or snobbish, he'd roll out a hostile, elegant little still life centered on the unctuous rosy brown velvet square studded with green pistachios and dark garnet pigeon breast, accompanied by hand-ground mustard and silky sheets of pickled turnip. He'd had to stop eventually. Pigeon was a pricey form of psychological warfare, and Shelley complained that cooking pâté made her hair smell of blood.)

Harry had met Shelley when he was in Ann Arbor, devoting himself to a now abandoned degree in comparative lit. He was financing his cooking habit with a job at a specialty foods store, which he took primarily for the discount and the tasting research. Shelley had worked there too, rotating from baking to cheese-making to counter serving as her various immune deficiencies allowed, and this flickering in and out of Harry's vision had been her best advertisement. She would appear, willowy and indifferently competent at any number of despised tasks, remote until Harry got her to laugh at least once. Laughter transformed her; he spent the next three years trying to coax it out of her. During those early weeks Harry would glimpse her at the deli counter, handing over beautifully composed and wrapped sandwiches the size of footballs, her wrist trembling with their weight, or ladling a batch of ricotta into tubs in the creamery, her hair pulled back in a way that emphasized her lemur's eyes and tiny coral mouth. When Harry showed up at work hungover and decimated after Catherine left for England, Shelley attached herself to him, all commiseration and lentil soup. It just went on from there, until Amanda Carroll came through Ann Arbor putting out feelers for people who were damaged, crazy, or zealous enough to move to a remote island year-round.

Any food lover who happened to wander through that corridor of the Midwest would end up at the store; in a region sparsely stocked with food destinations, the place was a Venus flytrap for gastronomes running low on inspiration or imported mostarda. So it was no surprise to walk into the bakery one morning and find a chef whose picture he recognized from *Food & Wine*. She was short and muscular as a fireplug, with rough blond hair and flat gray eyes. She'd been bent over the stainless steel work surface, pressing tart dough into shells in a blur of thumbs. At first Harry found it odd—why would a chef of her stature be screwing around in a Michigan pastry kitchen? But later, after a couple of years on the island, he came to understand. A cook cooked. Even while traveling, even while doing professional or personal research, a cook found it anathema to stroll through town like a tourist.

Amanda had bought an old restaurant building and set about calling on her contacts to staff it. She'd been leery of Milwaukee and Chicago cooks, fearing that anyone comfortable in a large city would go crazy on the quiet island almost immediately. He'd followed her to the island and persuaded Shelley to join him for one reason: he thought Amanda was a visionary. Her argument was that the island was locked in that destructive tourist-and-townie pattern that always ruined a place with more natural beauty than steady industry.

Harry agreed. He thought the psychology of tourist towns was like that of abusive marriages, a tangle of resentment and financial need. Or he thought so before he arrived, when he still had time and energy to theorize about things like the psychology of tourist towns. Once he was there, he was too busy being a lowly prep cook, the only one without significant kitchen experience and therefore the one dedicated to peeling vegetables, skimming stocks, picking over beans. At first it was awful. It was painful in the muscles and the back and the joints, and Harry realized that zipping around the store chitchatting with regulars about expensive sardines had not prepared him for the daily monotony of manual labor. He'd been snappish with Shelley and silent at work, mortified to have taken the two of them there so they could maximize both their penury and their misery. Shelley kept complaining about a cook named Jeff, whom Harry found abrasive and loudmouthed and who liked to enumerate his scars among the line cooks but nattered on about sun salutations and centering when he was on pastry next to Shelley. Her tone when she bitched about Jeff suggested that such a creature would never have come into her life without Harry's direct intervention, and maybe she was right.

Harry soon longed for department meetings, tedious subtitled movies, the stately green civilization of campus, and the petulant undergrads who answered their cell phones in class. Even at the salmon cannery he hadn't felt so lost—that had been dangerous and unpleasant work, but finite and edifying. It was worth knowing what a factory job was really like, how to go to a shady bar and hold his own. But on the island, with no end date in sight, Harry had felt completely unmoored. Why had he ever gotten this degree or that fellowship if the long-term plan was only to separate stones from beans? For the first time he'd felt that he might be slumming. Worse, that he was *trying* to slum and yet not even skilled enough to be above his own job.

But after a few weeks he began to settle into his routine. He realized he loved the frigid early mornings on the island, the sounds of wildlife outside the kitchen windows, the undulating shoreline of the stony beaches, the way a beer and a cheeseburger tasted shockingly delicious and earned when your muscles were tired and your brain fizzed with exhaustion.

As original employees began to depart, he took on more duties. He found himself within earshot as Amanda developed her dishes, and he got to see how many iterations they might go through before one met her standards. Usually he thought a dish was fine right from the start, but he learned to listen to Amanda talking about its proportions and food costs, how the wording on the menu suggested what the experience of a dish would be, and how plating naturally showed one the most enjoyable way to eat it. It was a lot like writing a thesis, actually, that same process of gathering information around a rough kernel of thought, a vague sense of flavor combination that might lurk in the back of the mind, and then the editing and revising and rearranging.

Soon he was learning how to cook on the line, starting with salads and apps and trying out the meat station on a slow night. When a line of tickets stretched before him, his mind went as quiet as it ever could—not truly quiet, perhaps, but hyperfocused on a series of concrete actions strung before him like beads on a necklace. The nights passed so quickly he sometimes felt a little drunk when they were over. And if Amanda became more irritable and silent as the busy season drew to a close, if that idiot Jeff kept sidling up to Shelley to talk about his great-grandmother's sourdough starter, which he claimed his family had nurtured for three generations, and if, most tellingly, Shelley had stopped bitching about Jeff altogether, Harry could take that. He barely noticed any of it for a full three years, until finally Amanda had to pull him aside and tell him the restaurant was closing. He'd been shocked, though he had no right to be. It should have been obvious from the dwindling tickets and the early nights, but Harry had been enjoying spending the free time trying out his own dishes, aping Amanda's process to see if it worked for him too. It was embarrassing to be a scholar, a close reader, who'd failed to look up long enough to take in what everyone else seemed to have known for months.

Amanda had planned to feed the restaurant and the island at once, and it would have worked if only none of them had been human. But they could do it just so long out there, gorgeous though the setting was. After a while it didn't matter if they were milling their own flour and smoking their own trout. You could labor away in obscurity for only so long before someone had to come in the door and give you money.

On his last night on the island, Amanda invited him to dinner at her cottage. It was just the two of them, because everyone else had already dispersed. The night had had an air of mourning and relief. Amanda's blond hair was down around her shoulders, and she wore faded black jeans and a T-shirt as she bustled around her kitchen while Harry sliced a few rounds of hard salami and set them on a plate next to olives and pickled peppers. An open bottle of red wine sat on the table beside two juice glasses. The rest of her glassware was already boxed. They'd cleaned out the restaurant supplies after the final night, hauling away the last wedges of cheese and tins of anchovy, a few quarts of cream and buttermilk. On a plate on her counter sat two pork chops and a handful of chopped bacon, which he knew had come from the walk-in.

"So where do you go tomorrow?" Amanda asked. She glanced at him over her shoulder, her gray eyes startlingly pale in the dimming light of the kitchen.

"I'm going to run through Ann Arbor and see a few people, I guess. And then I'm not sure. Just get a job while I decide the next thing. Maybe I'll finish my dissertation. I don't know. What about you?"

She lifted her hands in gesture of uncertainty and then sat down opposite him, took a slice of salami, and peeled off its wrapping.

"Sorry, I forgot to take that off," Harry said.

Amanda shrugged. "I have enough savings for a little while. But really the only thing to do at this point is get another cooking job." Harry searched her face for embarrassment, but she looked unperturbed. He was beginning to realize that the closing of a restaurant was old hat in this industry, an understanding that still shocked him a little. It hadn't occurred to him while he was killing himself that it could be so likely to fail. That was what had been harder than anything else, harder than Shelley ditching him, which turned out to be kind of easy. It had never occurred to him that the work, that insane and endless work, would not pay off.

Amanda was saying, "I'll probably start thinking about the next place, start looking for backers at some point. Right now I just want to put my head down and cook for a while. I'll just start talking to people, see who needs a new chef."

Harry had nodded thoughtfully. It sounded a lot better than returning to academia, which would require a certain amount of groveling before an adviser or two, and for what? To pick up research he now could barely recall.

"You'd give me a reference, right?" he said.

"I'd give you a limb."

"It's hard to imagine going back into academia. Maybe eventually. Or maybe I should keep going with this. Look for a line cook position or something."

"You can aim higher than that," she said. "You got a real crash course. Normally I wouldn't say that, but you did end up doing a lot here. Something to think about."

"Maybe my brothers need a sous chef," Harry had said. He laughed, trying to imagine an interview with Leo and Britt, how quickly it would devolve into some childhood mockery. They might even start there.

"You're from Pennsylvania, right? Where, near Philadelphia?"

"Sort of. It's a good hour and a half away, but getting more transplants from the city. My brothers' place is probably the nicest one in town, which is why it's at the edge of a far nicer town. A few years ago I think I'd have been doing chicken Alfredo day in and day out. But I hear it's starting to change."

It occurred to him that a few of the Italian and Eastern European grocery stores his parents had once taken them to might still exist. His parents had never been ardent eaters, except for the occasional adventure of hauling the boys into a different neighborhood for a particular item. Then they went back to chicken à la king and baked spaghetti until another craving hit.

As he thought about this, Harry experienced a longing to be in Linden, if only for a visit. He wanted to see if any of those places still existed, if any new ones had sprung up. Most likely there were now Middle Eastern, Indian, and Asian shops scattered around the area. As he sipped his wine at Amanda's table, he started thinking about an ice cream place he'd forgotten about till just then, about the doughnut shop he used to visit after the bars closed to buy apple fritters at three a.m., straight out of the fryer. Some of it was curiosity, some of it was nostalgia; most of it was weariness.

Amanda poured more wine into his glass and got up to start the bacon. Harry watched her work, feeling exhausted but peaceful, happy to observe the elegant way she flipped the bacon in its hot pan, the rush of the gas flame, the comforting sizzle of fat and the rich, smoky-sweet scent that filled the room.

THE KNOCK AT THE RESTAURANT WINDOW sounded just before dark, startling him. He'd been sitting at the bar, hunched over a spread of uniform catalogs and information on various types of point-of-sale software, all of which cost several thousand more than he'd intended to spend on servers with pads and pens. Well, Britt's money could cover the POS system. When Harry looked up, he saw only a homeless guy at the window, knocking and waving. He waved back, then raised both hands helplessly and shrugged. Just how many guys were going to be knocking at the kitchen door, or the front door, and asking for handouts?

The man moved on, and as he disappeared Harry sighed and picked up his phone. He'd been avoiding it for days, maybe weeks, but he was alone in downtown Linden in his empty restaurant space not long before the opening, and no one would know.

"Harry," she said, sounding entirely unsurprised.

"Hi, Shell. How's it going out there?"

A gusty sigh. "Oh," she said, "it's moving along. We got a nice review in the paper the other day. That's something. Except it was one of those lame ones where they just describe. You know, 'The salad has cucumber, tomato, and carrot and a choice of dressing.' That kind of thing."

"You're serving that kind of salad?" Harry said.

"No, we're serving local greens and a tarragon vinaigrette, Harry. I was making a point."

"Oh."

"Right."

Harry tapped his pen on the bar. It was never easy talking to Shelley. She always seemed to be responding to something happening just beyond your shoulder, or something you'd said in your last conversation but didn't remember. "I'm opening a place of my own," he blurted. "With my brother. He just signed on."

"I thought you hated your brothers," she said mildly.

"Of course I don't hate my brothers," Harry protested. "Jesus, when did I ever say that?"

"It was more something one sensed. You seemed to have a lot of unresolved feelings toward them. And they never came to visit."

"Yeah, well, it wasn't easy for them to get away from Winesap. You know how that goes. I certainly never said I hated them."

"Which one?"

"Which what?"

"You said one brother signed on. Which one, the shallow one or the serious one?"

Harry gave up. "The shallow one," he said, then amended: "Britt."

"Well, that should be helpful," Shelley said. "It's not like he has to be your spiritual guide. He probably has a good eye for color and whatnot. Jeff does too, but there's more to him than that."

"That's nice," said Harry. "Listen—"

"Let me send you a link," Shelley said. "To our website. I'd love your opinion. But also I think you might enjoy seeing the scenery out here. Why didn't we ever go to Northern California, Harry?"

"We were indentured to Amanda, for one thing. And for another, you hate flying and you were sure California would be a pollen-swarm."

"I don't think I thought that."

"I really do."

"Hmm. Well, I was wrong. Here, I sent it. Got it?"

Harry opened his e-mail, clicked the link in her message, and up popped the browser with their website. La Nonna. No bad Godfather music played; no scary mustachioed chefs leered out from the page. Harry couldn't help but be relieved. He'd had no idea what kind of horror show Jeff might come up with in service to a pizza place. You just never knew what people would do once they were making all the decisions. But the images looked clean and crisp, the restaurant interior warm and inviting and casual, farmhouse tables and high ceilings and a fire roaring in the background.

"You're right," he said. "It looks great. Good for you, Shell. You guys did a nice job. Never occurred to me Jeff would be capable of it."

"I know what you mean," she said, "but I'm proud of it too. Thank you, Harry."

"You're welcome."

"If you ever come out this way, we'd love to buy you dinner.

Bring your brother. Or bring a girl if you're seeing one. Are you seeing anyone?"

"Shelley. I need something from you." He heard the plea plucked from his mouth as if on a hook: his voice didn't even sound like his own.

"What's that?"

"I just want your input. I need your opinion on what I'm doing here."

She made a murmuring, noncommittal sound. "I don't think you need *me*. Why else do you have your brother?"

"That's why I need you," he admitted. "I prodded these guys for months and Britt finally either gains confidence in me or loses his mind and signs on, and now I think he's going to take a close look at what I've been doing here and know it's just a big clusterfuck. *I* don't even know what I've been doing here all this time. I mean, I've done a ton—you should have seen this joint when I leased it, and now it looks nice, it looks beautiful, even, but we open in a few weeks, and he's got me buying POS systems and leasing dishwashers, and I thought I would remember more from working with Amanda, you know? But I don't remember shit, or else I never knew shit to begin with. And you do, Shell. You grew up with this, you know it like the back of your hand. I just need a fresh opinion."

There was a long silence. Harry realized he could hear voices hollering and metal clanging about in the background. She must be at the restaurant, of course. The sounds of a thriving, bustling business place made him both nostalgic and terrified. Impossible to believe his place would ever be filled with voices and cooks and customers. But it had to be. He had an operating budget for two months after opening, and after that money had to come in. That was it. Money came in or they died and his brother never forgave him for decimating his finances—though Britt would be fine. It was Harry who wouldn't. Britt would go back to Winesap, and maybe Harry would get a job there too, as a dishwasher or shallot-peeler.

"Fine," Shelley said. "Send me your website materials and your business plan, send me your menu. I'll take a look."

Harry closed his eyes. "I was hoping you'd come out here, actually."

"That seems unnecessary, doesn't it? Besides, it's practically winter out there, Harry. Do you recall what happens to my skin in winter? I crack like clay. It takes weeks of moisturizing just to even it out again. And I don't know how Jeff would feel about that."

"I'm sure Jeff would be pleased to moisturize you."

"I meant me staying with you."

"Well, you don't have to," he said. "I've been staying with my parents anyway. Though maybe that helps."

"No," she said, "your parents don't like me. You'd better get me a hotel room, I suppose."

"They like you," he said. "What hotel?"

"It doesn't matter. Not one near a highway, please. Look, Harry. I'll come out for a day or two and I'll take a look around and tell you what I see. Next week, perhaps? There's some dried fig festival here that's going to cut into our business anyway. But then I have to get back. Jeff needs me here."

"That's all I'm asking. And if Jeff has any issues, just remind him he still owes me a girlfriend, so we'll call it square."

"Now you're being ridiculous. You left me mentally and spiritually long before I left you geographically."

"Maybe. Listen, thanks, Shelley. I mean it. Let me know your flight info and I'll pick you up."

Shelley's voice took on the pudding-smooth tone it always did when she was feeling ennobled. "I'll send it to you and you can reimburse me," she said.

CHAPTER 8

Istart with soup," shelley said. "I tell them to go in there and make me a soup, and then if the soup isn't a travesty, I tell them to make me a protein. You'll need to stock the cooler, obviously."

"Obviously," said Britt. "But I disagree about soup. How much soup are we ever going to serve here? Probably none."

Shelley gazed at him sadly. Her long brown hair hung in a braid down her back, and she wore some sort of knitted porridge-colored scarf or cap or babushka over the rest of it. The two of them faced each other across the banquette. Harry sat at the end of the table, eyes shuttling between them. He had not warned Britt about Shelley's visit, allowing him instead to show up that morning and discover her there like the corpse of a mouse. Now Britt had to make conversation until he could collar his brother out of earshot.

"It's not about soup," Shelley whispered. Britt had noticed that she liked to whisper when she wanted to convey a bone-deep weariness with others' foolishness. "I'm sure you'd rather they arrange a centerpiece or tailor a suit, Britt, but I'm trying to keep things relevant. The soup is just the medium. Can they build flavor? Can they work with what you have and keep their food costs down?"

"She's right," said Harry. "We did that on the island a lot. I had to make a soup."

Shelley laughed. "I remember," she said.

"The bisque!" Harry yelped.

"I don't think you can call that a *bisque*."

"Maybe a chowder."

"Okay," Britt interrupted. "I like the soup idea, you're right. We tell them to make soup. I'd like to suggest their protein be eggs, though."

"And why is that?" asked Shelley.

"Because it's easy to fuck up an egg," Britt said shortly. He knew a test when it was sitting across from him with its wispy hair and pursed lips.

"True," said Shelley grudgingly. "Agreed."

"Great," said Harry. He looked at his watch. "The first one's going to be here at eleven. Shell, you want to run to the store with me to stock up?"

"You and Britt should go," she said. "You know what you need, I'm sure. And I'm still a little tired from the flight. I'll just have a cup of tea and be restful. Do you have rooibos? Genmaicha?"

"We do!" Harry said.

"We do?" Britt said.

"I picked some up." When Harry brought her a tin of green tea, Shelley sniffed the cap and inspected the tea and toasted brown rice grains. She picked up a grain of rice and squeezed it inquiringly. Then she gave a wan smile to Harry and said, "I've gotten spoiled on the West Coast." Harry looked crestfallen. Britt considered setting fire to the tea but decided it must be doing Harry a rough kind of good, being reminded what it was like to have Shelley in close proximity.

Harry and Britt walked silently to the car. They said nothing until they'd reached the grocery store, gotten a cart, and were chucking essentials into it: olive oil, butter, heavy cream, broth. As Harry compared diced tomatoes in juice with whole tomatoes in puree, Britt finally lost patience.

"There is something so different about the restaurant today," he said. "It's hard to put my finger on it. It's like something blew in through the vents, perhaps. Have you had the ventilation checked?"

Harry placed both cans of tomatoes in the cart and turned to face him. Britt raised his eyebrows. "I should have told you," said Harry. "It was last-minute, and I want you to know this came out of my personal budget, not the restaurant's. I know how you feel about Shelley, but you have to remember she was grinding Italian sausage when she was eleven years old. I needed a fresh opinion."

His lack of combativeness was disappointing. Britt had been ready for a good pissing match. "A, I am your fresh eye," he said. "B, you can't be springing things on me. I can't walk in every day to find an exciting new employee I wasn't told about."

"Not an employee. I agree, but I still think we can make use of this."

"She has completely different taste," Britt complained. "How are we supposed to get useful input from someone who's going to tell us Sysco has a nice tempeh now?"

Harry nodded and started pushing the cart toward the produce aisle. "She's much more workmanlike," he agreed. "But I think that can be good. I don't know about you, but I need ballast sometimes. I need someone who doesn't get all flighty about inspiration but knows her basic food costs, you know?"

"Sure," Britt said, sighing. He threw onions, leeks, and garlic into the cart. He was mollified, but only slightly. He'd walked into the space that morning, two cups of coffee in hand and a bag of pastry under one elbow, whistling, and there was Shelley, gliding out from the kitchen like some kelp-colored apparition, Harry sheepishly in tow.

"Britt!" Shelley had said, as he found himself, trancelike, pressing cheeks with her. "It's been so long. You've barely aged at all. Maybe the tiniest bit around the eyes."

"Since last Christmas," Britt said. "You made that whole wheat pudding orb, if memory serves."

"And you brought a woman—Pamela, was it? Or Penelope?—who just seemed so in love with you even if she never said a word. Really, it's odd to see you without some woman trailing after you like a nanny goat."

"I guess I don't bring too many women to work with me. Most of them are busy running businesses."

"I know the feeling," she said. She crinkled her eyes at him as if they were old sparring partners. They smiled fiercely at one another and then turned to Harry, who was lurking near the bar.

It was this demeanor that worried Britt: the way he hung back at first, then eagerly pointed out this or that item to Shelley for her approval, as if Shelley were Thomas Keller. Watching him, Britt had felt downright uneasy: where was the steely resolve Harry had shown with hiring Hector, the lack of apology in his dealings with Leo? Because however uncomfortable those moments had been on a fraternal, social level, they'd also set off a welcome bell in Britt's mind, telling him that his feckless little brother was tougher than he seemed. Britt was just praying this was a minor setback, but nevertheless he now watched with a critical eye as Harry pawed a pile of collard greens and shook water off some chard. Where was the decisiveness? Get the water off with a brisk shake and get the hell on with it. But there was Harry, lifting a bunch of spinach to the light as if it were an offering for an angry deity.

THE FIRST INTERVIEW WAS WITH FREDDY, who'd been working as a line cook in Linden for ten years. Told to make a soup, he did a double take, then said, "Like what?" Told that it was his decision, he pressed for likes and dislikes, expressed dismay at the range in the cooler and coded resentment at the assignment, and eventually placed before them a roughly pureed tomato soup studded with seeds.

The second was Elliott, who was fresh out of culinary school.

He terrified all three of them by leaping up from the bar and running full-tilt into the kitchen for supplies, until Britt realized that Elliott thought he was being timed and hollered after him to calm down; it wasn't a quick fire. Elliott made a smooth carrot ginger soup with a garlicky crouton and a confetti of tarragon. He was jittery and high-octane as he moved about the range, murmuring to himself and to his carrots, dropping tasting spoons. When Britt asked where he'd found the fresh tarragon, Elliott blushed and confessed he had brought his own.

The third was Jenelle, who'd started working the egg station at the Breakfast Bar six years before, not long out of high school. She stood before them with hands on her hips, her short hair hidden beneath a baseball cap, thick brows gathered as she listened to the soup assignment. Then she nodded shortly, set a pot of water on to boil before she did anything else, and made a brisk, calm assessment of the contents of the kitchen and coolers. Jenelle moved easily and quickly about the station, slicing leeks, rinsing mushrooms, and in twenty minutes served them a silky mushroom and leek soup thickened with potato and cream and topped with crisply fried shiitakes. Britt detected a faint hint of sesame oil and took another sip, pleased.

Fourth was Marianne, two years out of culinary school, soft southern accent, hoping to open her own restaurant. "I'm a baker as much as anything," she said, causing Britt's heart to sink, but then she made a stunning cream biscuit to accompany a corn and shrimp soup with bacon, and he revised his judgment.

Fifth was Phillip, who caused a small fire.

Finally they saw Janet, who was in her forties and had been knocking around—her words—the kitchens of Linden for ten years. She worked clean and quick, didn't overthink it, gave them a chicken and rice soup.

Of the six, Jenelle, Elliott, and Marianne were asked to make an egg dish. "You're probably sick of that," said Harry to Jenelle, but she simply said, "Nah," and turned out three perfect, satin-yolked eggs en cocotte with Gruyère cream, spinach, and spiced tomato. Elliott made a thoroughly correct spinach soufflé bearing a faint whiff of shallot and nutmeg, during the baking of which he stood, back to them, at the oven, periodically peering at them over his shoulder. Marianne poached eggs and served them with hollandaise, sautéed spinach, and crisped prosciutto.

By seven o'clock the interviewing was finished and Harry, Britt, and Shelley were sprawled in a banquette, biliously eyeing their seltzer. Finally Harry hauled himself into a sitting position and clapped his hands.

"So, anyone we can just rule out?" he asked.

"Elliott," said Shelley.

Britt frowned. "He's well trained," he said. "Young and nervous, but his soup was fantastic."

Shelley sniffed at her seltzer and then put it back down. "If he calms down, I could see it. But he prepped a lot more ingredients than he needed, and don't forget, people are watching him cook out here." She gestured languidly in the direction of the empty space. "He'll make people nervous. Have you ever been around one of those animals who've spent too many years in a really tense household? And they just make you prickly and upset because their energy is so . . . so disrupted? That's what Elliott's going to be like out here."

Britt said nothing. He was trying to sort out his emotions. Shelley was possibly the most annoying person he had ever met, which made it extraordinarily difficult to accept when she was talking sense. Harry, perhaps sensing a watershed moment, was as still as prey. "Let's keep an eye on him," Britt said. "In a few years he might be good to know."

Harry took a deep breath, and Shelley smiled and closed her eyes.

"I like Jenelle," said Harry. Shelley nodded approvingly.

"She was good," said Britt. "It's just ... not a lot of fire, you know? Or creativity, maybe. She seems so stolid. We have all those kinds of cooks at Winesap and after a while you want some personality in there. And how much training can she have had to just do the egg station for six years? Don't get me wrong, I thought she was really solid, I just ... I don't know."

"But I want solid," said Harry. "You never go to the Breakfast Bar, but if you did, you'd see that they serve about six hundred people in a weekend. Maybe more. You cannot do that station without losing your mind if you aren't cold as ice. That chick was like a metronome."

"Hey, why'd you like the water?" Britt said suddenly. "You smiled when Jenelle set a pot on to boil."

Shelley turned to look at him, truly meeting his gaze perhaps for the first time all day. "Because she started her water before she even looked in the cooler. It takes the longest, and if you don't know what you need to make, it's just a smart way to get going—chances are you'll use it, and then you don't have to wait. It was just a smart basic move, that's all. We had a cook in St. Louis who liked to keep a big vat of water at a high simmer at all times. He said you never knew when you'd need it." Then she rolled her neck and resituated herself. "Oh, Lionel," she said fondly. "He was one of those tortured souls who stumbles through the world but fries a great eggplant."

Britt and Harry were silent for a long beat, waiting to see what had happened to Lionel, but Shelley just glanced between them and said, "So, my vote is Jenelle, but obviously my vote only counts for so much. I'm just a visitor. Harry, can you run me back to my hotel if we're done here?"

"Of course," Harry said. "You're not hungry, I know, but we could buy you a drink. A glass of wine."

Shelley gave a trill of laughter. "That sounds lovely. I have to tell you, though, that living among the vineyards has ruined me. I've become kind of an accidental connoisseur. You wouldn't believe how hard to please I am! I won't subject you." And because it really had been a useful day in the end, Britt stopped himself from thanking her.

CHAPTER 9

H ELENE'S HAIR WAS BOTHERING LEO. He kept eyeing her at the maître d' station whenever he walked through the dining room, noting the way her bangs flopped into her eyes. Leo understood that he was hovering. Maybe she was just trying out unpleasant new hairstyles now that Britt was over at Stray more often than not.

This was where Leo struggled, trying to match or mimic his brother's flawless taste. For all he knew, Britt would have told him that he was being an old man, that Helene's long side-swept bangs were solely responsible for a 5 percent uptick in bar sales.

"What can I do for you, Leo?" Helene finally asked.

"Oh, nothing," he said. "I just kept noticing your hair."

A frown crossed her pointed, miniature features. "My hair."

"It seems to be in your way," Leo said. He swiped at his own sparse hairline to demonstrate. "You keep brushing at it."

"I don't even notice," she said reassuringly, and looked back down at the book. Leo did too: thirty-eight on the books. Okay for a winter Tuesday. A moment later she looked up again.

"Leo?"

"It's just that I worry about guests being unable to make eye contact," he said. "People resist that. They like a nice, clear sightline."

"You're looking me in the eye right now," she pointed out.

"That's true." Leo began to feel very uncomfortable. "Maybe if you don't spend as much time looking down, the guests won't even notice."

"During service, I rarely do," she said.

"I'm sure you're right."

Helene returned to erasing table numbers and jotting servers' initials next to reservation names. "Leo," she said after a few moments, "how are you?"

"I'm fine," he said. "I'm better than fine. How are you doing without Britt here?"

She shrugged. "Fine. It's a basic Tuesday night. Alan's hoping for a bar diner or two. Erica and Apollo are opening, David's closing, and we have a backwaiter working-interview scheduled now that Christian's leaving."

"Are we still calling him that?"

"Apollo? I guess so. I can't even remember his real name. I think it's stuck."

Leo paused, trying to remember the real name of the newest waiter, who was so glowingly beautiful and creamy blond that on his first night Jason had said, "Get Apollo back here to pick up his halibut," and now no one could call him anything else.

"Kelly's trying out a new dessert at staff meal. Some kind of tart."

Kelly—tall, sturdily built, with near crew-cut black hair and two sleeves of tattoos—had just been hired for her deft touch with pastry and her ethereal sugar work. So far her desserts had been perfectly executed classics with one subtle switch or addition: the herbal bite of Chartreuse where one didn't expect it, a reversal in texture or temperature. The dishes were good—it wasn't that she wasn't good. It was just that Leo wanted to be stunned by the alchemy of it all, and she was amusing him instead.

According to Britt, Hector was spending the last few weeks before Stray opened perfecting some mad scientist's ice cream cone, cacao custard in a cup constructed out of malt or something equally odd, plus a salted, buttered popcorn ice cream. He'd created some kind of hot fried pastry with a cool Meyer lemon center, served with Thai basil cream and a sparkling drift of sugared zest. Britt had described them as otherworldly beignets.

"That sounds good." Leo sighed now. "But a tart? I don't know—didn't we hire her for her ideas? I thought we were branching out from this grand-mère shit, you know?"

Helene looked taken aback. "Were we?" she said. "I don't know the details on the tart. Maybe you should talk to Thea about that."

"Right, right." Helene now had the patient look of someone who had been playing rummy with her great-grandfather for several hours. "Well. I'll check in with Thea."

On his way to the kitchen he reminded Alan, yet again, not to set place settings on the bar until someone ordered food. He sometimes wondered if Alan was really worth the trouble. He sometimes wondered if *any* of them were worth the trouble. That was one thing Harry would get a taste of: the enduring, Sisyphean struggle, on any given day, not to fire your entire staff. But Alan had been working for Winesap for years; he knew their wine list, and now that he could back up Helene on hosting duties he was more central than ever.

Leo glanced back toward the dining room and saw that Alan and Helene were in close conversation, heads bent together. Now he'd pushed them together in union against him. It was as if he'd never managed people before; he was behaving like a neophyte. He couldn't recall the last time he'd dealt with the minutiae of the dining room. Britt had taken over so much of the personnel handling that Leo had forgotten how prickly and unruly a staff of thirty adults could be. The front-of-the-house staff was not only at odds with the world at large (who liked to ask what *else* the waitstaff did in their lives) but also with the kitchen staff, who resented their higher income and their requests for sauce switches and onion-free sautés.

The kitchen staff Leo could deal with. An early boss of his had said, *Nobody forced you to be a cook, so suck it up or go get a server job.* And of course the kitchen staff would never dream of it. They considered waiters the tender underbelly of the restaurant world, whimpering about guests and swanning in hours after they themselves had worked up a sweat.

Thea was at the table by the back door, going over a delivery while the driver stood beside her, his arms folded, in a mustard-colored down jacket and with a three-day beard. Thea held up a carrot from one of the delivery boxes and bent it like a licorice whip, then tossed it back in the box and made a sweeping series of scratches on her delivery form.

"You want to call the Makaskis and tell 'em why their order's just sitting on my truck instead of being in their walk-in?" The driver made a show of checking his watch.

"They're not missing much," said Thea, inspecting a yellow onion.

The delivery guy caught Leo looking at them. His face cleared, and he uncrossed his arms and raised his palms in supplication. "Hey, Leo. You want to talk a little sense here?"

Leo smiled. Thea glanced up at the delivery guy. "You want to wait outside while I do this?" she said.

"It's thirty degrees and sleeting outside."

Thea shrugged. "Up to you," she said. She picked up the carrot she had just discarded and inspected it with exquisite slowness and care. Then she laid it back down in the box and picked up a bunch of celery, examining it so minutely that Leo suspected she was counting the ribs on each stalk. She peered at its base, down between the stalks, sniffed at a leaf, and considered the scent. After a while she glanced over at the delivery guy. "This could really take a while. I have that feminine eye for detail."

The delivery guy looked toward Leo, who shrugged. "Could take hours," he said.

Thea said, "Hang out here and watch me go through this delivery so we can talk about credit for all the stuff I'm sending back."

Leo poured himself a glass of water and took a contented sip. Thea ran a kitchen staff of drinkers and brawlers and parolees; she had a kid just past the toddler stage—he'd have bet the restaurant itself on her. Finally the driver realized he had no backup and no choice and headed out the back, slamming the door behind him.

"Hi, Leo," Thea said over her shoulder. "Care to see what Gourmet Kitchen is trying pass off as food these days? I hate winter."

"Is it always this bad?" Leo rifled through the box with distaste.

"Britt and I have been discussing this for a while now. Didn't he tell you?"

Leo frowned. "He probably mentioned it. But if they've been getting worse, why are we still ordering from them?"

"We were giving them a second chance. Now they've officially gone downhill. We can't work with this crap till spring."

"Okay," Leo said. For a moment he said nothing, flummoxed. What had he come in to discuss? Watching Thea knock down the Gourmet Kitchen delivery guy had put him in such a good mood he couldn't quite grasp it.

The tart. "What's the new dessert again?"

"Kelly's doing a pear frangipane tart. She's been steeping vanilla beans in rum for two weeks for the ice cream. Wait'll you taste it, Leo, it's so potent it barely sets up."

He nodded. "Yeah, okay." He lowered his voice. "When we hired Kelly, didn't we talk about upgrading our dessert menu? Something a little fresher. This feels pretty Julia Child."

Thea looked up, perplexed. "Well, sure. She's working on some other things too, but they aren't ready yet. Britt wasn't worried. Plus we have a case of ripe Seckels and she's a whiz with puff pastry."

Leo had to take a deep breath. "Listen," he said. "I'm glad you and Britt were on top of this, but I'm going to need to be in the loop." Thea gazed at him impassively, one hand resting on a tomato stem. "And I'll concede it's my fault if I'm not in the loop already. Okay?"

"Okay," she said, drawing out the last syllable a touch longer than needed. "I just thought you didn't want to be bothered directly, that's all."

"Well, why would you think that? I'm here every day."

"I know, but you're upstairs a lot. I'm not saying I have a problem with it—you don't need to be watching over us down here. I'm just saying . . ."

"I get what you're saying," Leo said. He was realizing that he and Thea did not have a lot of sustained conversations; they simply ran through the basics and moved on. He'd been pleased with that until now. "I didn't realize I was being . . . uncommunicative." Thea shrugged in acknowledgment and held up the tomato with a questioning expression. "Yeah, go ahead." She returned to checking off her list. "But, Thea, I do want to branch out with these desserts. I'll talk to Britt next time I see him if you want, but I think it's important that we shake things up. If that wasn't clear, let's be clear about it now."

"Fair enough. But I thought we also were trying to work with our clientele, and you know they like a classic. Our clientele, Leo. Not the one Stray's hoping for."

That stung. "Our clientele isn't in the restaurant business," Leo said, setting down his glass of water. "They don't know what they want till we tell them. You think some random Joe decided he wanted salt in his caramel or foam on his sea bass? Of course not. We tell them."

Now Thea did set down her pen. "Do you think I'm not up on things, Leo, is that it? You want us doing some tired old *foam*?"

"Well, no, not foam. Just . . . something different. Something other than tarts and crisps and whatnot. I don't know. I don't know what."

"That's because you're not a chef. You tell the clientele, but the chefs tell *you*. And I am telling you that we're working on some ideas and that in the meantime Kelly's making a gorgeous dessert that's going to sell like crazy." She tilted her head and peered at him. "You look like shit," she said. "Are you sleeping?"

"Of course I'm sleeping," he said. She inspected his face with disconcerting intensity, while behind them the kitchen clamored. Nested and steaming pans hissed as they hit the dishwater, hotel pans clanked as Jason unstacked them and dealt them out over the stainless steel tables, and the Robot Coupe whirred as Kelly, looking reproachfully over her shoulder in Leo's direction, emptied a large bag of hazelnuts into the bowl and pulverized them.

"I'll be down later," he said. He cracked a smile. "It's miserable outside, by the way. Take your time on the order."

Upstairs, the servers had begun to arrive and populate the changing room, but he didn't stop to chat, just went into his office and closed the door. Half an hour later, the line buzzed.

"Are you coming down to staff meal?" Thea asked. "We're having chicken and rice."

"I'm a little swamped," Leo said. "I'll try to pop down for a plate."

"We'll send something up. You relax."

Leo went back to flipping through old menus, looking for dishes he wanted to revisit or revamp, looking for the moment when Winesap had begun to shift the way Harry and Britt insisted it had. And they were probably right, he knew. He suspected it was not long after the pasta makers arrived. Not that it was their fault—they made gorgeous pasta; Leo wasn't giving it up. But it had opened a door, he supposed. It had diluted a bit of focus.

A knock sounded on his office door and Jason's face peered around the corner. "You decent?"

"Come on in," Leo said, clearing a space on the desk before him. He turned to set a folder on the shelf behind him, and when he turned back he saw that Jason had set down a napkin and silver and a plate of food. The plate was filled with rich yellow rice, scarlet peppers, carrot dice, and silky golden onions. Two pieces of chicken, the skin perfectly, evenly browned, nestled in the bed of rice, scattered with minced parsley and cilantro. A few green leaves of salad were on the side, sheathed in vinaigrette, with shards of cheese shaved over the top.

The sear on the chicken was what he most appreciated: staff meal chicken and rice would be only the braised legs, delicious and shredding off the bone but not skillfully browned and crisped solely for the pleasurable contrast of the velvety meat and the rich, salted crackle of skin. Leo touched the golden edge with the tines of his fork. They dealt with such volumes of food at Winesap, all headed outward and never coming back in to his own table, that he forgot sometimes what it was like to have a dish made solely for him.

"This looks wonderful," Leo said. "Thank you, Jason."

But Jason, who believed not in God or human nature but only in even dice, hot pans, and being on time, who regarded emotion as a sucker's extra, like bottled water, merely shrugged. "No problem," he said, already turning to leave. "Thea told me to make you something special."

CHAPTER 10

A T TEN O'CLOCK THAT NIGHT, Thea took the evening's printouts up to the office, where she chose an empty desk—Britt's—and unfastened her hair and pulled her heels up from the backs of her clogs, letting them rest on top of the thick leather lip while she examined what had sold and what had sat. She missed the way they used to do it before the system was computerized, when the cooks ticked off hatch marks on a menu—the meditative scratch of the pen.

It was probably a sign that she needed to cook more, this nostalgia for such a simple, tactile thing. It was the same in any industry: you show your worth, you move up, you stop doing what you were good at. Now and again she imagined a return to the essentials of cooking, but it was just a fantasy. She made better money now than as a line cook, and she needed it all. Bryan was on time and reasonably generous with the child support, but it was always just enough, with nothing to spare.

Bryan had their daughter tonight, tomorrow, and the following afternoon. When Iris returned from her time at Bryan's house, she invariably was wearing some odd new hat or sweater, something Bryan's mother had decided was a crucial item for a three-year-old. Thea felt a fresh discomfort every time, seeing this evidence of Iris's life away from her. It never stopped surprising her, a three-year-old tromping confidently through more than one house and calling them her own, unafraid to be miles away from her mother.

She had no rush to get home. The house would be empty and dark except for a single kitchen light left burning.

Because no one else was upstairs, Thea ran her fingertips through her hair, massaging her scalp, enjoying the fresh looseness and even faint pain that came with letting her hair move in a direction other than the one in which it had been pinned all night.

She should go to Mack's. She had planned to go for months, the way one plans an unpleasant doctor's appointment, but there was always a reason to skip it. Yet tonight Thea was a strange cocktail of keyed up and tired. Normally she was simply exhausted, but her discussion with Leo had been running through her head all night. She wanted a deep glass of red wine, which she would not get at Mack's. But Mack's would have a short glass of bourbon, she supposed, and that would be almost as good.

She changed into her jeans and a gray sweater, kicking her clogs into her cubbyhole in the changing room and wincing at the feel of the leather boots she'd worn to work. By now they always felt stiff and cold, her feet swollen and heated as muffins. It was tempting to use this as an excuse to go home, but Thea knew she needed to go: show her face, remind the other chefs of her presence, of Winesap's presence beyond its line cooks. She would never admit this to Leo, who had been edgy for weeks, but she didn't like word of Stray filtering over any more than he did. Probably less: Thea liked Harry and Britt both, but they weren't her brothers; she wasn't invested in their success the way Leo must be, however complicated that investment was. Her fear was that Leo was right about Kelly, the new pastry chef, that the problem was not Leo's restlessness but Thea's judgment. Thea was thirty-six—younger than Leo, who seemed older than he was, and younger than Britt, who seemed poised at some eternal moment between youthful style and masculine maturity—but all the industry chatter about Stray's freewheeling setup and oddball menu made her feel staid and old. Who knew what was going on in the heads of her kitchen staff? They might be over at Mack's even now, complaining about Thea's staleness, her dishes' predictability and blandness.

She paused outside the bar door, then shrugged and pushed it open with a touch more force than it needed; now she had banged open the door as if to announce her presence like a sheriff's. Several heads nearest the door jerked in her direction. To her surprise, one of them was Leo's.

He was sitting at a table with a woman in her twenties, who was talking expansively and writing something on a napkin. She kept darting glances from the napkin to Leo and back again, a silky wing of black hair flipping into her eyes and back out with a flick of her chin. Was this Leo's type, androgynous and narrow-boned, wearing a sort of modified shag and no eye makeup, no jewelry but for a complicated series of leather rings looped around one wrist? The truth was, she looked pretty great. She just was not what Thea would ever have guessed.

Leo waved her over, and Thea stood next to the table, hesitating before sitting down. "Join us," he said. "Fiona, this is Thea, my executive chef. This is Fiona. She's the pastry chef at Hot Springs."

Fiona shot out a hand to Thea, rising slightly from her chair, and shook her hand heartily. "It is so great to meet you," she said. "I was telling Leo how much I love your place."

Thea was bemused to find herself relaxing a little, caught off guard by the mix of this girl's punkish look and her warm damp hand, her shining cheeks. "Thank you," she said. "I hear good things about you. Nice to put a face to the name."

Fiona blushed and looked away. After a pause they all jumped in at once, offering drinks all around. Fiona won and darted off to the bar, waving away any cash.

"What's on the napkin?" Thea reached across and turned the napkin in her direction: it was a dish diagram, showing a composition of what from her seat appeared to be circles and sticks.

"Some ideas she has," Leo said. "They're not bad, either."

"You wishing you'd gone after her?" Thea asked.

Leo looked contemplative. "Not really," he said, eyeing Fiona as she leaned over the bar. "She's good, but she's really young. You want to keep an eye on her over the next year or so?"

"Sure," said Thea. She couldn't resist defending poor Kelly. "Why, you think we have room for two pastry chefs?"

Leo smiled at her, turning his gaze away from the bar. He wasn't handsome, really: his thin hair often stood up in tufts from his scalp, and despite his good suits and shined shoes, he had the face and stocky build not of a smooth restaurateur but of a steamfitter or a short-order cook. His eyes were dark where Britt's and Harry's were flinty and pale, and the faint coarseness of his prominent nose and the lines bracketing his mouth suggested that the genes had been refined with each sibling. What Leo reminded her of, Thea realized, was one of those executives who had worked his way up from the shop and still had a touch of grease beneath his nails. She'd grown up among men like this, and she found them comforting. Leo's dark eyes turned down just a bit at the outer corners, and he had surprisingly long lashes, making his gaze seem both kind and a touch melancholy.

"I'm not gunning for Kelly," he said. "But we both know people move on sometimes. I like to keep up with who's out there."

Mollified, Thea nodded and accepted the bourbon Fiona placed before her. Fiona glanced down at the shifted napkin and blushed once again, turning it over. "That's just this thing I'm working on," she said. "I was boring Leo with it. I'll spare you."

"You weren't boring me—I asked," Leo said. "So how're Barbara and Donnie these days?"

Interested, Thea tilted her head as well. Barbara and Donnie Makaski were one of the more intriguing pairs in the local industry: to look at them, you'd assume that she was the heavy with the staff, what with her hawk's gaze and muscular build, but Thea had heard that it was Donnie who was a thrower and screamer.

Fiona sipped her drink determinedly, her gaze fixed on the table. "They're good," she said. "Business seems pretty good."

"I was there a little while ago," Leo said. "It was hopping."

"Yeah," Fiona said noncommittally. "They're pretty good at bringing 'em in." A silence hooked on to the end of the sentence. Thea and Leo waited, but then Leo seemed to take pity on her and delicately shifted the topic to the song that had come on the jukebox—a rap song, which he not only knew but apparently liked. Thea laughed, sipping her drink and enjoying the looseness blooming in her throat and her chest, the pleasurable mix of physical exhaustion and comfort. A hollowness opened in her belly; she was suddenly terribly hungry, though she'd eaten at staff meal. Still, that had been at four thirty. It was eight hours later, and there was something surprisingly draining about standing at the pass all night; she often ended up in her darkened kitchen at home, trying to be silent as she swiped spoonfuls of crunchy peanut butter over a pile of saltines or wolfed the leftovers from Iris's dinner. Sometimes she went all out and cooked, so that in the morning the house still smelled of a burger and sautéed mushrooms.

Fiona waved to a new crop of cooks entering the door. Thea and Leo exchanged a glance and a shrug; neither knew who they were. "I should say hi," Fiona said, reaching tentatively back for her jacket. "I used to work with those guys."

"Good talking to you," Leo said, extending a hand. "Keep in touch."

"Thanks for the drink," Thea said, raising her glass. After Fiona was gone, Thea eyed the remaining quarter inch of amber liquid swirling around the glass.

"Another?" Leo said.

"Better not. I have to get home at some point, and I just realized I'm starving."

"Me too," Leo said briskly. "Come on, let's get something."

Thea hesitated. "Shouldn't we stay? Make the rounds?"

"I see we're both here for the same reason," Leo said. He shifted in his chair and took in the room. "But I got here a couple of hours ago and I can give you the general drift. Fiona's too decorous to say that Donnie's been working on a serious drinking problem and Barbara's gotten really protective of the books. Do with that what you will. The barbecue place is going to expand its menu. They're trying out regional variations—I think even some Kentucky mutton, if you can believe that—rather than learning to make a decent brisket in the first place. Berlucci's is making money hand over fist despite the fact that they serve the blandest pizza crust and the soggiest pasta I've ever had. But they can barely fit the hordes in the door. Don't hate me, but I kind of want to go just to see what the hell they're doing there."

"Free booze."

"Must be. And that guy back there in the corner is doing some kind of Thai-French fusion thing, or planning to, but he hasn't found financing, and personally I don't think he will, because this town isn't interested in Thai-French fusion." Leo settled back in his chair. "Now you have what I have. I'm dying. And I owe you a meal. You coming?"

They walked back in the direction of Winesap, the air suddenly chillier. She was warm from the bourbon, but that superheated feeling she always had after a shift at the restaurant had departed entirely. As Leo unlocked the back door she felt a flash of exhaustion and impatience. Why had she agreed? She could be on her way home by now, closer than ever to some disgraceful, salty midnight gorging instead of whatever genteel little pasta Leo was about to whip up. But, flipping on the lights, she followed Leo into the kitchen anyway because he seemed so relaxed all of a sudden, so informal and friendly, that she was curious to see what lay beneath his general veneer of crisp aloofness and the constant sweep of his gaze.

"I'm going to cook," he said over his shoulder. "You want to hang out?"

"Sure," Thea said. She hopped up on a prep table and watched Leo gather two sauté pans and a couple of pairs of tongs. It was cool in the restaurant now that the heat had automatically turned down; he still wore his leather jacket. He disappeared into the walk-in and returned with a partial baguette beneath one arm, a carton of eggs, and a block of white cheese clutched in one hand. "You wanna slice this?" he asked, proffering the baguette, and Thea jumped down and went to work while he returned to the walk-in. When he came back, humming under his breath, he had two jalapeños and a package of dried chorizo. "Don't worry," he said, turning on the flame beneath the sauté pans. "I'll hardly use any of this. I'm not depleting your kitchen stocks."

"You're using staff meal cheese anyway." Thea shrugged. "It's just food from the mouths of your workers, that's all."

Leo chuckled. He swirled olive oil in one pan, took Thea's sliced baguette, and set the slices into the oiled pan. He sliced the chorizo thinly, fingers properly protected from the blade, Thea noted, and laid the sausage in the dry pan to render. A moment later she heard the spitting sound of the pork fat, and her stomach growled audibly. Leo was now clutching a bowl between his arm and his rib cage and whisking eggs rather madly, glancing back and forth at his pans as he did. The eggs slopped onto the counter, but he didn't seem to notice. Thea saw a pop of scarlet oil arc out of one pan, and though Leo started at the sound, he made no move to turn the heat down.

"I'm going to lower that just a bit," she said.

"You're the professional," Leo said. He was ignoring the tongs and turning the oiled bread slices with his fingers. Thea watched, fascinated and made faintly nervous by this slapdash new Leo, as he tipped the chorizo pan over a metal dish and spooned out the sliced disks of sausage, splashing several fat drops of red oil onto the counter, before pouring the eggs into the pan and stepping back with an air of satisfaction. It was the mess that made her so tetchy, she realized, the mess combined with Leo, who had never been known to cook, standing here, cooking away in what she considered to be her kitchen. She hated sloppy cooking, but there was nothing to say about it to him—though she felt a frisson of unease and an edge of hostility lurking just beneath it, in case he left the dishes when they finished for the cooks to clean up in the morning. A lot of owners would.

"Are you cooking the peppers?" she asked.

"I was going to slice them over the top with the cheese," Leo said. "Too much?"

"Nope." Thea let him handle the jalapeños while she shaved off a few thin slices of cheese, a mild cheddar the cooks kept on hand for baking into cornbread or slicing onto burgers at staff meal. It was just the sort of thing she would have been moved to eat if she'd been by herself, except she would have just toasted it on bread or eaten it cold on crackers, meditating on the ring of toothmarks she left in each slice as she chewed. Leo swirled his pan, tilting it to let the last soft rivulets of egg hit the hot pan, and then wordlessly reached one hand back toward her. Thea set the sliced cheese in his palm, realizing as she did that she was a little more buzzed than she'd intended to be, because she placed the cheddar on Leo's warm skin as delicately as if it were a piece of jewelry, a hollowed, painted eggshell. He laid the cheese over the eggs, then scattered a thick layer of chorizo coins over the cheese, and finally a handful of fresh sliced jalapeño.

"And we're done," Leo said. He paused, looking around frantically until Thea realized that he had forgotten where the plates were kept. She reached beneath the prep counter and handed him two.

"Thanks," he said. He ran a spatula down the center of the eggs and lifted a golden orange pillow onto each plate, dropping yet more paprika-stained oil onto the stove and the counter. He put several crisped slices of bread onto each plate and handed her one. "Don't think for a second I won't clean this up," Leo said, "but first let's eat," and Thea finally relaxed. They had jars of tasting spoons on the line but no forks, yet Leo just shrugged and handed her a spoon, keeping one for himself. They spooned up egg and cheese and pepper, the cheese dripping off in strings, and ate them atop the croutons, standing side by side against the prep counter, facing the stove and chewing silently. Thea had to slow herself from gobbling. The cool incendiary crunch of the chile peppers was the only thing that held her back from tipping her plate and its savory, oily contents straight into her mouth. Leo set down his plate and poured two glasses of water, one of which Thea drank thirstily.

"Tell your daughter I apologize for trying to kill you with a single meal," Leo said after a time.

Thea sighed, running a piece of bread around the edge of her plate. The meal had filled that buzzed, pleasingly hollow core in her belly and now she was good and sober again, warm and sleepy. "She can never know," she said. "If I make this for her, I might as well buy her some crack." Leo looked hurt. "Oh no," she said, "I mean because it's delicious. And because it'll kill us both. Do you eat this way every night?"

He shook his head. "I forget what I eat most nights, to be honest. Whatever's served at staff meal. If I'm off, I just have something simple."

"Yeah, like what?"

Leo looked embarrassed. "I really mean simple. Like once a week I make a big batch of oatmeal and then I heat up a dish at a time with some milk."

"That's not a bad breakfast."

"A lot of times it's dinner."

"Oh."

"And then I like sardines. I keep a lot of sardines in olive oil around and eat 'em on toast."

"Leo. You don't even like food, do you?"

He laughed. "I do, but I'm not passionate about it in my own life. When people get all sententious about flours and shit, I just want to laugh. It's a steak, it's not a cure for cancer, you know? But"—he raised his empty plate in Thea's direction to emphasize the point—"I'm not here to do this *badly*. In here, I care tremendously that we do it right, but I'd care the same way if I were running a tattoo parlor."

Thea nodded, trying not to show her surprise. The strange part was, she respected Leo even a little more now. It was easy to be exacting about your passion. But Leo's mania for correctness and his questing, constantly expanding business intelligence were both more innate and more cunningly applied than she had realized. He hadn't been predisposed or groomed to be a success in restaurants; he had made himself one.

Leo raised an eyebrow at her. She realized she was gazing at him. She looked away and said, "Well, if I'd known you were eating oatmeal every night, I would have had Jason cook you something really decadent for dinner."

"No way," said Leo. "I won't even joke about giving up that meal."

"Was it so good?" Maybe there was more to phlegmatic, corpse-pallored Jason than she'd thought; perhaps he'd wisely taken the opportunity to impress Leo. "What'd he do?"

"He just did it carefully," Leo said. "He did more for a staff meal than he had to. It wasn't super-innovative or anything. It was just what I needed, that's all. Thank you."

He turned to look at her, and Thea felt a flush rise through her cheeks. She thought of Fiona with a burst of compassion for her constant, visible shyness. Suddenly Thea was sure she had oil all over her chin. She swiped discreetly at her mouth, brushed crumbs from her sweater.

"Well, sure," she said. "Our cooks ought to be able to sauté a chicken, right?"

Leo paused and looked away, then took her plate. "Right," he said. "I'm going to clean up, okay? Give me five and I'll walk you to your car. It's late."

CHAPTER 11

EVEN AFTER BRITT HAD GIVEN UP on her, Camille—rather uncooperatively—continued to dine at the restaurant. She showed up with a couple in their late thirties, the woman heavily pregnant and so bejeweled that, next to her, Camille's elongated form in camel boots and ice-colored dress seemed as pure and cool as a blade of grass, a frosted twig. Britt issued a solemn cheek press and hand clasp accompanied with a faint smile. He told himself he was established, he owned two restaurants, an apartment, good scotch glasses, and real furniture. He would not vie with his little brother, not even for Camille. Besides, if she was intrigued by Harry, she must find Britt boring and staid.

"New business?" he asked. The couple had gone ahead to the table.

"College roommate." She looked him over. "Are you okay? You seem a little melancholy."

"Probably just winter," Britt said, gratified. He *did* feel a certain pleasurable martyrdom in giving up the idea of her, the possibilities of her wide mouth and long limbs. He was conscious of looking at her with a new gravity.

"Ah," she said. "I like to have a good cry when I feel that way. See if that helps." And she patted him on the arm.

HE SPENT THE NEXT DAY IN a trance of caffeine and exhaustion, interviewing servers and inventorying and rejiggering kitchen equipment with Harry before heading over to Winesap. Shelley's suggestions about the kitchen setup had turned out to be useful, even if Harry did keep texting her about the details when he thought Britt wasn't paying attention.

He was in the habit of expecting a gap of weeks or even a month between Camille's visits to the restaurant, but there she was at the Winesap bar less than twenty-four hours after she'd last been there, her hair in a loose knot and her chin propped thoughtfully in one hand. A glass of bourbon with an ice cube sat before her. Britt was tired enough and off guard enough to wonder if he was simply wrong about what day it was.

He shouldn't go to her. She left him feeling harried and sweaty every time, but he also knew he would not just smile and keep walking. He never quite knew what she would say to him, and he could never pass up the chance to find out.

When she saw him, she smiled and began putting on her coat. By the time Britt reached her, she was setting a bill on the bar. She didn't wait for Britt to say anything, just reached over and clasped his wrist as if she did this all the time, and said, "Can you step away for a minute?"

"Of course. Are you already done?" She had never just touched him, not outside their established ritual of a greeting or farewell, and the directness of it was a shock. His skin where she was touching him seemed hypersensitive, as if he could perceive the whorls of her fingertips, each curve in the smooth pocket of her palm.

"Oh, I'm not eating," she said. She slid off her barstool, so close that he was newly aware of her height, the way her eyes and mouth were on the same level as his own. "Come with me."

He left his coat though they were headed for the door, because he didn't want to stop the momentum of whatever she was doing. Maybe she simply wanted an escort to her car. There were people coming up the walk as they went out the front door, and she paused and waited for the door to close again before she spoke. Britt glanced behind them and realized he never saw the restaurant this way, the glow of its façade in the cold night air, the constant motion behind its lighted windows.

"Say we kept walking," she said. "How long before you ask where we're going?"

"Not long," he said. "But that doesn't mean I'd stop."

"That's good to know." She looked around them at the building and the cars, the quiet row of houses and shops down the street. He'd never seen her in the cool silver light of the moon and the streetlamps, in which her eyes seemed leonine and deep. Britt took a step closer, glad they were not standing before a window but before an opaque wooden door. "I want to know if it feels the same way," she said. "I needed to see you outside the restaurant—even right outside—at least once."

Something thrummed straight through him. Apparently he had never known what she was thinking. Even now she managed to be disarmingly straightforward without revealing much at all. He felt the dullness and exhaustion of the past few weeks slough off him like a layer of cloth.

"Why's that?"

"You know how the second you step out of your usual playing field, everything feels clearer? In there, it's your domain. And I was thinking maybe you're just a good host," she said. "Maybe you aren't interested at all—you're just polite."

"I'm not that polite," he said. "And you haven't taken me very far."

She smiled, a slow frank smile that seemed a reply to every part of him. "We're just getting started," she said. "You can go anywhere you want."

....

SOMEHOW BRITT HAD NEVER STOPPED to consider the problems of dinner—that was what a date was, a shared meal, for God's sake. His entire living was based on it. Yet the moment she'd said, "Where shall we go?" Britt had frozen. Where *should* they go? He knew all too well every restaurant within an hour's drive, and the prospect of actually relaxing in one of them seemed remote. What place had not recently gotten a halfhearted review that would lower their morale or a too-glowing one that would ensure a mob scene? What trendy new places had settled into a reliable but energetic groove, and what old stalwarts weren't lazy, boring, or under investigation for tax evasion, which had a way of distracting from quality control? Who wasn't doing blow with the waitresses and hadn't paid the staff in three weeks and the purveyors in five? Who hadn't gotten fined by safety inspectors and been forced to take a remedial HACCP class?

Camille cut off his deliberations and said she'd surprise him, freeing Britt and also leaving him adrift. Where had he taken his last few girlfriends? He almost called Leo, thinking to have a backup in mind in case Camille wanted to go someplace beset by hovering Makaskis or other enervating issues. Leo usually thought of some offbeat place, which was part of why Britt thought about asking him, but he had been so prickly lately. Leo was trying not to show it, but he could barely bring himself to look Britt in the eye when both were at Winesap.

And in the end Britt did not call Leo, and it did not matter. Camille delivered to him a brisk, sunny e-mail with a time and an address in a neighboring city. The address of the restaurant was unfamiliar. Britt walked up and down the street twice, marveling at how a city right next door to his hometown could contain these odd little triangles and alleyways that he'd never even come across. To reach the restaurant he'd passed a street filled with Middle Eastern groceries, Indian restaurants, and Irish pubs that pumped a miasma of beer, frying oil, and burgers into the air. On his third try, he finally realized that the flat, unmarked black door must be the restaurant. He gave it a tentative push and peered into a cool dark-green hallway, empty but for a stone bowl with a rounded loaf of agate in its center, water flowing continuously over it. A doorway opposite the fountain bore a Japanese character on it and nothing else.

Inside was a narrow room painted a cool stone gray, with long polished wooden tables. Running water was audible, but he didn't see a source. There were tables to the right and a sushi bar to the left, where Camille was already seated, in jeans and a black sleeveless top, talking with the bartender. Before her was an earthenware cup and a tiny sake bottle in a bowl. For a moment he fully expected to hear her conversing in fluent Japanese.

"I was just thinking I should come outside and wait for you," she said. When he kissed her cheek, her skin seemed warmer, softer, than he remembered. A flush bloomed over her cheeks, as if she'd jogged here. "You want the bar or a table?"

The tables were half full, and another couple was at the other end of the bar. Behind the glass case housing the fish and shellfish, a man dressed in white was slicing from a great, blood-pink length of tuna. "Oh, the bar," Britt said. "Let's watch him work." Not an Asian man but a white guy in his midthirties, with unnervingly pale eyes and close-cropped dark hair beneath a white cap. He nodded in Britt's direction. So this was the toro place, the one Harry had been so excited about, with its unmarked door and its relentlessly focused menu. Britt watched with new interest as the chef chose a slab of silver-skinned fish from the case and set about slicing a fine sheet from one end with a long, even stroke. The resulting square was a translucent pearl color of perfectly consistent thickness. Next to him, Camille murmured in appreciation. The chef didn't acknowledge any of his observers. He set about dressing the fish with scallion and nori and placed it before the couple a few seats away, never saying a word.

The restaurant was austere and beautiful, just as Harry had said, like the polished interior of a carved box.

"How're things shaping up?" Camille asked, turning to him. She gestured politely for an additional sake, told the bartender they'd put themselves in the chef's hands with the omakase menu, and then poured the wine for him, a gesture that struck Britt as strangely gracious and old-fashioned. On her right wrist was a wide band of matte silver, in her ears what appeared to be liquid platinum drops that shivered when they toasted with the sake cups. He watched her full lower lip pillow against the pale green of her cup as she drank.

Britt sipped his sake, which was smooth and as light as rice paper. "It's getting close," he said, "but I can barely tell whether that means we're ready or just that it's going to happen anyway. The friends-and-family's in a week, so I guess we'll know then."

She smiled. "You make it sound as if you've never done this before," she said.

"I have, but it's been years. It's probably like bringing a baby home from the hospital—you remember the overall sensation of frenzy and exhaustion but none of the specifics. And to do it well, it's all specifics."

"If it helps, I'm not concerned," she said. "I can't wait, to be honest. Linden needs something new—something just, I don't know, relaxed but interesting. I'm never *interested* anymore when I go out. Present company's other establishment excepted, of course."

Britt looked around. "I'm interested," he said. "I'm interested in this place. How'd you choose it?" It wasn't really fair, he knew, to try to tease out the nuances of her friendship with Harry, but he found it impossible to resist.

"Harry came upon it somehow—I think he met the chef at Mack's. And I kept meaning to try it, but this is the first I've managed it. It's not easy to think of a decent place to take another industry person, you know. I was hoping it was under the radar enough to interest you."

"Well, good job," he said. "It's pretty far under. Kind of risky, them hoping to sustain it long enough to bring in people through in-the-know chatter."

"You think that's what they're doing?"

"I'm just guessing. Then again, maybe they did a whole PR blitz and I just missed it. Harry and I've both been a little underwater for the past few weeks."

Camille hesitated. "He seems pretty frazzled. I know it's typical, but is Harry having a rougher go of it than most people?"

Britt said, "He does seem a little nuts, I admit. But I don't think he's ever had to work in quite this way before."

"Not even on the island?"

"Yes, but not with quite the same level of responsibility."

Now the first dishes were placed before them: translucent folds of fish, an ivory bed of rice, a gemlike cluster of caviar. They went silent as they ate. Britt chewed very slowly, thinking how heavy and oily so much food was compared to this faint salinity, this silky firmness, the succulent, dainty pop of fish eggs against the palate.

When the mouthful was gone, they sipped their sake, not looking at one another. Britt decided not to speak, just for a moment. He sensed where this evening could go, how easily he could push it in that direction, and the fact that already he was doing so. Camille's relentless polish, the shining surface of her companionship, didn't give him much purchase on how she truly felt about anything.

They could talk about restaurants, about where they lived and where they'd grown up, what she liked of her profession and what she hated, what Winesap was doing and how Stray was progressing, and then they would kiss on the cheek again at the end of the night and really that would be it, because there was nowhere else to go from there. The fresh clarity of the plate before them had had a bracing effect, made it all seem so dull and familiar.

"I'm sorry it took me so long to ask you out," Camille said.

Britt looked at her, startled, and was mercifully distracted when the chef placed two fresh plates before them: a crescent of coral shrimp, a golden thread of beaten cooked egg, a spear of scallion.

"Shouldn't I be the one apologizing?" he said.

She took a delicate bite of the shrimp from her chopsticks. "Why, because you're a man? I spent a lot of time with Harry this fall—it was probably on me to let you know whether that meant something or not. So no, I don't think you need to."

"Did it mean something?" Britt asked lightly. Her eyes were more golden-brown in this room, Britt saw; the fine velvet of down along her jawline glowed in the light of the bar. A faint burst of lines creased at the corners of her eyes as she smiled. She was gorgeous but not flawless, her nose with its touch of a downward curve, her disproportionately full lower lip, the faint tang of alcohol on her breath from the sake. And yet at such close range she made him sweat suddenly, the fantasy of her dismissed and replaced with this woman, whose skin was olive-toned and as silky as polished wood, who was looking him frankly in the eyes, and whom he realized he did not know at all.

"It did, a little," she said. "But not now."

THEY WERE STILL DINING while a number of other tables appeared, dined, and departed, which solved the question of whether this chef knew that Britt was a fellow industry person. Not that the man ever directly acknowledged it. During a tiny slurp of fresh oyster, a meaty, rosy octopus slice, and a selection of different fish that at first looked the same but were revealed to have an array of subtle but absolutely clear differences, they watched the chef, who somehow seemed to accomplish a great deal without moving a lot.

Britt waited for the telltale glance out among the tables, a natural scan to see how full the place was, what more might be needed as the night progressed, but this never occurred. The chef's silvery eyes stayed on his workstation until he placed a dish before someone with a brief, formal nod.

They were finally reaching the high point, the toro itself, and were on a third glass of sake. Why didn't Britt live on raw fish every day of his life? At least on every date. It was lightening and energizing; he could have gone for a run. He could have lifted Camille, who was nearly as tall as he was, without even trying.

"So who would you be having dinner with if not with me?" he asked.

Camille smiled. "On a Sunday? Probably my friends. You've seen them at the restaurant. Or one of an array of impressionable young men I keep in a stable. Or I'd be cooking something wonderful for myself and not sharing."

"Are you a good cook?" He had always pegged her for a non-cook. She seemed to dine out too frequently for someone who enjoyed cooking.

"I am," she said. "But I'm greedy. I used to live with a guy who liked pasta with littlenecks, but not as much as I did. And they're expensive, you know. So I always made linguine with clams when he was out of town, but with the same amount of clams as if I were cooking for two."

Britt laughed. "That *is* greedy." She shrugged, smiling. "Where'd the guy travel to?"

"He went overseas a lot. He was in computers. For a while he did a lot in developing countries, trying to get things up and running."

Wonderful. The only thing that would have made Britt look worse in comparison would have been Doctors Without Borders.

"I wasn't going to ask you about your work," he said, "except that I really do want to know."

She cast a sideways glance at him. "I love my work," she said. "Why wouldn't I want to talk about it?"

Britt colored. "Because it's the same thing you get asked on every date, I imagine."

"True." She took a swallow of sake, then shifted in her chair to face him. "But that's the game, isn't it? It's why we're here."

"Okay. Let's play the game. Tell me how you ended up here. The city, I mean, not dinner. We grew up here, so I never stood a chance, but you're from somewhere else." Britt often presented himself as a hometown boy, though he did not view himself this way and would have been insulted if anyone else really did. He had spent time in other cities; he'd traveled. He believed he had simply ended up here as a matter of chance.

"I grew up outside Philadelphia," she said. He noticed that she did not ask him why he knew she was not a local. "I spent some time in New York, worked in a few restaurants, worked as an assistant to a restaurant consultant—that was how I got into this. I couldn't handle the restaurant hours, to be honest. Once I got a taste of having my nights and weekends off, I couldn't go back."

"That *is* the problem. You have to love the craziness more than you hate the hours."

"You obviously do," she said. "Right? Tell me now if you actually detest your job and your life. Tell me why you opened a place in Linden and not in a bigger city."

"Leo asked me. That was where he was opening a place already. For a long time I was just doing the job where the job was. But I started to feel like there was a real point to this, to showing that you can live well here. I feel like we're part of the reason. I guess if you want to live on thirty acres of woods, this'll never be good living for you. But you know, if you want the amenities of a bigger city with a little less bull, Linden might be that one day. And I'm not trying to provide a restaurant that's okay for Linden—I want to run an objectively great restaurant." Britt paused, surprised to find himself declaiming at such length. He didn't know if he had ever quite articulated his feelings this way, but it felt very true.

"I know exactly what you mean," she said. "I came out here as a commuter, just trying not to go bankrupt on real estate, but I like how it's starting to change. It's as if you can feel the ground shifting."

The chef set out two square white dishes in his prep space, nodded at them, and disappeared behind a door. Camille uncrossed her legs and leaned forward on the bar, resting on her forearms. Her hair draped over her collarbones, her smooth shoulder peeking through. Britt reached over and hooked a skein of her hair in one finger, lifted it, and let it fall behind her back. She glanced down at his hand, as did he. He hadn't planned the gesture. He only wanted to see her clearly. For a moment they looked at each other, and then Camille smiled quickly, as if filing it away.

The chef reappeared, carrying a piece of pale fish. The other tuna they'd been served had been dark and richly colored, a gleam-ing garnet so firm it barely drooped when lifted between their chopsticks. But this was completely different. The chef's posture had even changed slightly; he held the plate a touch farther from his body than he had done before, his chin lifted just slightly. He turned toward the back of his workspace and brought out a fresh knife. When he began to slice the fish, it quivered as it parted for the blade. Its paleness wasn't the translucence of the raw hake or flounder; it was pale the way foie gras is pale, a saturated richness. Britt wondered if anything else would go on the plate at all.

Camille said, "Harry told me about a place in Japan his friends went to, where they sat by a window beside a little park. And once they'd ordered, the restaurant let kittens loose outside the window, to play for the guests' amusement."

Britt laughed. It was exactly the sort of detail Harry managed to pick up. "I'm lucky he hasn't ordered a gross of kittens to play in King Street. So, listen. How'd you start coming to Winesap?"

"I let the clients choose. They like Winesap, and Hot Springs, and that old-school pasta place. Berlucci's."

"I'm sorry," Britt said. "You shouldn't have to eat at that place. They parboil all their pasta and then finish it in the microwave."

Camille looked dejected. "I figured it was something depressing like that."

"What d'you think of Hot Springs? We've known the owners for years, in a grudge-match kind of way."

"The desserts are very good," she said, "but sometimes Barbara scares the crap out of me."

The chef now approached them with a plate in each hand, then placed the plates before them with an air of grave finality. Britt gazed down at the white plate and the unadorned pink fish centered upon it, feeling both excited at the climax of the meal and regretful that this was all ending. He remembered Harry calling the toro sea heroin, and looked up into the chef's lupine eyes with a faint chill of apprehension. Certainly he was about to taste something he might not taste again. That was the problem with such a place: once you'd had toro like this, fish like this, you developed a taste beyond your means.

"This looks amazing," Britt told him, "but now I'm sorry we're almost done."

The chef nodded, lifting one shoulder in acknowledgment. His expression suggested faint sympathy for the plight of two people about to taste an elusive and expensive form of glory, as well as a certain brusque acknowledgment that life ends, meals end; get over it.

They stopped speaking as they took the first bite. In Britt's mouth the rich fat melted almost instantly, as if the protein had been netted together only by prayer or memory. They barely chewed; they merely let the fish disappear.

After a moment, Camille murmured, "You could eat this through a straw."

Neither said another word until their plates were empty. As they ate, they watched the chef return to the fish, wrap it smoothly in plastic once more, and disappear behind the door again, carrying the knife he'd used to slice it.

"I bet he never uses the same toro knife twice," Britt said. "He's probably burying that."

Camille was looking around the empty restaurant. "I don't think anyone else was served that fish," she said. "Did you see it before?"

Britt felt a faint glow of pleasure. It wasn't pride so much as gratitude—maybe this guy had his own reasons for bestowing such a thing on certain people; maybe he had no idea Britt was in the restaurant business and simply liked the look of him.

A moment later, he thought about this again and almost laughed. So this was how the customer felt, how easily this was accomplished. He'd known it, of course, but he'd forgotten how effective it was to be on the receiving end of such treatment. And what treatment: the privilege of being served an extravagantly expensive meal, for which they would pay, of course, honored to be thought capable of it. Britt figured he could learn a thing or two from this silent chef.

They declined anything further. What were they going to do, follow up that heavenly, obscenely precious finale with some green tea ice cream? Even though it was probably delicious.

He was waiting for the check, inwardly dreading it now that the distraction of the food had ended, when a server set a wooden plate before Camille, on it a credit card receipt anchored with a polished stone. "Oh, you didn't," he said.

"Of course I did—I'm the one who asked you," she replied, signing it. "Britt. You should know this trick."

"I forgot it," he said wonderingly. How could he have forgotten? But he was also thinking that this was the first time he'd heard her say his name. The sound of it in her voice was a dull hot thud to the chest, as if he'd been eyeing her, unseen, from a distance and she'd suddenly met his gaze, having been aware of him all along.

Part 2

CHAPTER 12

L EO WAS EARLY. HE CIRCLED the block several times instead
of ringing the doorbell before eight and was rewarded by a
lengthy, suspicious look from a guy out shoveling his driveway as
Leo passed him for the third time.

Eventually he pulled into the driveway, where he hadn't been
for years, not since the grand pig feast Thea had hosted when she
was still married to Bryan. The light was on in her kitchen and he
could see her moving back and forth before the window, putting
dishes on shelves and closing cabinet doors.

He had asked her only last night, presenting it as a professional
outing to check on Stray's friends-and-family night, to support
their coworker and his brother, and to extend a hand to Harry as
well. He'd oversold it a bit. They'd been upstairs at the restaurant,
finished with the dinner shift, Thea back in her civilian clothes,
tired and shiny-faced while downstairs the last shift of servers began
straightening the dining room.

The night they'd seen each other at Mack's, Leo had walked
her out to her car and stood beside it, one palm flat on the hood,
while she threw her purse into the passenger seat and turned back
to him, her pale face lit with expectance and uncertainty. They'd
felt like old friends and also like people on a first date, some strange
blend of both.

He'd found himself more at ease than he'd ever been in Thea's
somewhat taciturn presence. When Thea had appeared in the

entrance at Mack's, looking startled by the thud of the door she'd just pushed open, her scuffed boots planted far apart as she'd surveyed the room, he'd known this was the last place she wanted to be. He was touched, because she was there because of the job, which was at least partially because of him.

As they'd finished their drinks and eaten their eggs and walked out into the crisp night air, Leo had felt the darkness of the past few weeks lift. The fretfulness and the unfocused discord that had infected every aspect of his day were just gone, soaked up by bourbon and a meal and by Thea's obvious pleasure at being cooked for and catered to. Alone with her in the kitchen, he had felt reckless and lighthearted, as if nothing he did could fail.

But by the time he'd walked her to her car, he'd come down a bit—they were back out in the quiet familiar neighborhood, the night was over, and they'd return in the morning, the spell broken, and have to work together again. So he just smiled and stepped back so she could close her car door.

The next day he'd braced himself for Thea to be dour and puffy from a night too late and too relaxed. Maybe he even wanted her to be less attractive in the morning, for all evening long, he'd wondered why he'd never noticed Thea's essential prettiness, the delicacy of her mouth and the fine point of her nose, the mink-brown tips of her un-made-up lashes, and it would certainly be easier if he had just been tipsy. But the next day she wore her hair in a bun that showed the tender hollows behind her ears, the arch beneath her cheekbones. At staff meal he'd strained to hear her voice at the other end of the table, and when he went into the kitchen to get more coffee, he'd caught a glimpse of her demonstrating some filleting technique with a branzino for Suzanne and Jason, one hand resting on the silver skin of the fish while the other guided a thin, sharp, glinting knife along the spine, all grace and mastery.

At first he was determined to enjoy a harmless imaginary interlude. He'd seen owners have affairs with the staff in restaurant after restaurant. How many uncomfortable dinner services did a person need to sit through to accept the lesson, how many scrambling, understaffed nights when someone walked out after a breakup? But he also thought about the many couples who opened a place together and made a life of this.

Then last night Thea had changed out of her chef's coat and into a sweater he would certainly remember if he'd seen it before, thin and dove-colored, wrapping snugly around her body and showing her long, narrow waist and the wings of her collarbones, and Leo thought perhaps he could have it both ways. They could go out in such an open and businesslike manner that really it was not a date at all—they could date without anyone noticing, maybe not even her.

Thea opened her front door and waved him in, her face startlingly composed and untouchable with its newly red mouth and eyes shadowed with makeup, her cheeks a matte pale pink. She said goodbye to her babysitter and tucked a hand in his arm as they headed down the icy walk to his car, and Leo reminded himself that the evening would be entirely beyond reproach, as long as he remembered not to say or do any of the things he desired.

HARRY HADN'T REALIZED HOW EARLY this city liked to dine. He and his staff had invited friends and family for any time between seven and ten, hoping for a natural spacing, but people crushed in at 7:10 and started ordering.

At first he'd managed to look over his shoulder here and there. He saw his parents seated at the bar, watching him raptly and waving each time he turned, and he glimpsed the pale blur of Britt's white shirt moving swiftly through the dining room among the scrum of people standing, sitting, talking across the narrow aisles. That was an unanticipated problem of a friends-and-family night; they all knew each other and kept trading bites and getting in the servers' way. People were tilting their heads back, or they had been, when he'd last been able to look, to gaze at the massive mirror or the sprays of silvered branches fanning out of pale blue-gray vases against the brick wall. Somehow it had all come together, visually at least, and the room was a mix of rustic and elegant, warm and cool, and Harry still wasn't entirely sure how it had been managed. Mostly Britt had done it; he'd exchanged a terracotta vase for the sleek ones the color of chalcedony, the stemware for Moroccan painted bistro glasses, the white napkins for oatmeal ones, and the ferns for more birch branches, until the clusters looked as if they'd come from Norway or a fairy tale.

Harry was moving, moving; his feet barely shifted but he never stopped reaching, turning, poking and flipping and brushing at the pans on the range to his right. On the other side of the range was Jenelle, her hair flat with sweat against the back of her neck, her thick dark brows furrowed and her thin mouth set in a line of concentration as she worked, lifting a basket of crackling shrimp and herbs from the fryer and letting it drain while she reached for a plate with the other hand. Out of the corner of his eye Harry could admire the crisp herb sprigs, parsley splayed like a doll next to the gold and coral crescents of shrimp. This batch looked good, but he'd been glancing over all night and he knew the shrimp kept changing color—she was pulling them out brown, pale yellow, all over the place; the temperature of her oil dropped when she had a crush of orders but then returned to the right one after a pause, and Jenelle, he could tell, kept forgetting to allow for it. She knew it too; she kept shaking her head in a sharp little twitch of recrimination. But this plate looked good, so Harry filed it away as he got a pan of olive oil heating to crisp the socca. On the range next to the socca pan was a wide sauté pan with four duck breasts—potatoes in the oven? Yes, he wasted precious time looking, but that was better than assuming—and then he helplessly watched a ticket print with yet more duck, his perfect self-saucing duck that Britt must have told everyone about because he'd already served ten of the goddamn things and it turned out it was murder remembering the last smear of mustard before the meat came off to rest; he had a bad feeling some had gone out without it, but there was nothing to do now but push through. Jenelle was plating the shrimp in a delicate little pyramid, plucking out the parsley and setting it near the top, scattering the plate with coarse salt and handing it back toward the server station, which was just the last section of the zinc bar nearest the dining room's back wall (guests kept crowding into the space and servers kept charming their way through, smiles dropping the moment they reached for the plates). She was already reaching with the tongs in her other hand toward the metal plate sizzling with confit that was crisping in the salamander. Hector was in the back room, prepping while he waited for the first dessert orders. They should have started the night fully ready, mise en place arrayed in its bins and perfectly prepared, but it just hadn't happened, and so Hector was back there amid a pile of produce, knife flashing and eyes flat as coins, a disconcerting faint smile playing at the corners of his mouth.

Harry reached up and blotted his forehead with an arm and kept moving. He couldn't hear the music anymore, didn't know if anyone could, but there was no time to worry about it anyway. Britt would have to deal with it; that was why he was here. Harry reached into the lowboy for a little oval stoneware dish filled with baccalà; it would go into the oven to heat and finish with a run under the salamander to brown it before it was plated with the socca and lightly dressed arugula. Already he disliked the monochromatic look of it. It needed more than arugula, perhaps, some piquancy, but there was no time to do anything about that. He couldn't think of what he would do later tonight or tomorrow. What was tomorrow? There was only right now, the varying stages of the dishes before him ticking forward in his head, the mental clicking punctuated by the occasional shout of laughter or his name (he waved wildly over his shoulder in the direction the voice had come from—no idea who it was) and here and there the faint sizzle of his forearm against the rim of a blazing sauté pan. He hadn't cooked like this in months, he was out of shape, and already his hands and forearms were dotted with burns. Another mistake: he should have found a way to do a stage or two to get back in fighting form, maybe at Winesap if Leo had allowed it, which was unlikely. Who had time to do that anyway? He'd been here every day for twenty hours a day, and he still didn't know what the fuck he'd been doing with it all, only that it hadn't been enough, it still wasn't enough, more remained to be done, and so he just put his head down and kept it all moving, rotating his proteins off the range and into the oven and under the salamander and back out again, spiking his tickets and talking to Jenelle in shorthand about tables and dishes and ordering and firing, until at some point the night would be done, doused like a flame, and he'd breathe.

BRITT WAS CIRCLING THE DINING ROOM, eyeing the servers, peering into the kitchen, where Hector was now working at his little minirange to fry off the hot and cold beignets, to warm caramelized pears and dulce de leche. Hector slid a square of coconut lime napoleon neatly off his spatula and onto a plate. The napoleon was the only dessert from Winesap that had ended up on the menu at Stray. Hector insisted that the recipe was his and therefore he had custody of the dessert wherever he chose to take it. Nevertheless, Britt wondered if Leo, when he finally showed, would order it just to make the point.

He kept looking at his watch and at the door, but Camille was not here yet either. Her time away from him seemed mysterious and tantalizing, all those hours in which she worked or read or drank tea, had dinner with her friends and was probably flirted with and cajoled by servers and movie-ticket-takers. Since their first date, they'd met for lunch and one evening walk; they'd embarked upon an ongoing series of funny and conversational e-mails and texts, but he had so little time between Winesap and preparing for tonight that things between them felt slightly tentative. She was unperturbed; as someone who'd worked in the food world, she knew exactly what these last few days had been like. But Britt felt hamstrung anyway. He didn't want to be apologizing already for his lack of time; he didn't want her to have to be understanding yet. He wanted to be out with her every night, drinking sake. He wanted her lounging around his house, or around her house, it didn't matter—he wanted them in some private interior, famished and spent, surprised to find it was daylight once again. Instead they had a teenage makeout session cut short by a text summoning him back to one restaurant or another, and one frustrating, sandwichy lunch.

But this was it. After tomorrow, the restaurant was open. It wasn't the last hurdle by any means, but it was a major one, and he believed some focus would now be possible, and this lent the night an additional thread of excitement. He planned to get her to stick around as they finished up the service tonight, take her home to a glass of red wine. He didn't have a fireplace, but who cared? He could set fire to something.

At the server station he paused, shaking himself out of his reverie. They still hadn't gotten around to replacing the griddle with an actual coffee-cup warmer, so he'd had to admonish the servers to keep the griddle on low so no one got burned. That was bad enough, but now he noticed that the shelves were too high as well. All the servers, except for one or two of the men who were as tall as Harry, were on tiptoe, swiping at the dishes and glasses. The shelves would all have to be rehung within reach of people of normal height instead of Harry's height, and it would have to be done soon.

The servers all wore jeans and dark shoes. Harry had wanted to allow tennis shoes as long as they weren't white, but Britt knew that would end up getting interpreted in some hideous way, try though they had to find waitstaff who wouldn't even think of owning white running shoes instead of sleek little Pumas in taupe or dark gray or chocolate. It wasn't worth the time it would take to describe it, so Britt just said dark shoes, no sneakers, and left it at that. (Actually, at first he'd specified leather, but Joshua's hand had shot up so he could inquire, ready for a fight, about vegan shoes, and Britt had backed off, bored already.) In their black T-shirts and denim, their messy chignons and facial hair and those awful spacers widening the holes in their earlobes, they could have been clientele but for the black aprons knotted around their sleek midsections. The bartender, Travis, was the one Britt was wondering about, getting steamy and red-faced from the heat of the range so close, losing precision and overpouring. This negated the whole reason the servers weren't pouring wine at the table—with the eyes of the guest on them, servers overpoured. It was human nature.

As he passed his parents, he let a hand linger briefly on their shoulders while he peered at their plates. They were down to crumbs, but that didn't mean they'd loved the dishes. Harry and Britt could have set a live possum before their parents and their mother would have coolly, maternally, sharpened her butter knife.

Years before, their mother had looked up a recipe for Harry's lamb tongue. When it was ready, she and Harry had each cut a tiny, brave piece of the ugly thing, which was sprinkled with parsley and marooned on its plate like a science experiment. Britt and Leo had watched them chew for what seemed a long time, until Harry swallowed and frowned, no doubt regretting his lost allowance.

"Lighten up on your pours, just a touch," he told Travis, who nodded and slowed very slightly. Ounce by ounce, lost booze drained away money when it should be the biggest moneymaker in the house—it was all markup and no prep.

Britt made his way yet again toward the front of the space, pausing to speak with tables as he did and then picking up plates as he returned to the back of the house. The duck plates were wiped clean, the baccalà not so much—people were running out of socca and reluctant just to spoon it up. They'd have to add another slice. The sardines lay denuded and separated from their nduja-spread toasts, a flavor combination Britt now confirmed was not working, since no one was eating it together. The cloudy-eyed heads of the fish were stoically averted from the bare fronds of their ribs. The baby octopus wasn't moving, but the few he'd seen looked perfect, purple and white beneath a yellow haystack of frizzled ginger.

He watched Joshua serve a table of four, placing a dish at an empty seat whose occupant had gone to the restroom. Britt sighed. When Joshua saw Britt watching, he reddened and sidled over to him. "She keeps *leaving*," he muttered under the din. "Is she feeding a freaking pet back there or what?"

Britt said, "If you can't hold the food another second, at least cover the dish and watch for her to come back, okay? I'll warn you now, this is one of my pet peeves." Joshua nodded and departed to replace the woman's napkin, darting an ingratiating smile in Britt's direction as he did.

The first desserts were now moving past him, and Britt raised his brows at a server to signal her to slow and let him look at the plates: the beignets a generous little pile of sugared pastry next to their glass cup of basil cream, the pears all plump, feminine round-ness beneath a veil of warmed dulce de leche. Next to these two playful, homey dishes, the napoleon looked too refined, its lime powder too vivid, like a dessert from a different restaurant, which it was. He shouldn't have let Hector serve it. Or Harry shouldn't have let Hector serve it. Britt was trying very hard to keep out of Harry's kitchen; he was front-of-the-house and therefore he issued opinions through the lens of what got the orders, what went back untouched, and what was exclaimed over at presentation and consumed in an instant. He'd bring it up later, when Harry didn't look so wild-eyed. Even the back of Harry's neck looked crazed, the muscles visibly bunched beneath the constant motion of his head.

He was doing okay, though, planted before the range with his back to the crowd, his height and long arms an unexpected boon in the tight space. Small Jenelle had to move her feet, but Harry did not.

By the time nine o'clock rolled around, the room was calming down. One or two tables sat empty, and the staff kept running out of coffee before the next batch was brewed—annoying, but at least a welcome sign of the end of the meals. Britt had had to remind the backwaiters only once to watch the water glasses—he despised an empty water glass—and when he poked his head into the restrooms, he saw just what he wanted to see: moisturizer, soap, folded towels, and a basket of tampons in the ladies', the same minus tampons in the men's. Plenty of toilet paper, no unsightly wastebaskets or towels missing the little linen-lined hampers.

By now Harry was starting to look normal again: Britt could no longer see the whites all around his irises when Harry scanned the room. In the kitchen Hector was in a groove, tossing beignets in the sugar with a practiced flick of the wrist. The cacao custard in its malted cone-cup was proving a tough one to serve—everyone wanted it, though people kept pointing at the word "cacao" instead of saying it, unsure how to pronounce it—but the delicate malt cup kept slipping out of the dollop of pastry cream that was intended to anchor it to the plate. The servers were all moving like zombies, eyes locked on the malt cup, and Britt was sure they were going to collide.

"Sourcing cacao beans," someone said behind him. "Such an esoteric skill."

Britt turned and found Leo standing just behind him, about to sit down at a table. Britt hugged him, ignoring the cacao comment because it seemed to be a joke anyway, and because in the adrenaline of the night he was now elated to see his brother, whose prior absence Britt only now realized had felt quite glaring. Leo seemed to be in a good mood too; he laughed when Britt embraced him and then turned to present his companion. For a moment Britt didn't recognize her: he saw a woman as tall as Leo, with dark brown curls and luminous eyes, broad shoulders, a simple black dress. He was reaching a hand forward, the other resting on Leo's shoulder for an extra beat to silently convey admiration for Leo's companion, when he paused, hand in midair, and realized with a shock that this was Thea.

"It looks wonderful," she said. She saved him by leaning forward to hug him, then made a little show of looking around. "How's it been? Did we give you enough time? We figured we both needed to check it out, so we scheduled a little professional dinner meeting."

Leo's hands were in his pockets. He and Thea offered Britt the same sunny, impenetrable smiles. "We wanted to be here sooner," Leo said, "but figured better to let you get the early diners out of the way."

"Thanks," said Britt. He was still recovering from recognizing Thea with his brother. It had to be business. There was no way Leo would cross that line; it was sacrosanct. When Britt had started at Winesap, that was one of the first lectures Leo had given him: labor laws and not screwing with the staff. Usually that meant waitresses, for some reason, but this was potentially far more explosive. There were a thousand waitresses out there, but try finding a new executive chef in a town this size. No, Leo would never show up here so brazenly if something was going on. Britt collected himself and said, "It's been a madhouse, but I think in a good way. We'll see how the postmortem goes tomorrow, but I'm feeling good. You just missed Mom and Dad."

"We saw them on their way out," said Thea. "I don't know how I've worked with you guys for years and never met them. They were lovely."

Who was this Thea, all sweetness and interest in parents? It was bizarre, and it made him worry all over again. Britt preferred grumpy, silent Thea, the Thea who understood that his parents were lovely but would drive her batty in the kitchen, insisting that they loved everything but then allowing their plates to go back half full, assuring the servers that everything was stunning, simply stunning, even as they refused to touch another bite of something they had clearly, distressingly hated.

"What did they say?" he asked.

"They said the duck confit was delicious—a trifle salty for their blood pressure, but delicious—and your mother is very concerned what people think of the lamb's neck."

"That damn lamb's neck," he said. "I don't even want to talk about it anymore. Listen, you guys have a seat."

Britt flagged down Anna, the head server. She had straight dark brows and yellow hair dyed a deliberately fake canary color, with a scruffy fringe of bangs and a silver nose stud.

"Got it, one of everything. Is that your other brother?" she asked.

"Yup. And the executive chef from Winesap," he said. "And don't think for a second that his being our brother is going to make him any nicer." But even as he said this, Leo was leaning back in his chair, laughing at something, nodding pleasantly at a neighboring table, and looking like pure charm and benevolence. Anna shrugged and headed off to get their drink orders. At the table, Leo and Thea looked over their menus. Their posture was straight; they weren't touching. They might have been at a menu meeting at Winesap. Still, it was another beat before Britt even remembered to tell Harry their brother was here.

When he got to the line, Harry was drinking a pitcher of water from a shelf beneath the counter. "Hey, Leo's here," Britt said, leaning over the counter. "With Thea." Harry nodded, swallowing. He didn't seem to find Thea's presence as provocative as Britt did, or maybe he was just too slammed to care. "How you doing back there?"

"Okay," Harry said. "I think okay. What are you sending to Leo?"

"Everything."

Britt looked again toward the front of the dining room. Where could Camille be? Harry might know, which didn't make him feel any less nervous. At first he had had the distinct sensation of being the interloper on Camille's existing friendship with his brother, but then Britt had the impression that Harry and Camille no longer saw each other quite so often. He didn't want to ask, or to look at their phones when they buzzed with a message or a call, but then again he did want to, too. Surely Harry's friendship with Camille had slowed a bit as he was swallowed by the restaurant as well.

"Hey, I thought Camille was coming," Britt said. "Did you talk to her?"

Harry turned back to his range. "Oh," he said over his shoulder, "I asked her not to, sort of. I thought it would be better if she came in when things had settled."

"Since when?" Britt said. "When was this?"

"This afternoon. She called the house phone to ask about a time and I just knew it was too soon, Britt—she should see it when we're really ready. I'm doing you a favor. You don't want her in till we're really flying."

Harry's words faded in and out over the clang of voices and sauté pans, but Britt had the distinct sensation of being dismissed. He would have liked to keep discussing this. Had she at least called his cell phone to say she wasn't coming? Since when did Harry direct his social life? Why let Leo see the place before it was perfect but not Camille? But Anna appeared next to him, flashing a professional smile at the patrons, and murmured that Leo was eyeing a neighboring table's octopus with great skepticism and did he still want to serve it?

LEO AND THEA WERE THE LAST TABLE in the place. By the time
Anna was clearing off their dessert tasting plates at eleven thirty, the
rest of the staff was gathered in the back, having cleared and reset
tables, restocked the server station, folded napkins, and polished
glassware and silver. Anna had hung the breakdown of server duties
in the kitchen by the espresso machine, and already Britt could see
that the laminated page might have to move until the servers had
their routines down; the espresso machine was mobbed with milling staff, peering at the list and trying to recall where to find the
coffee filters, the spray bottles, the polishing cloths.

They were both standing at the bar, Britt on the customer side
and Harry on the line, as Leo and Thea made their way to the door.
Britt swallowed, suddenly dry-mouthed. Anything looked good
when it was all you'd seen for weeks; you were so accustomed to
every dish and every movement that the brain automatically over-
laid all your good intentions and past failures on each dish, each
server and motion. But Leo was a fresh eye, and an unforgiving
one at that. Britt was used to being the one strolling inscrutably
alongside Leo toward the door, not the one waiting anxiously at the
bar, peering at his expression. He experienced a moment of kin-
ship and odd empathy for Barbara Makaski, the faint whiff of terror
he'd never before perceived in her sentinel's posture.

"It was really good," Leo said, without preamble. "You guys
want to talk more tomorrow, or you too busy?"

"Sure," said Britt. But even as he spoke Harry was shaking his
head.

"I don't think we have time," he said. "I *want* to, but I have to
be back here first thing and we have the all-staff meeting. I need
to rework a couple of dishes too. I'm not sure about our supplies,
either—I may have to make a bunch of calls. The stuff I thought
would move didn't, the stuff I didn't think would did." He was

leaning over the bar as he enumerated these issues, his hands gripping its edges. Thea's head tilted, just barely, as she observed him.

Britt said, "I can manage it, Harry. Leo, let's have breakfast—you can give me your impressions. Harry, how about if I'm here by ten?"

A complicated series of expressions crossed Harry's face: he looked first relieved, then vexed, then concerned, then resigned. All he said was, "That'd be great, thanks." All three watched him for another beat, waiting to see if he had anything to add, but Harry stood back, straightened his posture, and nodded with an air of finality.

"Hey," Britt said. "We should be celebrating. We got through our first service, and we did it pretty well."

Harry ran both hands through his hair, shaking his head. "We did okay. I've got a list in my head about fifty items long and I have no idea how I'm going to do it." Then he suddenly raised both hands, palms out, as if in surrender. "Hey!" he barked, startling them. "You're customers! You don't care. You *shouldn't* care. Get the hell out of here, go home, have drinks. We're not gonna do this. We're not turning you into consultants."

Leo looked puzzled. "I'm glad to help, Harry," he said.

"I know you are, and I appreciate it. Really. You two talk tomorrow and Britt and I'll catch up later. Okay?"

The kitchen door opened and Anna approached the bar. "Forgive me," she said to Leo and Thea, and then to Britt and Harry. "We're about done back there. You guys still want to check in with the staff?"

Britt glanced apologetically at Leo. "We have a couple bottles of champagne to crack."

Leo's face went blank, just for a moment, and then he moved into gear, bustling into his coat, assuring them that this was fine and that breakfast at eight would be fine, fine. As he talked, he was looping a scarf several times around Thea's neck, until she was wrapped all the way up to the chin. Discreetly, she undid a few loops and began the slow process of stepping toward the door, calling the same farewells over the brothers' various repetitions of plans and reassurances, until finally they had all exhausted the options for chitchat and the door closed behind Leo and Thea with a muffled click.

The two of them walked half a block without speaking, their steps slow and contemplative. Finally Thea said, "How odd to see Britt in another restaurant. I think he would have liked us to stay."

Leo looked at her gratefully. Her lipstick was long gone, and a faint sheen had reasserted itself on her cheeks; she looked again like the woman he knew. "Harry needs to be independent, I guess," he said, and though he knew this was true and that it was a sound idea, he was a little crestfallen nevertheless. "It was a good meal, though, wasn't it?"

"It really was," Thea said. "Forgive me for putting it indelicately, but the lamb's neck is fucking amazing."

Happy as Leo was that this was true, he felt a jolt of jealousy to hear her speak this way of someone else's food. "It's totally terrifying to look at," he said. "I mean, you're shredding meat off vertebrae. I think I saw a nerve."

"But the gremolata and the handmade cavatelli? It's stunning. Stunning. In the best possible way, it made me want to up my game."

"I don't think your game is in need of a thing," Leo said. And this was true, but he understood what she meant. The evening had been energizing; the space made him feel like he was in a bigger, better city; the food had been downright fun. He wanted only to be delighted for his brothers, but he could not quite banish the sinking feeling Thea's enthusiasm had left him with.

"Thank you," she said. "But I just mean I'm inspired. I had a great time."

They fell back into silence.

"Maybe it was a little unexpected that we went together," Thea ventured. They were almost to his car, and Leo was so uncertain how to answer this that he said nothing until they stood beside the passenger door. Surely this was his opportunity to state that any undercurrents were imaginary and their relationship was as it had always been. But the night had sped by so quickly. When would he have another excuse to see her laughing and swirling the wine in her glass, her posture becoming so relaxed and languorous?

"Well, we did say it was just business," Leo said tentatively. Thea's face lost its electricity, just for a second, and she looked away. Boldness surged through him, and Leo reached over, touching the curve of her jaw, the sharply lifting angle of it, with the tip of one finger. She looked back at him, a smile beginning to surface, and tilted her head very slightly into the cup of his hand. "We'll be fine," Leo said, "as long as that's what everybody thinks."

BRITT LOCKED THE DOOR, peering out into the empty, dark street. When he returned, Anna was gathering plastic cups for the staff and Harry had pulled out two bottles of inexpensive but decent champagne. Britt grasped Harry's shoulder as they headed into the kitchen and held his brother back as the door closed behind Anna. He'd intended a friendly clasp but ended up requiring a surprising amount of force to make Harry pause.

Harry turned, his eyebrows raised, and gestured with the bottles. "What," he said, "you think we need something nonalcoholic too?"

"Huh? No, it's fine. Well, maybe we do. Are you okay? You seem wound a little tight."

"You seem a little relaxed," Harry countered. "Listen, I can celebrate this for about ten minutes and then I have to get some work done. You mind sticking around?"

"It's fine," Britt said. "And if I'm relaxed, it's because I know we can do this. We have plenty to build on, but we did pretty well tonight." When had he taken on such a placating tone with Harry? There was something fraudulent in it, he thought, something too close to soothing a child or a pet.

Britt was about to bring up Camille when he saw that the kitchen was full, the staff was peering out at them, empty cups aloft, and he abandoned it. "You're okay, seriously okay? Because you seem a little too freaked out. And I'm telling you I don't think you need to be."

"Jesus, of course I need to be," Harry said, already turning away and heading toward the kitchen door. "You have Winesap. You'll be fine. I have all the weight of that success but none of the cushion. Now let's go drink a toast with these kids and turn 'em loose till we do it all again tomorrow."

It was late enough for Britt to send a text to Camille rather than phone her, and to his surprise an answer buzzed while he was still finishing off a swallow of champagne.

"I was banished," she said when he called. He'd left the restaurant and was walking to his car, keeping a watchful eye scanning the dark streets. "I'm so sorry. I called to let you know, but I knew you'd never hear it."

"No," he agreed, "I didn't even feel it buzz. It was a madhouse in here."

"I can't believe I missed it," she said, sighing.

"It's okay," he said, and decided that he meant it, at least as far as Camille was concerned.

"No, it's not. But I felt terrible for him. He was really roundabout and motormouthed about it—I finally realized he was trying to suggest that I wait to come in. You should be gentle on him, Britt. He seems pretty freaked out."

"That's Harry's general mode," Britt said.

"I guess you know," she said. She paused. "But I did want to see you in your new element." Her voice warmed. "I had a nice little plan for observing you from the bar all night and passing you my phone number on a cocktail napkin as I left. I was going to say nothing and tuck it into your pocket."

"My shirt pocket, I hope."

"Yes. It was a classy fantasy."

Britt laughed. His defensiveness and exhaustion had dissipated. Here they were, talking, awake, and the hurdle of getting the restaurant open was almost cleared—really, he decided, the restaurant *was* open, for all intents and purposes. "I want to see you," he said.

"It's almost midnight."

"I know what time it is. I want to see you. You want to see me?"

Camille lived fifteen minutes from Stray, in a Craftsman-style house on a quiet street. A light burned on the porch. She opened the door wearing stretchy black pants and a thin top, teeth brushed but hair ruffled, no makeup. As much as Britt enjoyed a woman who was smoothed to a high shine, this was suddenly better: the worn fabric of her clothing still heated from sleep, the top riding up to show a narrow band of skin at her belly. No bra smoothed her breasts into neutral shapes; instead he could see the clear outline of her nipples and the surprisingly rounded, heavy undercurve of her breasts.

Her hand rested on the doorknob, and a leaping pulse showed in her throat. Britt reached past her and closed the door. He was thinking that her wide mouth looked softer than he'd thought, the full lower lip a darker, more suggestive pink than he'd remembered. Everything from her dress to her manner was always so well controlled, and he'd supposed that in the middle of the night she'd be softened and even awkward, off-kilter at seeing him at such an hour, on such short notice. But she wasn't, not really—she wore dishevelment as easily as she wore a dress and heels. She wasn't surprised at all, and somehow he liked this even more.

He slid a hand around her neck, pushing her heavy hair up

against the hot curve of her skull. A faint breath of air—a gasp of surprise, desire, or just the impact—escaped her mouth as they backed to the door, and Britt hesitated. Their eyes met, and the room quivered for a still moment. His hand was still buried in her hair, the other flattened beneath her clothes against the velvety stretch of her spine. Her roving hands had paused, at his neck and at his waist, and now she moved them slowly, one finger slipping beneath the loosened hem of his shirt. He felt her arch her back, her hips pinning his hand between her heated skin and the rough wooden door. It hurt just a bit, as she seemed to intend.

WHEN BRITT AWOKE THE NEXT MORNING, he spent a long time listening to Camille moving around her kitchen. Wrapped in the warm duvet, he listened to the clink of glassware and the burble of pouring coffee and felt both content and slightly nervous; she was already up and about as if it were any other morning. When he emerged from the bedroom, she was sitting cross-legged on her couch, drinking coffee and working her way through the news-paper on her laptop. On the table before her was a neatly folded green linen napkin, a plate of sliced pear and oranges, and a small pitcher of cream, which she offered to him when he returned from the kitchen, where an empty white mug had awaited him beside the coffee machine. In the daylight her living room seemed serene and welcoming, with high ceilings, sage-green walls, and a pale gray couch. On the coffee table was a wide white bowl of apples.

"This is a great room," he said, sitting beside her.

Camille looked around as well, considering it. "Thanks. I painted it a few months ago. Before this it was orange, then taupe. I also tried painting something straight onto the walls, like a silhou-ette of a plant or something." He looked around to see if the ghost remained on any of the walls. "It's long gone," she said. "I have no talent for figurative painting, but I had it in my head that maybe I'd developed some without my knowledge."

"Stay with this for a while. I don't want to leave. I can just use your toothbrush and have some food delivered."

"You think?" She looked around the room, reaching over to touch his hand to indicate that she'd heard the rest of it too.

"Absolutely. Though if you still had some looming plant silhouette, I might not."

She laughed, taking a slice of pear and leaning back into the couch cushions, tucking her shoulder beneath his arm. "The plant did turn out looking like marijuana. Though my mother thought it fit the town. She likes to say things like 'This town is so earthy and real.'"

Britt made it a policy not to knock other people's families even when they were clearly trolls. He preferred neutral questions and gentle statements of the obvious. "You're not close, I take it," he said.

She shrugged. "My sister and brother and I don't talk much, but we're okay. That's just how she communicates. My parents are frequent-sniping types. Every now and again it devolves into a real conflict and then we have to get around that by not discussing it and having cocktails an hour earlier than usual. And then the holidays are over for another year."

She put her feet up on the coffee table, crossing them at the ankles. He was used to women who presented their familial troubles to him like a broken clock, something he felt obligated either to fix or to make disappear. Camille seemed to view her family with clarity but without rancor. It seemed something to aspire to. His conflicts with Harry were so petty, weren't they? Why not view Harry for what he was, a guy who got a little more into things than he should, who was still learning to modulate his approach? He resolved to let more go.

"I hate to leave, but I should go," he said. But he didn't get up.

"Do you want to shower?"

"I don't have any clothes here anyway," he said. "I might as well shower at home and change." He sounded so businesslike; it wasn't what he'd intended, not after a night like that. He should have been up first, arranging some grand gesture. He set his coffee cup down, pulled her over, and drew her on top of him. She had the scent of clean sheets and warm skin. "I don't care about a shower," he told her. "That's not what I'm thinking about right now, just so you know."

Camille grinned. "I do know," she said. "I know exactly what you're thinking about."

CHAPTER 13

THEA THOUGHT MAYBE WINESAP NEEDED another big staff party. No one had thrown one since well before Britt went off to Stray—not that Britt had been so integral to the staff parties, which were more about the kitchen staff than any front-of-the-house people, but she could tell the staff was still recalibrating around his absences. Stray had been open for a couple of months now, and while it found its footing, Britt was at Winesap only one night a week. The front of the house had lost a little of their smoothness, asking too often for repeats on the verbals, forgetting to communicate with the back. And in the kitchen Jason and Suzanne seemed peevish and out of it. Even prep for staff meal seemed a little depressed, as if they were waiting until the last minute for a dinner guest to arrive.

At staff meal one evening in March, the cooks clustered at one end of the table just as they always did, while the servers gathered at the other end, their ties tucked into their shirts, the women hunching carefully over their plates. Apollo sprawled picturesquely in his chair, long legs stretched out into the aisle while he tore pieces from a baguette.

Thea took a seat in the middle, where she could get a good look at both sides of the table. Something was brewing between two of the servers: Annette had ended up sitting next to David, but she never looked at him. David was staring straight across at Alan and talking in a carrying voice about a recent guest: "So this lady asks me what a pork cheek is, like it might really be a tenderloin or something, and I finally had to say, 'It's the face of a pig, ma'am.' Some people. They think they know everything but they don't know a damn thing. It's embarrassing."

Annette's profile never shifted, but her posture stiffened almost imperceptibly. Thea watched David smooth his shirtfront and shake out a napkin. So that was what it was: David was pulling the same thing he did with every female front of the house. Sometimes he gave it a week, sometimes they worked there for six months before the moment arrived, but invariably there came a day when David picked a little battle about how they poured wine or whether they were overheard too obviously bullshitting on a menu item or had folded a napkin poorly during sidework. He waited till someone was promoted to be his equal, then he reminded her that in his eyes she wasn't.

Thea noticed that he never fucked with backwaiters, and he hadn't bothered to give Apollo a hard time, either. He had some women issues, David did. Thea glanced over at Helene, to see if she was aware, and was pleased to see that Helene was observing David with a chilly expression. She wondered whether Britt just hadn't noticed or David was emboldened in his absence.

Leo had served himself with a plate of chili and salad and a few slices of baguette, then settled several seats down from Thea, among the cooks and one stray novice backwaiter, a girl in her early twenties who blushed when Leo said hello and then stared at her plate. New backwaiters were always intimidated by Leo and outright frightened of the cooks.

Leo seemed to take pity on the backwaiter. "Ginny," he said, and she nodded. "Remind me what you do when you're not here."

"I'm in school," she said, clearing her throat. She had brown hair pulled back in a bun and a dark sprinkle of freckles across her pink cheeks. "Zoology."

"Zoology?" Leo echoed, tilting his head. "So what'll you do?"

"Well, last summer I worked in the primate house at the zoo," she said. "I'll probably try to do more of that, I guess."

"The primate house," Leo said. "That probably gave you good training for waiting tables."

She laughed, then took a small bite of her chili and frowned as she chewed. Then she swallowed and ventured, "I ate at your other place last week. It was awesome."

The cooks were watching Leo closely. Thea ate some bread, trying to look at Leo with only as much interest as everyone else displayed.

Leo stabbed a few leaves of salad with his fork. "Oh, it's not my place," he said. "I'm glad it was good."

"Whose is it?" she asked, looking around from face to face. "I thought it was your brothers'?"

"Exactly," Leo said pleasantly, and Thea relaxed. "My brothers', not mine. What did you have?"

"I had the lamb's neck and the salt cod," she said. The cooks eyed her afresh. As if sensing it, she added with a note of defiance, "It was great. It's some serious neck."

"It's a terrific dish," said Leo. "They're getting a lot of press for it."

"They're getting a lot of press, period," said Suzanne.

Leo paused, a bite of chili in midair, then resumed eating. He said nothing.

"You know how it is with a new place," said Thea. She was careful to address the table as a whole. "Always a feeding frenzy for the first couple of months."

"And anyway, it's not all good," said David. "I saw a couple blog reviews that said the service was shaky and the dishes were overworked."

Leo looked up. "Let's not give credence to every moron with a blog and an immersion blender," he said sharply. "The real reviewers haven't covered it yet." David looked away.

Thea cleared her throat and picked up the menu from beside her plate. "Let's start the meeting, shall we?"

LEO WATCHED THEA RUN THROUGH the menu changes and additions, the items to push and the ones running low, while the servers took notes. Now and again she paused to tuck a lock of hair beneath her cap, revealing the pale underside of her wrist. Leo let his glance skate over it and back, in order not to stare at the twisting rope of muscle in her forearm, the violet thump of her veins. He felt he was becoming very Victorian, thrilled by the uncovering of a wrist or an ankle.

It was nearly April, which meant that local produce would be available soon. When that happened the dishes changed more quickly, as small crops of new items appeared and disappeared. There would be two or three verbals each night instead of one or none. Thea would spend longer hours in the kitchen, working her way through new dishes for the evening ahead, and Leo would have to taste them, extending this amiable form of torture by a few more crucial minutes each day.

Thea fell into step beside him as they all headed back to the kitchen, bearing empty dishes. She was carrying a hotel pan with the remnants of the baguettes.

"I have a few potential interns coming through this week," she said. Her eyes met his and slid away again as they neared the kitchen door, which Alan was holding for them. "Do you want to meet them?"

"Sure," said Leo. He nodded at Alan.

"Really?" Her eyebrows rose and her head tilted. "I usually only ask you as a courtesy."

Leo handed her a roll of plastic wrap to cover the bread. Cooks and servers eddied around them, holding pans and knives and cutting boards. "Really," he said, careful to keep his tone neutral. They were skirting awfully close to knowing banter. "I'd prefer to have a look at them."

The temptation to soften this with a smile was nearly overwhelming. This playacting was supposed to be hot, but being cool and professional with Thea made him nervous, as if they were always on the verge of a fight. He feared that even these gentle, silent admonitions of each other set a poisonous precedent for them the rest of the time.

"Of course," Thea said crisply. She tore off the plastic with a brusque movement. "I'll let you know when they're here."

Leo nodded and left the kitchen, ruminating on his dismissal. He was trying to recall whether, back when he was merely her boss, Thea had let him know so precisely the moment he went from necessary to unnecessary. Or had that been his prerogative, as the one in charge? Their interactions now had about three additional layers, and he was never sure which ones he was inventing. He'd have to ask her.

An hour later she stuck her head into his office. Downstairs the service was flowing at a good midweek pace, everyone occupied but not frazzled. "We're eighty-sixing the bison," she said.

"Thanks," he replied. He'd pushed his chair back from his desk automatically, thinking to get up when he saw her, but now sat back down. Anyone might be behind her, getting changed or grabbing stock. So he just smiled at her. No one would hear that. Thea grinned back at him, leaning far enough into the office for the door to block any view of her face from the hall behind her. Then she disappeared.

Leo returned to his work. His chest felt buoyant and full. There was no need for him to be told that they were out of bison. Her trip upstairs was a kiss hidden in plain sight, a little gift.

CHAPTER 14

Harry had never realized that it would feel so much like pretending. The friends-and-family night had felt like a huge, unending dinner party he hadn't adequately prepared for, but he felt that his lapses in it would be forgiven. But the next night, when he unlocked the doors at five p.m., turned on the sign, and went to his place behind the long zinc bar, he'd understood that now his folly was going to be absolutely clear to everyone. That the building and cooking and planning and borrowing had been unnoticed in the public sphere, just a fantasy he'd enjoyed all by himself, as a distraction from the things he should have been doing instead—finishing his doctorate, maybe, or learning to farm, or working an office job, as Britt had for years. At least you always knew what your paycheck would be.

Next to him, Jenelle had jittered about, repositioning dishes and knives, glancing around at the servers clustered by the zinc bar, at Britt standing behind the maître d' stand and reading a menu. Her mise en place was all set up; her pans were gleaming and clean; her knives were so sharp they severed the flesh of an onion or a chicken as softly and cleanly as a wish. She kept touching the flat of a blade as if to reassure herself.

Harry had regretted being out in the dining room right then. It might have been better to be hidden away in the kitchen, where the staff would at least be divided and could not all keep one nervous eye on him as the clock began to move forward and the door stayed closed and untouched. He was about to say something to Jenelle, just because she was closest to him and because he was sure she knew that he was terrified—something to dismiss that impression of him and yet elicit a reflexive reassurance. But then he saw that Jenelle was cutting an onion with such a slow, petrified motion, her eyes trained so fiercely on the moving blade, that he knew she must be realizing what a gamble it had been to leave the Breakfast Bar for this place. She was seeing the unpaid rent and the unemployment he must have set her up for.

Harry took a breath. He was the leader. It was his job to reassure her, not vice versa. "Hey," he said. "You want to try out pig's ear salad at staff meal tomorrow?"

She grinned. "Josh will faint," she said. Her shoulders lowered a quarter inch. "Let's do it."

They never did do the pig's ears—that evening the first wave of customers distracted him from ordering them, and the next night made him forget entirely. Harry soon moved on to exhaustion mingled with incredulity over the fact that this was what his life would look like for the foreseeable future.

It had hit him on a Friday morning at the end of April, as he sat at the bar with a pot of coffee and the previous night's receipts and the week's orders. There had been surprisingly few customer complaints. That might seem good, but it could be bad too, if people just didn't bother complaining because they knew they'd never come back. He poured another cup of coffee and pondered his failing Korean rice stick. He should be thinking of something to replace it, but he seemed unable to imagine any food that wasn't right in front of him.

Britt had had to be at Winesap the night before, so Harry had opened, cooked, and closed. He'd gotten home at two, slept for four hours, and then returned to work. Now he had a dull headache that would have gone away if he'd been able to sleep a few more hours, and his body felt limp and heavy.

Of all the things he'd done, none had been both so tenuous and so complex to undo as this. He didn't *want* to undo it. But it was hitting him that he had met a goal in opening the place and that the comfort of that next concrete goal was lost.

No one else was in yet. He turned on his laptop and visited some food blogs and industry sites, on the off chance he'd be inspired, but he got distracted almost instantly, so in another tab he opened a travel magazine. Singapore had a lot to offer. Plenty of street food, endless inspiration. Apparently the beaches in Croatia were stunning. He checked to see if flying out of Philadelphia would get him anywhere close.

The day before, Harry had discovered a few decent hotels in the Zamalek neighborhood of Cairo. Recently he had also, entirely by accident, memorized a list of autumn food festivals in Italy. He had his eye on the one celebrating the hazelnut. And even though he could not actually go—would not even think of going—imagining these escapes was so freeing that he couldn't stop, either.

Harry's great fear was that after everything, he might not be cut out for this. He had worried over the location, the staff, the reviews, the financing, the local economy. It had never occurred to him that he might find the relentlessness of the restaurant so overwhelming, as if it were a hungry baby that never got past the demanding newborn phase, or that owning the place would be different from being its most dedicated employee.

If they could make it to a year, their chances were good. Leo had been saying it since Harry was still in high school, and he was right. Most restaurants had a couple of months to find their way, but within weeks it was clear whose menu was generic or bizarre or poorly conceived, who couldn't keep a staff, who couldn't cook consistently, who had assumed that some magical presence would prevent them from doing this if they were unqualified. In just the time Harry had been working on Stray, he'd seen three new places open and close: a pan-Asian noodle house, an upscale diner, and a pasta place. The Texas barbecue joint was next. Everyone knew it. It had been six months and they couldn't get a brisket right—really, they had no business staying open.

Around ten a.m., Harry perceived a brown jacket two feet away and jumped, his body flooding with electricity. Hector had materialized at the end of the bar. "Jesus, Hector! Don't do that," he cried. "Whistle or something."

"Sorry," said Hector. He poured himself a cup of coffee and settled his baseball cap over his cropped black hair. Now he would stand, saying nothing and drinking his coffee, for five minutes. He never sat down. Then he would square his shoulders and disappear into the kitchen, commencing the sounds of whirring blenders and the occasional gasps from a nitrogen tank. Later that afternoon he would reappear and place a dessert before Harry and Britt, if Britt was here. Yesterday it had been a single chocolate orb that shattered with the tap of a knife, revealing shards of crystallized whiteness. "Chocolate-menthol geode," Hector had said, and watched them piercingly as they ate, the chocolate melting on their tongues while the menthol rose in vapors straight toward the tops of their skulls.

Jenelle appeared soon after Hector had disappeared into the kitchen, bringing with her a faint whiff of cigarette smoke, and began cleaning her station. Periodically she took a bite from a turkey sandwich she'd brought with her. Harry couldn't stand to look at it, the cold slick meat, the pockets of gristle and mayonnaise.

He joined Jenelle behind the bar and started in on his own station, both to avoid looking at the turkey and to prevent her from cleaning his station too. He didn't want her thinking she got treated like a lackey.

"Any word?" Jenelle asked.

"Not yet," said Harry. "It'll happen pretty soon. I'm surprised they haven't done it yet, but at least they're not rushing in here to review us before we have time to settle in."

"Maybe they've already been coming for a while and just haven't written about it yet," said Jenelle.

Harry froze. "Maybe," he said. He shook it off. "Probably. I don't know. I doubt a local paper can afford more than a couple of visits anyway."

Jenelle took a bite of her sandwich. "You want me to bring you one?" she said, chewing.

"No, thanks," Harry said. "I'm not hungry."

"I can always make another stop," she said. "I could bring you a burger."

"Nah," he said.

"The point," Jenelle went on, scrubbing at the flat top, "is that you don't really eat, ever. You never even join us for staff dinner. And you're pretty skinny."

"There's always too much to do. And I had a bagel today," Harry said. "With peanut butter." He was making this up; he had no idea what he'd eaten, and it was unlikely it had been anything more than coffee. It was true that he wasn't hungry lately, and that when he finally got hungry he was too busy to eat. But he assumed that would pass. "I'll eat when our review's in."

"Okay," Jenelle said dubiously. "Except what if it's not good?"

Harry looked at her. "Do you think it won't be?"

"I think we rock. But I'm not a reviewer."

Harry had been hoping that he was the only one worrying about this; it made him more anxious than ever to hear that Jenelle thought there was something to worry about too. "You know what? Even if it's not great, we learn from it," Harry said. "That's my motto. We can't see everything objectively." He was trying for a boss's Zen-like calm, but he could hear that he was speaking a little quickly. Nevertheless, his voice only got faster the more he tried to slow it down. "How *could* we be objective? We come in here and we just swim for our lives. I don't see anything objectively anymore. I'm looking forward to the review. There's no way we do everything perfectly. There's probably a hundred things I should see but I just can't, because I'm too close to it. A thousand. I look for it all, but I can't tell anymore. We may as well find out what we need to do. May as well fix it. May as well get the truth."

"Is there that much we need to work on?" Jenelle said.

"I don't know!" he said. He smacked the flat top with his palm. "That's the fucking point!"

From behind them they heard, *"Harry."* Britt was at the host's stand, a pile of menus in one hand and an expression on his face like the one he'd have if he'd found his brother watching porn in the dining room. A menu slipped out of his grip and drifted toward the floor without his noticing.

Harry looked over at Jenelle, who looked stricken. He shook out his stinging hand and said, "I'm sorry," to Jenelle. "I'm just saying I'll feel better when I get the feedback."

"Can we talk?" Britt said.

"Absolutely," Harry replied. He went back to scrubbing. "As soon as I'm done here, okay?"

"I'd prefer now," Britt said, but Harry knew his brother would tell him to calm down and not to swear at the staff, and he knew Britt was right, and he didn't want to take even more time to go over Britt's inevitable rightness. There was too much to do. There always was.

"Soon as I'm done," he promised, trying to sound confident, and he counted on Britt to be too worried about demonstrating cohesion in front of Jenelle to push it, and he was right. Britt left the room, giving him a dark look as he did.

Jenelle went back to work, scouring so hard her cheeks trembled. Every few minutes she cast a searching glance at him, which Harry ignored.

They were getting the pattern of the days: a weekday might be thirty guests, but when it rained it might be five. One wonderful Saturday had been close to seventy. They needed more—he needed at least thirty on weeknights and seventy-five on weekends—but they weren't ready to handle that yet. The servers were still getting comfortable with their systems; the cooks were still getting their rhythms down. Some nights they all hit it, just for a while. He could feel the energy humming through the place when it happened. All the ragged edges and darting eyes disappeared.

But other nights were just a farce. Earlier that week a server had dropped a full tray in the dining room, Harry had accidentally sent out a nearly raw duck breast, and Jenelle had forgotten the aromatics in the fried seafood, so it just looked like a platter at Long John Silver's. A server hadn't shown up and so food had sat too long, melting or cooling or separating, until Britt had to comp a small fortune in dishes and drinks. Even then the energy in the room remained grim. It had been the kind of night you gave up on salvaging and just hoped would end.

At least the numbers had begun to creep up, and though Harry had planned for this trickling start, he still visualized their funds as a deep and mostly empty bowl. At all times, sometimes peripherally and sometimes in the foremost space in his mind, he was aware of the bowl's inexorable depletion and its minuscule replenishment.

How had he never before fully grasped that the only way a restaurant got money was through selling food? You knew, but you didn't *know*, and seen in this light—in the light of his loans and paychecks and purveyors—he thought the menu was ludicrously, criminally underpriced.

Once he was cooking, his fatigue disappeared. It would drop back over him the moment the pace slowed, however, just as Britt would reappear so they could discuss Harry's latest screwup. But until then Harry could cook, and he could forget his constant hunger and the preoccupation that led him to forget to eat in the first place. He forgot the shifty-looking kids who depressed him by being across the street each afternoon, drinking generic soda and tugging at their piercings. He even came close to forgetting his loan payments. He just cooked. He eyed the golden crust of Jenelle's fried shellfish, he brushed the duck breast with mustard, he scattered herbs and olives.

The music was loud tonight, some weird jaunty mix of fiddle and drums, but the waitstaff was nodding along to it, and that pallid, pierced, and languid crew could be trusted in matters of taste, so Harry decided to like it too. He was just deciding that the fiddle worked for him in a June Carter kind of way when Britt appeared behind the line, where he never ventured, looking grim. "Well, first crisis," he said.

A few minutes earlier, Britt said, Juan, the dishwasher, had poked his head out the kitchen door and caught Britt's eye, his white apron appearing and disappearing in an instant. The kitchen staff were not to be on the floor during service, but there was Juan's face, his dark eyes round with alarm, for just a flash.

Britt had excused himself from a conversation at the door and headed back to the kitchen. He walked briskly; he did not run—he never allowed anyone to run on the floor.

He knew that panicked look, and he was hoping for a minor catastrophe—some broken dishes, a shortage of fish.

But in the kitchen he found Juan frantically placing buckets beneath two streams of hot water pouring from a pipe beneath the dishwasher. A busser was trying to move the racks of glassware from the dish sink to a far table, away from the wet floor, and another was throwing towels on the ground in a futile attempt to absorb the steaming puddles. Two feet away, Hector was serenely blowtorching a meringue.

Britt froze. This was not Winesap. These were not his expert cooks and longtime dish guys who knew what to do, but a bunch of newbies in a new place, including him, plus Hector ignoring the water lapping at his feet.

Britt realized that Juan was looking at him and snapped back to attention. "Turn the thing off," he said of the dishwasher. "And get the mop and bucket," he told the busser. "Start moving the water toward the drain. Juan, keep dumping the buckets so they don't overflow. You'll have to wash by hand for a bit. I'll be right back."

"I have to be on the floor," said the busser.

"Oh no you don't," Britt told him. He took out his phone and talked as he looked through his contacts and dialed the dishwasher service. "This is triage. They can bus their own tables."

He peered out at the dining room and counted tables. They were three-quarters full. If he'd had clean dishes, he would have been delighted. Without the bussers the dining room would get cluttered, fast. He needed a repairman and he needed the staff to be two people at once.

The crazy thing was that he was tempted not to say anything to his brother. Harry was working in a tight, focused rhythm on the line, and when Harry was in a zone it was much easier not to interrupt him, because you never quite knew how he would respond. He might get his rhythm back quickly or he might get so upset he'd be off his game for the rest of the night. It was exhausting managing Harry.

Finally Britt went behind the bar, calling "Behind the line" as he did so that he wouldn't get stabbed or burned by two cooks who were tightly attuned to each other's placement and assumed no one else was in their space. This was another problem with the public cooking setup. He couldn't yank his chef for a nice private crisis; he had to whisper it to him instead while the bar patrons watched over the rims of their wineglasses.

"Dishwasher's broken," he murmured.

"*Fuck,*" Harry said. He stopped all his motion, staring blankly at his pans and spoons and spatulas.

"Keep cooking," Britt said. Harry kneaded his forehead for a second, but then seemed to remember himself and started his work again.

"How broken? Fucked or fixable?"

"I don't know yet. We'll know when the guy gets here." Britt was aware that he was making his tone reassuring and calm, as if he were talking to a child. "He'll be here any minute."

Harry opened a drawer beneath the counter, pulled out two duck breasts, and slapped them on a plate to warm up. "And we do what in the meantime?"

"We clean by hand," Britt said, glancing sideways at Jenelle. Harry was moving more sloppily now. He set a pan down so roughly it made the other two jump. "This stuff happens," Britt said. He reached up to pat Harry's shoulder, unsure what else to do, but Harry batted his hand away. "Look, let's talk in the kitchen."

"Can't now," Harry said, not looking at him. "Can't relax, can't come talk in the kitchen. But tell me when he gets here. I want to see these guys at work."

Britt took a deep breath—he wasn't going to push Harry further in front of the staff or the guests. A sidelong glance toward the other side of the bar confirmed that a few were watching intently. He said, hoping no one else could hear him, "All we can do is move forward, Harry. Take a breath and keep going." But Harry didn't reply.

When a crisis hit, the whole world dwindled to a pinpoint: the next step and the one after that. Each task popped up before him and he knocked it back down. For the next hour Juan did dishes by hand, the busser wiped them dry, and Britt and the servers whisked them back out to the line. They swapped out buckets and managed to keep the floor from flooding again. Britt zigzagged between the floor and the kitchen, keeping the dining room clear and the dishes moving. The floorboards vibrated with the pounding feet of the servers. He had no time to see how Harry was doing. There was no end of the night or even end of the hour to consider—only this, until the repair guy finally arrived and Britt met him back in the kitchen.

He had to force himself to return to normal speed. At least Britt had dealt with this repair guy before. Not good, not bad, but it was always useful to have a familiar face. Britt dispatched the busser to the front to sweep the dining room again and then watched the repairman slither down beneath the dishwasher and poke around.

Harry came striding through the door, a towel in his hands. He chucked it into a kitchen linen bag and stood, arms crossed, beside Britt.

"What's going on?"

"I don't know yet," Britt said. The repair guy's shoes had worn tread and a wad of gum on one sole.

"I thought you knew this company," Harry said.

"I do," Britt said. "That's why they were here so fast. I've known them for years."

"We haven't had this thing very long," Harry said.

"I need a part," the repair guy called. He slid out from beneath the dishwasher and hauled himself to his feet. Britt extended a hand to help. "Let me run out to the truck." He looked at Harry. "You the chef?"

Harry held out a hand. "Co-owner," he said.

"Okay then," the guy said. "Shouldn't take long. Give me a second."

When the dishwasher guy had gone, Britt turned his back to Juan, Hector, and the busser and murmured to Harry, "Don't start antagonizing this guy. I've worked with him before—he's fine. It's not a conspiracy."

"I know that," Harry said. He glanced toward the front of the house, then eyed the back door again.

"I'll be right back," Britt said.

The dining room had filled further. Anna was covering the host stand, and he could see that three new tables had been seated already. Kelsey was removing a full plate of Korean rice sticks from a frowning couple; Heather had one plate too many stacked on her forearm and had to go utterly still when one began, sickeningly, to wobble. He did a fast circuit through the room, ensured that the new tables were covered, removed a tray of dishes, told Carrie to clear, and took three drink orders and dropped them with Travis. Jenelle shot him a pleading look. "I'll get him back here," Britt promised.

In the kitchen, Harry was towering over the repairman while Juan scrubbed at a plate and darted the occasional glance at the two men.

It was a shock to see Harry look so physically intimidating. He was well over six feet, and he'd gotten ropier since the restaurant had opened, which gave him a look not of skinniness but of intensity, even hunger. He looked, frankly, rather dangerous, as if he had been hunting his own food. The dishwasher guy had his hands on his hips and was shaking his head.

"—doesn't matter," Harry was saying. "Get the part. You should have it anyway. It should be in your truck. This thing has to be working right now, even if that means you call a coworker and sit there holding the fucking pipes together with one hand while you wait."

Britt laid a hand on Harry's shoulder, which felt like wood beneath his shirt. "What's going on?"

"Your chef needs his dishwasher—I get that," said the repairman. "I'm here to do my job, man, but I can't get the new valve while I sit here and talk to you, so you may as well back off."

Harry took a step closer to the repairman.

"Stop it," Britt said. His hand latched on to Harry's arm without his intending it to. Harry didn't seem to feel it. He reached out and touched the repair guy in the center of his chest. His forefinger landed with a delicacy that was somehow more threatening than a shove, as if Harry were a surgeon or a butcher, sussing out the tender space between the ribs.

"Don't," Harry said. "Don't talk to me like this is just how it has to be. I am here to do a job." His voice had gone soft and venomous. Britt saw Hector set down his tools and take a cautious step toward them. Juan had stopped scrubbing and was just holding a plate beneath the faucet while he watched. Britt was still uselessly clasping his brother's bicep, uncertain whether it was worse to intervene or not, because suddenly he had no idea what Harry would do.

"You are making that job difficult," Harry said. "You're making it difficult for my staff, and my staff is already working as hard as they can. So don't tell me why you can't do your job to fix this brand-new dishwasher." His finger tapped the man's chest with each of his next words. "Do. A. Better. Fucking. Job."

The repairman blinked. Everyone was silent. Out in the dining room the sounds of dishes and voices and music clamored, and as a server entered the kitchen with a tray of empty plates, the spell was broken. Harry seemed to notice his own fingertip on the repairman's coverall and withdrew it. He took a step back, looking slightly disoriented.

"I have to be back on the line," he said. It was not clear whom he was addressing. "Just—" He shook his head. "Just keep me posted."

The server trailed Harry back out the kitchen door. Hector returned to his workstation, Juan began washing the dish, and the repairman and Britt were left alone, looking at one another. The repairman brought out his phone. When he finished his call he said to Britt, "He'll be right here."

"Thank you," Britt said. He wiped his face.

"What happened to your other place?" The repairman looked around the cramped kitchen appraisingly, the buckets beneath the dishwasher, the shelves packed with supplies. Britt could feel him wondering if this place would be open long enough for any of it to be used.

"I still have it," Britt said. The guy nodded, and Britt could see that he was thinking Britt was a fool to be here but at least he'd kept his backup business.

"You're a stand-up guy," he said. "But if your chef ever touches me again, you're gonna have a problem on your hands."

THEY WERE ALL THERE UNTIL PAST one o'clock. The last tables departed by eleven thirty, but by then the backlog of dishes was formidable. Harry and Jenelle broke down the line and joined Britt, Juan, and Hector in the back to work their way through the racks. By then they had turned on music, and everyone's head nodded to the beat as they stacked and polished. The servers finished their sidework and joined them, polishing glassware and silverware.

At midnight Britt disappeared to the front; he returned a minute later with a pitcher of beer and a stack of the thick plastic cups they used on the line and in the kitchen. Harry took a long pull from his but then swayed slightly before righting himself. Britt watched him, then said, "How do you feel?"

"I feel fine," Harry said.

"We should talk tomorrow morning," Britt said. "Touch base on a few things." He would not air any grievances now, in front of staff, and probably not even tonight. They were all tired—Britt's back was sore, his head was pounding, and he just kept thinking of cool sheets and a blowing fan. But Harry looked ill. He had missed the staff meal again, appearing only at the very end to go over a menu change.

"Fine," Harry said. He slid a rack of steaming plates to one end of the dish station and grabbed the next. Britt took the rack out to the line and began to stack the plates beneath the counter. A moment later Harry came out with another rack. He set it down next to Britt's and began stacking the plates so carelessly that Britt thought they would chip.

"What was that?" Britt finally asked.

Harry sighed a grand, Shelleyesque sigh. "What was what?"

"You threatened a vendor. You freaked out the staff. Hector thought he was going to have to pull you off him."

"I didn't threaten," Harry said. "I made it clear we wouldn't tolerate this stuff, even if we are the new guys. You could see he was just trying to get away with slacking off, right?"

"Of course I did," Britt said. "But I would have fixed it if you'd let me handle it like a grown-up. I know this guy. I used to get along with him."

"Maybe," Harry said. "But he should know me too." His profile was stony.

This wasn't amusing in a man in his thirties. Britt didn't find it admirable, or fierce, or whatever way his brother was selling this to himself. What the hell had happened to him? He needed a haircut, he needed to eat, and his beard was scrubby and untrimmed, creeping up his gaunt cheeks. Britt was exhausted too, but they worked in public; he didn't go around looking like some short-order cook with a cigarette wedged where an incisor should have been.

The dining room was empty and dark, the street outside deserted. Soon one of their employees would probably be mugged and would sue them. His brother was either unhinged or—maybe worse—deliberately behaving as if he were. All of Britt's pride in this stylish room, in its great-looking servers and its eclectic menu, felt completely misplaced. A dishwasher repairman had taken one look around this place and seen its shabby, duct-taped heart.

Britt sat down on a barstool. "Is this really how you do things?" he said. "We had a problem tonight that should have been totally run-of-the-mill. You can't go around this town alienating people we work with. It never occurred to me that I had to say that."

"Would it have killed you to back me up on this?" Harry said. Britt could see the wetness of Harry's eyes in the faint light from the kitchen. His brother smelled of beer, cooking grease, and something sharp and adrenaline-heavy, like ozone. "You can take a buy-out whenever you feel like it and go back to serving foie gras and trolling the dining room for women. I have no other place. This is all on me."

"Why the hell am I here if that's how you see it? Why was it so crucial to have me on board that you could never just shut the fuck up about it?"

"Oh, please." Harry turned away and began chucking pans into a bus tub, shaking his head in disgust.

"All summer long!" Britt said. He was all pulse; his body was surging with an unbearable electricity. He jumped off the stool and began stalking in circles as he ranted. "'Oh, wouldn't it be perfect if we worked together, don't we all need to be in this together?' No matter what we said, you never listened."

"So why'd you buy in, for chrissake?" Harry said. "To placate me?"

"I thought you knew what you were doing. I *thought* I'd underestimated you. I was under the misapprehension that you wanted my help, probably because you badgered me for months—"

Harry hollered at the ceiling, "I wanted *Leo's* help!"

Britt stopped moving. Harry fixed his gaze on the wall just beyond his brother's head, shaking his own head.

"You little shit," Britt said. He breathed deeply, waiting fruitlessly for his heart to stop knocking in his chest, and then he got up and walked out.

CAMILLE WAS WAITING AT HIS HOUSE when Britt arrived. It was too hard to go from that aggression to the calmest sight on earth, which was Camille's sleeping profile.

She stirred when he got into bed. "You're late tonight," she said. She nestled against his rib cage.

"I'm sorry. It wasn't a good night," Britt said. "The dishwasher broke and Harry got all Cro-Magnon on the repair guy. I never know when he'll act like a normal person and when he'll Travis Bickle on someone."

Camille blinked, frowning. "Weren't you going to talk with him about this?"

"When did we talk about me talking to him?" Britt directed this toward the ceiling, but Camille detached herself from beneath his arm and leaned over him, making him look her in the eye. He lay there like a pinned insect.

"When he wouldn't let me come to the friends-and-family," she said. "I asked you to calm him down. Or maybe I just asked you to go easy on him."

She sat up and crossed her legs beneath the sheets, but Britt remained prone, hoping she would take the hint and lie back down. When she didn't, he finally sat up too and said, "You try talking to him and see how well it goes. It's like there's a language barrier or something. He makes it all about me backing him up or not."

"Well, are you?" Camille asked. "Backing him up, I mean?"

"Of course not!" Britt said. "How am I supposed to back up behavior like that?"

"I don't know," she said. "I just know he admires you and he may need a little extra from you right now."

"Maybe," Britt said. How could he possibly tell her that Harry had settled for him? It was too humiliating to admit. Camille leveled her exacting vision on everything from her earrings to the dish of apples on her coffee table to the lighting of a restaurant, and that had made it so satisfying to have her admiration. He felt he'd been selected for a prize.

Now Britt watched her face, that unknowable oval, and wondered if he'd been preening all along while she held her opinions in check. He felt a flash of empathy for Harry, asking Camille to wait till Stray was perfect. At the time Britt had thought it ludicrous.

Maybe Harry had told Camille months ago that he'd ended up with the lesser partner.

Camille looked at the clock. She seemed to make a decision, and in a lighter tone brought up a trade show she was attending the following week, but Britt was in no mood to be placated now.

"Do I not get to be pissed at Harry in front of you?" he said. "Am I talking to my girlfriend or my brother's friend? Because I just want to know for the future."

"I knew you couldn't get over it," she said. Britt went cold. She sat back against the headboard and crossed her arms.

"You said there was never anything to worry about."

"It hardly seemed worth getting into it. But now you're acting like I'm so unfair to you just because I don't instantly agree that you're right. I get it—Harry's being annoying. He's your brother. Don't you care why he's acting like this?"

"I don't think there's any big reason. He's stressed and taking it out on everyone else." This wasn't entirely what Britt believed—in truth he had never seen Harry behave quite so badly as in these last few weeks, but he had no intention of admitting this to Camille, not now. "All I want is to be able to talk about my business and my brother without you thinking you have to automatically play devil's advocate every time he comes up."

Camille said, "I hate to tell you this, but I actually disagree with you." She bent over the bed and fumbled around the floor, then sat up and began tugging on a pair of jeans. "And for the record, you've been talking about nothing *but* your business and your brother."

It occurred to him that she really would leave, and this frightened him, both because she wanted to be away from him more than with him and because it meant he'd never get his side of things across. Unsure which point to address first, Britt chose the easiest one. "Hey, come on. Camille. Look, I'm sorry I forgot to ask how you are," he said. "I was just looking forward to venting a little."

"*This* is not how you're supposed to be waking me up," she said, but she stopped moving and stood beside the bed, her white camisole bunched over her jeans. "Not with a diatribe, and without at least a perfunctory 'How's your day?' I *had* a day. I did things besides wait here like the interchangeable woman to see how yours went." Her voice had lost a tiny bit of its edge.

Britt leaned across the bed and grabbed her wrist. "I'm sorry." He felt drained of his anger and shocked at hers; till now they'd barely disagreed over what to have for lunch. "Stay."

"I don't want to commiserate with you about Harry," she said softly. "I'm still his friend."

"Okay," Britt said, though it wasn't. But he saw the chance to get their equilibrium back and he needed it. He and Camille were still too new to be addressing any deep wounds; there shouldn't even be any. His confidence was rattled, and right now he just wanted to make the whole night go away.

She watched him for a second, then pulled off her jeans, folded them neatly, and turned away to lay them on the chair. When she got back into bed, she seemed uncertain how close to come, and he pulled her to him, holding her narrow, fine-boned face between his palms.

He could not stop himself from insisting, "You know I'm not really worried about you and Harry, right?"

"I guess not," she said, and, pathetically, he decided to pretend that she had reassured him. "Okay," he said, and kissed her, hoping to dispel whatever had just sprung up between them.

CHAPTER 15

WHEN BRITT ARRIVED AT THE RESTAURANT the next morning, Harry was at the range, shaking a pan over a high flame. The two looked at each other for a beat, and then Harry said, "Have a seat. I'm trying something here." His tone was neutral but certainly not apologetic. Britt sat down at the bar, readying himself.

He had been too discombobulated to sleep soundly, and Camille had been restless all night before rising at six. At least she had kissed him before she'd gone, and it seemed right. Nevertheless, now he felt surly and uncommunicative, disinclined to offer a word.

Harry added several spoonfuls of an orange-red sauce to the pan and then a handful of scallion and tossed it all with a few deft movements before transferring it to a plate. He sprinkled sesame seeds over the top and set the plate before Britt, then handed him a fork and kept one for himself.

"This is kind of the traditional way of doing the rice sticks," Harry said, cutting a soft white square. "I woke up feeling hungover even though I didn't drink enough to be. Anyway, I was craving it. I figured I'd at least eat the real thing for once, or as close as I can make it, before we yank it."

Britt tried a steaming bite. The dish looked as if it would be fiery, but the chile sauce was surprisingly rounded and unvinegary. "They don't sell," he said.

Harry shrugged. "Off it goes." He took another bite and

chewed, gazing out the front window. "I'm sorry," he said. He spoke so conversationally that for a moment Britt misunderstood him. He thought Harry was apologizing for the failure of the dish.

"For what?" Britt asked, and he could see that Harry understood that he meant not *You did nothing wrong* but *For which offense?*

"I went overboard on the dishwasher guy," Harry said. "And with Jenelle. And I didn't mean it about Leo."

"Yes, you did," Britt said. "You did. Let's not sit here and bullshit each other."

"I wanted Leo in on this," Harry admitted. "I wanted all three of us in on it. And to be honest, I still don't know what the fuck Leo wanted that he didn't see here."

Britt shrugged.

"Leo has the most experience of any of us. He was in the business before you joined up. That's what I meant."

"I gave you a chance to tell me if you didn't want to partner up," Britt said. That was the worst part—how stupid he felt, having spent months sharing all his hard-won wisdom and guiding his little brother, now knowing what Harry must have thought all along.

"I wasn't sure how it'd work at first, with just the two of us," Harry said. "But it was working really well."

"You think so?" Britt said. Harry looked startled. "I never know what you're going to do when things go wrong," Britt continued. "Something always will—crises happen all the time. You have to thrive on that, not lose it."

Harry said, "I know. Last night was a bad night."

Britt didn't know what to say. Harry seemed to feel that a bad night still justified him.

"I kind of miss the school year," Harry said. "You work your way through the first chunk of fall, then it's midterms, then the next chunk, then it's finals. Time goes a lot faster."

Britt said, "It's been a long time since school, Harry."

Harry colored slightly but didn't look at him. "Well, sure," he said. "It's just something I was thinking about today."

Neither of them spoke until the rice stick was gone.

"You hear anything about a review yet?" Harry said.

"They'll let us know," Britt said. "Usually they need to take a photo. Harry, this person isn't going to be our new mentor—it's just going to be some reporter moonlighting from the sports desk or something, you know? It's not the *New York Times*."

"So it doesn't matter?" Harry said. "Is that what you're saying?"

"You're just expecting too much from it. They'll describe the food and say some stuff we agree with and some that feels completely random and deranged. That's how reviews always feel."

"I'm just trying to be positive about it," Harry said.

Britt sighed. "I know you are," he said. They seemed to have exhausted their capacity for overt conflict without actually resolving anything. The moment had slipped past them.

Britt gazed around the restaurant space. He could hear Harry drinking water, which irritated him more than it should have. He believed the two of them could work together that night without any hostilities spilling over, but the mutedness and evasiveness of Harry's apology left Britt feeling as if Harry hadn't really heard half the conversation. His manner now seemed to leave no room for Britt still to be angry—and he was. Because he'd let Harry cajole him into a few moments of regular conversation, it would appear churlish to return to the problem. Apparently Harry got to decide not only when to set a fire but when it pleased him to extinguish it.

Their reflections in the grand mahogany mirror looked hazy and distant, Britt's face a blur set with two smeared eyes and a grim mouth. He watched the reflection of the back of Harry's head, his bony shoulders and his wristbones like pebbles, as the image began to gather dishes. Britt had always imagined Harry's years away from home as carefree and picaresque, but maybe they'd been darker and more violent than that. Perhaps that was how his brother had become this other man, whom Britt felt he might not really know and might not have chosen.

"I think I was wrong about that mirror," Britt said. "It brings the whole room down."

"No, I like it," Harry said. "For a while I didn't, but I do now."

CHAPTER 16

L EO'S HOME KITCHEN WAS A DISGRACE. He'd been meaning to renovate it for years to get rid of its ancient gas range
and crappy oak cabinets, the white paint left over from Frances's
first paint job, which was now a yellowed ivory. Who had time to
renovate a kitchen he never cooked in? The kitchen that mattered
was at Winesap.

Thea looked all wrong in here, which was what bothered him.
Her white limbs only made the older paint and appliances seem
duller by comparison—the surroundings failed to elevate her. A
chef like Thea should be cooking in a renovated kitchen.

But at least it was private. Her car was parked in his garage
while his was in the driveway, and he had pulled the shades down.
This wasn't a big city; who knew who might be driving past his
house and see her at his stove, hair pulled back in a ponytail, dressed
unmistakably casually and intimately in a T-shirt of Leo's and a pair
of cut-off leggings?

It was just after ten. Was it embarrassing that they'd left the
restaurant at nine—it had been a quiet night—and had already had
time to dash home to his bedroom *and* to start dinner? Leo tried
to draw things out, but they never managed this until they'd rushed
each other the first time and then settled in to luxuriate for the second. And they were always so hungry, depleted either from sex or
from work or from both, a blend of exhaustion that was strangely

satisfying, because it left them wallowing in pure sensation until they were tired and sated, their clothes trailing through the house.

Thea barely tired over a ten-hour shift, thanks to running and swimming. The disparity in stamina between them had become a little embarrassing as he had started to realize that her portion sizes were half his, that in her free time she really liked great bowls of fresh vegetables and brown rice. Leo had the distinct sense that the first thing he'd cooked for her, the eggs and chorizo, had branded him. He'd only been pleasantly buzzed that night, still grateful for the dinner she'd sent up earlier and trying to impress her by doing something like rendering fat from dried chorizo instead of copping out with a drizzle of olive oil. But now he was convinced that part of the reason Thea had avoided introducing him to her daughter for several months was not just sensible maternal caution, and not just that she wasn't sure the relationship would last, but that she thought he might drop dead at any moment.

Leo had no idea what one did with a three-year-old, and he wasn't entirely certain why he had been lobbying to spend time with this one, whom he had met only once, in passing, at a staff party. There was always a slight air of gamesmanship in his time with Thea, a pattern set by their working relationship and still in place in their romantic one. Maybe his desire to meet this child came about only because Thea had hesitated, and maybe she'd hesitated at least partially out of the habit of not immediately accommodating him. Or perhaps she wasn't wild about drawing a three-year-old into an illicit relationship. You couldn't count on a child not to spill secrets.

Another thought occurred to Leo: maybe it simply felt sleazy to her, the rush to sex, secret lunches, separate cars.

Leo watched Thea toss the spaghetti in tomato, olive oil, and scallions. How was it that she was so calm about it all? She was too sensible and professional to be doing what they were doing, but here she was. Leo didn't know whether to be ecstatic that he'd managed to tempt her to cross a boundary or worried that this meant she was not as levelheaded as he'd always believed her to be. Being at work with Thea but unable to touch her left him in a constant state of anticipation, suspended between the workaday present and the vivid, saturated past and future. It was a pleasurable ache but an exhausting one. He was the only one who knew her this way, he often reflected. He'd once thought of her gaze, when it landed on him, as chilly and searching, but now he found her thrillingly direct.

He hadn't told Britt. He hadn't told anyone, and he couldn't imagine a circumstance in which he would be able to. But he was a terrible liar. If anyone asked him straight-out if he had been dating his own executive chef, he'd probably get out a calendar and chart it for them. No one did ask, however, and he tried to believe that this was because no one suspected. This contradicted everything he'd ever seen in the restaurant business, where knowledge was shared osmotically, flashing from busser to cook to waiter to owner like a nerve impulse. He comforted himself by remembering that he and Thea were all business everywhere but here. Yes, people might have seen them leave Mack's together, but they were colleagues. And yes, Britt had looked suspicious at Stray's friends-and-family, but he'd said nothing to Leo since. Could anyone really know anything just from seeing two people go through a doorway one after the other?

They could, of course. He could. He'd seen it a thousand times, in owners and managers who were foolish enough to do what he was doing.

Leo kept watching her bare feet against the floor, the flex of tendons and the spread of her heels as she shifted her weight.

She glanced over her shoulder at him. "How is it?" she said.

Leo looked at the laptop, forgotten before him on the table. "It's good," he said. "It's really good."

The first real review of Stray in the *Star* was a two-pager by a critic who had written up Winesap a number of times, a woman with whom Britt had cultivated a relationship for years—one in which he managed to suggest simultaneously that he was intimidated by his respect for her yet also on the verge of devouring her at any given time. It was the sort of thing Britt could do.

Britt had run through the restaurant that afternoon, on his way to Stray, brandishing an advance review he refused to share. "I can't," he'd said. "Harry'll freak out if he doesn't see it first."

Britt still appeared for two shifts a week at Winesap, and soon he would need to renegotiate a long-term schedule. Two and a half months into its life, Stray was settling in, and Leo knew from experience that by now each night should not be a fresh terror. Helene was getting tired of her extra shifts each week, while Alan had discovered that he preferred the bar to the maître d' stand after all. He did seem to enjoy the aura of power conferred upon the host, however, and now and then Leo caught him hemming and hawing, for the pleasure of it, over an easily granted request. He'd also turned out to be an enthusiastic updater of blue cards, which were now filled with his notes on conversational preferences, suspected marital issues, and probable food aversions.

The disturbing part was that Alan had turned out to be quite perceptive. So far he had correctly predicted two divorces (the spouses later appeared with new people) and had taken to casting an appraising eye in Leo and Thea's direction. They gave him nothing; under scrutiny, Thea smoothed her expression as blank as a mannequin's. They never touched; they did not even pause in the office when they thought they might be alone. But now that he was downstairs and in the kitchen so much more often as they worked on a new menu, this distance was torturous. Leo could swear he knew where she was at any given moment—every day at work he could feel her move through the restaurant's space. He recognized her profile and the set of her shoulders from across a room, from another room altogether.

"So read it to me," Thea said. She began portioning out the pasta in two bowls. A baguette sat on a platter before him. Thea sat down and tore a large chunk from it. "No, wait, let's eat in the living room." They carried their bowls and the computer to the couch, where Thea liked to drape her legs across his. This was another surprise to him—she didn't like to go from bed to the formality of the table. She said they had all day to sit across from one another at a table. Now they set the laptop on the coffee table and read the review as they ate.

When he'd first read it, he couldn't help but feel a faint satisfaction at the reviewer's characterization of the location as "equal parts bold and foolhardy," but when he spoke it aloud he felt offended on his brothers' behalf—as if they weren't wise enough to make a considered choice! He shook his head and continued. The reviewer extravagantly praised the interior and noted approvingly Britt's less polished demeanor in this new setting, all before she got around to discussing the food.

"It's kind of like those reviews where they tell you all about their Christmas vacation for two paragraphs first," Leo said with a snort.

"She's got a bit of a thing for Britt," Thea said.

"Okay, finally, the food. 'The signature lamb's neck with gremolata and cavatelli is a gauntlet thrown before the diner. Will you see past the restaurant's refusal to prettify the cut in order to enjoy its tender richness? Only the cavatelli feel as if they ought to be on another dish—one could imagine a lamb ragù with these little mouthfuls, but here they feel overly rich.'" Leo frowned. "I thought the cavatelli were excellent," he said. "Didn't you? The gremolata keeps it all from feeling over the top."

He shook his head and continued: the socca and baccalà got high marks, as did the octopus with ginger, the duck, and all of the desserts, though the reviewer also felt that many of them seemed to be coming from a different restaurant. Thea said nothing as he read a listing of Hector's most recent triumphs: a chocolate menthol geode, a hot fried dumpling with a startling cool center, the malt cup of cacao custard, and a flight of shiso leaf, lemongrass, and yuzu gelati with black rice crisps. They were both silent as the last word lingered in the air, and then Thea reached over and closed the laptop.

"She says Harry's physique is 'cranelike,'" Leo said.

"He *does* need to eat more," Thea replied.

"Harry's wound a little tight. That, we knew. We'd hear about it from Britt if there was really a problem."

"Maybe," said Thea. She took a bite of her spaghetti and rubbed her foot against his shin absentmindedly.

"Should we have found a way to keep Hector?" Leo said.

"I don't know if we could have," Thea replied, running a crust of bread around her bowl. "It would have been nice to have him longer, I know, but I don't think he was right for you, Leo. He drove you batty, if you recall. He never talked except to deliver the names of these dishes or just to say things like 'umeboshi.' Let Harry deal with it! And I think Kelly has come into her own, anyway."

Leo nodded. Kelly was doing nicely. She lacked Hector's pure fearlessness, but he had to admit that she worked beautifully within the confines of Winesap's menu. Her desserts felt intriguing but not overly challenging.

"We just can't do some of that sci-fi malt shop stuff Harry can," Leo said morosely.

Thea frowned. "Leo. What do you want to do to the menu? Seriously. We've streamlined it. We've made it simpler, more elegant, we've integrated the random influences and lost the ones that just didn't fly. We gave up on that damn brittle. And I think it's working—the comments from the diners are really good. What more do you want to do?"

Leo sighed and sat back. It was an affront not to finish Thea's spaghetti, but he wasn't hungry anymore. "I don't want anything," he said. "I really don't. I feel like the place is running fine, that even without Britt the floor is run well, the cooks seem productive, it's all fine. I just feel a little bored with it all, I guess."

He was expecting Thea's hand on his, a sympathetic look on which they could segue back upstairs, but instead Thea's expression hardened. She stood up, removed his bowl and hers, and before he could stop her went into the kitchen, where he could see her scraping his remaining pasta into the sink.

He followed her into the kitchen. "What?" he asked.

"I have a kid, you know?" Thea said.

"I know you do," Leo said. "I've been hoping to meet her."

Thea ignored this. She leaned against the sink and crossed her arms. "I have a kid to think about, and a job I work hard at and that I am excellent at, Leo, and if you think some vague sense of ennui from you is enough to start shaking things up at work *again*, you'd better find yourself another chef. We run a good place, and if it needs a reset now and again that's fine—but we gave it one, and it's been successful. So let well enough alone. If you wanted to go in with Harry, you should have. But you didn't."

"No, I didn't," he said. "You're right about that."

"Okay, then," she said.

The dressing-down left him weirdly soothed. This felt like the old Thea—the unsentimental, straightforward self she'd been before they got together, unsoftened by affection. That Thea was not the sort who liked being placated, and so he did not embrace her. He got up and began to wash the dishes instead.

It was a relief to hear Thea's complete willingness to say what she thought, even if it wasn't nice, even if it was directed at him. She hadn't fallen in with him in a daze of boredom or sudden-onset madness. She was her same old self, but now she was also with him. Leo gave in to the urge to whistle. Thea looked searchingly at him, but Leo gave her a smile in return.

"It never occurred to me that he'd have a knack for it," he said after a while. "I know that sounds terrible, but I never paid a lot of attention to whatever he was doing, and I just figured he'd quit before it went too far. I mean, if anything, the closer it got, the more I freaked out, you know? I just thought, *This kid has no idea what he's doing, and he's going to be up to his neck in debt and have nothing to show for it.*"

"I know you did," Thea said. "So why did Britt disagree?"

Leo shrugged. "He saw the space. He saw possibilities."

"He learned a lot of that from working with you."

Leo set the bread plate in the sink. "Did you know Harry used to hang out down there when he was a kid? It wasn't so down-trodden then. He told the reviewer he's had his eye on that crappy waterfront since he was a teenager, just wondering how to come home and revitalize it."

A smile fluttered at the edges of Thea's mouth. "You think it's true?" she said. "Or an invention of Britt's?"

"It might be true." He relaxed a little, relieved to see her smiling. "Those stores my parents took us to weren't far from there—that might be what they meant. And Harry's more of a planner than he seems. My mom used to order a separate pizza for the three of us when we were kids, you know, when Britt and I were teenagers and Harry was maybe seven. It was always kind of a frenzy. And he got so pissed off if we got more pizza than he did that he would sit there with his finger jammed in the middle of the next piece he wanted while he ate his first one." Thea laughed, but Leo just shook his head. He rubbed his hands over his scalp. His hair was thinning even more—soon he would just have to shave his head. You couldn't fight this sort of thing.

"Are you going to call them?" Thea asked. She leaned one hip against the counter and faced him, hooking a finger in his belt loop.

Leo was embarrassed. Of course he should call them; he shouldn't have to be asked. "I'll call them now. They're probably out celebrating."

He was dialing when she said, "Leo, don't you want to go out and join them? They're probably all at Mack's."

He hesitated. "It's pretty late."

"Since when does that bother people who work at night?"

"I should, I guess. I hate to leave you."

She made a gesture of futility. "You know I can't go there with you. And I really think you ought to go."

He knew she was right, but still he said, "I've been looking forward to being alone with you all day."

This was a bit much for Thea. She flushed, looking equally embarrassed and annoyed, and said, "Oh, me too. You just wanted to make me say that."

MACK'S WAS JAMMED WITH STRAY EMPLOYEES, the cooks still smelling of hot oil and toasted bread, the servers in their off-duty attire, which included things like metal cuffs around their biceps and battered but closely fitted leather jackets in odd hues like olive and oyster. It was nearly eleven. They'd moved the whole staff over almost as soon as the last table left at ten. Harry and Britt gazed out from the center of the maelstrom, a head above everyone else.

"Our employees are such stylish pocket people," Britt marveled. He felt terribly fond of their employees at the moment, even the servers who drove him to distraction most nights. Right now he liked the look of them all, their insouciant posture and neck tats offsetting their glee at the shitty free beer. He was pretty sure several had changed into fresh eyeglasses postshift. Well, this was why you hired the young: not because they were reliable but because the right ones created an atmosphere that drew people in—they were doing that even now, milling about in a knot like a portable hipster zoo while the other bar patrons, faintly intrigued, observed from the perimeter. If only Britt could keep them from showing up to work smelling of cigarettes and unisex cologne, he'd almost love them.

He'd gotten to Stray just before staff meal. His eyes met Harry's through the window, and for a second Britt had paused before waving the paper. He should have been elated. Finally Harry could stop waiting for the sky to fall. This ought to have been a salve for his relationship with Harry, a sign that they were on the right track. But he was discomfited and morose, unable to put his finger on exactly why.

When Britt held up the review, Harry's brows had shot up and disappeared into his hair, and one hand flew up in what seemed to be an involuntary wave of excitement. After a few weeks of a muted, careful peace between them, it was a relief to see his brother's posture straighten that way and to watch his face take on an expression that made him look like a very tall, scruffy ten-year-old.

But Britt could not get past that panicky, cornered feeling, and it was only as he was walking into Stray's front door that he understood why. A rave review said they were on the right track, it was true, but it seemed also to say that they had no choice but to stay on it together.

Britt wasn't certain he wanted to. He didn't know if his trepidation about the future with his brother was wise or just grudgeholding. But he knew he was here in his brand-new restaurant, filled with the staff he and his brother had hired, and the only correct thing to do was celebrate.

So they'd read the review aloud, pausing for cheers. Harry had seemed subdued but pleased, at least. The moment the last table departed, everyone raced through sidework on the promise of free drinks at Mack's. Britt had noticed that the napkins were folded a little sloppily, and Harry had nudged a few crooked plates back into place, but it didn't matter. The same people would fix their sidework tomorrow. Tonight they would celebrate their first acknowledgment from an actual professional critic, even if she had complained incorrectly about the cavatelli and correctly about the need for more cohesion in the menu. It truly was a good review—he was getting into the spirit of it.

"I was thinking," Britt said. "We don't have any good non-alcoholic drinks. I don't think a good place can get away with that anymore, you know?"

"We have those expensive little sodas," Harry said.

"Yeah, but we need a good cocktail. Something not sweet. Something sophisticated."

Harry shrugged. "Sure. I got it."

Britt decided to drop it. Harry sometimes drew an arbitrary line over certain back-of-the-house decisions. You never knew when he'd get protective, but it wasn't always worth pushing it.

"Anyone would think we got a bad review, looking at you," Britt said.

Harry made an effort to smile. "It was great. Hardly any criticism. Did everybody already read it over at Winesap?" he asked.

Britt didn't have to clarify whom Harry meant by "everybody." "I just told them it was good," he said. "They've probably all seen it by now—I'm sure it's online."

Harry nodded, looking out over the group. Someone had put Marvin Gaye on the jukebox. Jenelle and Anna were dancing beside one another, heads tilted dreamily in opposite directions, beers slopping out of their plastic cups. Watching everyone's celebration selves made Britt feel both hopeful and lonely.

After a pause, Harry said, "He excited?" and Britt turned to look at him. Harry's glasses were smudged and slightly crooked; his hair had grown so far beyond shaggy that it was starting to look kind of good again. He seemed so vulnerable and little-brotherish that Britt felt protective whether he wanted to or not.

"I'm sure he is," Britt said. Harry looked away. "You know Leo's not the biggest talker."

Harry finished off the last of his beer and looked over at the bar. "I keep thinking about the cavatelli. I thought it was great, but maybe it's not. You and Leo had reservations about it. What do you think?"

"I had reservations," Britt said. "I think Leo liked it."

"If Leo said something to you, you can tell me."

"I know that," said Britt. "But he didn't say anything."

"I just know that sometimes people hold things back if they think you can't take it all at once. I'd rather just hear it, you know? Otherwise I spend all my time trying to figure out what people aren't telling me. I can take it." Harry reached for a pitcher they'd bought for the staff and refilled his cup. He drank half of it and filled the cup once more.

"Slow down," Britt said. He placed a hand in the path of Harry's wrist as the cup traveled back up to Harry's mouth. "No one's holding anything back from you."

But Harry kept shaking his head, and now he started talking and seemed reluctant, or not quite able, to pause. He wasn't looking at Britt as he spoke. He focused just above Britt's head, at the door, at the bar, anywhere but at the person he was addressing.

"It's just—it's such bullshit," he said. He repeated it, as if surprised to discover this. "You work your head off and you know it isn't perfect but you count on people to give you feedback. You count on professionals to give you feedback. That's why they're professionals. Or supposed to be. But instead they go on about how everything is great except for two things any idiot could see. Except me, I guess, but you know what I mean." Harry took another long gulp from his beer. He looked a little sweaty.

Britt said, confused, "Are you pissed that the review is too *good*?" He poured the rest of the pitcher into his own cup in order to keep Harry from drinking it.

"I just thought it would be helpful. It wasn't the slightest *bit* helpful. I don't know how we get better if I can't see what we need to improve. Take the lamb's neck." Harry wiped a beer mustache off his lip. He seemed not to be talking to Britt; Britt even glanced over his shoulder to be sure Harry had not been addressing someone else the whole time. "I love that fucking thing. There is nothing I would change on it. Not one damn thing. That reviewer doesn't know what the fuck she's talking about. There are probably a hundred other things we actually do need to fix and she was so busy talking about our best dish she didn't say what any of them were. I *know* there is stuff we need to fix. I know it. I feel it every day when I come in, all that shit I'm not getting right that just lurks in plain sight, and everyone can probably see it but me. But nobody tells me. And then the day gets away from me and I can never just concentrate and figure it all out. I can't see what I need to *do*."

On this last syllable, Harry's beer slopped over and onto the floor with a smack. The sound seemed to shake him off his track. He just stood there, as if he were trying to think of something to say.

Throughout all this Britt had gone from slight discomfort to alarm. It wasn't that Harry's words were irrational, but they did not quite fit the situation—not in content, not in the rabbity cadence of his speech. Maybe he'd simply had too much to drink, but then he should be slower, shouldn't he?

Britt took the cup from Harry's hand and Harry reached for it just as quickly, almost automatically, but Britt cupped a hand over each of Harry's shoulders and looked hard at him. "Harry. I can't even tell exactly what you're upset about anymore. You don't have to fix anything. It's all fine." He saw a few staff members look over at them and lowered his voice. He brushed off Harry's shoulders and let his hands drop. "You want me to drive you home?"

Harry looked startled. "No," he said. "I'm fine. I don't want to be alone."

Britt opened his mouth to question this, but then Harry looked over Britt's shoulder and jostled past him. Britt turned to see Harry let out a whoop and pull Camille to him, lifting her easily into a hug and letting her down with a resounding kiss on the cheek. Camille's pink cheeks and the gleam of her teeth made her look both embarrassed and pleased, as if she'd admonished Harry a hundred times not to do this but had done so only halfheartedly. And indeed Harry had reached for her as naturally as if they'd been doing this for years, as naturally as if he had not just been behaving like a different person altogether.

Camille's eyes met Britt's over Harry's shoulder. She pushed herself away from Harry with a hand on his shoulder and stepped back, swiping her hair off her face. The gesture seemed to compose her, and she turned to Britt and kissed his cheek. It was all so quick that Britt wasn't quite sure what he'd seen, if he had seen anything at all. He was not sure his own perceptions were sound in any way—hadn't his brother just seemed so upset? But here he was, ebullient again. And what had that hug really been but his brother embracing a friend? She'd always been clear that they were friends.

Harry was already gone, and Britt watched him make his way through the crowd, accepting congratulations and back slaps. He was suddenly Harry again, triumphant and relaxed, the host of a raucous party.

"Well, hello," Camille said, smiling. Having materialized so unexpectedly, stripped of the familiarity of her house and the restaurants, she was somehow taller here, more vivid and rangy among the smells of popcorn and beer, the peeling red booths and the cloudy mirrors. Britt was aware of the staff glancing over in amusement and interest.

"This is a surprise," Britt said. He leaned over to kiss her because that was what he always did, but he was moving robotically, one eye still on his brother. Where Harry had touched her, her cheek was warm, smelling slightly, and confusingly for an instant, of Stray. "How'd you know we were here?"

"Harry," she said. "He said you'd be at Mack's."

"Harry called you?"

"Texted me," she said. "Honestly, I would have thought *you'd* call me."

"It was already late," Britt said.

Camille looked uncertain for the first time. "Do you not want me to be here? Is that why it was him and not you?"

"Of course I do," Britt said, but some element was missing. They were looking at each other with a mix of trepidation and annoyance, and neither of them seemed entirely ready to name the reasons. But it was late now, and the tension of the past several weeks had left him depleted and inarticulate. More than Britt wanted to dredge everything up so he could address whatever had just happened with Camille, he wanted everything to be easy again.

"He's a little worked up about the review," Britt said. It was a relief to change the subject, but he found it difficult to articulate exactly what had made him uneasy.

"He seems anxious," Camille said carefully.

"I'd think he'd be relieved," Britt said. "But he's freaking out about how to fix whatever might need fixing. And about what Leo thinks."

"Have you talked to him about . . . I don't know, just taking better care of himself?" she said.

"I try," Britt said, but he wasn't sure that was true. He talked to Harry about not flying off the handle; it wasn't quite the same thing.

"Because he seems a little wound up," she continued, a touch more forcefully. "Is this typical for him?"

"Kind of," Britt said, frowning. "Listen, can we not discuss him the whole night? Let's just have a good time."

Camille blinked. For a time neither of them said anything, and then she took a look around the room and shrugged, gazing away from him. "Fine. Whatever. Maybe Leo can calm him down," she said.

"Meaning what?" said Britt. He sounded petty even to himself.

Camille was staring at him. "Meaning there's Leo, over by the bar, and maybe he can calm him down."

And so he was, making his way through the scrum. Harry slouched just a little as he accepted a hug from Leo, his posture suddenly sagging between exhaustion and relief, so that for a moment it looked as if Leo were holding him up.

Britt looked away. Was it just petulance? He thought it might also be exhaustion, from the constant vigilance Harry seemed to require even as he saved his best self for everyone else. Britt pulled Camille a little closer to him, wanting her then, even if her loyalty was divided, even if he was angry with her too. He could see by the change in her expression that he wasn't looking celebratory now, if he ever had been. She opened her mouth to speak but then seemed to change her mind. Instead she just pressed her forehead against his temple. The night seemed to have been going on forever.

"YOU'RE LOOKING PRETTY TIRED," Leo said. Leo looked Harry up and down, taking in his frame. "You ever eat?"

"Of course," said Harry.

"I didn't mean when your body has to consume itself. I meant a meal."

"Jesus, you and Jenelle should get together. Suddenly everyone's so concerned about my diet. I'm just not cooking for myself a whole lot."

"Who's Jenelle? The reviewer said you were cranelike."

"Oh, right. That's helpful, eh?" Harry swirled the liquid in his glass. "So, what'd you think?"

"I thought it was great!" Leo said.

"Seriously?"

"Listen, by any standard it was a great review. I'm proud of you." Harry looked toward the door, and when Leo turned he saw the back of Britt's head as he slipped out. "That means a lot to me," Harry said, but his voice had lost some energy.

"Well, I'm psyched for you," Leo said, a little desperately. He wasn't sure how many more ways he could say it.

"Could've been yours too," Harry said. "All the glory, I mean." He gestured in the direction of a group of dishwashers chugging beers in unison.

"Let's not take it there," Leo said, but Harry shook his head.

"It's not a dig," he said. "Well, yes it was. But I can't figure it out, Leo. I made this great space. I built an amazing menu. I was bracing myself for a review because I thought that would tell me, but basically she loved it except for a couple things like the lamb's neck." Harry was standing very close to Leo, his gaze darting searchingly around Leo's face.

"Is that it," Harry continued, "the lamb's neck? Was that why you passed? Because it's one plate of food. And I keep fucking looking at my restaurant and trying to figure out what's missing, and it's making me nuts, because as far as I can tell, nothing is. But something must be, so just tell me. Tell me what you see that I don't."

"It was just me," Leo said softly. He had to take a step back; beneath the beer on Harry's breath was a desperate ketonic edge. "Harry, I don't know. I thought it was the right choice at the time. I don't know if it was. It was what I thought back then. And now it's done."

CHAPTER 17

T HE POSTREVIEW RUSH BEGAN like a shot at five o'clock the next night and kicked the shit out of them straight through until midnight. Each subsequent evening hurtled over them the same way. Every Stray employee was on deck until the end. The tables filled; the bar was crowded with people both standing and sitting, chomping on appetizers and waiting for tables or just there to have a drink and a snack.

Harry had always imagined success as a happy clamor of inquisitive faces and ringing glassware, but the reality was chaotic and even a little frightening—he had dreams of running through the streets of Linden, pursued by a smiling crowd that increased each time he looked back.

He upped his orders of food and booze and upped them again, trying to walk the balance between running out and having product that went bad before he could use it. Who knew if the rush would continue? But it did. Each day he got to the restaurant earlier than the day before, as the amount of food he had to prep continued to grow. In the last moments before sleep he often saw piles of shallots in his drifting mind, heard the thunk of the Hobart mixer, or found that he was holding the fingers of his left hand in the clawed position in which that hand remained much of the day, holding food in place while the knife continually rose and fell.

Spring streamed past them and became summer. By the time June came around, the restaurant had been at high speed for two months, and Harry couldn't see any sign that it was letting up. Now and then he caught a glimpse of Britt moving about the dining room, where there were never quite enough servers. Britt looked as tired as the rest of them did. Jenelle and Hector were even less talkative than before, too busy hunched over their workstations even during prep to converse beyond the basics of position and tools. Even the servers, whose general pallor had always suggested a variety of unsavory pastimes, were paler than usual, with pouches beneath their heavily lined eyes.

But Harry thought he and Britt might be okay. They hadn't fought again, at least. He was taking this as a good sign. Once a week or so Camille appeared at the bar to meet up with Britt, and when she did Harry often slipped an extra tempura shrimp into the fryer or sliced off a crisped bit of chicken and made it into an amuse. She ate the dishes, she arrived and departed with a wave, but she seemed to him to be a distant celebrity, shiny and eye-catching, friendly but remote.

He left the lamb's neck on the menu, but he could not stop tweaking it. He tried it with artichokes, with toasts and little coins of new potato. He tried it with no starch at all, just carrot and parsley. He tried skewing it sweet-tart with gooseberries and skewing it savory and dark with thyme and garlic and braised cipolline onions. They all sold about the same—regularly, if not flying off the shelves. The dish was a more of a cult item, one a guest ordered as much to announce himself to the restaurant as to allow the restaurant to show itself to him. The point was, nothing revealed itself to Harry as the obvious course of action. He liked the dish no matter what, he would eat it no matter what, and he knew that this was a problem. A chef should be able to break down a dish to its components in a few bites, not view it as a mere lump of tastiness that had just appeared on a plate. The more Harry tried to fix it, the more confused he became.

On the Saturday when he got the idea to try it with pesto, he began his day at the farmers' market. There was a little weekend market about fifteen minutes away, where he often shopped in a chef's coat, not only to buy supplies but because people loved to see a chef at the market. They asked questions about where he worked and what he'd do with garlic scapes. It was better than a commercial. The facts that this summer was hotter than the last and he felt dizzy and damp standing in the blaze of the morning sun, that it took longer to get in and out when he had to stop and chat all the time, and that every moment he was not barreling through his prep list it felt like something was drawing more tightly around his chest were not enough reason to skip the chef's coat.

The pesto was going to be made with garlic scapes, which shouldn't have been difficult: blanch them, shock them, puree them with olive oil, lemon juice, cheese, and nuts. Boom. The result was supposed to be a vibrant green paste, garlicky in a subtler, greener-tasting way than one made with bulb garlic. He'd do a toast with pesto, maybe, serve it alongside the neck, or toss little new potatoes in it.

The problem arose once he was back at the restaurant with his produce. All he had to do was choose the right nut. Pine nuts, walnuts, almonds? He knew he should simply make a tiny batch of each and taste it, but he got caught up thinking about the rest of the menu. You didn't want almonds on too many dishes, and they were already in a tart. Walnuts? He was low on walnuts, and anyway they might disappear into the pesto. Or maybe they'd be a kind of stealth ingredient.

While he ruminated on this he started to put together flatbread dough, but as he was hauling out flour and yeast he began picturing how the bread would work on the line. To get the best from a flatbread, to get its blistered edges and those chestnut-crowned bubbles, one had to cook it like a pizza, with last-minute intense heat. He couldn't dedicate one whole oven to the heat he'd require, and anyway it might heat up the whole bar. He supposed he could do it in a hot oiled pan, but his range was crowded as it was, and he didn't know if he had room for yet another dish cooked in a big sauté pan.

By this point Harry was standing before the mixer with an empty bag of flour, several pounds of which he'd already dumped into the bowl, working through calculations that should have been brisk and simple but that felt impossible to reconcile. Maybe he'd skip the flatbread and throw the flour back in its bag, but he could not recall whether he had added salt and yeast yet.

He began sifting through the flour with a spoon, looking for traces of yellowish powdered yeast or the coarser grains of salt. As he was doing this, he began thinking about the nuts again. He was wondering if he should toast them instead of blanching them. Maybe toasting was one of those things no one did but they ought to, one of those little tweaks that elevated a whole dish. Maybe toasting would work better with almonds than walnuts, or maybe walnuts over almonds, but then again maybe toasting would bring pine nuts back into play.

He realized that he was still standing there, hunched over the bowl of flour, stirring it with a spoon. He'd forgotten why he was digging through a bowl of flour in the first place.

Harry decided to leave it for a while, while he went out for almonds or walnuts or whatever. Whatever was cheapest, he decided. That was a reasonable way of making a decision—do what won't bankrupt your restaurant.

And then he was out in the sunlight, and it was nine o'clock in the morning, and he was walking to his truck and trying to concentrate on pesto-smeared flatbread beside the lamb's neck. Was pesto too much of a cliché? Was flatbread a cop-out? Then he was back to the flatbread question, wondering if he could use the salamander for flatbread, if that would be genius or if it would irreparably slow everything down.

He got into his truck and began to drive, but he did so unthinkingly, turning according to some hazy instinct rather than logic, ending up going in the opposite direction from the store where he'd intended to go. The drive kept proceeding in these fits and starts—he'd correct himself, turn in the proper direction, then start thinking about some minutiae to do with nut variety or yeast or the end of the garlic scape season and whether anyone even wanted them anymore, because for a while there it seemed as if everyone was cooking with garlic scapes. Except why should seasonal produce become a cliché during its brief heyday? Was a tomato a cliché? A zucchini? Maybe the garlic scape would soon become as commonplace as carrots, so that it didn't feel like such a trend to use them.

There were too many variables before he would ever get that far.

He had just thought of pistachios and was digging in the glove compartment for a scrap of paper on which to write that when the van pulled out in front of him. Or maybe it simply pulled into traffic at a reasonable distance and he failed to see it. He became aware of the van's dull blue paint looming before him the moment his truck collided with it, creating a terrific bang and a flutter of broken glass.

Harry sat there clutching the steering wheel as the van doors opened and began to disgorge a number of flustered but unharmed senior citizens.

The driver of the van, a man in his sixties or seventies with thick square glasses and a floppy hat that hung down his back on a string, came rushing around to Harry's truck. Harry gazed down at him, at the man's fingers curled over the lip of the half-opened window.

"Young man," the driver said. "Young man, are you all right?"

Harry knew you weren't supposed to admit fault, and he wasn't even sure it *was* his fault, but the man seemed so flustered, his glasses opaque and his white hair endearingly fluffy in the sunlight, his head turning this way and that as he fretted, explaining that he was supposed to be driving a group of seniors to the theater that night and with a broken taillight he couldn't.

"It's my fault," Harry said, and he got out of the truck and joined the circle of people inspecting the damage. The truck was nearly unharmed, with a small dent in its fender, while the van's taillight was pushed inward, the glass shattered on the roadway. The disparity seemed to convince the van's driver of Harry's guilt, and he turned rather cool and brusque as Harry wrote down his information. But when Harry pressed the paper into the man's hand, that palm was extraordinarily soft, like a child's, and a shudder of relief and retroactive fright coursed through him. The others got back in their van, busily discussing him, and left him standing beside his truck.

Harry wasn't sure what to do. He should call his insurance company, but there was no need to phone the police. He got back in his truck and started it up. His hands were still shaking from the shock of the accident, but driving seemed to calm him. He forgot that he had begun the drive looking for a grocery store. He was just moving, in a rickety truck, and the pure uncomplicated motion felt so calming that he merged onto the highway. The blacktop stretched out before him, smooth and flat and flanked by Pennsylvania's rolling hills.

The idea of his brother pinged like a bell in the distance. Maybe Harry ought to call him—but Britt no longer found Harry useful. He frowned when Harry spoke at staff meal; he frowned when Harry said hello to Camille; he frowned and shrugged when tasting the very best dish Harry could muster. Harry never even looked at Britt without knowing that he had disappointed him.

The flatness of the road seemed to quiet his mind a little. He almost managed to stop thinking about pesto, even though pistachios probably were the best idea, even though pesto changed so much depending on whether it was on bread or vegetables or pasta. And which shape of pasta. And which brand. Or homemade.

He was driving faster now, edging up over eighty as the truck began to vibrate. He didn't know whether he had passed a sign for an Amish farm stand or the idea had just arrived and rooted itself unbidden—things did that to him now; they took hold before he knew where they'd come from—but suddenly Harry was thinking about pie. It helped him forget the pesto and the lamb's neck as his mind listed all the fruit pies one could make at this time of year, then all the pies one might make at any time. In his head he listed cream pies and meringues and custards, things too gloppy and rustic to serve at the restaurant. He tried to enjoy the image of each pie as it passed through his mind, but the pies kept turning into great vats of dough and uncertainty about thickeners, numbers piling up as he scaled up recipes.

After a while it stopped helping. The attempt to focus was just too difficult. He was realizing now that *trying* was the problem—all that effort that never solved anything. Every day broke over his head just like the one before, no matter what he'd done to prepare.

Harry let the word "pie" tap a beat in his head until it didn't mean anything at all. It was just a syllable he could say, his dry lips popping in rhythm with the stripes on the road.

Now he did pass a sign for an Amish roadside stand, which seemed not only fortuitous but a little chilling, as if he'd conjured it.

Sometimes this kind of thing happened to him at the restaurant. He had to ask Jenelle if they had already discussed the new lamb prep or if he had only thought about it, if he had told her what to do or she had somehow known without his verbalizing it. He was always a little surprised to learn he had told her, surprised to learn he still needed words to communicate his thoughts. He could no longer feel the division between himself and the entity that was the building and its teeming needs and movements. Stray was an animal, Harry not its owner so much as its parasite.

He veered into the right lane just in time for the exit and pulled off the expressway and onto a two-lane road, following an arrow and a sign with a silhouetted horse and buggy.

The landscape was all green fields and sprawling farmhouses, a single ancient gas station. There were no kids with cigarettes and tattoos. No one here had ever heard of his restaurant, an idea that left him feeling both exhilarated and frightened. If Stray could release him for this long—for by now it must have been many hours—then perhaps it didn't exist after all.

He'd hoped for something small, like a lemonade stand, but the Amish farm stand was a building with a parking lot and a big sign among tables of lettuce, snap peas, and zucchini. The produce looked like play food. Harry got out and walked slowly among the tables, picking up a zucchini and sniffing it to determine whether it was real.

Inside the open doorway, he found what he'd been looking for: white-boxed pies lined up on a long table—labeled, he was saddened to see, with printed stickers. He'd expected something handwritten. He picked out a blueberry pie and a strawberry-rhubarb pie, because he couldn't think of what else to do.

The girl at the cash register wore one of those mesh hair covers over a bun at the back of her head. One hoped an Amish girl would be fresh-skinned, her eyes luminous, bottomless, her scent that of peaches and linen, but this girl had narrow, rounded shoulders. The tops of her ears flared pinkly in the light through the window, and her eyes were a flat, pupil-less doll blue.

"Twenty-five dollars," she said, and gazed off beyond Harry's shoulder at the road. He turned to look, his wallet still clutched in his hand, as a car raced past. It occurred to him that she was probably waiting for someone. Not only was this Amish girl not going to be an oasis of compassion and tranquillity, she was actively trying to get away from here herself.

"You looking for someone?" he asked. She met his eyes, startled, and then looked away. Harry blushed and began counting out his bills, trying to remember how much the pies were. He gave her a twenty, a five, and a ten. She slid the ten back across the counter at him.

"I mean, are you waiting for someone?" he clarified. It sounded like a proposition, and when the girl opened her mouth, lifting the bill from the counter, he was too embarrassed to let her speak. "Forget it. I came out here thinking that no one wants to leave, but that's probably what everyone comes out here thinking. You must get sick of it. The tourists, I mean. I'm not really a tourist, I'm just driving. I own a restaurant, but I had to make pesto today and anyway I saw your sign. I never make pies"—he'd been struggling to find his point, but here Harry began to suspect that he might be getting back on track, and he sped up, trying to catch up to his idea—"they're too homey-looking and they don't slice the way people think they do unless the filling is too thick. But I wanted to try yours. Your pie. I got blueberry and strawberry-rhubarb." He opened one of the boxes, peering in at the golden circle of pastry, the ooze of filling staining the perimeter of the steam vents. He might have gotten the wrong kinds.

The girl cleared her throat. The ten-dollar bill was still on the counter. "The strawberry-rhubarb's good," she said, and Harry waited for her to tell him about the blueberry. But she gave the money a little flutter instead, waiting for him to understand that it belonged to him. Finally she set the money on top of the pie box and turned away, her smile the same chilly and dismissive sort Britt was always trying to train out of his servers.

LEO HAD WON HIS CAMPAIGN to meet Thea's daughter, which meant that today he was having lunch with a child who for all he knew was pure hell. Maybe the daughter was a biter, a screecher, or an expert administrator of convenient lapses in potty training. Leo had gotten what he'd asked for, but now he had his doubts that he even wanted it. He kept trying to remember his brothers at that age, or at least Harry, but came up with only a lot of tickling, freckles, and wailing.

Last night he'd popped down to the line on the pretext of getting a glass of water—he was immensely well hydrated these days—and was whistling when he'd joined Thea. She had just fired a plate of buttered pasta. "Who got that?" Leo asked.

"Little kid in the house," she said. She shook her head. "Why anyone brings their kid to a place like this is beyond me."

"Agreed," said Jason. He slid a plate of lamb loin into the window and spiked the ticket. "If your kid won't eat beef heart, it doesn't deserve to leave the house."

"Oh, please," said Suzanne. She was tossing the pasta in a sauté pan and had to assert this over one shoulder. "It. We charge them a lot for some silly buttered noodles—what's the harm? We're above children now?"

"It's not about being above," said Thea.

"Yes it is," Jason said.

"It's just a waste of money."

"Maybe not," Leo heard himself saying. "Maybe they wanted a family evening. Maybe the kid is who he is and they like having him around anyway. Or maybe buttered pasta is his favorite thing in the world and it's his birthday. Maybe he's a Torsini, you ever think of that?"

"The Torsinis never use their discount," Thea said. "I get the feeling they think they can do better at home."

"Yeah, well, I'm going out there," Leo said, "and I bet you both a drink it's not some little demon brat but a perfectly nice kid who has the good taste to like homemade pasta with butter and Parmigiano. There is Parm on it, isn't there?"

Thea nodded, one eyebrow quirked. "Aha! My point exactly."

The server had been slightly amused to find Leo carrying the plate of pasta, but Leo insisted, feeling a mixture of giddiness and pugnacity, a weird happy buzziness in which he was drawing ever closer to doing something ridiculous and public for the sheer joy of it, like sweeping Thea into a low dip right there on the line, just for the pleasure of feeling the curve of her back beneath his palm.

The table was indeed a family, a couple, a child, a teenager, and two grandparents. The child was about six or seven, Leo guessed, just a little boy in navy-blue pants and a white shirt, with slightly messy brown hair and—this moved Leo suddenly and unaccountably—two of those little rubber bracelets, an orange one and a blue one, showing beneath the cuff of his shirt. Leo had no idea what charitable cause the colors signified, or if these bracelets signified anything at all, since no one really wore them anymore, but for some reason he was touched by the decision of it, the fact that this boy had chosen to wear something he liked, something he thought looked nice. All the jangly effervescence Leo had been riding on coalesced into something else inside him, a sort of clear, suffusing warmth and calm. He delivered the plate and chatted up the table with the same aplomb as ever, as beautifully as even Britt could have done, and when he finished he headed right back to the line.

Thea looked up with a sardonic half-smile, ready to give him a hard time, but something in his face made her say nothing. She watched him approach, one hand on her towel and the other still reaching up toward the window for a plate of gorgonzola-crusted beef. For a moment her expression was strangely gentle, but then she looked away and attended to the beef, using a kitchen torch to caramelize the cheese and then wiping the plate rim in two swift motions.

"Well?" Jason said. "Cried? Wants chicken tenders?"

"Nope," Leo said. He coughed into his hand. "Just a kid. And you're a complete misanthrope, Jason, but I'll buy you guys a drink tonight anyway. I just want you to briefly experience what happiness feels like."

Later that night, Thea called him from her car. "You want to come for an early lunch tomorrow?"

"Sure," he said uncertainly. He didn't want to ask whether this was his invitation to meet her daughter, in case Thea's natural contrariness reasserted itself. Maybe she'd forgotten she had Iris this weekend. "You want me to cook?"

"I miss cooking," she said. "I just expedite most nights. I have to be at work by two, but I'll make lunch, you bring dessert. Okay?"

Thea's house was a little cream-colored ranch with navy trim, with a plum tree out front and a scattering of wildflowers adorning the lawn like weeds, a two-person cedar swing on the front porch. For a moment the house, compact and charming as it was, made Leo feel disheartened and lonely. It was the house where Thea had lived with her husband, who might have been the one to plant the tree or make the swing. And even if he was gone now, the place still bore a cozy air of someone else's family, and it made Leo wonder suddenly how Frances was. She had e-mailed him an announcement when her baby was born, with a photo of a perplexed-looking infant with spiky black hair and black eyes. It had been a long time since he'd been married to Frances, and they'd stayed friendly enough to exchange the occasional e-mail, but the image had felt both too familiar and depressingly distant all at once. The baby looked so much like Frances that she only reminded Leo of the infant he'd once intended to have with her. His ex-wife was further gone than ever, a state of affairs he no longer minded but that took him aback now and then with its sheer completeness.

He shook off the melancholy and paused outside the door. Normally he'd knock and open it, but now he rang the doorbell, ran a hand over his hair, and checked his grocery bag. He was sweating.

Thea came to the door in jeans and a white T-shirt. She gave him a conspiratorial smile. "Hey there," she said. "Come on in. We're making gnudi."

Her daughter was sitting at the table with a small bowl and spoon, stirring something. Thea said, "Iris, say hello to Leo." Iris glanced his way, seemed unimpressed, and went back to work. "Iris."

"Hello," she said, but she said it into the bowl, into which she was peering not with sulkiness but with great concentration.

"Ricotta and herbs," said Thea, nodding in the direction of the bowl. "Are the eggs mixed in?"

"I think so," Iris said. "There's a little yellow."

"Okay, well, be gentle and mix it just enough to get rid of the yellow."

Iris had Thea's wonderful hair but shorter and darker, a messy headful of curls. She was wearing orange shorts and a blue-and-white-striped shirt, and when she glanced over at Leo her eyes were large and dark brown. She had Thea's serious set to her mouth, the shape of her eyes, but it was somehow a relief to be reminded that she was not the replica of her mother that he'd had in his head. She was an actual person instead, and he found this, and her utter lack of interest in him, comforting. Some of his nervousness departed, and so did the temptation to cajole her into talking to him. He set his grocery bag on the table and began removing things from it while Thea stirred a pan on the stove.

"You brought dessert," Iris said.

"Well, I brought the stuff to make it," he said. "I'll just get started." He set out a quart of strawberries, a bunch of mint, and a glass bottle of heavy cream. To Thea he said, "I went to the farmers' market this morning and guess what they had? Araucana eggs."

"No kidding. Who had them?"

"No one I knew. Just a guy who had some honey, some eggs, some foraged stuff. I brought you a few."

The eggs were small, not much larger than quail's eggs, pale blue, pale pink, a nutmeg-freckled celadon green. Iris gave them careful consideration, reaching out to pick up an egg with one eye trained on him to see if he'd stop her. "Do you have a few bowls for the berries?" he asked Thea, who reached into a cupboard and handed him two. When he returned to the table, Iris was examining a green egg. It filled her palm perfectly. She looked up at him and carefully set the egg back in the carton. Leo didn't touch the carton, just sat down and began sorting through the strawberries, pulling off the green stems and placing them in one bowl and the berries in another.

He worked in silence for several moments, until Thea came over and retrieved the ricotta mixture from Iris. "Do you need a cutting board?" she asked.

"It depends," he said. "I can't decide if I want to eat these whole or cut in half."

"I'll get you one just in case," she said. A moment later she set down a cutting board and a paring knife beside him.

"Thank you," he said, and kept stemming the berries. He could feel Iris looking at him now and then, mildly interested in the gem-like berries, the miniature pastel eggs, and the glass bottle of cream. Then she left the table and went into the next room. She was sturdy and purposeful, and she walked with her shoulders back and arms swinging, like a cowboy or a teamster. He and Thea exchanged a glance, and Thea tilted her head to see into the next room. Then, apparently satisfied by what she saw, she returned to sprinkling flour into the egg and ricotta mixture in her bowl.

Iris returned, holding a good-quality small metal saucepan and cover, both of which had clearly been repurposed for some use in a playroom. She set the pan down on the table beside the eggs and stood there expectantly. Leo forced himself not to smile. "I wonder if those eggs taste any different from regular eggs," he said, as if to himself, "or if they just look nicer. Probably no way to tell."

Iris took the measure of his limitations with a regretful look.

"You cook one," she explained, briskly but not without kindness, "and then you eat it and see."

Behind them, Thea snickered. Leo told Iris that he agreed this was the only sensible way to approach it; silently he noted that this would keep him on track next time he thought he'd patronize a three-year-old. He was filling the little pan with water, letting Iris drop in the whole eggs with care, when his phone rang.

"It's Britt," he said to Thea, looking at the number. He went into the other room to answer it, closing the door behind him. "Britt, what's up?"

"Where are you?" Britt said. He was breathing in an odd way, as if he were moving frantically around and talking at the same time. Something clattered in the background. "Are you at Winesap?"

"No," Leo said. "Am I supposed to be? What's wrong?"

"I just got here and the kitchen's a mess but nobody's here. It looks like he emptied all our flour into a mixer and just left it there. There's a big pot at a full boil with a bunch of green beans or something in it. He's not with you? Did he call you?"

Leo felt as if Britt were resuming a conversation he didn't remember having. "You're at Stray?" he asked.

"Yes, I'm at Stray! Jesus. I'm here and Harry's not."

"He's not with me," Leo said. "You sure he left all that? He might have just stepped out. Or maybe Hector was there and he quit."

"No," Britt said. "Mom and Dad haven't seen him either. I think I freaked them out—now Mom wants me to call her back."

"Listen, I'll call them," Leo said. "You just call Harry or look around or whatever and keep me posted. I'm sure he was there and he just ran out for something. It's not that late yet."

"For him it is," Britt said. "He's usually here by eight in the morning."

"Is he doing okay? He seemed a little touchy last time I saw him."

Britt sighed. "Leo, for chrissake, that was weeks ago. And he's not a little touchy, he's really getting off the wall. He's changed the stupid lamb's neck dish about a dozen times in the last month. The staff can't even keep it straight anymore."

Leo sat down on Thea's couch. "Why didn't you tell me?"

"You knew," Britt said bitterly. "You saw him. You're just not paying attention." Leo heard the catch in his voice, as if Britt had sat down suddenly and heavily. "I can see where the water started in that pot and it's almost boiled away. He's been gone a while."

CHAPTER 18

B RITT TURNED OFF THE FLAME BENEATH the pot of water and threw out the soggy vegetables, but left the flour in case it was salvageable. He tried Harry's cell phone, which went straight to voice mail, and then he tried a text and an e-mail too. He did this every half hour, in case the previous messages were somehow not getting through.

He examined the doors and windows, but there was no broken lock or even a cracked window. Out on the sidewalk he looked at the building's façade, trying to tell whether it appeared to be the kind of place that was easy to break into, where someone might be working alone with a bunch of cash. It wasn't—not the cash part, anyway, but people might not know that. Teenagers were smoking on the curb in one direction, and shadows were shifting inside the grimy bodega windows in the other.

Through the scrim of cigarette smoke the teenagers' skin was pale and pebbled with acne. They hadn't seen Harry. "You didn't see anything unusual, did you?" Britt pressed them. "Anyone hanging around the restaurant?"

"You mean like us?" one kid said, and they laughed longer than necessary. Britt stood there for another beat, wondering if they'd just told him something, but then he realized it was only a joke, at his expense. They'd forgotten him almost before he gave up and left to talk with the bodega owner.

None of them seemed very concerned, but he couldn't tell

whether that was because the neighborhood was safer than he thought or just so sketchy that the locals were inured to its dangers.

When he hadn't heard from Harry by twelve thirty, he phoned the police. As he dialed he had the sensation of observing his own actions, as if he were watching a movie in which the clueless brother is about to get terrible news, and he did not know whether this was detachment or insight. But the police had no reports of anyone like Harry doing anything at all. They agreed that it was odd for someone to leave his prep work half done, but not so odd that they would pursue it yet.

"But he's been under a lot of stress," Britt said. Was he being alarmist or not alarmist enough?

"Are you worried he would harm himself?" The man's voice was brisk but faintly disappointed, as if Britt should have led with that.

"No," he said automatically, but he wasn't sure that was right, either. "Deliberately? Or accidentally?"

"Deliberately," the policeman said. "Anyone could hurt himself accidentally."

"I don't think so," Britt said. Harry had been under duress, but he had also been coming to work and going home and generally doing what needed to be done; he was just being ornery and touchy about it. Still, Britt had hoped for some kind of reassurance from the police—he hoped they'd be so used to real issues that they would scoff at his. *Obviously Harry is fine*, he wanted someone to say. *Nothing you've said sounds that bad*. Instead the police were taking him just seriously enough to be frightening, sounding just disapproving enough for him to begin to realize that in his own story he sounded lax and irresponsible.

The policeman interrupted, newly brisk. He seemed to have abruptly reached his limit. "I have your information and your brother's information. If you don't hear from him by this time tomorrow or the next day, give us a call back. And call the hospitals, just in case. Keep trying him. Ninety-nine percent of the time there's just a misunderstanding."

"That often?" Britt asked hungrily.

"Something like that," he said.

Britt stayed on the line, not knowing what to say. Nothing had really been accomplished; it seemed wrong to hang up. Finally he realized that the line was dead.

When Hector arrived, Britt tried to casually feel out whether there was any chance of his working the line. This was around one o'clock, and Hector was standing before a table stocked with bus tubs of produce and chocolate and bottles of liqueur and vanilla. He was holding a prep list with only one item crossed off. Britt started to ask, but then he recalled how recently Hector had rebelled against some perceived slight by filling the kitchen with trays of marshmallows and a fudgy, throat-coating penuche.

In the end, he just lied. He said that Harry was ill and possibly contagious, that he couldn't be sure whether it was even safe to let him work tonight. Hector nodded shortly and returned to his work, but although Jenelle maintained her placid expression, her dark eyes were as watchful as a crow's.

"I can't work the line by myself," she said. "Not on a Saturday night."

"No," he agreed. "Of course not."

"I don't suppose you could work it with me?"

He laughed a little bitterly. "I wish I could," he said. He looked around the room and checked his watch once more. "Just keep going for now. I'll take care of it. If you can prep extra, though, do. I'll call one of the dish guys and ask them to come in early and you get 'em doing the prep they can handle, okay?"

"Okay," she said, and gave him one last glance, a sight that tightened Britt's gut into a fist. Skepticism in one's employees never boded well long-term. He would rather have seen outright rage.

By now it was nearly one thirty. This time he tried Camille, on the off chance that Harry was with her and had persuaded her he wasn't much needed in his own restaurant to prepare for a jam-packed Saturday night.

"Listen. Any chance you've talked to Harry today?"

He was expecting defensiveness—they had tacitly buried the night at Mack's and their argument after the dishwashing episode, and Britt believed that recently she had not even spoken to Harry except to say hello when she came to the restaurant. But she must have sensed that he wasn't asking out of jealousy, and her voice shifted crisply into office mode while in the background music continued to play jauntily. "I haven't. What do you need?"

"I need my brother in the restaurant," Britt said, ducking behind the office door. "I don't know where he is. He hasn't called you, e-mailed, anything? He's about six hours late to work."

"What?" The music disappeared. "He's not there? Are you sure he's not at home?"

"He's not. I tried my parents. They're starting to freak out. He left at the usual time this morning, and he was here at some point, but then he left."

"That doesn't sound so bad," she said soothingly. "He probably needed to get something."

"He left all his prep work in the middle," Britt said. Each time he said this it sounded worse. He wanted not to say it anymore. "He left pots on the stove, flour in the mixer."

There was a long silence. "I'm checking my phone. Nothing. What should we do? Did you call any hospitals?"

Britt rubbed his brow. "Not yet."

"I'll do it," she said. "It'll give me something to concentrate on. Let me help you."

"That'd be good. I have to call Leo," Britt said. "We have this lean, mean kitchen staff and there is not one extra hand in an emergency, which it's now clear to me was a terrible business plan. I need a pair of hands up here."

"You're opening anyway?"

"Should I not be opening tonight?" he asked, stricken. "Do you think this is that bad?"

"I don't know," she said. "It just popped out. No, you should be open. You'd feel stupid otherwise, when he comes back in half an hour and you've closed it all down."

"You're right," he said. He'd never been so relieved by a statement so obviously made up, but Camille sounded sure. "Listen, I have to go fix this. Call me if you see him, okay?"

"Okay, then. I'll be there in about half an hour."

"You don't have to come here," he said.

"I'm coming. I'll help you set up the dining room while you deal with other things. I can cut vegetables and do basic kitchen help if your cooks give me a little direction. I'll bring something decent to wear in case you need me on the floor."

For a moment Britt felt slightly weakened by emotion for her—for her complete reliability, her willingness, and her universal competence. When she spoke so calmly and authoritatively, it made him think Harry must be fine, as if Camille must somehow know Harry better than he did. For once, this seemed like a positive thing.

"You're okay, aren't you?" he said, wanting confirmation.

"Sure," she said, but she sounded less confident now. "Harry must be too. He's just . . . I don't know. He fell asleep somewhere, maybe."

They both paused, letting that idea hang there in all its implausibility. After they hung up, he took a breath and then stared at his hands for a long moment. He wanted to work, to address the immediate needs of the restaurant, because that was such a manageable problem. You needed bodies in a restaurant. You had the necessary number of hands or work failed, and that was all there was to it. He could find people. But that felt wrong too, to focus on something as small as call sheets and prep work when his brother was gone. He should be driving the streets or combing the neighborhood.

Leo answered on the second ring. In the background Britt could hear the sounds of people moving around and yelling to one another, and he wished he too were in the office of Winesap, where it was hectic and active with people. "Any luck?" Leo said.

"No," Britt replied. "The cops say to wait, and Camille's trying the hospitals. I'm just trying to focus on the restaurant for now."

"The hospitals? Jesus. I guess so. Did you take a walk around the building, around that neighborhood? That place has a million little alleys."

"I *looked*," Britt said. "I asked around, I looked around—he's not here." He took a breath. "Listen, I have to open as usual and I need a set of hands, Leo."

"Shouldn't we be looking for Harry?" Leo said.

"We *are* looking. But what am I supposed to do? We can't skip a weekend night, and we can't just have a closed sign up for no reason. It'll make us seem like we're circling the drain." The needs of the restaurant may have been many, but they were simple too.

"How come you never lined up any backup kitchen staff?" Leo said distractedly.

"We were keeping costs down. I guess it was a bad plan, but this is the one thing I can fix right now. Is there any way I could borrow Thea? You could expedite for one night—"

"I don't think that'll work," Leo said.

"What, you can't expedite?"

"I can do that, but I can't spare Thea," Leo said. "I'm sorry, I know you're freaking out, but she's my executive chef."

Britt said nothing, trying to control his temper. Leo's voice was as sharp as if Britt had asked him to send over the entire Winesap staff.

"I know it's a big favor," Britt said slowly. "And I'm sorry for even asking. But this is a pretty special circumstance—"

"Jesus," Leo blurted. "I said no, okay?"

Britt could hear the sound of a door closing, and he knew Leo had shooed away whoever might have been in his office and was probably now standing at the locked door. And Britt would not have brought up what he did then, except that he'd been running on adrenaline and uncertainty for several hours, he was exhausted and the night had not even begun, and he had no idea where his brother was, whether he'd been so tired or distraught that he'd fallen asleep at the wheel or failed to see a mugger until one was right behind him, or had gotten in a fight and taken the brunt. Leo had been so happy that he hadn't paid any more attention to Harry than Britt himself had.

"Leo," he said, drawing it out. Actually, he savored it, because this was the one moment in this terrible day when he felt absolute certainty. "Just because Thea tears herself away from you for one goddamn night doesn't mean she's dumping you. All you had to do was suggest someone else. This is why everyone knows about you—because you cannot lie. Not even to save your life. You never could."

The silence stretched out for nearly a minute. Britt started to wonder if Leo was going to respond at all. "I know you heard me," he said. "I can hear you breathing."

"Everyone knows what?" Leo finally said, and this was what finally set Britt off.

"About you and Thea, obviously! How dumb do you think I am? Do you think a person without a kidney condition needs to be walking past the line to get glasses of water *that* many times a night? You're not acting like a boss, you're acting like a jealous boyfriend. What d'you think I'm going to *do*? Because right now I don't even care. Another time I might have the patience to pretend that everyone from the newest busboy to the sous chef to your *brother and business partner* doesn't know about you guys. God knows I have been trying to be discreet until you came to your senses. But I don't know where our brother is. I don't know if he's okay, and I don't know who can do his job. That you have lost your fucking mind is a topic for another time."

He stopped, out of breath, and waited.

Britt had been debating how to address this situation for weeks, and now he had chosen the worst possible tactic. He didn't even care. Outside his own office door, he heard Juan arriving, Jenelle's voice heading into the kitchen to start him on prep. He had almost forgotten Leo was on the line when he finally heard him say quietly, "Hold on."

Britt listened to the sounds of the phone being set down, doors opening, faint voices, boxes being thumped to the ground.

What had Camille planned to do today, before he'd called? Sometimes you felt that loneliness on a bustling summer Saturday, as the restaurant geared up for service—or a crisis—while outside, people strolled happily around yards and shopping malls, wondering where to eat that evening, distant as a fairy tale.

Leo's voice was suddenly there again, cheerful and false and loud. "Jason says he would be happy to help you out," he said. "We can work out the pay tomorrow, but he's on his way over now."

"I'll pay him whatever he wants," Britt said.

"You can tell him in a few minutes, then," Leo said.

"I will," Britt said. "Listen—"

"I'll keep trying Harry," Leo said. "Let me know the instant you hear from him." His voice was the silky professional one he used with job candidates who had fatally failed to impress him, with vendors who would never see another order from him.

CHAPTER 19

LEO HAD REFUSED TO BORROW a chef's coat. He was not about to don that uniform without having earned it. He just put on the striped navy apron, draped two clean dry towels over the tie at the waist, and stationed himself at the pass.

He felt a little ridiculous in his suit pants, dress shirt with the sleeves rolled up, and the borrowed apron. It did not help that when told he'd be expediting, the employees reacted with surprise of an intensity that was the tiniest bit unflattering. But how could they have realized he knew how to do this? He hadn't expedited for years, not since the earliest days, when they were still gathering a stable core staff and he was sometimes required to step in. Only David, who had been at Winesap since the very beginning, was blasé. Of course, David enjoyed reminding his coworkers of his longevity, so he too might have forgotten and merely nodded sagely out of sheer habit.

On the line across from him, Thea was talking to him while she set up her station. "Apps take about ten minutes. Same with desserts. Dennis has a cold amuse all set to go, the servers just grab that themselves when they fire the app. They'll let you know if you need to delay a fire on the entrée." She glanced up as she chopped a last-minute bin of chervil and parsley. Leo winced, fearing for her fingers, as he watched the smooth motion of her chef's knife. "Otherwise, when the apps go out, fire the entrées. Cross the served items off your tickets, move 'em down to the left as you go from app to entrée."

"Got it," he said. He'd forgotten how tight the timing really was back here. To the dining guest, the progression of the meal seemed leisurely and measured, but in fact the staff dealt with increments of five and ten minutes. And of course if the expediter timed it badly, if an extra five or ten minutes passed while the guest awaited a course, that felt like an eternity.

"You have your menu?" she asked. "Your list of finishings?"

"Got it," Leo said again. His menu was carefully marked up; the correct one-word terminology for each dish had been high-lighted, the cheat sheet for how to finish each dish jotted in the margins. For the most part he simply had to wipe plates and scatter them with fresh herbs or a drizzle of fragrant olive oil, but for the vegetarian tart he would have to brulée the Gruyère-scattered top with a kitchen torch. That he was looking forward to.

His phone beeped with a text from Britt. "Nothing," he said to Thea after looking. She met his eyes, trying to discern whatever he wasn't going to say in front of the other cooks, the backwaiters slicing bread, and the staff darting back and forth with armfuls of coffee cups and folded linens. Leo looked at the message again, as if the meaning would change.

The text was completely unlike Britt's usual texts, which used full words and capitalization. Maybe Britt reserved his formal texting style for people he respected. Leo had been knocked down to those undeserving of vowels.

He looked up again at Thea and shrugged. He had not told her what Britt had said about them. He'd told her only that they needed to help out and send over a cook, interrupting her before she could volunteer. He didn't know now why he had felt so vehemently that it must not be Thea. Simply the need to have her in-house? Dread—obsolete now—that she would give them away during a postshift drink? Or just fear that she would march into Stray, be energized by its youth and verve, and never return?

It was a relief to be able to look up and see her. She made him feel calmer than he ought to, distracted him from texting his parents to say there was no word. It was maddening to hear nothing, but reiterating the silence to them would make things worse. They had phoned him twice in the past couple of hours, and he was regretting having asked them to call him and not Britt. They were coming up with more detailed scenarios than any Leo had invented—Harry pinned beneath the truck on a deserted road, wandering the streets with amnesia after a blow to the head, the victim of a brutal, casual stabbing.

"Leo," Thea said. He looked up, startled. His ticket machine and the line's were already spitting out the first tickets. "You ready? Here we go."

THE NIGHT PASSED IN A RUSH of one-word conversations and slashes of his pen across tickets, the satisfying pop of paper impaled on the spike after the ticket was complete. Leo had no time to look out into the dining room, so he had to content himself with updates from Helene as she passed by.

For the first hour he was sweating and uncertain. The kitchen jargon sounded false in his mouth, and as neatly as he wiped down plates, replenished his serving trays and dish covers, as effectively as he wielded the kitchen torch, he felt adrift, an impostor.

At first he kept a close eye on Thea. She moved with reassuring grace and ease back there, her knife work smooth, her tongs so deftly handled they barely made a sound when clamping around a sizzling metal dish. Watching her, though, Leo began to worry. Her flawless confidence, her immersion in the job—she was irreplaceable. And maybe she knew this. She must. Why would such a practical, professional chef risk herself with him? When Leo asked himself why he had begun this affair, as thoroughly ill-advised as it was, it was easy to answer: there had been something so freeing in Britt's absence and Leo's own reemergence downstairs, something so intimate and partnered in his resulting work with Thea, that it seemed not at all transgressive. This was what he'd been unable to say to Britt, who clearly thought he was simply having a midlife crisis. But he wasn't. He wasn't engaging in some sad, boozy waitress-boffing. No, there had come a moment with Thea, just before the first time he gave in and kissed her, when Leo had felt a sensation of fearsome intensity, as if his head had breached a wave he hadn't known he lay beneath and the air above it was nearly too pure and densely oxygenated to bear.

But what did Thea feel? Watching her work, Leo knew her both better and yet less than he ever had. He might be a fool—he could accept that—but what could she be thinking? Maybe she was willing to be with him because she already knew she was leaving and therefore risked little. Maybe she was more reckless than he had ever suspected. It was a disloyal thought, to punish her for what he'd wanted so badly, but for a long time as they worked across from one another, he could not entirely shut it down. He watched her slice a duck breast on a neat, even bias and expertly slip the flat of her knife beneath the meat to plate the slices, watched her gauge a meat temp with a touch of her fingertip, and wondered who she really was.

But soon, to his tremendous relief, he had no time to worry about any of this, nor to keep checking his phone or think too hard about where Harry might be. There was no time to wonder what Thea truly felt for him or for her job or whether he sounded like a poseur calling out the orders coming down the road or firing the next batch of entrées. He was calmed by the precision of the plates being handed to him over the pass, by the vibrant greens and scarlets of Dennis's Edenic salads and his patchwork-quilt terrines, by Suzanne's head-on shrimp gazing tenderly out from their fragrant tomato-based graves, and by Thea's textbook meat temps and tight, elegantly centered plating. The rhythm of the service built and built until the seven-thirty rush began, and then the velocity peaked and just kept barreling forward, steadily frantic, for the next two hours.

During those hours Leo felt nothing, no hunger or thirst, no uncertainty over Harry's well-being or Britt's anger at him or Thea's unknown and unknowable depths, no fears for the next day or even the end of the night. His consciousness was focused entirely on the next few steps, on perfecting what was imperfect, on ticking off each plate and dispatching orders with gratifying efficiency to the endless rotation of backwaiters and servers who appeared instinctively just as he needed them. He was part of the machine; around him the gears turned smoothly and cleanly; together they rolled right over obstacles and buffed away the jagged edges, and the hours rocketed forward, with mercifully little time to think.

ONCE BRITT HAD TOLD THE LIE, he had to stay with it. He didn't lie to women, preferring the simple clarity of frankness to nicer explanations that only dragged things out. Nor did he did lie to his employees—he asked a lot of them, and honesty seemed a basic courtesy in return, so basic it had never occurred to him until now to articulate his position on it at all. And now, as he walked away from a group of servers who thought that Harry had something that sounded like food poisoning, he knew he was a liar, not simply someone who wisely kept his mouth shut when the need arose. Another problem Harry was responsible for.

Britt had an image of himself in a day or two, after Harry had been found somewhere, bloody and dying, when he would regret all he'd blamed on his brother when he should have been saving him with the force of his mind. The loop was impossible to stop; when anger was at the surface he thought he might regret it, when his fear was foremost he could only hope he would get a chance to be merely angry again, and then the switch began again.

Camille was back in the kitchen, wearing a baseball cap, comfortable shoes, and a long-sleeved, snug cotton shirt. Of course she knew to protect her arms and pamper her feet, to secure her hair and avoid any loose fabric—she'd worked in restaurants years ago. Hector and Jenelle had given her bins of shallots and carrots and greens to rinse and peel, and each time Britt went back to the kitchen he saw she was working on something a little more involved. Just before staff meal, she'd been beheading squid with Jenelle's ten-inch knife and peeling off the transparent purple skins. As he watched, she drew the soft yellow innards from the sac and dropped them in a trash bowl, then cut the tentacles from the other end.

She seemed to be doing fine, but then her knife stopped moving. She stared down at the blade beside her fingers, her face a blank. She remained still for so long that Britt thought she'd cut herself and was in shock.

She startled when he touched her, looking up into his face before she knew who it was, and for an instant her expression was naked and empty, her eyes dark with worry, and then she saw it was Britt. Her face transformed into a perfect facsimile of her usual arch, alert self, a metamorphosis of such will that he didn't dare ask her about what he'd seen a moment before.

AT STAFF MEAL HE HAD INTRODUCED her and Jason to the rest of the crew, repeated the feeble story about Harry being indisposed, and then had to hope his brother wouldn't show up and prove him wrong.

The waitstaff was far less interested in Harry's absence than they were in Camille's appearance on the floor. Jenelle, Jason, and Hector were watching Britt closely—he could feel their eyes on him the entire night—but the servers merely shrugged and assumed that kitchen changes were typical, not caring who handed them their food as long as someone did, and for once Britt was profoundly grateful for their attitude.

They got through it. Jason's station started off slowly as he tried to remember the components of each dish, and he and Jenelle had to try to hear each other under the din without making it obvious to the guests that Jason was new. But after a spate of delays and questions, he managed to find a groove. If every dish didn't look exactly as Britt would like, the dishes were plated, they were at the right temp, they were going out to tables and not coming back. Once or twice Jason even made an accidental improvement, adding chorizo instead of arugula to the socca and baccalà, upping the basil and chile in the tuna conserve. The socca became richer and heavier than Harry had intended, the unctuous, oily flakes of fish turned herbal and brisk with heat, but the guests were exclaiming over both.

Camille was a glorified food runner-slash-busser-slash-hostess. She'd easily memorized the table numbers and seat positions, knew never to waste a trip out of the kitchen or the dining room by not carrying something with her, and never stopped clearing, watering, and refilling. Now and then he caught a glimpse of her, the dangle of a glittering earring as she reached for a plate, the swivel of her hips as she moved between waitstaff and tables, the sheer egolessness with which she'd taken on the most menial tasks in the place, and felt a surge of gratitude for her. Her efficiency calmed him; he found it reassuring that she had changed her clothes after staff meal and now looked like the woman he saw each day. She had twisted her hair as she always did, threaded earrings through her earlobes as she always did, and somehow these rituals suggested that all was well.

He was thinking about this when suddenly a gentle, thorough wash of nostalgia overtook him, like a wave rolling up behind his knees. He had a vivid déjà vu of childhood, of Sundays in his parents' kitchen at the weathered wooden table, of his brothers hollering and punching one another in the arm. He was so struck by the intensity of it, the calm of such a respite in the night's tension, that he very nearly stopped short right there on the floor, first to enjoy the memory and then to figure out its source.

Something—a scent, he realized—was evoking the most comforting sense of sun through windows and the pleasant blend of hunger and an abundance of food, of maple syrup and something golden and toasting, an empty day stretching before him in which he and Leo could play a game of basketball, sneak a cigarette over by the city baseball diamonds.

He was approaching the server station as he snapped out of the reverie, and as he did he saw Josh glance furtively over his shoulder, see him, and whip back around. Two of the other servers were clustered beside him, and all three turned around and smiled guilelessly in Britt's direction. Then they darted back out to their tables.

Britt strolled over to the station, refusing to let it show that he was investigating anything—not because of the servers but because of the guests, who could see straight into the station if they happened to look. When he got there, he realized what had caused that olfactory memory: on the coffee-cup warmer—correction: the *griddle*—the cups had been shoved to one side and three silver-dollar-sized pancakes were bubbling. A cream pitcher of batter and a small spatula—a plastic spatula, he noticed; were they actually being careful not to scratch the griddle with a metal spatula from the kitchen?—sat innocently next to the folded napkins. Behind the napkins was a bread plate bearing a pancake with a single bite taken out of it. His brother was missing, his other brother had lost his reason, his girlfriend was working like a dog, and all these little fuckers could think to do was make pancakes on the coffee griddle.

He stayed very calm. He unplugged the griddle, set the plate and its pancake, the spatula, and the pitcher of batter on the cooking surface, and carefully wound the griddle's cord into a neat loop. Then he carried it all back to the kitchen, the warmth of the metal seeping through the napkin to his fingertips. Hector looked up, smiling when he saw the whole setup and then losing the smile when he saw Britt's face. Britt gave him a dignified nod and kept going, past Hector to the back door that opened onto the alley, into which he stepped, looking both ways to see that no one was nearby, and hurled the entire mess—pan, cups, dish, utensils, and plate—against the brick wall.

WHEN THE LAST TABLES DEPARTED, the servers turned up the stereo as they finished cleaning the dining room. The door to the kitchen got propped open so that the room filled with the sounds of the dishwasher thrumming and the silver clinking, waiters laughing as they polished glasses and flatware. Camille reappeared periodically with a bus tub of folded napkins or polished silver and then strode back into the kitchen once more.

Britt asked Jason for his cell-phone number. He'd told himself at the beginning of the night that by this time he'd know, he'd have heard from Harry, from the police, from someone, but he'd heard nothing. They would need a hand tomorrow.

When it was over he left his car and Camille drove him home. He'd realized that he was too sapped to drive. At his apartment they stood in the kitchen and shared a beer, then peeled off their sweaty clothes and got beneath the shower. There was nothing sexy about it—they were both sore and spent from emotional tension and physical labor. Under the stream of the water their bodies seemed slick and pale.

The pleasure of being cool and dry in the soft sheets of the bed was almost unbearable. They lay side by side, hands clasped. "I don't know how I can sleep," said Britt into the darkness.

"He's fine," she said firmly. "He's probably on his way back by now." They let this fiction settle between them like a soap bubble while they waited for sleep.

CHAPTER 20

Leo met britt at winesap the next morning. The empty restaurant seemed cool and forbidding, all the energy of the previous night long gone.

Leo wished that Thea hadn't had Iris last night. He'd had no choice but to include her in the communal farewell he'd bestowed on everyone. When Leo had left she'd been sitting at the bar, a beer before her, laughing at something Kelly had said. She'd looked loose and happy, her cheeks and eyes glowing. He'd been jealous of his employees, of everyone who got to enjoy this version of Thea when he had to leave. None of them saw her this way with any frequency, not even Leo.

His parents had already called that morning, his father focusing on Leo's failure to keep Harry out of the restaurant business.

"I mean, it's ridiculous," his father said. "The hours, the failure rate. You all went to college! For what, so you could serve people and worry about the quality of . . . of"—he spluttered—"carrots?"

Leo couldn't think of a thing to say. That his father might have harbored this feeling toward his career—toward the restaurant he'd named for a childhood memory!—had never occurred to him.

Britt was waiting for him in the dining room. They had both brought coffee and white paper bags, so each shrugged and set to work on the first of two coffees and the first of two pastries. Leo couldn't tell if Britt's offering meant anything at all, but either way they seemed to cancel each other out.

"Jason did a great job," Britt said eventually, wiping his mouth with a napkin. "Which we knew he would, of course. Thank you, Leo."

Leo nodded. "No problem. Thank him."

"I did. I'll come up with something else for him. A bonus, something." Britt rubbed his face and pushed his hair back over his skull. He looked tired and papery around the eyes. "Anyway. How'd you work things over here?"

"Thea took Jason's station and I expedited."

Britt said, "You did, huh? Been a long time. How did it feel?"

Leo smiled. "I felt like a total fraud for the first hour. But I have to say that after that it felt good. Too busy to worry." He stopped smiling. "I was afraid he wasn't ready. But I thought that would mean, I don't know—staff problems, low numbers. A problem menu."

"Not this," Britt said, and Leo had to agree.

"Britt," he said. "You ever get the feeling that Dad's disappointed we went into this business?"

Britt glanced up from his phone. "Sure," he said. "You think he was happy when I said I was leaving a nice stable white-collar job to work at a restaurant?" He laughed. "Of course, when Harry did the same thing it was a sign of fearlessness. I can't control what he thinks. Why?"

That was Britt: reasoned, brisk, a little chilly but also enviably serene.

"I just never thought of it before," Leo said. "He's upset that we let Harry get in over his head."

Britt's composure cracked, just for a moment, showing only in the vehemence with which he crumpled an empty coffee cup.

After a moment Britt said calmly, "I haven't expedited since you made me learn back when we first opened. If we could fit an expediter in, I might try it again, just to show the kids I know how." He tipped his chair back precariously and rolled his neck.

"We miss out, just watching," said Leo, grateful to discuss business again. "It felt really good to be in the mix. Thea had a blast on the line. She's really kind of made for that." Britt hadn't changed posture, but now he was eyeing Leo, his grayish-green eyes appraising.

Britt returned the front legs of his chair to the floor with a decisive thud. "You know what the first thing you said to me about this business was?"

"Yeah," Leo said.

"You told me to stay away from the staff."

"At the time I was thinking more not to go after the waitresses."

"This is worse," Britt said wearily. "Not to be crass, but there're a lot of waitresses out there. I don't know of anybody else of Thea's caliber in this area. What do we do if you blow this? Recruit someone from Philadelphia or Pittsburgh to come to Linden? That's not happening. You know of anybody already here who might grow to fit her shoes? Me neither. And we're not even talking about labor laws. She could sue the shit out of us."

Leo ventured, "She's not going to sue us."

"No one ever starts off bad, Leo. Things go bad when you don't expect them to."

"Oh, well, thanks for that."

"I'm sorry, I thought I had to state the obvious now. You seem to need it."

"So what are you hoping to achieve?" Leo said. "You think if you come here and shame me, I'll just dump her?"

"Would you?" Britt said, watching him cannily.

"Not a chance," Leo said.

Britt nodded. "Then I guess there isn't any more to say. We have bigger things to worry about."

Leo took a drink of his coffee. "Do you think he'd go see any of his old school friends, or anything like that?"

"I thought maybe he'd go see Amanda," Britt said. "He could have driven to New York in a couple of hours. Or maybe he went camping."

"Maybe he's in California, trying to win back Shelley."

Britt paused. "Actually, that's not insane."

Leo watched him dial his phone and asked, "You have Shelley's number in your phone?"

"Don't ask," said Britt. "She was briefly our consultant."

It was early in California, only seven, but Britt didn't care, and when Shelley answered her phone, she sounded as if she'd been up for hours anyway.

"Shelley!" he said. "It's Britt."

"Hello, Britt," she said. "To what do I owe the pleasure?"

"I'm looking for Harry. You haven't by any chance talked to him, have you?"

"No," she said. "What's going on?"

"He disappeared yesterday," Britt said, and it sounded both melodramatic and not dramatic enough. He cleared his throat. "I got to the restaurant, and I think he'd just left in the middle of his prep work. I haven't heard anything from him."

"How has he been?" she asked. "Has he seemed tense? Tenser than usual, I mean."

"Yes," he said. "Why? Do you know something?"

"I know the same things you know—how he gets in that vortex he can't get out of. Maybe his dosage is off."

"What dosage?" Britt said. Leo looked up.

"The milligrams, you mean? I can't recall—I never take prescription drugs."

"Dosage of what? What's he taking?"

"It was an antidepressant, last I checked. But it's been a while—for all I know he's taking something else now. Or maybe he stopped altogether? That could be the problem. He doesn't tell me these things. But then, I guess he doesn't tell you either."

LEO LOCKED UP AFTER THEM and then stood in the Winesap parking lot, wondering what to do. He didn't want to see his parents worried about their investment, or about the son whose exploits always seemed to have delighted them. Until Harry had come back and opened Stray, Leo had felt much the same. Perhaps the family had always operated with the tacit belief that as long as the older two remained stable and successful, Harry was free to take any risk he liked. They could feel pleased about their real estate and businesses and vicariously enjoy and be worried by Harry's deliberate poverty, his exuberant itinerancy. Somehow it had all balanced out.

He wondered if Thea was home and if Iris was with her. Maybe Bryan had taken her to church. Did he go to church? Leo didn't even know if Thea did. He assumed not; he had never heard her express an ounce of religious feeling, but who knew? Who knew what his girlfriend did on Sunday mornings when he was not allowed to be with her? Maybe she and Iris had some Sunday morning ritual—waffles, a walk in the park—so dear that she told no one about it, ever. Leo despaired of ever having such a ritual with Thea himself. Any ritual at all, except sneaking out doors at separate times.

It was a bad idea, of course, but he began to drive in the direction of her house. He understood now that it was crucial for him to see her and confirm whatever he was trying to confirm. That he could touch her, that she did indeed look at him differently outside the restaurant, that this was not all some desperate mirage he'd concocted out of loneliness or anger.

When he reached her house, he turned off the ignition and sat in the heating car for a long moment, peering at the windows to see if she was home. Her garage door was shut, so no help there. As he got out of his car, he listened for the sound of Iris's voice in the backyard. He looked up and down the street like a criminal, and finally went up the walk.

At the last moment he decided to call instead, believing that phoning her from her front porch was somehow less of a breach of their code of conduct than ringing the doorbell. When she answered, he couldn't bring himself to lead with the fact that they'd been outed. Instead he stood there on her porch, saying that no one had heard from Harry yet.

"I think you'll have to cook again tonight," he said.

"We can't ask this of Jason for much longer. Whatever happens, I want to keep him in-house. I'm afraid if he gets all comfy there we'll lose him altogether."

Leo realized that he could hear her moving on the other side of the door, her footsteps and the echo of her voice. His being out here was too creepy to continue. When she began to speak again, he interrupted her. "Thea—I'm here. I'm outside."

"You're what?"

He sighed, mortified. "I'm on your porch. I wanted to call before I rang in case Iris is there and you want me to go away."

"She's at Bryan's," Thea said. The door swung open, and she stood there, barefoot, in cutoff jeans and a white tank top, magenta bra straps showing. She looked baffled. "Get inside."

He followed her in. The air smelled of fruit and sugar. "Baking?"

"Muffins. Iris likes them. I usually send a few home with Bryan."

This was worse than he'd imagined: she still baked for her ex-husband; she saw him throughout the week and planned the care of their daughter with him; she probably kissed him hello and good-bye and wondered why they'd ever split when they shared such commonalities as offspring and fruit-laden baked goods.

"Are you close with him, with Bryan?"

"No. I get the feeling Iris likes me to cook for him in some little way, so I do. He cleans the gutters in the fall for the same reason, I'm pretty sure, but we don't discuss it."

"Oh." He sat down on the bench at her kitchen table, where two platters of blueberry muffins, sparkling with sugar, sat cooling in the center. Next to them was a bowl of bananas and nectarines. Thea placed a glass of water before him and sat beside him, facing him. She reached for his hand and asked, "Why are you here, Leo?"

"I have something to tell you," he said, and her hand froze over his. Her mouth went white.

"Okay," she said slowly.

"I'm sorry—this must be unnerving. I'm having a hard time saying it, I guess."

"They're going to be here soon," Thea said, "and if you have something to say to me, I'd prefer to hear it alone."

Leo looked at her. Her lips and the tip of her nose were bleached of color. "You think I'm here to end this," he said. She didn't answer. He shook his head and admitted, "I'm not. I'm definitely not. But Britt knows."

Thea exhaled; her spine seemed to droop. After a moment she said, "Britt's not dumb."

"No, but he also said everyone knows. 'From the newest busboy to the sous chef' were his exact words, I believe."

Thea looked away. Two spots of color bled into the apples of her cheeks; a flush crept up her chest.

"I know you're embarrassed," he said. "I don't know what I thought would happen. This business is like a . . . a beehive. Or an anthill. They all know everything without even saying it aloud, I swear to God."

"I'm not embarrassed," Thea said.

Leo continued. "I know why I did this, but why you? What do you get out of this? Even the ones who would blame me can't really blame me."

"'What the hell was I thinking'—is that it?" she said.

Leo looked at her. "Well, yeah. It's not too late if you regret this. No one really *knows*, they just think they know. It would all go away if you want it to. They'd think they were wrong, that's all."

"Is that what you want?" Thea asked. "Shall we hit the reset button and forget it ever happened?"

"It's not at all what I want," Leo said. "I just can't figure out why you wouldn't."

Thea picked up his hand and looked it over, as if she were examining an item before buying. She didn't look up at him for a long time. In the silence of the kitchen he began to fear that her face was taking on the last intimate expression he would see from her, one of chagrin and farewell. He let himself hope that her eyes might be filling with tears—this might be the best that he could hope for, a regretful break.

But when she finally did look up again, her face was composed.

"I would offer you a blueberry muffin," she said, "but they're kind of ex-husband muffins."

Leo's throat was tight. He took a sip of water, coughed slightly, and finally managed, "Do you not want to share?"

"I don't, actually," Thea said. "Not those, not with you. I don't know—I've given these to him too many times, as in I don't take him back, but I give him muffins. I can't give him love anymore, but I can give him breakfast. I don't want to give you the same thing, is my point. I want to give you the opposite. What can I make that says the opposite, Leo? You tell me."

"You don't have to make me anything," Leo said. "Just give me saltines. Ritz crackers."

"Is that so?"

He cupped her face in his hands, tentatively, because she looked slightly angry, even if her eyes seemed tender. Her jaw was so narrow, he was thinking, its angles swept so steeply up from the point of her chin. He had seen the planes of this jawline in profile for years; sometimes he was still taken aback by the privilege of looking at Thea head-on, at a range so intimate that he knew the slightly uneven peaks of her lips, the faint freckles that dusted her nose.

To his relief, she let him kiss her. It wasn't until he felt her—her warm mouth, her satiny neck, the rough abundance of her curls where they tended to knot at the base of her skull—that he realized he had talked himself out of expecting to touch her like this ever again.

"You don't need some kind of reassurance?" Thea said. Her hand came to rest on his neck, her fingers curved lightly over his earlobe. She smiled very faintly. "Something a little nicer than a basket of divorce muffins?"

"Give me unpopped popcorn," he said, his voice a croak. "Matzo meal."

"You're not a well man, Leo."

"Dry rice," said Leo, still trying for lightness, for she seemed to be trying too, but neither of them quite achieved it. Their voices were tinged with shakiness and bravado. Leo tried not to sound as naked as he felt. "A bag of flour," he said finally. "Any old flour in the world."

CHAPTER 21

T HE CREW AT STRAY MANAGED to do it all again that night, at slightly slower velocity. Chastened, the servers were deferential to Britt and extra-charming to the customers; the coffee was served in room-temperature cups. Jason and Jenelle worked smoothly together, and Camille came in for the busiest hours and departed again when it slowed. No one dared to ask about Harry.

The night was nearly done, with only one last table finishing a shared portion of gelato, when Britt's cell phone rang. He froze—he was as frightened now of answering the phone as he was of its silence.

"Yes?" He walked swiftly back toward the office, ready to slip behind the door if it was Harry.

"Britt?" It was a woman's voice, one he vaguely recognized, and Britt pulled the phone away from his ear to look at the ID and frowned in confusion. "Oh, good, it's you. This is Barbara Makaski. I'm sorry to call you so late, but I thought you'd want to know. I seem to have your brother Harry here."

HOT SPRINGS HAD EMPTIED OUT when Britt arrived, with only two cars left in the lot, which he assumed belonged to Barbara and maybe another staff member. Harry's red truck was parked across two spaces.

The front door was unlocked, but the music had been silenced and the dining room broken down for the evening: flowers gone to the cooler, candles doused, tables reset. Britt poked his head into the bar.

Barbara Makaski was sitting on one of the barstools, her posture regal, reading a copy of *Food Arts*. The light cast coppery threads in her hair, which was as rich a magenta as ever. She turned with a start at Britt's voice, then laid a hand on her chest and flapped the other in his direction. "So silly to be startled," she said. "I knew you were coming."

"No, it's late," he said. "Thank you for calling."

She made a rueful face. "Well. It seemed the only real option. You'll see." Barbara got off her stool and brushed a few nonexistent crumbs from her black dress. "Would you like something to drink? No, no, of course not. Well. Come on back."

Britt followed her past the bar and toward the back of the restaurant. He was calculating how long it had been since he and Leo had been here for dessert—nine months, give or take, in which he'd taken on a new relationship, a new restaurant that was already drowning one of its owners. Not a slow rate of change for less than a year.

They passed the windowed kitchen door, the restrooms, a server station, and finally came to the office door. Britt hesitated, suddenly hoping to stall. "Donnie here tonight?" he asked.

Barbara observed him, her head to one side as if she weren't sure he was serious. Her eyes were the caramel brown of a lynx or a fox, and her teeth were frighteningly white in her tanned face. In her earlobes were two flat onyx discs that, if you looked closely, were revealed to have faces carved into them. "Donnie and I split up," she said. "I figured everyone knew by now. But perhaps you're being polite."

"I don't think I did know," Britt said.

"But you may have heard a rumor or two. It's okay. We all know how this business loves to gossip." She paused, and Britt wondered if she had heard about Leo and Thea. He waited, not sure how he'd deflect it if she had, but then she said, "We're still working out the details, but the gist of it is that Donnie's off doing . . . something else now. The restaurant stays with me." She said this as if it were a child, Britt noted, but he understood.

"I'm sorry, Barbara," he said, and was taken aback at how sincerely he meant it. He had never really liked Donnie, or even Barbara for that matter, but right then it didn't matter. A restaurant was a terribly public place to undergo a dissolution, be it of a partnership, a marriage, or both. It made you wish you were in some faceless corporate environment where no one cared whether you had limbs, much less a spouse.

"Thank you," she said with dignity. "I'm choosing to regard this as one bad year. When it's done, it's done. What Donnie will do, I can't begin to guess." With that, she opened the office door.

His brother was stretched out on a brown leather couch, feet dangling over the edge. His arm was draped over his glasses. His chest rose and fell, and his mouth hung slightly open. He was wearing an old T-shirt and jeans, which Britt was relieved to see did not bear evidence of some traumatic incident, no rips or mud or blood. He looked extremely long and skinny, limp as a shot egret.

"He came in around ten," Barbara said, "and ordered a very odd dinner and a bottle of white wine, though he didn't drink more than half a glass. At first I just thought he was doing a little research, but the server let me know he didn't seem well. She didn't realize who he was."

Britt nodded, appreciating the unstated assurance that at least one person might not know to publicize this, though the rest of the staff had probably told her by now anyway. Mack's was probably already abuzz with it.

"Anyway, I asked him if he'd like to come talk to me in the

office, just industry chatter, but he looked so exhausted that I suggested he might like to lie down. I must say he seemed more than willing."

"What did he order?" Britt said.

"I'm sorry?"

"You said it was an odd dinner."

"Oh, yes. He ordered two molten chocolate cakes and the sardines. He asked for the cakes first, though, and that was after he called the server back three times to change his order."

"Ah."

"Yes." Barbara glanced at Harry, seemed to reassure herself that he had done nothing to ruin her office, and withdrew discreetly to her seat at the bar.

Britt turned back to Harry, who still appeared to be asleep. He wasn't entirely sure what he wanted to do now. It was tempting to see if Barbara could keep him overnight, but of course this wasn't an option. He would have to wake Harry up and drag him home, install him on the couch. He realized that he didn't even trust Harry not to bolt as soon as he awoke, but at the same time, what was Britt going to do? Lock the doors from the outside, tether him by an ankle? He thought wearily that Harry would do whatever he was going to do, and he himself might have to proceed without him.

He had feared that seeing Harry in person would enrage him, the way sometimes people's physical presence—their large-pored noses, their swampy chewing sounds and braying laughter—could grate unbearably. But Britt felt only slightly more alive than his unconscious brother appeared. Harry seemed defeated and emptied out. Britt felt his own energy drain from him, as if once he had his brother safely in his sights his adrenaline could finally depart, leaving his system with only the faint memory of a staff dinner and a half glass of water. He was teetering and fragile, made of thinned blood and hollowed bones. He felt a frustrating mix of tenderness, relief, exhaustion, and stymied anger.

Britt pulled the desk chair beside the couch and dropped into it with a sigh.

He reached over and lifted Harry's arm from where it lay across his glasses and set it on his belly. Harry's nose bore a deep crimson dent from where his arm had pressed on the glasses. His brow furrowed and his eyes began to open. When he saw Britt, he blinked furiously. His eyes filled briefly with tears and then squeezed shut for a long moment. Britt waited silently until Harry's eyes opened again.

"It's me," Britt said. "Barbara called."

Harry nodded, raising a fist in front of his mouth to cough. He removed his glasses and wiped them on his shirt, swiped his knuckles across his eyes. He looked around the room, getting his bearings. "I figured she would," he said finally.

"You want to sleep at my place? I'll drive you back if you're not going to duck out before I get up."

Harry nodded and heaved himself into a sitting position. "You know Donnie's gone?" he said.

Britt stood up and returned the chair to the desk. "I know. You want to help me out and just not talk about that for now? I'm pretty tired, Harry."

"I know. I know that's my fault."

Britt shrugged. No point in pretending otherwise. "Come on. You can text Leo and Mom and Dad from the car, so they know you're alive."

Harry nodded, shamefaced. They headed back to the bar, where Barbara was turning off the lights.

"Let us walk you to your car," Britt said. "It's late."

Barbara began to protest, but she seemed to do so out of habit and then consented to let them accompany her into the parking lot. Britt suspected she was so accustomed to walking out beside Donnie that this was one of the little ways in which she was being reminded of that absence.

The night air was warm and humid. Britt wondered what had been on the menu at Winesap that night. Cold shrimp, poached chicken, blanched snap peas?

Barbara beeped the locks on an SUV and opened the door. "Thank you," she said formally.

"Thank you," they replied in unison.

"I'm sorry to have been in here in this condition," Harry added, but she shook her head.

"I've seen worse," she said, and closed the door behind her.

They stood back and watched her car reverse and take a left out of the driveway. Britt wasn't looking at Harry when his brother said, "I wanted to get in touch with you. I was just too embarrassed to do it myself."

CHAPTER 22

B
RITT HAD ALWAYS BEEN ENERGIZED by the relentless forward motion of a restaurant, but as Harry's disappearance was buried beneath the following week's rhythm of preps, seatings, and closings, he found himself hoping the story would not die. When Harry returned to Stray the day after Britt picked him up from Hot Springs, he embroidered the illness story with a few vivid details of the sort that shut down further inquiry, and to Britt's astonishment no one pressed. He barely restrained himself from dropping sarcastic comments at staff meal, and often peered around at the others' faces, seeking a clear hint of doubt or discord, anything to suggest that it was not only him who felt as if Harry had gotten the satisfaction of flaming out in the most spectacular way possible without any of the fallout.

He had learned the details the morning after he retrieved his brother: Harry had driven into Pennsylvania Dutch country with no more plan than satisfying a craving for pie, which he had accomplished by purchasing two and picking at them with his hands and a penknife, leaving his front seat littered with pastry and jewels of baked fruit. He hadn't slept at all; he'd simply driven around, or stopped at a gas station and stared out the windshield for a while before starting up once again. He'd had the notion to tour Hershey or Kellogg's but ended up turning back before he reached either. Hungry, exhausted, he saw Hot Springs as he returned to town, wanting something familiar. Time, he said, had seemed to stretch and leap at once, and he'd lost most of it trying to follow each potential decision toward its eventual conclusion. None of it really made sense to Britt, but it was clear that this was not unfamiliar to Harry.

"Didn't you want to call me?" Britt had asked, imagining his brother tooling around tourist areas and chatting up Amish girls. "Or just say *something* to let us know you were okay?"

Harry had looked him in the eye. "I wasn't okay," he said, and Britt colored, ashamed of himself.

Now Harry finally told Britt about the times he'd needed treatment in college and on the island, but he also seemed to feel that Britt should understand how distant and implausible those events had seemed as soon as they were over, just as this one now did. He seemed genuinely aghast that he had endangered his own business and his brother's by failing to admit or address his problems. Britt was left to wonder what else he could want from him.

Leo was so delighted to find Harry unharmed and to have his staff back in their places that he barely bothered to commiserate. (Also Harry had known about Leo and Thea and had said nothing, which infuriated Britt all the more because he had done the same thing.) Their parents were so relieved to see Harry that they might have forgotten that either restaurant even existed. And Camille, who, after Leo, should have been the one with enough restaurant experience to grasp fully just how irresponsibly Harry had behaved, had been more concerned about doctors and treatment plans. She brushed aside Britt's comments about the depth of Harry's failures with a cheerful opacity that managed to silence, soothe, and admonish him all at the same time.

The first Saturday after Harry returned, she appeared at the end of the evening to have a drink. Britt allowed himself a glancing touch of her shoulder blades as he kissed her hello, anticipating cool silkiness, but, more provocatively, her skin was warm and humid from the heat outside.

"So," she asked Harry, "how're you feeling?" She was perched on a barstool, a glass of rosé before her. Her hair was pulled into some complicated, fountainy knot at the back of her head, and she wore flat sandals and a precarious pale green dress, the spaghetti straps of which kept falling off each shoulder.

"My hair hurts," Harry said. Her greeting to him had been a hug followed by an affectionate but vigorous tug at his hair. Somehow, with these gestures Camille conveyed more frustrated angst than anger. Every time Britt tried to clear the air with a joke, he sounded venomous.

"Yeah yeah yeah," she said. She leaned across the bar, glancing to be sure no one was close enough to hear them. "You're taking care of yourself?"

"Yup," said Harry. "I'm doing what every successful chef does, eating regular meals and spending ten minutes every morning and night writing in my fear journal."

She laughed, looking toward Britt, who nodded. "Really?" she said.

"Really," Harry said. "It's supposed to be better if I have a specific place to address anxieties. Other than, say, Amish country."

Camille laughed, but Britt did not. Harry had been back a week and already his breakdown had become a comic set piece.

Britt excused himself to check on the backwaiters' sidework and returned to find two of the servers perched beside Camille at the bar, chatting with her and Harry while a room full of dirty tables languished behind them.

"So where'd you get the batter?" Camille was asking them, but before the servers could answer they saw Britt and bustled off to clear the dining room.

"I'm still trying to figure that out. Jenelle couldn't have made it," Harry replied once the servers were gone. "Not out here." He was leaning back against the counter with a seltzer.

Britt glanced toward the front of the restaurant, where the servers were stacking dinner plates. "Josh brought it from home," he said, keeping his voice low. This made the other two burst out laughing. "It's not *funny*. What would you think if you'd been the guests that night, paying a hundred bucks to watch a new chef scramble while the waitstaff acts like teenagers?"

"Did anyone notice?" Camille said, peering toward the server station.

"I hope not. They only managed a few pancakes." Infuriatingly, this made Harry start to laugh again. As the servers passed them carrying bus tubs filled with dishes, all three of them went silent. Britt could tell his brother and Camille were fighting smiles, gazing downward in collusion, as if not only the pancakes but Harry's disappearance were a charming prank.

When the servers were in the back, Britt said to Harry, "So now you're all relaxed?"

Harry paused, and then seemed to decide to ignore the bitter note in Britt's voice. "Only with your staff," he said, finishing the last of his seltzer. "I'd already have fired one of them."

"That seems premature," Camille noted. "For all you know they were excellent pancakes."

Harry smiled but said to Britt, "I support whatever you need to do to get them back in line. But I wouldn't be surprised if no one noticed."

"No, you could smell them," Britt said. "I had an olfactory flashback."

"I love pancakes," Camille said. "They smell just like childhood."

Harry snickered. "Just like crepes after dressage practice."

Camille and Harry had an air of comfortable, intimate enclosure that struck Britt as more worrisome than a sexual spark. It wasn't that Camille was attracted to his brother, he realized. It was worse. Somehow Britt had ended up being the one asking her for help in the restaurant, leaning on her for support in the madness of its early life. Harry had made him into the needy boyfriend. Now

Harry was the entertaining one. It wasn't too much to ask that his brother seem sincerely contrite instead of mining his behavior for laughs. Britt wanted Harry abject; he wanted him mortified. He wanted some fucking shame.

"I could have told them not to bother with pancakes," Harry was saying. "Fun is roadside pie."

Harry took a long, satisfied drink of his water, as if he needed some reward beyond Camille's cascade of laughter—which to Britt sounded so loud and showy, so prodding, as if it were Britt who needed a cue to behave reasonably. Britt listened to the sound of the liquid sloshing around Harry's greedy mouth, stared at the lurch of his knobby Adam's apple.

"It's all just funny now," Britt said, "is that the idea?" Camille and Harry turned toward him, their expressions tentatively pleased to hear him joining in the conversation, until they realized what he'd said and their faces went still. He was gripping a water glass so hard he had to force himself to set it down carefully on the bar; the temptation was to ram it down, just to feel the tremor run up his arm.

Neither of them spoke, so Britt continued. "Everything's happy and no one ever acted like a crazy person." His voice came out wobbly, which only enraged him more—he didn't want anyone mistaking this for some crying jag of relief at having his brother home. No, that tremor was the vibration of his pulse, the heart that was suddenly an uncontrollable motor inside him.

"It was just a dumb joke," said Camille. She reached a hand to him, and he stepped back in order to prevent himself from knocking it away.

"I'm not making light of it," Harry said. "I just want you to relax."

"*Bullshit*," Britt spat, and Harry started. "The staff sees you laughing and they know you don't care."

For a moment, seeing Harry's face bleached of its merriment

felt satisfying and right. It felt like something Britt needed, like something he was owed. He saw Camille look around the room, which was empty of guests though the staff was clustered up at the front, noisily rearranging furniture and clearing tables.

He tried to keep his voice low, but he was leaning across the bar toward Harry, jabbing a finger into the zinc bar top. "You took your little holiday, your fucking little walkabout, and no one even knew if you were dead or alive, but the moment you get back it's all perfect, it never happened, everyone's just so glad to see your little *face*. And that is the *best* part. That's my favorite part of all. You've arranged it so that all you have to do is take care of *yourself* to make it all better."

Camille stood up, but Britt ignored her. He shoved his phone and car keys into his pockets. Let her enjoy Harry's company now that it was so laid-back.

"So now your big progress is to remember to . . . to what? To have feelings? To eat when you're hungry and sleep when you're tired? And this is supposed to be enough for me to trust you?"

Harry hadn't moved throughout the whole diatribe; he stood there and absorbed it. As Britt left the restaurant, he was already losing the fierce pleasure of his righteousness. However much Harry deserved it—and he did, Britt reminded himself, he did—his brother had still looked as stunned as if Britt had smiled at him before throwing a punch.

HE DROVE TO HIS OWN HOUSE instead of Camille's but wasn't surprised to see her car pull in a few minutes after his. She didn't come in, though she had a key, but knocked.

She followed him back to the kitchen and sat down beside him at the table.

He took a long drink of beer. "Sorry about that."

She shook her head and laid one hand on the back of his neck, a gesture he'd grown used to, and had looked forward to for its sweetness and urgency, the protected sensation of a palm cupped over a vulnerable spot. But now he felt coddled, her hand seemed unpleasantly maternal, and he reached up and removed it.

Camille looked stricken. "Why are you angry at *me*?"

"I'm not," he said automatically.

She sat back on her chair, propping one foot up on the seat. In the light from the lamp above the table her face looked sculpted and cold, and his bravado flagged. Suddenly it seemed so much more important for them to communicate calmly, kindly, for her not to look at him with this kind of chill.

He aimed for conciliation. "I wish you wouldn't joke with him, okay? I don't think he needs a partner in acting like everything's fine."

"I want to joke with him," she said. "I was friends with him before I met you, and I'm relieved I have the opportunity to joke around with him at all."

"You know I'm glad too, Camille," he said. "But he's acting like nothing happened."

"He saw a doctor, right? He's getting some treatment."

"I told you he is."

"Then isn't that what he promised? He's trying to put things right."

"Well, what am I supposed to say to that?" he asked.

She looked not at him but up at the lamp above the table. "All spring he got more and more anxious," she said, "and I kept waiting for you to do something, but you never let me talk to you about him."

"I'm sorry it felt that way," Britt started to say, because he could not quite apologize for anything else. Maybe he was sorry for something now—for that unfamiliar look on her face—but he no longer knew what it was. He reached out to stroke her arm, thinking they could stop this if only he could reset things somehow.

He knew that touching her was a mistake, but he couldn't quite believe it when she pushed him away—she actually shoved his chest to get him away from her; he found himself sitting there with his palms against his chest where her hands had been. "Oh, *fuck* your fake apologies," she said. "You didn't care that he was struggling, not enough to do anything, and you made damn sure I knew I couldn't talk about him. Not even when he was gone! We should have been helping each other, but you put all your energy into the restaurant. You barely even talked about him, Britt! You just worked and acted like it was a regular busy night, like he was on vacation."

She had gotten up and was digging through her purse as she headed toward the door, and Britt went after her. "Oh no," he said. "What did you want me to do? Collapse? I didn't know that the whole time I was so grateful to have you there, you were just thinking I'm inhuman. He's my brother! It's a given that *I'm* upset—why the fuck are you so upset?"

The keys jangled to the floor and Camille batted his hand away when he reached to retrieve them for her. She swiped them up and straightened, pointing a finger at his chest.

"Don't even try it," she said. Her mouth was quivering, and she tightened her lips and took a shallow, jittering breath. "Don't you even think about trying to insinuate that I'm not trustworthy, not after I called hospitals and ran around being your gopher and your busser and I never burdened you with how frightened I was. And you didn't even ask! I know he's your brother, but you couldn't just ask? When do you ever hear me talk about my family? We've been together for months and you haven't seen them since the night we met, because I barely talk to them myself. But you have one and you don't even care. If I had the relationship with my family that you have with yours, I wouldn't be so cavalier about destroying it."

In the doorway she turned around, pulling her dress strap up, and Britt thought that maybe she was coming back.

Maybe now she'd had her say and was as empty and scraped

dry as he was. He felt as if this had been going on for hours, but the last table at the restaurant had left only forty-five minutes ago. He took a deep breath to slow his pulse and was about to speak when Camille said, "You should have seen what was happening with him," and that was when he gave up and let her go.

CHAPTER 23

Harry went into the restaurant at eight. The first morning he'd returned, he'd been nervous just to be there, as if the air itself would go to work on him. But every morning since then he'd come in early, enjoying the silence and the methodical process of cleaning, organizing, and prepping.

At nine his watch beeped to remind him to stop for breakfast, which consisted of a couple of bananas and a handful of nuts from a container he kept on the line. He was trying his best to be one of those guys he used to laugh at for being weak, who paused for two minutes to eat, who kept dried fruit on hand and drank a lot of water and limited booze to one shift drink. It was like being either very young or very old. Did other people do this? Did they do it so naturally that they simply did not require the kind of attention he had to give it? Maybe Harry had just assumed that everyone did to themselves what he did to himself, that because they didn't make a show of eating meals and sleeping soundly, they weren't eating and never slept, just like him. But it turned out that no one needed to discuss it.

Harry was reasonably certain that Britt had been adding to his almond stockpile, for the level never seemed to dwindle. He never asked, but the image of his brother surreptitiously tipping bags of almonds into the stash made Harry feel simultaneously frustrated and chastened. Last night he'd realized that Britt might not ever forgive him, which meant that he might not ever trust him again.

Somehow Harry had never thought of their relationship in these terms. He'd always thought of his brothers as impervious and distant, secure and stationary in their partnership and their maturity, while Harry himself flitted about, gnatlike.

He finished his breakfast, wiped his hands on the towel at his waist, and went back to the kitchen. He'd eaten, he was doing his work, he was here taking care of his restaurant. He would concentrate on the next few steps. Finish the shallots. Get the stock bones into the oven. Clarify the butter.

AT LEAST IT WAS EASY TO PARK at this hour. Britt pulled in directly in front of Stray, where no one was around on a weekend morning for anything but cigarettes at the bodega. A warm summer wind was kicking in from the river, and Britt slowed down to let it soak in. He was already late anyway.

He hadn't slept so much as drifted into the occasional whiteout during which the clock had leapt forward. After Camille left, he wasted an hour debating whether to go to her house, but by about twelve thirty he realized it wasn't going to happen. He wasn't going to go dashing after her late at night, as if they were twenty-one and drunk—as if they were servers at Stray. That had at least given him a bitter little smile.

At least if he were still that young, a fight like this might feel dramatic. But you bought a place, you opened a business, you were nearer forty than thirty, and being up all night was simply desolate. They'd unearthed something wretched, and it sat there with him while he dug up a bag of potato chips from the back of one cupboard and then went to bed and tried to sleep, his phone silent on the table beside him.

This was not the same mess he'd thought it was; his position was not the purely victimized position he'd felt so certain of. He tried to stoke the belief that Camille had heaped something on him he didn't deserve, but it did not entirely work. So she didn't like how he'd dealt with Harry's disappearance; it didn't mean his response was invalid. She could have talked to him. She didn't have to suffer in silence and then lash out at him a week later. And Harry was a grown man—Britt didn't ask him to manage his life, so why would Britt have to do this for him? He ran through all these arguments, and he knew plenty of them were reasonable, but he wasn't sure that would ever matter.

He hadn't had a real argument with a woman in years—nothing ever got that heated; they just dwindled until the final conversation was as quick and dry as a kiss from an aunt. What was a fight and what was a breakup?

As he turned back from the river and toward the restaurant, the Ethiopian guy waved from the coffee cart. Baklava seemed no worse an idea than anything else. The guy was already pouring two coffees and wrapping up two pieces of baklava. Britt had only intended to buy one for himself, but he let the man pack two pieces and clap lids on both coffees. Then he stacked the coffees on top of each other, tucked the bag beneath one arm, and made his way to the restaurant.

He was feeling strangely experimental. In the past several months, not one thing had gone as he'd expected, in his restaurant, in his relationship, in his family. The walk to the restaurant seemed to take a long time, with the tree leaves looking sharp and crystalline in the sunlight. He felt a not unpleasant weightlessness, a general willingness that was not focused on one particular thing. Whatever awaited him at the restaurant would be no worse than what he had left last night.

When he got to the restaurant, he set the coffees and baklava on the bar. Harry came out of the kitchen, carrying a bus tub full of pans, and paused as the door swung shut behind him. "You want some breakfast?" Britt said. "Or did you already eat?"

Harry came around the back of the bar and set down his tub.

"I can always eat more." He began lining up his pans and utensils, folding towels and stacking them on the counter. "You look like shit," he said after a time.

Britt shrugged. "You look okay. You look better than you did a few weeks ago, anyway."

Harry nodded. Britt watched Harry move from the pans to the cutting board to the walk-in and back, trying to tell if he was still missing some clue in Harry's behavior, as he obviously had before. But Harry moved with the same quick grace that Britt had been so surprised to see last fall.

Britt watched Harry's knife slide through some onions. There came a time when you were either going to turn someone loose or stick around. He could keep punishing Harry—he probably wouldn't even be wrong to demand a new apology from his brother, maybe even every day, and he knew Harry would do it if he asked. But Britt wanted his brother back to his old fearlessness, back to what Harry used to be, or whatever Britt had thought he was.

BRITT MADE A PROJECT OUT OF the rest of that day and the next. Before he went running off to Camille, before he even phoned her, he would assume that they were finished. Maybe it would feel better than he expected. Perhaps it would be an unexpected relief.

In service of this idea, he thought a lot about her flaws. She'd told a story about her first restaurant job more than once, and the second time she'd hit precisely the same beats and all the same jokes. She often texted when she could have called, and her texts always read as if a robot had written them. She had said a particularly obnoxious novel was inventive and enthralling.

The idea was for him to realize that he had been miserable with her without actually knowing it, but this was, on its face, such undiluted bullshit that Britt very nearly impressed himself at how long he kept it up. He kept getting twisted around and ended up thinking about the things he found endearing: the occasional silky patch of golden hairs under her arms; her insistence on overtipping; the overheated passion with which she had stated that she would never try horsemeat.

She did not contact him, and he tried to take the hint, but her absence was yawning and tangible. It seemed impossible that she lived so near him, that she was going about her day and seeing people and talking to them, that her friends could simply drop by, that some jam-maker could call her up and actually *see* her. The nadir was on the morning of the third day, when he sat morosely over his coffee, thinking of all the random accountants and telemarketers who could talk to her at any time at all. He became aware that he'd begun to think of her less as a woman he could call, as a grown-up might, and more as some type of mythical creature. It had been long enough; he was going over there. She'd won, and he didn't even care.

HE PROBABLY SHOULD HAVE KNOWN that her house would look the same. It had been only three days. Still, when Camille let him in, he looked around in disbelief at the bowl of fruit on her table, the plate of half-eaten toast beside a cup of tea.

When she appeared at her front door, she looked unsurprised. She was wearing gray yoga pants and a long, belted sweater. She had no makeup on; her face was pale and slightly worn around the eyes, her hair loose around her shoulders. "Hi," she said, and waited until he asked to come in.

That plate of toast made him very nervous. He didn't think a distraught person would bother to spread her toast with butter and honey, or to replenish the fruit on her table.

She gestured him in the direction of her couch and sat down opposite him in an oversized armchair. She waited for him to speak, her face as bright and enigmatic as it had been when he'd first met her.

Now that he was here he wasn't as sure of himself. He'd smoothed over countless little disagreements with countless women, with varying degrees of difficulty, but the irony was that the less invested he was, the easier it was. He could offer up whatever people wanted to hear if he was interested only in a few more good weeks or months.

And Camille did not seem to be trying to torture him, necessarily. She sat cross-legged, her hands on her knees as if she were meditating, and observed him with what appeared to be mild interest. The tea steamed on the table beside her.

Maybe he should have brought flowers. It seemed so childlike and stalkerish, though, to present a bouquet of roses and baby's breath as if it wiped everything away. But it might have been nice to be occupied by the business of fetching a vase and trimming the stems.

"I didn't realize Harry's leaving was so upsetting for you," he finally said, when the silence had stretched out too long. "And I'm sorry I didn't listen. I just thought you were being easy on him because he might still be interested in you."

"That's flattering," she said. "You thought I was keeping him in reserve?"

"No," he said, and now he meant it. "I just thought you had a soft spot for him."

"I do," she said, but her tone had changed. "But he's my friend. That's all."

They looked at one another, waiting to see what else there was. Britt had nothing else to add—this was as far as he'd planned on the drive over, because he'd thought she'd start talking. The clock ticked gently on the wall; the tea sent up a curl of steam that disappeared into the light coming through the window. Camille leaned back in her chair.

He found it very hard to meet her eyes without smiling from nerves or self-consciousness, or both. Finally he couldn't bear the stillness and said, "Camille. I came to you, I apologized. I have no idea if we're making up or just having a very yogic breakup."

She blinked at him. Then she lowered her head and covered her face with her hands. Uncertainly, Britt rose and took a step in her direction. When she lifted her face she was laughing, weepily, and she shook her head, looking at the ceiling.

"I didn't know until just now," she said. She reached out her hands for him to pull her up from the chair, and as he wrapped his arms around her he breathed in the scent of clean wool from her sweater, the scent of her hair. Every time, she was taller than he remembered; her chin was wedged tightly over his shoulder, her cheek against his. They stood that way for a long minute, as if to ease the transition, and finally she pulled back and kissed him, tasting faintly of honey.

"What are you smiling at?" she asked.

"Your toast scared the shit out of me."

Camille laughed. "I'm one of those people who eats normally even when I'm miserable." She reached up and clasped his hand, sending such a deep sense of relief through his body that Britt could think of nothing to do but raise her hand to his mouth and kiss it. He waited for her to tease him about the toast, to let him know she'd been just fine really, but she leaned her forehead against his and closed her eyes. "I was miserable," she said.

CHAPTER 24

HARRY AND BRITT HAD SPENT three weeks developing a menu and spreading the word about Monday night family-style dinners, Britt calling up a few local columnists, Harry releasing a stream of witty little updates on Facebook and Twitter, and both warning all reservations about the different menu. After that, there was nothing to do but open the doors on a Monday and give it a shot.

Harry and Jenelle had tried out the dishes at staff meal, but Harry still had his doubts. Lamb shank, flatbreads by the yard with an oily, fragrant salumi, great platters of fritto misto, broccoli rabe, or roasted eggplant, a rabbit fricassee with porcini and bacon and white wine. Suddenly they were an Italian restaurant on Mondays, it seemed, but when they'd brainstormed dishes, that was what had popped into their heads. Something about these dishes, plus the cooling fall air, had felt comforting and generous, just what the staff was feeling desperate to eat, and so they decided to go with it. "Maybe we'll try out a new region every week," Harry had mused as he and Jenelle stood over a dish of rabbit, tasting shreds of its lean little haunches. "We do Italian this week, we fry up chicken and biscuits next week, in the dead of winter we do couscous and tagines, coq au vin, or daube, maybe."

Jenelle had shrugged. "I have no idea what daube is," she said, "but if we can serve it in a vat, I'm on it."

"It's just French stew, with beef or lamb," Harry said. He slid the house copy of *The Food Lover's Companion,* much thumbed by servers, across the zinc bar, thinking that this was both Jenelle's curse and her blessing: she came to the line without pretension, having cooked for years not for passion but to make a living, the same way she would have worked at upholstering chairs or carving wood or any other craft one did with repetition and attention to detail. So what if she never showed up wanting to try a new spin on pho crossed with laksa? You could give her rabbit, you could give her quail eggs, you could give her whatever, and after a test run or two she had it down. She was a quicker study than Harry had ever been, and he prided himself on having picked things up fast. But he'd always been busy trying to impress Shelley or Amanda, and as a result his early cooking had been a slideshow of muddled influences and pretensions. But Jenelle's cooking, while not high in flourish, was so crisply executed that Harry almost never had cause to correct her. Now and again he said a little silent thank-you to Shelley for pushing him in that direction, tempting though it had been to listen to Britt and consider talented, schizy Elliott, who after a few years and drug therapy trials might be a powerhouse.

Their first Monday was passable: the servers seemed nervous explaining the setup to the tables, the guests kept looking around uncertainly to see if other tables had gotten the regular menu, and the staff had to keep pushing tables together to accommodate each new crop of large groups, a process Harry found inelegant when it occurred during service. Harry decided that they would do a shorter menu for these Mondays in the future, two main course choices at most and one side. On the plus side, Hector had amused himself by making a fig and mascarpone crostata and grappa ice cream; for the largest tables, they simply served the crostata whole in its round dish.

There was something disconcertingly smooth about the entire evening. Though the numbers were not impressive, they were sound, and at the end of the evening, no one looked beaten or crazed. And this was the whole point.

Harry was still amazed that it had been Britt's idea. Normally Britt was a much bigger believer in anything that pleased the guest, regardless of the extra work for the staff. (Britt was under the impression that this was primarily a failing of Leo's, but in fact he was just as bad.) Nevertheless, he'd come bustling in one morning, barely recognizable in faded jeans and ancient work boots, and said, "Once a week, we are going to relax."

Britt's idea was to serve a different menu each Monday, family-style, with some tweak to the dishes to make them so interesting that the clientele would actually make the trip for them. That was what the big idea came down to: bigger plates.

Harry had been secretly receptive—though as a matter of form he had debated it—to any solution to the exhaustion they were barely managing to assuage even with added waitstaff and a search under way for another prep cook. "But it isn't what we do," Harry had said at first. "What about all those places that we say never know what they want to do, that have no focus?"

"We'll keep it within our focus," Britt said. "That's what menu planning is for—we make sure we do this so it feels like us. What about paella?"

"People like trying a lot of different things, though," Harry said. "It's kind of why they're here."

"So we'll make a lot of booze part of the variety somehow—we'll get some great hard-to-find wines, or make cocktails tailored to each week. If there's one thing the restaurant business has shown me, it's that people think drinking's just as much fun as eating."

"I don't know," Harry said. "I feel like we're just getting our feet back under us." Britt raised an eyebrow. "Okay, I feel like I'm just getting my feet back under me. I'm a little scared of changing up the systems. Maybe we should just keep rolling. And we'd need new tableware." But even as he said this he was thinking of grand platters of one perfect dish. Such simplicity.

"We can hire more people," Britt was saying. "We can rethink the line setup. We can just put our heads down and hope we all come out intact when things settle, whenever they do settle. I mean, we don't even *want* them to settle, we just need to be able to meet the burden and be sure we keep our staff in the meantime. The servers are doing better, but you and Jenelle still need help. Hector being Hector, every day could be the day that he finally builds a life-sized marzipan version of himself and leaves it in the kitchen instead of showing up. I'm just saying we can try out a few weeks of service that might be fun for the guests and give us one night of breathing room. We can roll this out and roll it back up if we need to."

"That's true," Harry conceded. It was a perfectly reasonable, small-scale, and, yes, reversible idea. "But I don't want you feeling like you have to carry the kitchen." He said a silent apology to Jenelle and Hector for including them as "the kitchen" when he really meant himself. "Carry *me*," he corrected.

They looked each other over for a moment. Britt's clothes and hair looked a little creased and faded, as unthinkable on him as a backward baseball cap, but Harry was noticing his brother's expression, which was somewhere between wry and affectionate, and just as unexpected. Finally Britt shrugged. "I have plenty to do without carrying the kitchen," he said. "I'm not suggesting this because I think you're going to lose it again. I'm suggesting it because I think you'll do this well."

CHAPTER 25

Leo sat in the office, the windows open to the sounds of the staff breaking down the dining room. Alan had turned off the evening's usual mix and turned up hip-hop instead. Leo didn't know the name of the song, but he listened for it whenever he was here this late, tapping his fingers to the beat.

He would go home without Thea, who had Iris that night and preferred him to show up the next day instead of staying the night. He had never dated a woman with children and had been taken aback to realize that he didn't quite want to stay the night there just yet, not when Iris was home. He kept imagining her being startled to see him in the kitchen one morning, all bedraggled and dragon-breathed, in a stained white tank top he didn't even own. Children were an unending source of unwelcome self-awareness, he had discovered. Next to Iris he often felt overgrown and whiskered, a hideous creature smelling of garlic and coffee and strong cheese.

"She's not an angel, you know," Thea had said when he expressed this. They were in her living room, having a glass of wine while Iris slept and before Leo left. Thea was in her yoga pants and a Bucknell sweatshirt, her long cold bare feet pressed up against his belly beneath his shirt. Leo loved her feet; they were elegant and battered from years of standing on the line, with long toes and prominent jade-green veins. "She likes raw radishes with butter, for one thing.

Some days she comes home from her dad's and breathes horseradish pastrami all over me. It's like being mauled by a very tiny old man in a deli."

"I don't think she's some kind of cherub," Leo said, though privately he felt a flare of annoyance at Bryan for making rounded, apple-scented Iris come home reeking of deli meats. Had he never heard of nitrates? "I just don't want to be lurking in the kitchen, you know, all hairy and unexpected."

"Well, you would be dressed," Thea said. She resettled her feet against his skin and Leo cupped them, through his shirt, with both hands. Anyone else would just put on some socks. "When that time occurs. If it occurs."

"I would," he'd said, rubbing her feet. "I'd wear a three-piece suit."

Downstairs he heard the volume of the music rise and Britt's voice joining in the chatter. Leo opened up the books for Monday night. He recognized most of the names but checked their blue cards anyway. Apparently the husband of one couple had stopped drinking and wanted no alcohol in his food either. A pharmaceutical rep hadn't wooed a crew of doctors here in months, but another had taken her place and had been here three times in the past six weeks. Another couple had divorced. *Don't mention Alice*, the card warned.

He opened Britt's card, half wondering if there'd be a snide reference to his brother's absence. But it was the same pithy two-word joke it had always been, *Mouth breather*. And yet just below Britt's name he now saw his own. Of course he had always been aware of the fact that the servers had never made a blue card for him, not in all the years they'd had the system. He'd never known if they skipped him because they didn't think of him as someone to joke with or because they thought he'd be angry if they got it wrong. Or maybe they'd just never given him much thought. He opened the file, feeling weirdly trepidatious. It would probably be something about the temperature he liked his steaks.

Likes his desserts traditional except when he doesn't, Leo read. He smiled, then started to laugh as the lines scrolled up. *Vehemently believes bar is for boozing, not dinner. Too modest to admit his past as a professional synchronized swimmer—but note the grace, the grace!*

CHAPTER 26

WINESAP'S ANNUAL STAFF HOLIDAY PARTY was traditionally held during the doldrums of mid-January, when everyone had recovered from the holidays and the restaurant could afford to close for a night. What the event lacked in Christmasy effervescence it usually made up in sheer alcoholic fortitude. This year it had doubled in size and potential for mishap, for Britt and Leo had insisted on combining the parties for Stray and Winesap into a single melee at Leo's house.

The party always helped take Leo's mind off a slow business moment that he loathed and enjoyed in equal measure. The guilty sweet spot arrived every year in early January, after the preholiday parties and between the cash-cow amateur nights of New Year's and Valentine's Day. As a matter of pride, Jason and Thea had tried for years to prevent the tasting menus on New Year's and Valentine's from settling into nothing more daring than lobster, cream, and warm chocolate cake, but the brutal truth was that those items sold. The guests who came out twice a year were there for lobster with chanterelles and saffron-scented cream, for oozy chocolate cake and flutes of champagne. And so they did their best to lend the stalwarts some interest and accepted the necessity of charging sixty-five bucks a head for a menu that they could produce and serve almost without coming in at all.

A part of Leo always feared that the crowds would not return. But they always had in the past, and so this year he was doing his best to enjoy the two-server weeknights, the last reservations arriving at eight thirty instead of nine forty-five.

Harry had been having a difficult time attempting to take the same approach. He had become accustomed to a full house, had staffed up for it, and now he faced the drop in numbers as if someone had thrown a rock through the front window. All of Leo's and Britt's assurances that this was normal, recommendations to take it as a breather, had failed to reassure him. There was nothing to be done but let him ride it out, as everyone had to do in his first year. This was just how the business went. He'd manage.

Right now Harry was standing with Britt and Camille in a corner of Leo's living room. All three were consuming steamed pork buns with pickled vegetables and heroic dollops of chile sauce. Leo happened to know that Harry was on his fifth.

Thea was turning the pork buns out by the dozen in Leo's kitchen. Jason stood at her side, splitting the soft, steamed rolls and adding a squeeze from a bottle of hoisin before layering on the sticky glazed pork and the pickled cucumbers.

Leo had had three himself, healthful diet be damned. There was a sort of creepy eroticism to those pale, yielding steamed rolls, the sheer ease and silkiness with which they pillowed up, and the deceptive, infantile lightness that suggested you could and should eat half a dozen. All around his living room, cooks and servers were tearing into them, shaking their heads in disbelieving pleasure. Even vegan Josh looked delighted with his roasted mushroom version.

It was always disconcerting to see these employees outside the confines of the restaurant, dressed not in whites or in work clothes but in their jeans and sweaters, to see who wore motorcycle boots and who knotted scarves prettily around their necks. Helene had exchanged her swishing skirts and spike heels for tight jeans, flat brown boots, and an artfully dilapidated violet T-shirt. Apollo, who'd recently cut his surfer's hair and gotten new tortoiseshell glasses in a vain attempt to downplay his looks, was hovering near her, amplifying the glow from an adjacent lamp. Despite wearing faded jeans and a bright sweater, Jenelle somehow still gave the impression of being dressed for the line. She was awaiting her moment to produce the next course, lurking near the kitchen doorway, where Leo was loitering as well.

Jenelle was on noodle duty, having spent the previous weekend simmering the thigh bones of a pig with kombu into a cloudy ivory broth. Harry had warned them it smelled like a stockyard during simmering, but some alchemy had occurred, and the broth warming on Leo's stove now smelled less like pork than some savory, rich emulsification of everything meaty in the world.

Britt materialized next to Leo. "Shouldn't we get these things catered?" he said. "All the cooks are working when they're supposed to be relaxing." His gaze wandered over to Camille at the other end of the room, where some of the Stray staff were hoisting up their clothing to display their new tattoos.

"I tried," Leo said with a shrug. "I offered, I had Thea offer in case they were just being polite, I even circulated a few caterers' menus so they knew I was serious. But you know these guys. They think caterers are hacks, and they couldn't stand to miss a chance to show each other up. I think that's what makes it a celebration to them."

"Yeah, I tried too. Jenelle got pissed at me for even mentioning a caterer when she'd already sourced twenty pounds of pig femur. Hector just stared at me as if I'd insulted his entire matrilineage. I haven't been permitted to know what he's doing."

"Harry wouldn't have minded a caterer," Leo said. They both looked once more toward their brother, who had finished his pork bun and was now looking furtively around, clearly considering a sixth.

"No, but now the poor sap has to pitch in anyway," Britt said heartlessly. "Can't let your cooks do all the work at their own party. I mean, we are, but we bought the alcohol."

They shrugged in unison, content with their contributions. This was the one time when a decent boss had to know his place: they did what they were good for, supplied drinks and a venue, and even went so far as to close their restaurants on a dead winter Monday just to be sure the employees didn't feel burdened by their own party on the one day the restaurant was closed. Then they got out of the way for the rest, allowing Leo's kitchen to become as densely packed with secrecy and competitiveness as any palace kitchen. Hector and Kelly had arrived at the same time, or maybe they had arrived together, bearing coolers draped with tablecloths for extra discretion. They set the coolers just outside Leo's back door and now hovered near the entrance as if to guard them.

Leo made his way into the kitchen, gently displacing a number of the Winesap cooks, to where Thea was stationed at the counter beside the stove, slicing the last of the pork belly. She'd brought her own knives—all the cooks had brought their own knives; the counter bore a neat row of black knife rolls—but Leo had sharpened his anyway, for credibility. He paused, enjoying the sight of Thea at work, the smooth motion of her knife through the strata of fat and meat, the curl of her fingers, her mouth turned down at the corners in concentration. Thea could cook an entire meal and barely shift her feet, she was that good at her setup, that efficient in her movements. Even the coil of curly hair gathered at the base of her neck barely shivered as she worked. Already Iris was the same: Leo had given her a small cutting board of her own, a dulled butter knife with a red handle, and a flat-ended wooden spoon that no one else used. When they set her up with a banana to slice or herbs to tear, she got the same expression Thea did, suggesting grave responsibility and faint wariness of her ingredients, as if they could not be trusted to become delicious on their own.

He laid a hand briefly on Thea's shoulder. Even this small acknowledgment, he knew, was bold. They might not be actively hiding anything anymore, but neither did they allow themselves a demonstration. Nevertheless, Leo decided, it *was* a party. Jason's gaze strayed to his hand against Thea's black-shirted shoulder, settled there, and then shifted discreetly away. But Thea merely glanced over her shoulder at him and smiled, and Leo felt relief and delayed adrenaline race through him, as though he had just come through some perilous event. Her hands, slick with mahogany glaze and pork fat, stayed where they were above the cutting board, but she lifted her shoulder just long enough to let her jaw rest on his hand before she went back to work.

When the steamed buns were finished, Harry and Jenelle took over the kitchen to dish up the ramen. Back out in the living room, Thea watched the two restaurant crews mingle exuberantly, prodding one another with chopsticks, slipping out front to stand on the porch, smoking cigarettes and waving through the windows. The age disparity seemed to be no obstacle to bonding, whether because of the pleasures of industry kvetching, the products of an afternoon's competitive cooking, or just the fresh sexual possibilities in cross-restaurant socializing. Earlier that evening, one of Winesap's servers had even sidled beerily up to Harry and stood very close, just about to hit on him, until Britt saved them both with a specious question about pork broth. It all made Thea feel a little parental and affectionate.

Leo watched her head back to the kitchen, since the noodle course had been served and Harry was now seated there with Jenelle and Britt. Harry was holding up a piece of pork between his chopsticks and examining it, probably considering the fat-to-meat ratio and whether he liked the purveyor, whether the sticky, savory marinade had penetrated a sufficient few millimeters into the flesh. His brows were drawn together, his jaw working meditatively as he chewed.

Leo thought perhaps he too should use every day, even a party, as a chance to improve his culinary understanding. Harry devoted this same concentration to everything from Saturday morning scrambled eggs to staff-meal chicken tacos. Britt had mentioned it with some admiration, for it had begun to dawn on both of them how all Harry's exploits had had a gustatory purpose, from the raw Alaskan salmon to homegrown goat. Yet Leo hadn't felt the same pure admiration as Britt seemed to. Instead he felt—both then and now, as he watched Harry dip the pork into the broth and take a small, considered bite—a sort of vexed tenderness, a wish to give his brother some respite from his striving.

HARRY HAD HIS THEORIES ABOUT Hector and Kelly's dessert, and they involved fire, shards of iced substances that had never before been iced, or maybe mochi. After the demise of the Korean rice stick dish, Hector had gotten very into glutinous rice flour; several of his desserts had taken on a chewy edge that was terrifically satisfying. And yet Harry really had no idea what they were serving, nor was he concerned about it beyond the pleasant expectation any guest might feel awaiting dessert. For once, whatever Hector wished to do had no real bearing on him, on customers, or on the restaurant. Hector could candy a rat if he wanted to—it was all fine with Harry.

He'd never gone so long without socializing, and he hadn't realized how essential it was, and not just to the restaurant business, which thrived on it. Even at the salmon plant there'd been a certain level of lightly armed camaraderie at the bars after shifts. Now Harry regretted the fact that this party was not his doing or even his idea. At first he had resisted combining the two staff parties, in case Britt and Leo's offer was only polite, but he ended up sounding pissy and ungrateful, and he had understood that he had to stop slapping down every attempt his brothers made, that he was being not self-sufficient but petulant.

Harry looked into the kitchen, where his brothers had gravitated once more. "Any idea what they're making?"

"Not yet," said Britt.

Leo reached behind a cooler and brought out a single pork bun on a paper plate.

"Take it!" he cried. "It's all we have—take it and leave us alone!"

Harry accepted the plate. "You think you're shaming me, but I will indeed take it."

"I told him you would," said Britt. "Leo doesn't see you at staff meal every day."

"Hey," Harry said a few minutes later, pork bun now a memory. He wiped his mouth with a napkin. "I found a place. You don't have to look quite so surprised. Mom and Dad were always temporary."

"It always starts off temporary," Britt said. "Then next thing you know it's thirty years later and you're still there, sharing a truss."

"Where's the apartment?" asked Leo. "I'm assuming you rented an apartment and didn't buy an old warehouse to renovate in your spare time."

"You know where the Stray neighborhood stops being crappy and gets almost totally unscary? I rented a place about one foot over that line."

They tapped beer bottles and drank. After a moment Leo added cheerily, "I'm not helping you move."

"I have it down to a science. Also I don't own anything."

"True. You're as monastic as it is possible to be while still eating duck-fat-fried potatoes once a week," Britt said.

Harry poked around the cooler and found a bottle of porter. At the counter by the stove, Hector and Kelly were placing the last layer on a towering stack of crepes, aligned with an architectural precision between layers of dark chocolate and topped with what looked like salted almonds. Harry had expected to see something spectacular and aflame, but the sheer technical care of the cake seemed more impressive to him somehow, even moving. He loved a cook who could embrace the sheer repetition and minute attention of the process. They made it look simple: all you had to do was execute a task flawlessly, then do it a hundred more times.

Next to the crepe cake sat a platter of caramel-brown, disk-shaped pastries, glistening with sugar and what Harry assumed must be huge quantities of butter. Kelly glanced up at them and said, "Kouign amann."

"Holy shit," he said. Britt and Leo looked blank. Kouign amann, which he'd heard of once or twice but never tasted, was an unspeakably fussy and arcane Breton specialty, essentially a means of incorporating as much salted Brittany butter into pastry as the laws of physics allowed. The recipes he'd seen had required such care in ingredients, temperature, and precise handling to achieve the right layering of pastry that he'd never considered trying, but the rounds before him were stunning, rich, glossy, and crisped.

He was so busy advancing on the kouign amann that he was startled when Hector turned from the counter bearing a grand pâte à choux ring, split in half and filled with what looked like a tawny-colored mousse of some kind. It looked magnificent and ridiculous, like the Sun King's take on a doughnut.

"What *is* that?" Britt murmured. Hector and Kelly drew themselves up with an identical air of hauteur.

"You disappoint me," said Kelly. "At least Harry recognized a kouign amann! This is a classic Paris-Brest, I'll have you know. We filled it with cinnamon-scented cream instead of plain whipped cream."

"It's named for a bike race," Hector said.

"Jeez, you guys," Leo said in wonderment. "They're mind-boggling. They're so traditional."

"I can do traditional," Hector said, shaking his head. "Everyone forgets that." He nudged an almond back into place.

They all went silent, as if waiting for someone to dim the lamps or light a candle and sing, and then Kelly shrugged and broke the moment by sinking her knife into the heart of the crepe cake.

Harry almost laughed, because all three of them had flinched, as if the last thing anyone would expect for a cake was to slice it.

The rest of the party surged in to get their desserts, and the three backed over to one wall to let them through, listening to the exclamations over the desserts ("A Paris-Brest!" Alan cried) and the remnants of conversations that carried on as people picked up their plates and forks. The little kitchen was humid and loud, there were great piles of dishes to be washed, and the staff moved like one animate mass of hunger, swarming the table and then dispersing more quickly than seemed possible.

Harry, Leo, and Britt waited until all the employees had returned to the other room amid conversation about the glazed fruit, the light pastry, the richness of the cream, and then they stepped forward to serve themselves.

The table was empty, its platters cleaned of all but a scattering of crumbs. They looked around to see if any further desserts might be lingering on a counter or above the fridge, but there was nothing but empty plates, beer bottles, and utensils. On the stove, two stockpots each held a half-inch of pork broth, and nearby sat an extra tray of naked steamed buns without filling. The kitchen was finally quiet, but the rest of the house swelled with a comfortable volume of laughter and the clinking of china and silverware.

There was one lone swirl of cinnamon cream left on a platter, just enough for each of them to taste a dollop of it. Harry managed to collect a few shards of pastry from another serving dish, enough for each of them to manage a bite. Even the remnants—the faint tang of salt, a shattering medallion of browned caramel clinging to a shred of soft dough—were enough to incite a murmur of appreciation and contentment from each brother. Then they sat at the table, slouched peacefully in their chairs. The three of them listened as their guests, oblivious, devoured the last of their meals.

ACKNOWLEDGMENTS

This book would not exist without the efforts of a small army of readers, writers, and restaurant gurus. My novel group—Susanna Daniel, Judy Mitchell, Jesse Lee Kercheval, Jeannie Reynolds Page, and Melissa Field—allowed me to hijack our meetings for several months until I'd completed a first draft, and they fed me delicious snacks to boot. Rae Meadows and Sarah Yaw provided the kind of trenchant reads that make me hound them to quit their jobs and neglect their children in favor of being my full-time readers, and sometimes I am kidding. Edenfred is no more, but when it was a gracious writing space for Madison artists, you can bet I used it to complete yet another round of revisions.

Though I worked in the restaurant business for a number of years, that was a long time ago, and when I sat down to write about the business's day-to-day workings, I needed professionals. Leah Caplan and Daniel Momont let me pick through their knowledge and their psyches, and any inaccuracies are all my fault. The staff at Lombardino's let me hang around the kitchen during service and never once admitted that I was in the way, which I absolutely was. Michael Ruhlman's wonderful series on the life and career of the modern chef was invaluable, and not just for the excuse to read the books all over again, in the process kiting at least one Michael Symon dish. I have yet to make it, but Harry can prepare it in his sleep.

Emilie Stewart's guidance and tenacity were once again instrumental in getting this book out in the world. Liz Duvall and Nora Reichard caught every inconsistency and repetition. There are not enough superlatives in the world to heap at Jenny Jackson's feet for her faultless ability to find the crispest solution to the fuzziest manuscript issues and her supernatural ability to read each new draft afresh. Working with her has made me not only a better writer but a better editor.

Emily Dickmann, Farah Kaiksow, Jeremy Kraft, Tom Kuplic, Daniel Momont, Ryan Narzisi, Tara Waldron, Alison Weatherby, and Kate Zurlo-Cuva are some of the best friends and extended family the world has to offer, and one of these days I will set us all up on that commune to which I am pretty sure they've implicitly agreed.

There is no better husband and father than Steve O'Brien, who is my cheerleader, my structural support, the funniest man on earth, and the most memorable childbirth class participant the world has ever known. And finally, I spent a long time dithering around with the first seventy pages of this novel, until Holly O'Brien set a firm deadline. That's my girl.